BALTIMORE LOGIC

BASIL TRUSCOTT

PREFACE

This novel is dedicated to and inspired by my late father and his brother, my late uncle. Intensely serious and hard men, they taught me to value courage above all things and appreciate the humor and irony of daily life.

First and foremost, this is a work of fiction, a product of my imagination. Set in the 1939 to 1941 timeframe, any reference to historical events, real people, or real places, are used fictitiously. Other names, characters, places, and events are products of my imagination, and any resemblance to actual events or places or persons, living or dead, is entirely coincidental.

To avoid anachronism and simultaneously avoid inadvertently offending any individual or group of people, I have used the terminology prevalent in *The Baltimore Sun* and the *Baltimore Afro-American* newspapers during the timeframe of this novel to characterize individuals and groups of people discussed herein.

I am eternally indebted to the following organizations for the extraordinary assistance they provided to me in researching and writing this novel: Adirondack Editing, the Enoch Pratt Free Library, the Baltimore Museum of Industry/The Bendix Radio Foundation, the Glenn L. Martin Maryland Aviation Museum, the National Electronic Museum, the American Radio Relay League, the Vintage Radio and Communications Museum of Connecticut, and LifeSafe Training. In the interest of preserving the privacy of those courteous, knowledgeable and patient individuals in the aforementioned organizations who helped me as I researched and wrote this novel, I have decided not to acknowledge any of them by name. **Any errors in this novel are mine and mine alone.**

Finally, I would be unpardonably remiss if I did not thank my remarkable wife, who has guided, supported, and tolerated me in all of my endeavors over the past forty-eight years, for her encouragement regarding this project. Rainey, I could never have written this novel without you.

Basil Truscott

Connecticut

July 10, 2019

1

A Warm Welcome

"ENTER!"

And so he did. Opening the opaque glass door, Lieutenant JG Martin Victor took three steps forward into the office, snapped a smart salute, and stood at attention.

The US Navy Captain seated behind the large desk took off his watch and placed the timepiece at the apex of an isosceles triangle bordered by his forearms on the polished wooden desktop.

"Do you know why you are here, US Naval Reserve Lieutenant Junior Grade Victor?"

"No, Sir."

"This is your job interview for a position in the regular US Navy. Judging by what I see before me, I believe our conversation will be brief. Just answer my questions concisely and let's get this over with."

"Yes, Sir."

"Why did you join the Volunteer Naval Reserve Training Unit program at Saint John's College in 1925?"

"Three reasons, Sir. First, the VNRTU was an innovative new concept for American university education at the time. Saint John's jumped on the idea and I wanted to be a part of something no one had ever done before.

Second, as a student of ancient Greek history, I yearned to be a modern-day Themistocles or Phormio or Lysander. Third, I liked the way the US Navy Dress White Officer Uniform and cover looked, Sir."

"And how did that work out for you, Lieutenant Junior Grade Victor? In the year you joined the VNRTU, the Navy rejected Saint John's admission into the real Naval Reserve Officer Training Corps program because it wasn't as good a school as Harvard, Yale, Georgia Tech, Northwestern, the University of California, or even the University of Washington. Furthermore, having inspected your personnel folder, I do not see any evidence whatsoever of tactical acumen, individual gallantry, or success leading men in combat. All I see is a naval reserve officer who likes radios, teaches high school history during the day, and is studying to become an ambulance-chasing lawyer in Baltimore at night. Finally, I can see by the way your uniform fits you that you are out of shape, Victor!"

"With respect, Sir, today's date is September 13th, 1939. Six days ago, the President declared a Limited National Emergency in response to war breaking out in Europe. On September 11th, I received an RCA telegram ordering me to report to this office in the Navy Department Building at 09:30 on September 13th. Despite the limitations you noted regarding my resume and physical condition, someone, somewhere in the US Navy requires my service. Sir, I am ready right now to defend the United States of America against all enemies foreign and domestic. Just tell me what you want done and I will do it."

A wry smile—actually, a predator's smirk—appeared on the weather-beaten face of Captain Charles McLaughlin, Annapolis Class of 1910. Replacing his watch on his wrist, he fixed his hard, hawk-like eyes on Victor.

"Fair enough, Lieutenant Junior Grade Victor. You are to report in uniform to the FBI training center in Quantico, Virginia, on September 15th for eight weeks of intense physical conditioning and instruction on counterespionage, surveillance techniques, industrial plant security, firearms training, close-quarter hand-to-hand combat skills, and the finer points of how to deal effectively with Jap and Nazi spies. Should you survive Quantico, you will return to this office and work with me. I will decide whether you make the varsity ONI team or not. Get a good night's sleep on the 15th. The formal training will commence at 06:00 on Saturday, September 16th. I will be receiving regular reports from the FBI instructors about your performance. **Do not let me down!** Here is an envelope with your orders as well as funds for you to return to Baltimore and travel to Quantico. You are to advise your current employer, as well as your night school, family, landlord, and what few friends you may have, that the Navy has called you up for the foreseeable future, but nothing more. Make no mention of the Office of Naval Intelligence, the FBI, or anything pertaining to the nature of the missions you will be called upon to perform to anyone. Think of yourself as a ghost with one point of earthly contact: me. Any questions?"

"No, Sir."

Lowering his head of immaculately coiffed steel-gray hair to read the one sheet of paper on his desk, Captain McLaughlin icily said, "Dismissed, Lieutenant JG Victor."

Alone in his office, the door closed, the Captain picked up the black telephone handset from its base and dialed three numbers. At the other end of the internal Navy Department line, a sultry woman's voice he knew so well said, "ONI."

"Good morning, Catharine. Is the Rear Admiral available?"

"No."

"Catharine, would you advise the Rear Admiral that I think we have our Baltimore Man, and that he should be operational in mid-November 1939."

"Captain McLaughlin, I would be delighted to do so for you."

The Captain heard Catharine hang up her phone. He conjured up the image of her elegant body before him as it would be tonight and whispered to himself, "My God, I just cannot get enough of that woman!"

And that was that.

SHENANDOAH TO BALTIMORE

The B&O Shenandoah departed DC's Union Station at 4 PM. Martin Victor pondered precisely how to manage his Baltimore goodbyes. Arriving at Camden Station at 4:58 PM, the putrid scent of Baltimore harbor in late summer enveloped him as he briskly walked north on Greene Street to the entrance of the University of Maryland Law School.

Seated at his desk reading Agatha Christie's latest novel, *Murder Is Easy*, the avuncular dean and professor of law, Thurston Bell, slowly looked up at Martin Victor in his uniform, standing somewhat stiffly before him. With a perfectly straight face, the legal scholar said, "And what can I do for you, Admiral Victor?"

Martin responded, "With respect, Sir, I am a Lieutenant JG. The US Navy has today mobilized me for full-time service. As a consequence, I will have to withdraw from my fourth year of evening school classes, effective immediately."

Rising from his chair and walking around his desk, the dean grasped Martin's right hand with an astonishingly firm grip. "Lieutenant JG Victor, your nation needs you and I know that you will do whatever necessary to defend her from the totalitarian wolves at her doorstep. For two years—1917 through 1919—I served as an infantry Captain in the US Army in the Great War. After the Armistice, I returned home to practice law, became a law school professor, married, and raised a family. My hope, my prayer for you, is that following your military service, you have the same good fortune that I have had."

At this point, the dean's eyes narrowed. In a granite hard voice, he continued. "My advice to you now is concentrate exclusively on your responsibilities as an officer in the United States Navy. Be smart, be shrewd, be strong and, if conditions demand, be lethal. I commit to you that once you complete your service, you can resume your legal studies here. I will prepare a memo to this effect and place it in your permanent file at the University of Maryland Law

School. I look forward to having you in my admiralty and administrative law courses in the future."

"Thank you, Sir. I will take your advice to heart."

And that was that.

THE EQUITABLE BUILDING

Martin Victor now strode purposefully east for ten blocks to The Equitable Building at the corner of Fayette and Calvert Streets. On the third floor of this Renaissance Revival architectural masterpiece worked Milton Victor, Esq., Martin's eldest brother. Thirteen years older than Martin, Milton had served as his surrogate father. Their biological father, a violent alcoholic from Cracow, Poland, and their invalid mother (also from Cracow) were not up to the task of parenting the six children—three males, three females—that they had recklessly produced. The six Victor siblings survived the mean streets of Baltimore through their cunning, resilience, and utter absence of empathy for others. Milton, the oldest of the six children, however, marveled at Martin, the youngest of the Victor brood. Logical and iron-willed, Milton protected his intuitive and charming baby brother, Martin, from the city of Baltimore's ever-present perils.

It was 7 PM. Martin observed Milton pacing the green and black linoleum-tiled floor in his office, rehearsing his opening argument for the jury trial that would commence tomorrow. Milton's well-deserved reputation for methodical case preparation and flawless courtroom performance typically caused opposing lawyers to settle cases rather than risk losing to him. Jurors, judges, court reporters—even the retired Baltimoreans who regularly observed trials for entertainment purposes—believed in Milton and trusted him because he never exaggerated, raised his voice, or displayed emotion. They recognized his total mastery of the facts of the case and the issues of law. Milton's relentless, yet respectful, cross-examinations withered opposing witnesses, to the consternation of their counsel, and amused everyone else in the courtroom. As the Chief Justice of the Fourth Circuit Federal Court of

Appeals once averred, "Milton Victor is a lawyer's lawyer!" Martin idolized his big brother, but he rarely let him know it.

Martin walked into the office just as Milton's oration ended. Now Milton's inquisition of Martin would commence.

"Where have you been, Martin? Why have you not answered your phone? Why are you in uniform? I tried to call your landlord, Dr. Basswood, at 5 PM, but of course neither he nor his 'hillbilly' wife would pick up the phone because it is the Jewish New Year. What is going on?"

Staring into his brother's impenetrable gray-green eyes, Martin smiled and said, "Why, I have been at the Navy Department Building in Washington, DC. Milton, I got called up on account of the State of Limited National Emergency declared by FDR."

"Damn it to hell, Martin! Why on earth did you persist with this naval reserve nonsense? I put up with your wasting your time as a public school teacher, but I should have put my foot down when you continued your infatuation with those high-class anti-Semites in Annapolis! Jesus Christ, they are going to get you killed! Martin, what will I do without you?"

With these words, Milton's eyes glazed over, but no tears fell.

Martin had never seen or heard Milton, "the man of iron," behave in such an emotional manner. Martin momentarily wondered whether he might be in way over his head.

Too late now, he thought and then replied, "Milton, I cannot tell you much." Martin decided to lie in order to ease the pain he had clearly inflicted on his brother. "I am being trained for a desk job and will be away at a Navy school for a while, perhaps two to three months. I will not be going to sea. My orders specifically forbid me from providing you or anyone else with any more facts. Now, can we go get something to eat? I am starving."

Milton knew when Martin prevaricated for the purpose of deflecting difficult, potentially emotional, discussions. Milton went along with Martin's hoax, looked at his brother's handsome face, and said, "I guess I will have to pay for your dinner…as per usual. Since you're now such a big-shot, top-secret naval officer, let's go over to Haussner's and get some crab cakes from those purportedly naturalized Germans. Since I have a full day in Superior Court tomorrow, we will have to skip having a beer together and make this a quick, but expensive, meal."

The two brothers left The Equitable Building and walked east on Fayette Street and retrieved Milton's pride and joy, his burgundy 1936 DeSoto Airflow SG coupe.

"You want to drive, Martin?" Milton said with a wicked grin on his face.

"Absolutely NEVER!" responded Martin, knowing that no one other than a factory-trained DeSoto mechanic would ever be permitted behind the wheel of Milton's beloved mechanical marvel.

Milton let out a laugh and said, "You finally got something right today!"

Driving past Baltimore City Hall, the War Memorial, and the fortress-like Central District Police Building, Milton made a sharp right turn onto East Falls Avenue and then turned left onto Eastern Avenue, carefully parking the DeSoto near the entrance of Haussner's Restaurant. Martin enjoyed wading through the immaculate sea of tables covered with white linen tablecloths almost as much as he enjoyed flirting with Haussner's exceptionally trim young waitresses dressed in their crisply starched white uniforms. This evening, however, Milton was in no mood for Martin's dallying or dalliances. The two brothers promptly ordered crab cakes and devoured them with gusto. Martin and Milton then completed their ritual Rosh Hashanah repast by savoring generous slices of Haussner's famous strawberry pie and swilling cups of the restaurant's somewhat less renown coffee.

Smiling broadly, Milton poked Martin with his crowbar-like right-hand forefinger and said, "You will not get food or service like this wherever it is you are going, Martin."

"Milton—I mean, Your Honor—I appreciate your pointing these facts out to me!"

The two brothers chortled at their comedy routine.

Then Milton delivered his closing argument.

"Seriously, Martin, the damn Nazis, Japs, Russians, and Italians will come after us after they overrun the pathetically weak and incompetent Poles, Frogs, and Brits. You know that I served as a chemical warfare officer at Edgewood Arsenal during the Great War. As a former chemist, I have a pretty good idea of what our country is capable of throwing at these bastards if they get too close to our borders. Whatever you do, stay the hell away from chemical weapons. And do not volunteer for combat duty. You are thirty-three years old and not cut out for committing homicide. Leave the shooting, stabbing, strangling, smashing, and other mayhem for the millions of young men whom FDR will draft for such purposes when the appropriate time comes. Finagle your way into a secure, stateside radio communications base, like that huge one the Navy has in Annapolis. Do not try to be one of those ancient Greek or Roman heroes you fantasized about at St. John's College! Do you hear me?"

Again, Martin lied to his brother. "Milton, of course I hear you. I agree with you. And I will follow your advice to the best of my ability."

There he goes, lying to me again. Hopeless. He is just plain hopeless, Milton thought.

Martin continued. "Now I have to face Dr. Basswood tonight and the principal of Baltimore City College tomorrow morning and let them know that their tenant and faculty member, respectively, will be leaving town for an indeterminate period of time."

"Martin, what about the dean of the University of Maryland Law School?" Milton inquired.

"Oh, he is taken care of, Milton. He promised that when this situation is over, I can come back and complete my law degree."

"Good, Martin. I want you as my law partner. Remember that!"

Milton paid the bill and drove his brother to 14 South Broadway, a three-story red-brick building built in 1920. Martin's third-floor walk-up apartment was cold during the winter and stiflingly hot during the summer, but it afforded him the seclusion he craved.

"Give my regards to Dr. and Mrs. Basswood, Martin. Wish them a healthy and a happy Rosh Hashanah."

"Will do. I will keep in touch as best I can during the next two or so months, Milton."

"I will miss you, Martin." Milton could not bring himself to say "I love you" to another man, not even to his beloved kid brother. Just the same, his heart ached.

Lightheartedly, Martin replied, "Milton, do not worry. I will see you soon."

Milton drove the DeSoto to the two-story building he owned at 3454 Auchentroly Terrace. Next door stood the Shaarei Tfiloh Synagogue, an imposing, domed neoclassical building facing Druid Hill Park. The synagogue was dark. All its congregants were no doubt dining with their families on this first night of the Jewish New Year. Milton retrieved his mail before climbing the stairs to his second-floor flat. Once inside, he stripped off his clothes, showered with ice-cold water, and brushed his teeth. As he lay in his bed wearing just his underwear, he stared at the ceiling and thought of his brother. "Martin, Martin, Martin," he said softly, mournfully, and then fell soundly asleep.

Milton awoke at 4 AM, as usual, ready for trial. The former South Atlantic Conference 154-pound-class wrestling champion eagerly anticipated pinning his opposing counsel, Hilton Carruthers, in the courtroom. Carruthers's law firm, Drummer and Polk, an old-line Baltimore law firm, proudly hired no Jewish attorneys and waited until Yom Kippur to file complaints, notice depositions, and otherwise ingeniously inconvenience Jewish lawyers. Milton Victor lived to vanquish such gentry and the gentry knew it. While they played golf and tennis at country clubs that barred Jewish membership, Milton prepared for trial. While they vacationed at Palm Beach and Hilton

Head Island, Milton prepared for trial. When they celebrated Christmas with their families, Milton—a solitary bachelor—prepared for trial. He could not be outworked. He could not be outthought. He could not be intimidated. He took no prisoners. Firms like Drummer and Polk settled cases on the courthouse steps rather than go head-to-head with Milton Victor. Every now and then, a dandy like Carruthers would get into the ring with Milton and suffer the predictable consequences. Milton hoped that today would be just such a day.

Dr. BASSWOOD'S PRAYER

Martin walked up the four marble steps to the frosted-pane glass front door, unlocked it, and entered the foyer at 14 South Broadway. The short, wiry figure of Dr. Henry Basswood—arms folded, chin down—blocked the stairs leading to Martin's apartment. Basswood's cold blue eyes looked through Martin like an X-ray.

In a hoarse, bass voice, Dr. Basswood declared, "*Shanah Tovah*. A healthy, sweet, and happy New Year to you, Martin."

"And the same to you and Grace," said the naval officer, somewhat sheepishly.

"Martin, you left very early this morning dressed in that uniform of yours. Have we gone to war and no one had the decency to tell me about it?"

"No, Dr. Basswood—America remains at peace. However, I have been mobilized by the US Navy for the foreseeable future. Do you have a moment to discuss the implications of this call-up with me?"

Still examining his tenant closely, Henry said, "Certainly, Martin, but first we must say a prayer together tonight before engaging in such a mundane, worldly conversation."

The novelty of this late-night revival meeting amused Martin. *If only Milton were here*, he thought. *I can see my big brother's eyes rolling in his head, appalled at the superstitious, illogical conduct perpetrated by an alleged man of science.*

"OK, Dr. Basswood. Where should we pray?"

"Upstairs in my second-floor study."

In his six years as a tenant, Martin had never been admitted to Dr. Basswood's second floor "Holy of Holies." He had, however, dined with Grace and Henry Basswood in their first-floor apartment. On occasion, the secular Martin grudgingly accepted their invitations to celebrate religious holiday meals with them and their Orthodox physician friends. Martin had even been treated as a patient in Dr. Basswood's three-room medical office in the front of 14 South Broadway. Martin now wondered, *What could trigger such unusual behavior by this stone-cold, Johns Hopkins–trained surgeon who had performed an autopsy on his own mother and kept the tumor that killed her in a jar of formaldehyde on a shelf above his office desk?*

Well, Martin thought, *I will soon find out!*

Martin followed Dr. Basswood up the steep flight of stairs. At the landing, Henry pivoted on his left foot to face the door to his private study. Inserting a key that he had retrieved from his pants pocket, the doctor unlocked the door and turned on the lights. Martin beheld a room lined floor-to-ceiling with bookshelves on which rested religious tomes, small bronze statues of Eastern European Jews, and tiny framed paintings of Oriental Jews perched on equally tiny triangular stands. On the floor next to a sofa stood a large tuba resting on its bell. Throughout the cluttered sanctuary appeared to be souvenirs from foreign lands, as well as from states in the western part of the United States. Dr. Basswood slowly lowered himself onto the black hardwood chair emblazoned with the logo of Johns Hopkins Medical School that faced his rolltop desk. Like a schoolmaster, the prematurely wizened doctor beckoned Martin to sit facing him on another Johns Hopkins University chair adjacent to the desk. Henry fished out a miniscule book—two inches by three inches—from his shirt pocket, handed it to Martin, and said, "Let us recite Psalm 140, a prayer popular with Jewish Confederate soldiers during the Civil War." Martin read Psalm 140 aloud while Dr. Basswood recited it from memory.

Deliver me O Lord, from an evil man; from a man of violence do thou keep me....

After praying, the doctor inscribed the pocket-sized book of Psalms "To Martin" and signed "Henry" with the date and "Baltimore, Maryland, USA" underneath the signature. Dr. Basswood then handed the gift to Martin.

"Now, Martin, what do you want to discuss with me?"

"Dr. Basswood, please understand that I have been ordered by my commanding officer not to disclose any information to you—or anyone, for that matter—other than I am now an active duty officer in the regular Navy and that I will be departing on Friday to take a two- to three-month course at an undisclosed location."

"So, Martin, neither you nor I know whether you may be returning to Baltimore at the end of the two or three months. Correct?"

"Correct."

Squaring his slight-but-sinewy shoulders, the former-farmer-turned-physician asked, "And you want to know what Grace and I will do about the apartment on the third floor of 14 South Broadway that you have been renting from us for the past six years?"

"Correct," replied the tenant Lieutenant.

"Well, Martin, Grace and I will let you keep the apartment rent-free while you are away. If the Navy stations you back in Baltimore at the end of the course, we would be delighted to have you back under our roof. If they ship you out to destinations unknown, we will deal with that eventuality when the time comes. Is this acceptable to you?"

Clearing his throat, Martin replied, "Dr. Basswood, thank you for your generous and thoughtful offer, but I cannot deprive Grace and you of the rental income to which you are entitled."

Basswood shook his head. "We are the ones who are benefitting from your service, dear Martin. We can certainly do without the rental income for two to three months. Now, let me tell you some things only Grace knows about me and I think you will more clearly understand why mere money means nothing to me in this matter."

Reaching for a framed photograph on his desk, Henry showed Martin the fading image of a seated, unsmiling sailor in a uniform with Russian letters woven on the band of his service cap.

"This, Martin, was my father, Avram Kotzebue, a member of the crew of the battleship *Suvorov*, a part of the Tsar's ill-fated Second Pacific Squadron in the Russo-Japanese War. In late May of 1905, when I was sixteen years old, my father perished along with 908 *Suvorov* sailors slaughtered by the Japanese at the Battle of Tsushima. With my father dead and anti-Jewish violence escalating in our hometown of Odessa, my mother and I fled to the German port of Hamburg and purchased one-way tickets on a ship bound for Baltimore. So you see, Martin, if your mission will be directed against the Japanese, you will be the instrument of my revenge against the murderers of my father. If your mission will be to fight against that psychopath Hitler and his Nazis, well, then you will be my avenging angel against the tormentors of Jews. Lastly, if you are ordered to fight against Hitler's ally, Stalin, you will be punishing the evil successor to the Tsar whose ignorant followers hounded my mother and me out of Russia. Any way you look at it, Martin, it is I who should be compensating you for destroying my enemies and the enemies of the United States."

At first, Martin thought, *This guy who took the Hippocratic Oath has a hit list longer than God's!* However, after a moment of reflection, the US naval officer realized that he might soon be ordered to engage in combat with members of the armed forces of the Empire of Japan, Nazi Germany, Soviet Russia, or maybe even Mussolini's Fascist Italy. Martin took Dr. Basswood's hand, shook it firmly, and said, "Doc, you have got a deal!"

Henry Basswood smiled at Martin. *Another first*!

"Now, Martin, one other thing. And this is serious. As you no doubt know, I treat at least a hundred sailors a year for various venereal diseases. These filthy men contract these awful illnesses by having sex with filthy women—

and sometimes with other filthy men. They wander up here to my office from their ships in Baltimore harbor seeking complete cures for their afflictions. Martin, complete cures without serious side effects do not yet exist for diseases like syphilis or gonorrhea. Please behave yourself, Martin. If you cannot behave yourself, wear a condom and do not practice oral sex. One day, God willing, you will fall in love with a virtuous woman, get married, and have a wonderful family. Venereal disease would destroy any possibility of your having a happy life. So conduct yourself appropriately, Martin. As my teacher, the great Dr. Osler, advised me in medical school, 'Be clear-eyed, clean, and pure!'"

What could Martin possibly say in response to these admonitions from the doctor known as "Baltimore's Vice Admiral of Venereal Disease" other than, "Roger that, Dr. Basswood!"

To break the tension, Martin asked, "One last question, Dr. Basswood. How did the surname 'Kotzebue' become 'Basswood?'"

"Well, Martin, the immigration officer at the Port of Baltimore could not pronounce or spell 'Kotzebue,' so he renamed my mother and me 'Basswood.' The name seems to have successfully stood the test of time. Do you have a problem with it?"

"No, Sir—none whatsoever. See you in the morning."

Extending his arms and placing his hands on top of Martin's head, Henry said, "May the Lord bless you and keep you. May he cause his countenance to shine upon you. Amen."

"Thank you, Dr. Basswood."

And that was that.

AN INTERLUDE WITH GRACE BASSWOOD

Martin awoke, as usual, at 4:30 AM. He showered, shaved a bit too closely, applied Old Spice aftershave to his wounded face, performed 50 push-ups and 50 sit-ups, and shadowboxed for ten minutes. Next he donned his somewhat-rumpled uniform and walked down two flights of stairs. As he attempted to exit 14 South Broadway, Grace Basswood called his name from the door to her apartment at the end of the narrow hallway behind him.

"Grace Basswood, to what do I owe this unexpected pleasure?" said Martin in his most engaging voice.

"Henry told me all about his conversation with you last night, Martin, and I wanted to let you know that for once, I agree with everything he said!"

Grace Basswood hailed from the hills of western Maryland: Hagerstown, to be exact. Her father, a peddler, and her mother both emigrated to the United States from Russia in 1881 after anti-Jewish pogroms triggered by the assassination of Tsar Alexander II made their life in the town of Minsk unbearable. Born in 1895, Grace Leontieff was the youngest of eight children produced by her refugee parents. Grace grew up poor, but proud. She was nobody's fool.

After graduating from high school, Grace headed to Baltimore to become a nurse. She received her training at Johns Hopkins Hospital. In June of 1919, she met Henry during a gruesome surgery he was performing to repair the groin of a man who had been kicked by a skittish police horse that he had foolishly approached from the rear. Things did not turn out well for the patient, but Grace and Henry fell into their minimalist version of love and married several months later. Childless, Grace served as Henry's medical office nurse, bookkeeper, receptionist, and critic. She was an ardent follower of fellow Baltimorean Henrietta Szold, the founder of Hadassah, a women's Zionist organization. Grace admired Henrietta's faith and courage. She would have joined Ms. Szold and gone to Palestine in 1933 to assist in rescuing Jews fleeing Hitlerian persecution, but Henry would not allow it. Grace and Henry bickered incessantly, but to Martin, their relationship appeared to be infinitely superior to the callous indifference of his own parents and the turbulent, sometimes violent, households of his married siblings. Martin Victor, like his unmarried brother Milton, took for granted that there were no happy husbands and no merry wives in the city of Baltimore. Gordon Turk,

Milton's best friend from high school and an incomparably acute raconteur and wit, famously observed in 1937, "In Baltimore, you have to go to Sol Levinson and Brothers Funeral Home on North Avenue to see spouses care for each other."

"Grace, you know that I cannot thank you and Henry enough for all that you have done and continue to do for me," said Martin sincerely.

Grace then surprised him. "Martin, you need to know that Henry and I view you as a member of our family. We respect your commitment to teaching history in a public high school during the day while studying law at night. We admire your devotion to the US Naval Reserve, your attending those shortwave radio training meetings each week at the Richmond Armory, and doing whatever it is you do for the Navy each summer on those long cruises. We even like that odd brother of yours, Milton, and the way you two look out for each other. Most important to me, Martin, is that you have always shown us the utmost respect. You have never been late with a rent payment. You have never brought women into your apartment, and you have never been loud or inebriated in our presence. You are a decent young man. Now Martin, you take care of yourself, son, and remember, as the Talmud says, 'If a man comes to take your life, rise up and take his first!'"

Martin could not quite believe his ears. He thought that he knew everything about Henry and Grace. But clearly, he did not. This call-up by the Navy had unleashed sentiments, emotions, truths, and commitments that Martin had never known or believed could exist.

My God, he again thought. *Perhaps I am in way over my head.* Nonetheless, Martin understood that there was no turning back on the road to his destiny.

"Grace, I will take your advice. Now have a good day and I look forward to seeing you and Henry tonight."

Stone-faced, Grace waved to him as he headed out the front door.

She never smiled. Ever.

A KNIGHT DEPARTS FROM THE CASTLE ON THE HILL

Still pondering his impromptu chat with Grace Basswood, Martin boarded the Baltimore Transit Company streetcar No. 16 bound for the junction of Baltimore and Aisquith Streets, where he transferred to the northbound No. 19 streetcar. After passing unenticing urban landmarks such as the Maryland Penitentiary/Baltimore Jail complex, the Greenmount Cemetery, and the Clifton Park Golf Course, Martin transferred to the T Line bus at the intersection of Harford Road and The Alameda. At 33rd Street and The Alameda, he beheld his alma mater and soon-to-be former place of employment, Baltimore City College High School.

Founded in 1839, the all-male Baltimore City College High School was the third oldest high school in the United States. In 1928, at a cost approaching $3 million, BCC moved from a wholly inadequate building on Howard Street to its current location, a 37-acre tract of land from which rose an imposing three-story gothic-style collegiate edifice with a tower standing 130 feet tall. The approximately 3,000 young men who attended "City" in 1939 arrived each day by automobile, bus, on foot, and by streetcar from Baltimore's numerous ethnic enclaves—Anglo Saxon, Dutch, French, German, Greek, Irish, Italian, Jewish, Polish, Scottish, and Ukrainian. The building was appropriately called "The Castle on the Hill."

Martin walked from the bus stop up the knoll on which the massive gray stone building stood. Arriving at the office of Dr. Vincent Caldwell, the principal who had hired him after his graduation from Saint John's College in 1929, the US Navy officer rapped on the closed door.

The stentorian voice of the principal, a Johns Hopkins PhD Latin professor, responded. "The door is not locked; please enter."

The tall, lean, silver-haired patrician rose from his swivel chair as soon as he saw the uniformed Martin Victor cross the threshold of his office.

"So, Lieutenant JG Victor, let me guess: The United States Navy has called you to the colors."

Smiling broadly at the playfully perceptive face of this erudite educator he so respected, Martin replied, "Now I know why you are the person running this institution."

They both laughed.

"Professor, my orders require me to report for training immediately. My commanding officer sternly admonished me not to say any more than this to anyone. I am embarrassed to leave you, my students, and my history department colleagues in a lurch like this, but I must, as your friend Virgil would say, '*Dare fatis vela*… Spread sails to fate.'"

At this, the classics scholar grinned and, also quoting from the *Aeneid*, replied, "*Nunc animus opus,* Martin. *Nunc pectore firmo*… Now, Martin, is the hour for courage, now for the dauntless of heart.

"Martin, is it not wonderful to have a fellow graduate of Saint John's College as your friend and patron? Who else could capture this moment in history—this moment in your life—and share it with you in Latin, the language of Scipio Africanus, Julius Caesar, and Augustus? Do not worry about me, your students, or your colleagues. Somehow we will survive without you. I will break the news to them. When America declared war against the Germans in 1917, I had been teaching at BCC for ten years. Faculty members inconveniently got called up then, too. I have had considerable experience handling these sorts of matters. Virgil, as always, put it best: '*Experto credite*…' Trust me, Martin, I have gone through it. Soon, no doubt, many of your young scholars will be following you to defend our *patria* against the barbarian hordes threatening us from both the East and the West. Men like you and the students we shape and mold at Baltimore City college High School will win through when the time comes. Of this I have no doubt. My advice to you—and to all who must in the future face our foes on the Field of Mars—is Virgil's sage dictum: '*Durate et vosmet rebus servate secundis*…' Endure and keep yourselves for days of happiness. Martin, I look forward to your return to teaching history at BCC with a triumphal wreath atop your noble head."

Once again, Martin had misjudged the reaction of a person he thought he knew well to his sudden departure from Baltimore. He had expected at least an expression of mild irritation from his employer for the disruption that he was causing. Instead, he was given a pep talk in Latin from Professor Caldwell, a scholar he revered. Martin extended his right hand. The principal grasped it and said, "Look with favor upon a bold beginning."

"Prof, that quote is from Homer's *Odyssey*. Nothing Roman about it!"

Looking down at his soon-to-be former employee, Professor Caldwell replied, "Martin, every now and then quoting a little classical Greek will not hurt! Now get out of here before you get trapped in numerous conversations that you are not supposed to have."

And that was that.

SOUTH ANN STREET

Martin Victor exited Baltimore City College and retraced his bus and streetcar route back to South Broadway and Pratt Street. He walked east to South Ann Street to the dilapidated building in which his biological father, Leon, lived. Martin expected that his father would be stretched out on the worn old living room sofa, semiconscious from the effects of liquor. But again his expectations were proved wrong. There on the brick steps sat a temporarily sober Leon, his narrow-brimmed black felt hat covering his bald head and shading his desiccated face. As Martin got closer, he noticed that his unshaven father's wrinkled white shirt, lined front and back by black suspenders, desperately needed to be laundered. Looking down, he observed that the cuffs of the old alcoholic's winterweight suit pants could not quite hide the cracked black leather on Leon's one pair of never-polished shoes.

Leon smiled impishly at Martin, the stubble on his face glistening with hot Baltimore summer sweat. Martin, who reviled facial hair, struggled to say, "Hi, Dad!"

Leon replied, "Vere are you going dressed like dat? On a boat or someting?"

"I am going away to school for a while, Dad. I probably won't see you until early December. Milton will let you know when I will return to Baltimore."

"School? I thought you vent to dat law school in Baltimore."

"No, Dad, this is a different school. I cannot tell you anything about it."

"OK. You haf a good time avey at school. I vill see you ven I see you."

"Great, Dad. Take care of yourself."

"I vill, son. Vit your mother gone, I haf to take care of mineself."

"Now, Dad, you know Milton stops by all the time to take of you."

"No he does not. He takes my bottles from me every time he visits."

"Dad, Milton is just trying to keep you healthy."

"Vot nonsense! I am strong as a horse. *De schnapps* preserfs me. Your brudder is mean to me just like your mother voz. He hates me."

Leon's inaccurate and unfair criticism of both Milton and his dead mother was the final straw. Martin thought, *This conversation should have been over long ago. Time to end my charade of civility.*

"Dad, Milton—like Mom—has only your best interests at heart. I must go now."

With that, Martin put his hand on Leon's bony shoulder, did a quick about-face, and marched back to 14 South Broadway to pack for his train ride to the FBI National Police Academy in Quantico, Virginia.

On September 15, as former high school history teacher and night-school law student Martin Victor rolled south on the Richmond, Fredericksburg, and Potomac Railroad route from Washington, DC, to Quantico, Virginia, he cleared his mind of thoughts and concerns from his past. Martin focused only on the future. He would give this course, and whatever missions came afterward, everything he had.

2

A BRIEF LOOK BACK IN TIME

SEPTEMBER 1, 1939; 2516 MASSACHUSETTS AVENUE, NW, WASHINGTON, DC: THE EMBASSY OF THE EMPIRE OF JAPAN

Approximately two weeks before Martin Victor packed his distressed leather suitcase for his trip to Quantico, Captain Saigo Masuji of the Imperial Japanese Navy waited patiently for a decrypted copy of a top-secret cable sent to him by Lieutenant Ito Yuji, an engineer at the IJN's Technical Research Center. The Captain's official diplomatic title was naval attaché. His real role was to spy on the US Navy. He was a master of the art of collecting "human intelligence," adroitly recruiting as his agents cash-starved US Navy officers and enlisted men. Masuji's specialty, however, was accessing military secrets from sex-starved secretaries he seduced who worked at naval installations and industrial enterprises performing sensitive weapons work for the American Navy. Additionally, Masuji utilized the talent-spotting services of two resident deep-penetration Imperial agents, Taiso Tadatomo and Kimura Katsuie, who had spent years cultivating pro-Japanese attitudes among Negro individuals and organizations such as the Pacific Movement of the Eastern World, the Development of Our Own, and the Ethiopian Pacific Movement. Both men were members of the Black Dragon Society and had previously served as intelligence officers in the Imperial Japanese Army. Unfortunately, Tadatomo's recent arrest by US immigration officials in Detroit on July 7,

1939, deprived the Captain of any access to Taiso's American Fifth Column contacts.

Broad shouldered and ramrod straight, Captain Masuji stood 6 feet, 2 inches tall. He towered over the rest of the embassy staff. Behind his back, even high-ranking diplomats nicknamed him "Benkei" after the mythical Japanese warrior-giant renowned for his skill with weapons. A 1904 graduate of the Japanese Naval Academy at Etajima, Captain Masuji served on Admiral Heihachiro Togo's flagship *Mikasa* during the Battle of Tsushima. Though shrapnel from an exploding Russian shell severed both the pinky and ring finger from his right hand, Captain Masuji remained at his post commanding a fast-firing three-inch gun crew throughout the entire naval engagement. For his intrepidity in this and other battles, Captain Masuji received numerous honors, including: the Order of the Rising Sun, the Order of the Golden Kite, and the Russo-Japanese War Medal. Ruggedly debonair, fluent in unaccented English, and a superb ballroom dancer, women in the DC diplomatic community viewed him as a mature, mustachioed Japanese Gary Cooper. Husbands of these women had another name for him: "Lothario."

Kinuyo Hara, Captain Masuji's secretary, climbed the spiral staircase to her superior's office, bowed, entered, and approached the seated spy. With her porcelain arms fully extended, Hara held in her graceful hands the sealed, letter-sized envelope containing Lieutenant Yuji's decrypted cable. "*Arigatou gozaimasu,*" growled Masuji. Hara knew not to say another word to Benkei. She continued to bow toward him as she backed out of his office door. The Captain deftly slit open the envelope with his razor-sharp *kunai* and read the following:

Intelligence Collection Request
To Captain Saigo Masuji

Admiral Toyotomi Mitsuhide, Chief of N-3, Imperial Navy General Staff, requests that you commence comprehensive and persistent collection of all significant public and nonpublic data regarding the use of radio waves and devices using radio waves to detect the presence, movement, speed, distance, and direction of ships and airplanes. Without limitation, data collection sources should include US academic, industrial, and military institutions, and individuals. All communications between you and Lieutenant Ito Yuji regarding this subject must be encrypted using the latest level of the IJN fleet code. Whenever possible, send relevant radio-wave documents by way of diplomatic courier. Documents regarding this subject must be maintained in your embassy office safe when not being used by you.

Inhaling air through his teeth, Captain Masuji asked himself if technology might be moving faster than an old sea-samurai like himself could comprehend. Answering the question he had posed to himself, he replied out loud, "*Chigau yo* [Definitely not]!"

With this declaration of war against self-doubt, he stared across his office at his new RCA Model 40X-56 radio with the 1939 New York World's Fair Trylon and Perisphere molded into the electrical device's Syroco wood cabinet. Masuji walked to the table on which his 5-vacuum-tube treasure rested and turned the power knob to the right. The vacuum tubes heated quickly and he could hear WRC broadcasting a report about Nazi Germany's invasion of Poland. Turning the dial to the left, the sound vanished. The Captain lifted the radio to eye level and inspected its back panel. He then raised the device a few inches above his head and examined its bottom. And there they were! Seventy-two US radio patent numbers—displayed in eight columns with nine patents per column—listed by RCA for all the world to see. He placed the source of his inspiration back on the table. A grim Satsuma samurai grin crossed his face.

Lifting the telephone off its receiver, he asked the switchboard operator to connect him the Japanese embassy's economic attaché.

Hiroaki Shima quivered as he heard Captain Masuji's military command voice say, "Shima, come quickly. I need you!"

As he approached the spiral staircase leading to "Benkei's Chamber," the economic attaché noticed on the wall to his left a painting of what appeared to him to be a bullseye. *How appropriate*, he thought. *The bullseye is on me.*

Winded before he even reached the top of the stairs, the chain-smoking bureaucrat heard Captain Masuji say, "Shima, my good man, ENTER!" Bowing deeply, he crossed the threshold of the office, and as the 5-foot, 3-inch, 125-pound economist straightened himself, he beheld the fearsome eight-fingered giant towering over him. He then felt the powerful grasp of the three-fingered, right claw-hand of the Captain on his puny left shoulder and the vice-like grip of the spy's intact left hand on his pitiful right shoulder. For a moment, Hiroaki Shima thought that he might faint from fear.

"Shima, what I am about to discuss with you is classified top secret. You must not tell anyone, including the ambassador, that you are assisting me on this mission. Do you understand?"

"*Hai*, Captain Masuji," replied the diminutive diplomat, summoning all of his limited courage as he made brief eye contact with the formidable naval officer.

"Good. Very good!" Directing Shima to the couch in his office, Masuji said, "Please sit down. This may take a while. May I pour you a drink?"

Shima could barely utter the words, "Just water, please."

The Captain graciously placed the glass in the economic attaché's tiny hand.

"Shima, I know little about patents. What precisely are they? Do you have a copy of any American patents that I could examine?"

"Captain, in exchange for a very detailed public disclosure of a product or process that solves a specific technological problem, a government grants the inventor a patent, the exclusive right to exclude others from making, using, or selling the disclosed invention for a limited period of time. I do not have a copy of any US government-granted patents. However, in response to requests I receive from Japanese industrial enterprises desirous of preserving their anonymity, I have the science and technology attaché instruct a trusted *gaijin* law firm to place a watch at the US Patent Office for all patents granted in a specific area—say, aircraft engine technology—in one of the law firm's attorney's names. The S&T attaché provides me with copies of the patents provided to him, which I then forward to the Japanese firms that requested them."

"Shima, this is excellent. Please confirm: You could, in the ordinary course of your work, tell the S&T attaché that an undisclosed Japanese company has requested copies of all existing US patents regarding the use of radio waves to detect the movement and direction of ships and airplanes. Correct?"

"*Hai*, Captain Masuji."

"And, Shima, your request will not raise any suspicion in the mind of the S&T attaché?"

"*Hai*, Sir. As I think I may have mentioned, we have an ongoing watch on all US aircraft engine patents. The S&T attaché never asked which Japanese enterprise wanted the information, and he has never displayed any particular interest at all regarding my request."

"Shima, this American law firm and its lawyers… How discreet are they?"

"Captain Masuji, at the present time, under current US laws and regulations, US patent lawyers care primarily about the timely payment of their outrageously excessive fees. Also, they are like US doctors: they take client confidentiality very seriously. Patent lawyers disclose in minute detail important inventions for their US and non-US inventors all the time. They routinely advise their clients, both US and non-US, how to design and build products that do not infringe on existing patents. I do not believe that a request by our attaché for published patents regarding radio waves will raise any eyebrows at the *gaijin* law firm. In their minds, he is a good, longstanding client who never quibbles over fees and pays promptly."

"Your experience and logic have persuaded me to approve your taking this step. Execute this patent sweep first thing tomorrow and provide me with the results no later than Friday, September 22nd. One caveat, Shima.

Do not extend the search for existing radio-wave detection patents into a watch for future patents. Make the requested search a one-time event. Leave as few tracks as possible.

"The S&T attaché must never know that I am the source of this request. If he demands to know who requires this information, tell him the name of a Japanese electricals firm—say, Nihon Musen, or some other plausible Japanese electrical corporation with which you have excellent relationships and will support your cover story.

"*Hai*," replied Shima.

Glowering, Benkei admonished Shima. "I repeat, even the ambassador must never know that you are working with me on this project. The project's code name is '*Hinode*' [Sunrise]."

"*Hai!*"

"Finally, Shima, once we collect these patents, we will have to build profiles of the US companies, academic institutions, and individuals working on radio-wave detection technology and devices. Be prepared to move very quickly, very precisely, and most of all, invisibly. Your secretary must not prepare any documents for you or have any knowledge of *Hinode*. Maintain all *Hinode* documents in your office safe when you are not using them. Never take these documents outside of the embassy."

Shima replied, "*Hai!*"

"Let us continue our *Hinode* conversations after the embassy staff has departed this evening."

"*Hai!*"

Hiroaki Shima bowed and returned to his office feeling oddly invigorated by Benkei's trust in him. He vowed to follow Captain Masuji's orders perfectly and with all deliberate speed. For once, Shima knew no fear.

Benkei, alone in his lair, awaited his next inspiration. It was not long in coming.

On Saturday morning, September 2, 1939, Captain Masuji sat at his desk reading a compendium of recent articles from *The New York Times* prepared for him by Miss Hara. A headline from the August 4 edition of the newspaper seized his attention. **FBI Spy Training Underway For A Year.**

According to the article, Director of the FBI J. Edgar Hoover had personally participated in implementing a year-long secret program educating FBI agents in techniques to uncover espionage, sabotage, and subversive activities. The FBI announced that it now offered its counterespionage training courses to agents of the Office of Naval Intelligence, the Military Intelligence Division of the US Army, state and local police forces, and even private detectives providing security for industrial firms. Military bases, aerospace and defense plants, and critical national infrastructure elements such as ports and oil reserves were specifically mentioned as areas of concern for Director Hoover and his FBI. Apparently, a nonpublic Executive Order by President Roosevelt had authorized this coordinated activity, targeting foreign spies like Captain Masuji operating in the US.

"Diplomatic immunity in a law-abiding nation like the United States is a wonderful thing." Benkei laughed. "If I get caught spying, the Americans will declare me *persona non grata* and simply send me home. My way, the Japanese way, would be different."

Grasping his glistening *kunai*, he said to himself, "If I detect someone—*anyone*—committing espionage or sabotage against Japan, it will not be pretty."

Unreported in the media that morning was the fact that J. Edgar Hoover got along quite well with the Rear Admiral serving as Director of the ONI. The two men met weekly to discuss counterintelligence matters in Hoover's private conference room in the recently constructed Department of Justice Building at 10th and Constitution Avenues. On his own initiative, the FBI Director had offered ONI personnel access to his state-of-the-art counterintelligence course in Quantico, Virginia. Agents from both organizations were now being trained together and expected to work together to defeat threats to US national security. The gloves were coming off, and an army of US counterintelligence agents would increasingly employ a comprehensive array of sophisticated and tough techniques against spies that even the formidable Benkei had to respect.

6 AM, MONDAY, SEPTEMBER 11, 1939; CAPTAIN MASUJI'S OFFICE: AN OP PLAN EMERGES

Mr. Shima bowed deeply before Benkei and said, "*Ohayou gozaimasu.*"

Captain Masuji, barely bowing at all, replied, "*Ohayou*, Shima. Please be seated. What news have you received from your *gaijin* lawyers?"

Beaming with pride, Shima delivered the information sought by Captain Masuji ahead of schedule. He handed his superior a 5-inch-thick, 3-ring binder divided into four tabs: Summary, Radio Wave Patents, Radio Wave Companies, Radio Wave Inventors. The economic attaché then launched into his report.

"Three researchers at the US Navy Research Laboratory—Taylor, Young, and Hyland—filed a patent application for a system for detecting objects by radio on June 13th, 1933. Patent No. 1,981,884 for this invention was granted on November 27th, 1934. One of the inventors, Lawrence A. Hyland, left the US government lab and became an executive at Bendix Radio Corporation in 1936. Apparently, Mr. Hyland has continued his radio-wave work, as he assigned to Bendix a Patent No. 2,151,917 for 'radio apparatus' that was granted to him on March 28th, 1939.

"Interestingly, an article in *The Baltimore Sun* dated November 15th, 1937, indicated that Bendix opened a plant to manufacture 'special radio equipment for aircraft' not far from DC—in the city of Baltimore. This Bendix facility is located at 920 East Fort Avenue, near to Baltimore harbor's Locust Point docks, where Japanese merchant ships not infrequently load products such as scrap metal bound for Japan. Located approximately four miles northwest of this Bendix plant is a Westinghouse plant that, according to a *Baltimore Sun* article dated July 17th, 1938, manufactures 'highly specialized radio equipment … for the federal government.' While no specific Westinghouse radio-wave detection patent grants have been identified by our law firm, this company may well be involved in such important research. Similarly, while Raytheon Manufacturing Company in Newton, Massachusetts, possesses no radio-wave detection patent grants, the company likely has the capabilities required to pursue such advanced technology electrical systems work.

"As you will see, other US entities and their researchers receiving patent grants for inventions pertinent to radio-wave detection devices are:

"Radio Corporation of America, or RCA. Researchers Irving Wolff, located at Camden, New Jersey, and Ernest Linder, located at Philadelphia, Pennsylvania.

"Bell Telephone Laboratories. Researcher Horace T. Budenbom located at Short Hills, New Jersey.

"And Stanford University. Researchers William Hansen and Russell Varian located at Paolo Alto, California.

"Finally, Captain Masuji, our lawyers have heard credible rumors that the Government of the United States, under its 1917 Espionage Act and 1928 Foreign Agent Registration Law, will soon require attorneys working for foreign governments to notify the US Department of State of their activities. While we have no further radio-wave detection patent search or other radio-wave detection work with the law firm, I cannot guarantee that our efforts to date will not be reported should these new regulations take effect."

"Thank you for this prompt, efficient, and thorough work, Shima. Keep your antennae discreetly trained on our law firm's response to this unfortunate change in US surveillance practices, and report to me when and if there are any moves by the US Government in this regard."

"*Hai!*" replied Shima crisply.

Leaning forward in his chair, the muscles in his stomach, shoulders, and neck tensing, Benkei growled, "Now, Shima, let us discuss this Bendix Corporation."

Shima sat ramrod straight, pen in hand, and placed his notepad on the Captain's desk.

"Shima, for the moment we must concentrate our limited resources on Bendix. At some point, we may have to make a surreptitious entry into the Bendix plant. So we need to understand thoroughly the tactical situation we will face before making an uninvited visit to an American defense factory. Specifically, you should obtain detailed maps of the area of Baltimore in which Bendix is located. What government buildings and offices, commercial enterprises, and residential dwellings surround or are within one mile of the Bendix building? How close to Bendix are the nearest Federal Bureau of Investigation, Maryland State Police, and Baltimore City Police Department outposts? Are there any US Army or US Navy bases nearby? Are there any Federal Communications Commission monitoring posts near Bendix?

"Without attracting any attention, we need photographs of this entire area. Find out which Japanese merchant vessels will be docking at this Locust Point area within the next six months and the names of the Captains and Executive Officers of each ship. Americans do not get concerned when drunken Japanese sailors pose for group photographs. Perhaps I will be able to use my connections to IJN resources to generate precise images of the plant and its environs. Find out where Mr. Hyland and other senior Bendix Radio engineering executives reside. Collect significant personal details regarding these men so that we can construct profiles of them.

"Finally, let us both read *The Baltimore Sun* newspaper each day to maintain our situational awareness of the zone of our potential future operations. I want to review your progress on these matters in one week, September 16th, at 6 AM."

At this, the undersized attaché rose from his chair, bowed, and said an enthusiastic, "*Hai!!*"

After Shima departed, Masuji called Miss Hara into his office. Hara bowed submissively and Benkei told her to contact Kimura Katsuie using secure channels and ask him for the names and biographies of his and Tadatomo's most trusted agents with connections to or residing in the city of Baltimore. Alone in his office, Masuji mulled over his next moves.

9 AM, SEPTEMBER 14, 1939; CAPTAIN MASUJI'S OFFICE

Miss Hara delivered to Captain Masuji the decrypted response to the questions he previously posed to Kimura Katsuie on September 11.

> Greetings. I can provide you with three Negro males capable of performing a range of complex surveillance, extraction, and armed activities in the Baltimore-Washington area of operations. These individuals support Japan's efforts to break the power of the white race and, despite these men's intelligence and academic attainment, they are essentially "invisible" to white Americans. One of the men is a youthful, early middle-aged physician who works part time in a Negro hospital and maintains a private practice with no Caucasian patients. The other two individuals are young men in their early twenties who are recent graduates of segregated undergraduate schools.

> I await your further instructions and look forward to assisting you in your important work for our Emperor, our Empire, and the Imperial Japanese Navy.

Benkei deduced from his daily newspaper and magazine clippings—as well as his confidential sources within the US government—that he would have to move expeditiously, as the American's internal security apparatus improved each day in terms of the numbers, training, and sophistication of its personnel. Even American industry and academia appeared to be cooperating with the Federal Bureau of Investigation efforts to blunt foreign penetration into their facilities and secrets. Masuji understood all too well from his education at Etajima, combat experience, and work as a spy how technological advantages, combined with incessant drilling, harsh discipline, and attention to minute detail, provides the victor's edge. At Tsushima, Admiral

Togo crushed the Russian's Second Pacific Fleet in no small part due to the Imperial Japanese Navy's superior rangefinders, rigorous target practice regimen, sophisticated wireless communication system, swifter ships, and excellent torpedoes. Whatever the Americans were up to with this radio-wave detection technology, he intended to get it and transfer it to the IJN. His duty to the Emperor weighed heavily on him.

Masuji looked up at his secretary standing impassively before him. "Hara, send the following message in code to Kimura:

Kimura,

Please arrange to get your most competent "invisible" agent employed at the Bendix Radio Corporation plant and office building in Baltimore, Maryland, located at 920 East Fort Avenue. Ideally this person should get a job providing him with access to the offices of managers of Bendix Radio and electrical engineers. Inform me, as soon as your invisible is hired, of his job title and job description. We will give him a few weeks to establish himself in his job before briefing him on his precise mission.

Separately, prepare your second invisible agent to serve as a conduit—or "outside Bendix" agent—who will report the information collected by the inside Bendix agent to me alone, either in face-to-face meetings or at dead drop locations I will arrange for him.

Finally, alert the physician that he will be the controller responsible for overseeing the day-to-day activities of the two younger agents and providing them with logistical support.

Meetings between your three agents must appear, even to trained watchful eyes, as natural and above suspicion.

For Your Information Only: The inside Bendix agent's initial mission will be to identify any Bendix projects for the US government that involve the research, design, engineering, manufacture, and service of devices using radio waves to detect military aircraft and warships. Identifying Bendix employees and US government officials involved in such radio-wave detection activities will be part of this phase of the mission. Should your agent uncover radio-wave detection projects at Bendix, phase two of the mission will involve gathering information, documents, drawings, specifications, etc., to forward to the relevant interested bureaus within the Imperial Japanese Navy.

DESTROY THIS MESSAGE AFTER READING.

Hara bowed and, as always, backed humbly out of Benkei's office. Once in the hallway, Hara righted herself. While quite satisfied from her secret weekend tryst in Potomac, Maryland, with a puissant *gaijin* who dwarfed even Captain Masuji, she knew that she was playing with fire. Violating Benkei's rule mandating no relationships with white men would, at best, get her sent back to Japan. At worst, Benkei would torture her, interrogate her, and murder her, or have her tortured, interrogated, and murdered before reporting her missing to the embassy consul after she "failed to report for work." Hara's body would be found eventually. However, there would be no evidence as to who perpetrated the crime. Her ashes would be transported to her family in Matsumoto by a representative of the Foreign Ministry, who would duly express the profound grief of the Empire over a perfidious act inflicted on an innocent young Japanese woman by despicable American gangsters.

Masuji picked up the phone and asked the operator to connect him with the cultural attaché, Hiroshi Sakamoto. He heard the effete bureaucrat say, "Sakamoto. What can I do for you, Captain Masuji?"

Benkei said, "Sakamoto, I need your assistance. Will you be sponsoring any Japanese embassy events in the city of Baltimore anytime soon, where either I or one of my agents might accompany you?"

After a brief silence, Sakamoto replied, "Why, yes. We will soon be sponsoring an exhibit of Japanese art and a children's art competition at the Walter's Art Gallery. I would be particularly delighted to have someone with your military background present, as the children will compete to draw a samurai sword and scabbard on display at the museum. Does this event meet your requirements?"

Masuji grinned into the receiver and said, "Very satisfactory. Could you arrange for us to spend one night in a Baltimore hotel, either before or after the event?"

Sakamoto said, "Of course. I will find a hotel that has no objection to serving Japanese patrons and get back to you with all of the travel details."

"Fine," replied Masuji, replacing the phone handset on its cradle.

The thought that there might be any issue at all with obtaining a hotel room on account of his race infuriated Benkei. He looked forward to the day when Japan would shame the Americans, just as it had humiliated the Russians in 1905.

Then he read Shima's radio-wave detection patent file cover to cover and thought some more about ways to accomplish his mission.

3

SEPTEMBER 15, 1939; QUANTICO, VIRGINA

Martin Victor saw the man in a dark suit and fedora as he exited the train.

"Lieutenant JG Victor, please come with me. I will drive you to the Academy."

Martin retorted, "I would appreciate seeing your credentials before we go anywhere."

The stranger smiled, opened his suit jacket, and pulled his FBI badge wallet from his belt, making certain that Martin also saw his holstered Smith & Wesson .357 Magnum revolver. Proffering the identification materials to Martin, the armed man said, "Special Agent William Murphy."

Satisfied that he was not being shanghaied, Martin walked with Murphy to a black Chevrolet coupe. The FBI agent opened the trunk of the car and Martin placed his small suitcase in between a 12-gauge riot gun and some electrical components necessary to operate the vehicle's two-way radio.

"What? No Thompson submachine gun?" Martin said in jest.

"I did not want you to scuff it up with your luggage, so I left it in the armory. I will retrieve the .45-caliber beast after I acquaint you with the Academy," replied Murphy…not in jest.

Pressing his luck, the new recruit asked, "Do you live in this town?"

"Nope. I live in Baltimore. Stoneleigh, to be somewhat more precise."

Another Baltimorean! Now Martin was interested. "Really? Let me guess… You attended Calvert Hall High School."

"*Vitae via virtus,*" responded Special Agent Murphy with the Calvert Hall motto. "Virtue is the way of life."

Pushing his well-armed chauffeur yet further, Martin asked, "Where did you go to college? Loyola?"

"Nope. Johns Hopkins, and then Georgetown Law School."

Martin knew enough to stand down at this point. "Pleasure to make your acquaintance, Agent Murphy."

"The pleasure is all mine, Lieutenant JG Victor."

Neither Martin nor Murphy believed this last line at all.

Arriving at the Academy, Murphy introduced Victor to Special Agent in Charge (SAC) Gilbert Horan, who would be serving as the overall administrator and concierge for the participants in this special eight-week class. Horan appeared to Martin to be about forty years old, nondescript, and comfortable being in command.

"Mr. Victor, you are the first person to register. Congratulations!" Horan said affably as he extended his right hand, which Martin shook firmly. Politely, Horan then stated, "I suppose you would like a little lunch before we take you to your barracks and have you sign for your equipment."

"Actually, Agent Horan, if you are amenable, why don't we take care of all of the administrivia and then have lunch." Martin had decided—once again—to assert himself enough to impress his minders, but not enough to irritate them. Horan smiled, nodded, and led the way to a small, locked warehouse where he provided Martin with a wealth of athletic clothing, uniforms, a pith helmet, bed linens, bath towels, a loose-leaf notebook, writing implements, and toiletries.

"When do I get an FBI fedora?" joked Martin.

Murphy frowned, but Horan, somewhat amused, said, "Once you make the team, Victor."

They walked to the dormitory where Martin was assigned a ground-floor room near the front door that appeared to accommodate an additional two "campers." Martin placed his gear in his dresser and his writing materials on the desk across from his bed. He made his new berth and then the three men marched to the mess hall. Each man took a prewrapped bacon, lettuce, and tomato sandwich on toasted white bread and a Coca-Cola from the metal display case. They sat together at a corner table in the empty cafeteria.

After finishing his sandwich and downing his Coke, Horan drilled Martin with his eyes. "How about you and me taking a walk around this medieval manor?"

"Fine with me," said Martin.

Standing up slowly, Murphy took his leave, saying, "I have to complete some paperwork and then get back to the train station to pick up another Baltimorean. See you all this evening."

Horan and Victor both nodded in Murphy's direction, deposited their trays with a mess hall attendant, and walked into the sunlight.

"So, let me tell you why you are here, Victor."

A WALK WITH SPECIAL AGENT HORAN

"Pursuant to Executive Order 8247, President Roosevelt assigned Director J. Edgar Hoover and the FBI the leadership role investigating espionage and sabotage matters in the US. We are building a security structure across the country to deal with the growing internal threats posed by the Nazis, Japanese, Fascist Italians, the Soviets, and their Fifth Column allies. You are going to be a part of this structure. My job for the next eight weeks is to prepare you as an ONI agent to work with the FBI to identify and surveil individuals and groups who intend to do harm to the United States, uncover their precise plans to damage America's will and ability to defend itself, prevent them from executing their plots, and bring the malefactors to justice. Baltimore's port, aircraft plants, shipbuilding yards, steel plants, electrical companies, rail-roads, airports, and academic centers, like Johns Hopkins University, have become prime espionage targets. Special Agent Murphy and I are based at the FBI's Baltimore Field Office, which is located not far from your brother's law firm. Once you are fit for service, you will work with us and a Baltimore City Police Department Detective named Gareth Messenger to make Baltimore a 'hard target' for our enemies. Messenger should be arriving at Quantico today to train with you. Any questions?"

"Sure. A lot of questions, but just four that are relevant regarding what I need to do for the next eight weeks. My orders are not to mention my rela-tionship with ONI with anyone. Do you know my commanding officer?"

"Yes. Captain McLaughlin," replied Horan.

"And has Captain McLaughlin approved my participation in the entire program that you have just outlined?"

"Yes. He will remain your commanding officer. You will report to him at the end of this course and he will give you orders regarding your handling of specific missions pursuant to this program. I will provide Captain McLaugh-lin with regular evaluations of your performance here at Quantico. Should you graduate, I will report on your field performance in Baltimore to Captain McLaughlin."

"Roger that. Now, does Special Agent Murphy know the facts about me and the program?" said Martin, his eyes narrowing.

"Murph knows everything I know. We are all part of the same team."

"Finally, does Messenger know anything about me and this program?"

Horan cleared his throat. "Not quite yet. I will brief him, probably today. In the meantime, you can maintain your cover and just talk about City College with Detective Messenger."

"You know that he and I were in the same graduating class at City?" Martin tossed this out to get more intel from Horan.

"Martin, we know pretty much everything about you and about him. You were both on the BCC wrestling team. Neither of you were assessed by your teachers or coaches at City as gifted intellects or gifted athletes. Nonetheless, both of you today have been rated by your respective commanding officers as persistent and resilient men who will do whatever it takes to complete a mission. You will need these characteristics to make it through this course. You will need a bit more training, however, to survive and operate effectively against the Nazi, Jap, Fascist, Soviet, and Fifth Column agents operating on the streets of Baltimore, DC, and elsewhere in the United States."

Martin stopped walking at this point, turned to Horan, and said, "I guess we are not in Kansas anymore!"

Horan smirked. "Great movie, Martin. I was in the Loew's Century Theater on Lexington Street when you and your 'secret' lady friend saw *The Wizard of Oz*."

Martin now knew that Horan had talent. He had never seen Horan before, but the FBI man clearly had been following him closely. Victor thought, *I had better pay much closer attention to what is going on around me.* Martin replied to Horan in Navy fashion. "Roger that, Special Agent Horan. Roger that."

Gertrude Kowalska was Martin's secret love. Even Milton knew nothing of her existence. Martin was Gert's secret "*kochanie* [sweetheart]." Her parents, her friends—no one in her Patterson Park neighborhood—knew or could know of her "Jew boyfriend." Tribal hatreds were never more than a millimeter beneath the social surface in Baltimore. Battle lines had been drawn between Poles and Jews long ago. Both Gert and Martin courted disaster, but their attraction to each other could not be denied. He remembered the first time he saw her standing behind the counter at Mr. Cohen's radio and electrical components store on Howard Street. Martin laughed to himself as he recalled asking the statuesque blonde to check his triode tube and seeing her blush. He also recalled vividly the last time he saw Gert and told her of his imminent departure from Baltimore. That single solitary tear gently gliding down her magnificent left cheek. *What a goddess Gertrude*

Kowalska is! But duty called. *Stop thinking about Gertrude and stay focused on excelling in this program*, Martin thought.

The two Quantico men walked on in silence.

REUNION

Detective Gareth Messenger of the Baltimore City Police Department (BCPD) took the initiative in all things. Inquisitive and bold, even the most taciturn of criminals surrendered to his all-knowing visage and magnetic Baltimore flamboyance. Of course, Messenger's well-deserved reputation for inflicting physical damage on individuals "resisting arrest" also enhanced his fact-finding effectiveness, even with the toughest of Baltimore's tough guys. Gareth's boss, the Chief Inspector of the BCPD—a perfectionist intensely loyal to the equally perfectionist Police Commissioner—appreciated Messenger's talent on the street, in the courtroom, and as a leader of lawmen. Gareth Messenger was, in the Baltimore vernacular, "Good police." When the FBI offered a Quantico counterespionage course for one Baltimore City Police Department officer, there was no doubt in the Chief Inspector's mind that Messenger was the man for the assignment.

As he stepped out of Murphy's Chevy near the red-brick FBI schoolhouse, Gareth saw Martin and called out his name. In unison, they pointed their respective right forefingers at each other, grinned, and then pulled their respective arms to the center of their respective sterna and saluted each other with their middle fingers.

"This country is in big trouble if it thinks it needs the likes of you here," said Messenger as he swaggered toward Victor.

"Right. And that goes double for you!" said Martin to Gareth. With that they grappled with each other as if they were back on the mats in Baltimore City College. Gareth, 5 feet, 11 inches, and 200 pounds of streetwise sinew, dominated Martin, who stood three inches shorter and weighed 35 pounds less.

"Still soft and in need of a bodyguard," taunted Gareth, until Martin deftly broke his hold and assumed a boxer's stance. "Oh, so now you think you are Jack Portney?"

The reference was to Baltimore's outstanding, recently retired Jewish welterweight fighter. Martin answered Messenger's derisive remark with two quick jabs followed by a sharp left hook, and then a snappy, straight right that stopped just short of striking Gareth's surprised face.

"So, in fourteen years you managed to learn something from your big brother Milton, did you?" mused Gareth. "It won't be enough, *boyo*, as you will find out real soon in the gym here." The two long-lost friends, now room-mates, shook hands and commenced singing an off-key but spirited rendition of their school fight song, "City Forever."

Just like old times.

SEPTEMBER 16, 1939; SCHOOL BEGINS

On Saturday morning at 06:00 sharp, ten teams of three men—one ONI agent, one local or state police officer, and one FBI agent from towns and cities in Virginia, Maryland, Delaware, and New Jersey—assembled in their sweat suits and tennis shoes for morning exercise. The drill instructor, a ferocious forty-year-old Marine Corps sergeant with a pockmarked face and an almost incomprehensible Southern drawl put the candidates through an hour-long battery of calisthenics, followed by a 3-mile run.

Before releasing them for breakfast, Sergeant Bedford Forrest Young told the heaving mass of men, "Listen up, you old ladies. To successfully complete this part of the course, each one of you must demonstrate that you can do 20 chin-ups, 50 push-ups, 50 sit-ups, 50 jumping jacks, 50 squat thrusts, *and* run three miles in 40 minutes or less. See you tomorrow morning—same time, same place. Now, shout 'THANK YOU, DRILL SERGEANT YOUNG!'"

The winded thirty-plus-year-olds yelled as ordered. Sergeant Young bellowed back, "I CAN'T HEAR YOU, LADIES!"

The trainees screamed back as ordered. Sergeant Young roared, "PATHETIC! YOU PANSIES MAKE ME PUKE!"

He sneered at them one last time, squared his shoulders, and marched off to another Quantico site to inflict much greater punishment on a new class of Marine Corps officer candidates.

After a shower, change of clothes and breakfast, the class marched to school three abreast in rows ten men deep. Special Agent Horan greeted them at the front door and directed them to a first floor classroom and their preassigned seats.

Horan minced few words.

"Gentlemen, everything we do here over the next eight weeks is classified top secret. You are not to share any of the provided course materials with anyone except your CO and teammates. This includes notes that you take; skills that you acquire; policies, practices, techniques, and/or technologies we employ; and the identities of your classmates and instructors. The FBI has identified key areas of national vulnerability that must be fixed immediately. We will train you to assess the risks in your geographic area and eliminate them. You will be the sharp point of the spear in this effort. You may think that the US is not at war with Nazi Germany, the Empire of Japan, Fascist Italy, or Soviet Russia, but an undeclared war is being waged right here and right now. Approach each day and each activity with all the seriousness and determination of a soldier, sailor, Marine, or airman preparing for combat. Now let's get cracking. Open your binders to tab one."

Martin opened the loose-leaf notebook on the center of his desk. Tab one read Industrial Security. The instructor, an FBI agent from Camden, New Jersey, took the class on a slideshow tour of an RCA vacuum tube manufacturing plant, as well as an RCA research and development facility. He used each image to demonstrate FBI procedures for identifying and correcting security vulnerabilities. He presented case studies of actual attempts by foreign agents to bribe or otherwise entice company personnel into disclosing program information and related technical data regarding secret and top-secret Navy Department weapons programs, communication systems, and intelligence gathering and processing systems. Martin, a skilled US Navy radio officer, could appreciate the implications of this presentation more than most people in the classroom. Electron tubes—diodes, triodes, tetrodes, and pentodes—were fundamental to effective military radio communications, direction finding, and intelligence gathering. Martin had been trained to track hostile fleet radio transmissions and use them to target adversaries for destruction. He was also aware of the US Navy's ingenious efforts to intercept and decipher the Imperial Japanese Navy's radio communications. The innovative militarization of vacuum tube technology by physicists and electrical engineers at the Naval Research Lab in DC, the Army Signal Corps in Fort Monmouth, New Jersey, and America's universities and corporations constituted a crown jewel that had to be protected. Martin harbored no doubt that inattention to efforts by the Nazis, Japanese, and the Soviets to rob America of its edge in electrical systems and components would cause his country to lose the coming world war.

BIG GUN

After lunch, Horan announced, "For dessert, we are going to the firing range. We have a special treat in store for you today. Special Agent Dalton Broadside, a member of the FBI's National Championship Pistol Team, will demonstrate the proper use of the .357 Magnum revolver, the most powerful handgun in America today. Let's move out."

Like most surface warfare Navy men at that time, Martin fervently believed that if the guns mounted on your vessel were bigger, more powerful, more accurate, faster firing, and more reliable than your opponent's weapons, the better were your chances of prevailing in a sea battle. This logic applied to handguns too. Firing a 158-grain bullet at 1,500 feet per second, the blued carbon steel Smith & Wesson .357 Magnum revolver with a 3.5-inch barrel instantly appealed to Martin. Broadside, a sharply dressed gunslinger from New Mexico, put on a fast-draw, rapid-fire, deadly accurate show with the S&W revolver that sealed the deal for the former Baltimore city public school teacher. Martin just had to own a Smith and Wesson Magnum of his own. This mechanical device would set Martin's finances back $60. He could just imagine the frown of disapproval on Milton's face at his kid brother's profligacy. *Well*, Martin thought, *I will just have to deal with disappointing my big brother yet again*!

Following Broadside's virtuoso performance, Horan announced, "Gents, now you see what is possible with the right weapon, the right training, and a lot of practice. To pass this course, every one of you must take the basic FBI pistol test and qualify at least as a marksman. Our expectation, however, is that each one of you will do better than that and perform at the sharpshooter or expert level. Every day you will practice specific FBI pistol test skills until you can complete them all in in 5 minutes and 45 seconds or less. Today we will work on Skill No. 1—firing five rounds of .38-caliber ammunition from a prone position at a man-sized target 60 yards downrange. As Special Agent Broadside taught you, put each bullet in the heart—the center of mass, the bullseye. Tomorrow we will add reloading at the 60-yard line and running ten yards to a low barricade set up on the firing range's 50-yard line. There you will fire five shots at the man-sized target downrange from a prone position and five more shots from a seated position. Then you will practice reloading and firing ten more rounds—five left-handed and five right-handed—from a standing position behind the barricade. On Tuesday we will add sprinting 25 yards to another barricade—a high one—where you will practice speed loading and firing 15 more rounds of .38-caliber ammunition at the target— five shots seated and ten rounds alternating left and right-hand pistol grips. On Wednesday, we will add one last skill, running from the 25-yard line to the seven-yard line, reloading, and firing ten shots at the target from the hip.

"From Thursday forward, you and your local police partner and FBI partner can and should practice the pistol skills together until all three of you are ready to take the test on the same day. You are a team. No one succeeds unless you all succeed! Finally, never forget that we only shoot in self-defense at the individual or individuals trying to kill us. We do not shoot innocent bystanders. And when we shoot, we shoot to kill! Period. Do you copy?"

Every trainee shouted, "Yessir!"

Horan then said, "Oh, one last thing. Whoever gets a perfect score of fifty bullseyes when they take the timed test becomes a member of the 'FBI Possible Club' for scoring as high as possible. There are fourteen members of this prestigious club at the present time. I would like to see at least one of you become a member of this select fraternity. The practice ammo and targets are on the house. Use as much of it as you like as often as you like."

And so, daily target practice began. Martin pledged to become a member of the Possible Club.

HAND-TO-HAND COMBAT

After 1.5 hours of shooting at torso targets 60 yards away, Horan called for a cease-fire and directed the trainees to retrieve their targets, return to the range armory, clean their weapons, and lock them in the safe assigned to them.

"Let's go get ourselves a little exercise before dinner," Horan said gleefully. The trainees marched to the gym where they were greeted by two muscular uniformed Navy lieutenants with pilot wings standing in the center of a large wrestling mat—their feet akimbo and arms folded. The larger of the two instructors, whose nose had been broken at least once, spoke first.

"You can call me Spike. My partner here, with the cauliflower ears, you can call Mike. Our job is to train you how to fight dirty. Real dirty. Mike and I took a post-graduate course in disabling, maiming, and killing people—without using any firearms—from a Limey Police Chief in Shanghai, China. We have been ordered to pass on to you in eight weeks everything he taught us during our fun-filled year in the Orient. To achieve proficiency in this style—if you can call it that—of martial arts you will need to devote yourself to dispatching your adversary quickly and mercilessly. We will demonstrate specific techniques each day. You and your partners will practice these moves over and over again until they become a natural or automatic reflex. Let's get going."

Mike chimed in. "Fellas, you want to know how to end a fight fast? You attack your opponent's groin. You kick, punch, smack, squeeze, and crush his gonads, his balls. Go all the way with them before they go all the way with you. Your mom would not approve of these tactics. Your priest or reverend would not approve of these tactics. But I am tellin' ya, you do not want to fight a Hitler-loving Nazi or an Emperor-loving Jap or a Stalin-worshipping Commie fairly. Just get the thing over with as quickly and as unfairly as possible so you get to go home and have breakfast with your wife and children in the morning. Anybody here from Baltimore?"

Gareth and Martin looked at each other and raised their hands.

Mike directed his question at them. "What do you two Baltimorons call the principle underlying this philosophy of fighting?"

Messenger spoke first. "Baltimore Logic. Some problems in life can best be solved by the judicious application of force."

Mike looked at Martin. "You agree with that statement?"

"Totally," said Martin with no hesitation.

Mike grinned an evil grin. "We are going to get along just fine." Pointing at Gareth, Mike said, "You wanna put one of those boxing foul-protectors on so I can demonstrate some awful things to your classmates and not make you a candidate for the Vienna Boys' Choir?"

"Sure," said Gareth as he walked to the edge of the mat, picked up, and put on one of the new Montmarquet protective devices the FBI had so generously provided each trainee.

"OK, my Baltimore friend, why don't you sneak up behind me and apply a rear stranglehold?" Mike turned and proffered his back, neck, and head to Gareth.

Gareth moved quickly to attack Mike from the rear. He wrapped his right arm around Mike's neck and pulled forcefully on his right hand with his left hand so that his bicep and Popeye-like forearm would pinch off the flow of blood to the instructor's brain. Messenger thought, *Oh, I got you now, tough guy.*

Not quite. Using his powerful right hand, Mike grabbed Gareth's right forearm and applied exquisitely painful pressure to the ulnar nerve, causing the astonished Baltimore City Police Detective to loosen his hold on the instructor's neck. Mike quickly lowered his chin, turned his head to the left, and slapped Messenger's testicles hard with his free left hand. As the Baltimore Detective gasped and doubled over, Mike seized Gareth's right arm at the elbow with both of his hands, dropped to his right knee, and executed a vicious flying mare move on Gareth. Next, Mike added insult to injury by putting the dazed and flattened BCPD Detective's right arm in an elbow lock. Gareth tapped out and Mike ceased punishing him. Like a matador, Mike loomed over the figure lying on the gym floor.

"Jesus Christ!" uttered Messenger. The class knew better than to laugh.

Mike finished his tutorial. "Let's pick a partner and practice these moves. Spike and I will be walking around, correcting your form. By the end of this lesson, you will know how to dispose of anyone launching this kind of attack from behind."

For an hour, Special Agent Murphy and Martin, along with all of the other recruits, worked together to perfect each other's execution of this defense against a rear stranglehold.

Spike called on the trainees to form up at the edge of the mat. "Good, solid work. Why not learn another new maneuver before dinner?"

Turning to Gareth, Spike posed the following question. "In Baltimore, what do you do when a guy you are questioning suddenly attacks you by wrapping both of his arms around your arms and chest?"

Gareth responded, "I do not know for sure, Spike, but somehow I have to resist kissing him and instead attack his groin, right?"

"Right you are! Now, Gareth, let's show them how to counter a bear hug."

Spike and Gareth squared off. Gareth placed both of his strong arms around Spike's upper torso. Spike dropped his hips downward, grabbed Gareth's hips with both hands, and created just enough space to launch a series of ferocious knee strikes into Gareth's groin. Though protected by the Montmarquet device, Gareth released his hold and slumped to the floor.

"See? Easy peasy!" said Spike to the trainees while offering a hand up to Gareth.

"Now why not practice this a few times so one day you can crush Adolf Hitler's one little testicle when he tries to hug you!"

The students got down to business. After the training session concluded, the men showered their aching bodies with hot water and went to dinner.

9 AM MONDAY, SEPTEMBER 25, 1939; QUANTICO, VIRGINIA: HAND-TO-HAND COMBAT CLASS

Ten days into the FBI program, Martin, Gareth, and Special Agent Murphy were working well as a team. Martin's marksmanship skills with the .357 Magnum made him a class standout. Gareth's' ability to knock out or disable an adversary with vicious knife hand strikes to the carotids, swift palm strikes to the chin, hammer fist strikes to the mandible, brutal elbow strikes to the sternum and, of course, devastating knee strikes and kicks to the groin, earned him accolades from Spike and Mike. Murphy excelled at everything—academic as well as physical. Martin and Gareth agreed that despite his arrogance, "Wild Bill" Murphy possessed an incomparable intellect. Murph could envision five moves ahead on the counterespionage chess board and checkmate anyone in the class, including the instructors. The two City College graduates were eager, even at this early stage of training, to hit the streets of Baltimore with "the Calvert Hall guy."

The skill to be taught in this morning's self-defense lesson—taking suspects into custody—seemed easy enough to master. Spike demonstrated how one man armed with a revolver might attempt to arrest three suspects.

First, the instructor—gun in hand—marched three burly fellows numbered one, two, and three in a lineup to a wall. Spike ordered the men to stand three feet from the wall and face it. He then directed them to lean forward and place their foreheads on the wall with their hands behind their backs. With his left foot looped around suspect number one's left foot, Spike searched the man for weapons and found a knife in a scabbard on his belt, brass knuckles in one of his pants pockets, and a snub-nosed revolver in an ankle holster. Spike handcuffed the man and ordered him to move to the right of suspect number three and assume the forehead-to-wall position. As the instructor moved to inspect suspect number two, suspect number three quickly moved his hands to the wall, pushed off, spun around, and swung at Spike with a blackjack that came from his right shirt sleeve. As soon as suspect three made his move, Spike used his left leg to pull suspect two's left leg out from under him. With suspect two flattened, Spike dodged suspect three's blackjack and fired four rounds from his pistol into the attacker's belly. Screaming and grabbing his abdomen, suspect three fell backward to the floor. Suspects one and two froze, as did each of the members of the class.

Astonishingly, suspect three stopped screeching, got up off the ground smiling, and said, "Guys, it's all OK. Spike only fires blanks. Just ask his wife!"

Mike then addressed the group. "Never attempt to take even two men into custody alone. You must have at least one, and preferably two or more, partners covering, processing, and subduing prisoners. Your adversaries know everything you know—and maybe even a little bit more—about hand-to-hand combat. They are spies operating with (or without) legal cover outside of their own homeland. They do not take prisoners. They will not simply tie you up or knock you out. They want no witnesses. They will eliminate you. Plan your arrests carefully. Always outnumber, surprise, and overwhelm your targets. Pick the circumstances and surroundings most advantageous to you and least advantageous to them. You have the home field advantage—use it!

Mike paused for effect and then resumed his lesson. "Now, one last thing. The local law enforcement agencies of the cities and towns in which you will be operating frown upon the sound of gunfire and the presence of bodies—even of spies and traitors—disturbing the tranquility of their streets. Each team here has at least one local police or state police officer who will take the lead in maintaining good diplomatic relations between your counterintelligence group and the host constabulary. At the conclusion of the course, the non-FBI team member will accompany the local or state law enforcement team member to meet with the senior state official responsible for issuing pistol permits. You will impress this Police Commissioner or magistrate or whomever with your maturity and self-restraint regarding the use of deadly force. Your local law enforcement partner will vouch for you. The FBI will also vouch for you. The Office of Naval Intelligence or the Military Intelligence Division of the Army will, of course, vouch for you. But remember, this is America. If the responsible local authority refuses to issue you a permit, you will have to operate unarmed. So conduct yourselves appropriately during your interview. Nobody wants you out there without a gun. Got it?"

"Yessir," replied the class in unison.

10 AM MONDAY, SEPTEMBER 25; 106 NORTH HOWARD STREET, BALTIMORE, MARYLAND

Gertrude Kowalska had just completed the sale of an RCA Model U-111 Victrola with Radio for $39.95 to a downtown dentist who had been shopping for an expensive birthday present to give to his wife. Gertrude looked out the Sun Radio Company shop window and thought she saw her Martin. She ran from behind the counter to the door, but the man standing on the sidewalk was not her *kochanie*. Shalom, the store owner, said, "Miss Kowalska, what is wrong with you? Is the store on fire?"

"I am sorry, Mr. Cohen. I thought I saw someone I had not seen in a long time. I just wanted to say hello."

"Well, Gertrude, control yourself. This is a place of business, not a missing persons bureau."

"OK, Mr. Cohen. It will not happen again."

"Good. Now please go over the books or inventory the new equipment from RCA or straighten up the showroom."

Gertrude longed for Martin. She wondered what he might be up to this morning. She wondered how much longer she could endure waiting for him, daydreaming about him, before descending into that dark pit of loneliness that seemed to be her lot in life. The war in Europe had cut off all news from her relatives in Warsaw, which further intensified Gertrude's sense of isolation and helplessness. Her entire community—the Poles residing in Patterson Park—grieved over the Nazi and Soviet invasion of poor defenseless Poland. Even her saintly parish priest, Father Wojtecki, could not provide any relief for Gertrude and her devout parents. Wojtecki's fears for the lives of his own dear mother, father, sisters, and brothers in Crakow depressed him so severely that he had to be admitted to the Shephard Pratt Asylum just north of Baltimore in Towson, Maryland.

Gertrude returned to her own imaginary escape routes from her gloom. She dreamed of dancing the fox-trot with Martin at Carlin Park's Forrest Gardens. *The man sure knows how to make a woman feel like she is all that matters in the world to him as he leads her gracefully, sensually, across a dance floor*! she thought. But just then a new customer required her attention and ended her reverie. There was no relief for her in sight. Martin had told her he would have to be "radio silent" for at least two months. She had not heard a word or received anything in writing from her *kochanie* in weeks.

"Mr. Cohen's advice is correct. I have to control myself," whispered Gertrude. And so she did.

Later that day, Gertrude sat down at her desk and worked on Mr. Cohen's books. New business with the Radio Intelligence Division of the Federal Communications Commission poured money into the Cohen Manufacturing Company for something called an "aperiodic receiver." The device fit into a wooden box, with cooling holes drilled into its sides and back. The solid front lid was detachable. Serious-looking, well-dressed men with fedora hats drove up to the store in new Hudson automobiles without any notice or warning and Mr. Cohen would hop into the backs of these odd vehicles and disappear for hours at a time.

The back of each of the FCC Hudson sedans was packed with electrical gear. A loop antenna would, from time to time, protrude through the roof of the cars. When Gertrude once asked Mr. Cohen what this new business was all about, he told her sternly, "Forget about it," and not discuss anything to do with the FCC with anyone, not even her parents or priest! Mr. Cohen meant it. Nonetheless, Gertrude could not forget what she overheard while quietly working at her desk early one morning. One of these mysterious FCC men told her boss that the receiver had helped them locate a transmitter in New York sending coded messages to Hamburg, Germany.

Gertrude was wary of Mr. Cohen, but not frightened of him. In fact, Gertrude feared no one, not even Mr. Cohen, who carried a pistol inside his waistband and had once even shot a man looking into the window of his home. Gertrude had no idea how her boss had not been prosecuted for this odd form of urban target practice. *The Baltimore Sun* briefly carried the story, but nothing came of it. *Maybe the men in the fedoras protected Mr. Cohen.* She had no way of knowing. All she knew was that Shalom, though mercurial, was a genius and treated her respectfully. His sole friend, Mr. Evans, who paid for the FCC's "aperiodic receivers" and other electrical equipment, appeared to operate at the same serious, brainy level as Cohen.

"My job is interesting. It sure beats working at Bickford's automat or some noisy factory floor," she would tell her two best friends from Patterson Park High School, Basia and Ella. They could not comprehend how their friend could enjoy working for a Jew. Gertrude was confident that if either Basia or Ella found out about Martin, her friendship with B & E would be over.

Gertrude, Basia, and Ella graduated together from the commercial program offered by Patterson Park High School. "B & E," as Gertrude called them, now worked as secretaries at the giant Glenn L. Martin aircraft engineering and manufacturing campus in Middle River. The three young women operated by the same rules: Do what you are told by your employer, keep your mouth shut about work-related matters, and always keep your eyes, ears, and mind open and alert for trouble. Gertrude, Basia, and Ella were "pure Baltimore."

4

A LOOK BACK IN TIME: RECRUITED BY THE EMPIRE

Junius Jordan Johnson (aka "J3") met Kimura Katsuie by accident on the campus of Howard University in May of 1939. An honor graduate of Baltimore's segregated Frederick Douglass High School, Class of 1935, Mr. Johnson was now a senior at Morgan State College pursuing a degree in education with a minor area of concentration in US history. J3, however, desired to apply his considerable intellect to something grander than teaching in Baltimore's "separate but *unequal*" public school system. He wanted to become a lawyer and challenge America's systematic subjugation of members of his race. Attending the state of Maryland's only law school was out of the question. Everyone in Baltimore knew that the University of Maryland Law School had barred Thurgood Marshall—one of Douglass High School's best minds—from admission in 1925 solely on account of his skin color. Junius, therefore, decided to explore the possibility of attending Howard University's Law School in Washington, DC.

Junius had a high school friend, Coleman Braxton, who was completing his senior year as an engineering student at Howard University. After graduating from Douglass, Junius would see Coleman in Baltimore at parties, dances, and the movies during breaks in the school year, usually around Christmas, Easter and the summer months. In April of 1939, during spring break, Junius told Coleman about his interest in Howard Law School. Coleman offered to show Junius around the campus and meet a few acquaintances of his who attended the law school. It was during this exploratory visit to Howard University in May of 1939 that Coleman invited Junius to participate in a small private meeting with a Japanese scholar named Katsuie.

"Junius, there is a scholar who has come all the way from Japan to talk to us about colored pride," announced Coleman to J3. "George Jones, a Howard University Law School student from West Baltimore, and Jefferson Daniels, a graduate student in mechanical engineering from New York City, say this yellow man should be listened to carefully. They think he understands our problems here in America and provides sound ideas for putting an end to all the demeaning stuff we put up with each day. Look, I respect George and Jefferson. They insist that I come. I do not want to let them down. Will you go with me?"

Realizing how earnestly his host Coleman wanted him to hear whatever this Japanese guy had to say, Junius Jordan Johnson replied, "How could I possibly refuse?"

Since Katsuie's arrival in America in 1920, the intelligent, soft-spoken Japanese Imperial agent had studied Negro Americans carefully. He admired their indomitable response to pervasive racism and cultivated colored Americans from all walks of life, from menial laborers to scholars, encouraging them to view Japan as their ally in their struggle for liberation against white oppression. Katsuie's message to rapt audiences at Negro colleges and universities was concise, clear and compelling.

Just as a unified, proud, educated, scientific, industrious, and militarily trained Japan overthrew powerful white Tsarist Russia in 1905, so too could America's 12 million Negroes overcome white domination today by aiding their Japanese brethren in the coming war against the United States.

Junius, Jefferson, and George were moved by Katsuie's message. Junius became an instant convert to Katsuie's cause. So too did Jefferson and George.

Junius thought that Coleman had been swayed. But Coleman had been anything but swayed. In fact, Coleman had been repulsed by Kimura Katsuie's incitement to racial warfare.

Junius lived with his parents in a row house at the intersection of Laurens and Calhoun Streets in West Baltimore. He loved both his mother and his father dearly and they believed that the sun rose and set on their handsome, scholarly son. Junius ate breakfast and dinner with them nearly every day, pleased them by performing exceptionally well academically, and attended church with them each Sunday. He comported himself at all times as a gentleman. However, his parents had no idea that their beloved only child silently seethed with anger at the daily indignities he experienced as a Negro man in Baltimore. Junius reviled the political system that employed a separate but inferior education system, carefully designed to keep colored people down. He despised the devious techniques used by realtors to keep nonwhite Baltimoreans ghettoized into crowded, substandard housing located in a tight circle surrounding the commercial and governmental center of the city. This decaying core of colored neighborhoods was compressed by modern, more spacious, exclusively white suburbs. Junius felt suffocated by both Baltimore city and its surrounding suburbs' segregation of restaurants, movie theaters, amusement parks, swimming pools, bus stations, bowling alleys, ball fields, department stores, and even hospital wards. Junius's mother, a kind, immaculate, devoutly Christian woman, could not even try on a dress in a Baltimore department store on account of her race. Her uncomplaining acceptance of second-class citizenship pained her son. Junius knew, however, that questioning his parents' willingness to accommodate inequality in America would be a waste of time. They just wanted to "get along" in Baltimore. So Junius struggled each day to suppress his hatred of the arrogant Caucasians who abused his family and his people at every turn. To please his parents, Junius pretended to be a carbon copy of them, but just beneath the surface, Junius longed to get even.

Junius's father, Isaiah, had happily worked at the central post office on Lexington Street in downtown Baltimore since his return in 1919 from serving as a noncommissioned supply officer at the Port of Saint-Nazaire, France, during the Great War. For reasons Junius could never comprehend, his father loved America, and even loved living in the city of Baltimore. Frances, Junius's revered mother, had matriculated from Frederick Douglass High School, where she had first met and fallen in love with Isaiah. Though unmarried, Frances became pregnant with Junius the night before Isaiah went off to war. Upon Isaiah's return from Europe, the two married, and like everything else in their lives, they took their vows seriously. Frances pursued a college degree in elementary education by taking evening courses at Morgan State College. To facilitate his wife's ambition to become an educator, Isaiah would hurry home from work each day to care for Junius. When Junius entered first grade, his mother could walk him to school in the morning and back home in the afternoon because she had become a faculty member at his elementary school, PS 108. After graduating from Douglass High School, Junius too took evening classes at Morgan State and earned his BA in education in June of 1939. He looked forward to abandoning his day job as a car jockey at the DeSoto dealership on Howard Street and commencing his teaching career at one of Baltimore's colored high schools in September of 1939. To all the world, the hard-working, God-fearing Johnson family represented all that was best in segregated Baltimore.

Appearances, however, can often be deceiving. During their first meeting, Kimura Katsuie accurately diagnosed Junius's carefully camouflaged contempt for white-run America. He erred, however, in his assessment of Coleman's willingness to commit espionage and treason. Katsuie offered each of the young men entrance into a "summer training program" that would prepare them as leaders in the revolt against the US government when the race war with Japan came. Junius, George, and Jefferson accepted the offer. Coleman did too, but with his fingers crossed.

Katsuie drilled deeply into the souls of the four recruits with his eyes, and in a voice which was barely audible, said, "In late May, each of you will receive a signal from me through the United States Postal Service. An affectionate letter written in a woman's elegant hand will provide you with the date, time, and location of our next meeting. The letter will arrive at your current residence in a light pink envelope that will have the slight scent of feminine perfume. The envelope will have no return address. To the outside world—your parents, your roommates, your friends—you will appear to be engaged in a love affair. Use this secret relationship as cover for attending training sessions and arriving home late at night, or even the next day. At our end-of-May meeting, I will provide you with details about the summer weekend training sessions designed to provide you with the specific skills required for you to execute future missions against the Nordic oppressors efficiently and safely." Katsuie bowed slightly toward the four young men and departed.

"Finally we are going to change things around here!" Junius told Coleman. "Finally we will fight and bring down American bigotry. Let's see how they like being *our* servants!"

Coleman nodded and reminded Junius that he had to catch the bus back to Baltimore. "See you soon, Junius. This training is really going to be something!"

"Can't wait." said J3 with a broad smile as he waved goodbye to his friend.

Coleman waved back and then headed to his Uncle Hercules's house on U Street.

5

HERCULES BOULANGER

Hercules Boulanger won the Croix de Guerre on October 31, 1918, during the bloody Meuse-Argonne offensive. His regiment, the 369th, had been put under the command of the 4th French Army in July of that year. Outnumbered and initially overrun by German infantry near the Aisne River, Hercules's unit counterattacked, inflicting startling numbers of casualties on the Germans, who broke and ran for their lives. Using his rifle, bayonet, trench knife, and bare hands, Hercules singlehandedly killed six enemy soldiers. Hercules never discussed his role in the Great War with his nephew. However, Coleman could read French and deciphered the story from the text of the official citation behind the decoration displayed in a glass case hanging discreetly on a wall in Hercules's bedroom. Hercules lived alone in spartan simplicity. The man did not even have a radio in his home. To the best of Coleman's knowledge, Uncle Hercules had no significant human relationships with anyone, outside of Coleman and a few fellow police officers.

Coleman was wrong. Hercules had married a French woman named Genevieve Rocard in Paris five months after the Armistice of Compiegne ending World War I took effect on November 11, 1918. Genevieve and Hercules were introduced to each other in early December of 1918 by a 4th French Army Captain, Emil Massu, who had observed the gallantry of Corporal Hercules Boulanger at the Aisne River on October 31, 1918. It was

Captain Massu who wrote the recommendation for Hercules to receive the Croix de Guerre.

Captain Roland Rocard, Genevieve's brother and a close friend of Massu, died for his country at the Aisne River on October 31. Captain Massu figured—correctly, as it turned out—that he would both honor his deceased friend's life and cause something humane to come from the butchery at the Aisne River by helping to unite the stoic Genevieve with brave Hercules. At first, Hercules found it difficult to believe that a cultured white woman could ever truly love him. Over time, however, she won the heart of the hardened combat infantryman. She taught him to communicate fluently in French and exposed him to the profound beauty of her nation. Most important, Genevieve and Emil got Boulanger to see the United States through the eyes of sophisticated French people who were grateful to America and all Americans for rescuing France from German barbarism.

Hercules viewed his experience in France as a second baptism, stamping him for eternity with the spiritual seal of the United States and its Constitution. Later in life, when asked by a skeptical senior FBI official why he would spy on "his own people," Hercules looked into his inquisitor's eyes and said, "World War I taught me that all Americans are my own people. If some Americans want to break the law and endanger my great nation, I will do the necessary to stop them. Now, *never* question my fidelity and loyalty to the United States again." The stupefied FBI executive got the message and repeated the story to his superiors as well as other agents when similar questions arose about trusting African American citizens' commitment to the United States.

Not long after their marriage on April 14, 1919, Genevieve contracted the Spanish Flu that was spreading across Europe and the rest of the world. She died on July 4, 1919. After her funeral, Hercules swore to Genevieve over her grave that he could not and would not ever love another woman. He never did. Hercules never broke a promise.

Hercules returned to Washington, DC, in September of 1919 and joined the Washington Metropolitan Police Department as a patrolman. He worked his way up to the rank of detective by the age of forty-three in 1935. An excellent interrogator who understood firsthand how a person's feeling of guilt can create a deep need for confession and absolution, Hercules could break down the resistance of all but the most psychopathological criminals in DC. He had the highest conviction rate of any WMPD detective. In 1937, the Federal Bureau of Investigation counterintelligence group retained his services to spy on radical Negro organizations such as the Development of Our Own and the Ethiopian Pacific Movement, and identify members likely to pose a threat to US mobilization efforts in the event of war with Germany, Italy, Japan, or the Soviet Union.

Since the first semester of his freshman year at Howard University, Coleman enjoyed his monthly private dinners and conversations with his gray-haired uncle. "Herc" listened attentively to his nephew's concerns about everything from career opportunities for colored engineers to his lack of success with women, and guided Coleman's efforts to find solutions for his various problems. Uncle Hercules was his trusted advisor, moral compass, and source of strength. Coleman needed him now more ever.

Coleman knocked on the door to his uncle's house. "Who's there?" came that low, gravelly voice.

"Coleman."

The door opened and there stood Uncle Hercules, still dressed in the dark blue suit, white shirt, and red tie that he wore to work. "Well, come on in, my good man."

Coleman smiled. His uncle Hercules would help him get over his fears about the meeting of subversives that he had just attended at Howard.

"Uncle Hercules, I have a problem—a big problem—and I have to tell you that I am frightened."

Boulanger did not like to hear such talk coming from his nephew. Getting right to the point, Hercules said, "You are frightened?"

"Yes, Herc. Frightened."

"OK. What is going on? Coleman, you know I am here for you and there is no problem that we cannot solve."

Coleman sobbed and said, "A Jap named Katsuie is recruiting students on Howard's campus to lead millions of American colored people in a rebellion against the US when war comes with Japan. My God, he just convinced three of my friends to train to fight against the United States. I know Katsuie thinks that I too have joined him in this…this conspiracy. Hercules, what am I going to do now? I do not want any part of this. However, I fear that this guy may kill me or have me killed because I know too much. Maybe I need to get a gun. Can you get me a gun?"

At this point, Boulanger placed both of his hands on top of Coleman's shivering shoulders and said, "Now, Coleman, there's no need for you to arm yourself. I know just the right people to deal with this problem. They will be delighted that you have come forward to provide me with this important information. Let me ask you just a few fact questions and then I will make a phone call. You and I will see this thing through together and as God is my witness, nobody—certainly no Jap—is going to fuck with my nephew!"

Coleman had never heard his uncle use the "F" word before. He had never seen the man display anger before. *Well*, he thought, *there is no one better than Hercules Boulanger to have in your corner when the boxing bell rings*. Coleman was right.

Retrieving a small notebook in his left interior suit jacket pocket, Uncle Hercules motioned his nephew to sit down at his dining room table.

"Precisely where did this little meeting take place?"

Coleman responded, "Jefferson Daniel's dorm room on the Howard University campus."

"What time did the meeting begin and when did it end?"

"Started at noon. Ended around one thirty."

"Who arranged this get-together?"

"I do not know for certain. It may have been George Jones, a Howard law student, or Jefferson Daniels, a clever guy from New York City. Hercules, if I had to guess, it was probably Jefferson."

Hercules's dark eyes narrowed. "Coleman, from now on, no guessing! When you communicate with members of law enforcement, say only what you know to be true and accurate. When asked a question and you do not know the answer, just say that you do not know the answer. You must never mislead police. Period."

"Got it!" said the young man forcefully.

"Coleman, when and where will the next meeting occur?"

"I do not know. But this Katsuie guy said that we would receive orders in the mail to report for training soon."

"Coleman, I cannot thank you enough for reporting this incident to me. You have done well. This is important—really important. Now I am going to contact my team and we are going to discuss this situation with two seasoned FBI special agents. You ready?"

"Yessir, Uncle Hercules. I am so sorry about all this."

"Coleman, no need to be sorry about anything. You need to be smart. You need to be alert. You need to be brave. You need to be strong. And you need to follow my directions."

Coleman nodded his assent. *When you are in over your head*, he thought, *you need to submit to the authority of a real man, like Hercules Boulanger.*

Hercules got up from the dining room table and walked into his bedroom, closed the door, and picked up the only telephone in his house. He dialed the FBI hotline monitored around the clock every day of the year. After the required five rings, he heard, "Special Agent Smith" at the other end of the line.

"Agent Smith, this is Special Agent Hercules Boulanger. I have a Confidential Informant at my home right now with firsthand information concerning a Japanese organized espionage conspiracy involving several Howard

University undergraduate and graduate students. I need two national security team agents to debrief this informant now, as I have reason to believe he may volunteer to serve us as an inside informer."

"Roger that, Special Agent Boulanger. Sit tight, the cavalry will arrive soon. I am dispatching Clarence Walker and Louis Clyde. You will be in good hands."

MAY 12, 1939; DC EARTHQUAKE

FBI Counterintelligence Agents Clarence Walker and Louis Clyde parked their black 1938 Ford Model 81 four-door sedan in front of Hercules Boulanger's house after driving around the neighborhood to determine whether the alert they had received was a prelude to an ambush. As always, Clyde did the driving. A Bureau of Internal Revenue agent prior to joining the FBI, Louis Clyde could outrace the best of the Southern moonshiners. He had killed two such alcohol entrepreneurs by deftly running their automobile off a cliff during a pursuit in Arkansas' Ouachita Mountains. Acerbic and gruff, Clyde derived great satisfaction from intimidating people.

Walker, on the other hand, had a knack for making just about anybody feel at ease. He had acquired his exceptional social skills from both his late father, a refined and unflappable State Department diplomat, and his mother, a stately Vassar fine arts graduate. Walker developed his profound pastoral skills, however, all on his own. From early childhood on, Walker's total devotion to the teachings of the Catholic Church concerned his essentially agnostic parents. Despite their misgivings, they were not prepared to dissuade their bright and obedient son from following the faith that came to him so naturally and so intensely. In high school, Clarence observed the kindly and encouraging manner with which Monsignor Capodanno ministered to troubled individuals and families. At confession with the Monsignor, Walker experienced the serenity that comes from being listened to, understood, loved, and forgiven. Walker also absorbed from Capodanno a strong sense of what was right and what was wrong. Graduating at the top of his high school class, Walker publicly pledged his commitment to advancing goodness and righteousness by combatting evil and sin in his valedictory speech.

After high school, Walker focused on the study of logic while pursuing his undergraduate degree in philosophy at Princeton. He graduated from Yale Law School in 1930, clerked for the Chief Judge of the United States Court of Appeals for the District of Columbia, and became an FBI agent in 1935. Fluent in French, German, Italian, and Latin, Clarence Walker could spot someone prevaricating in five languages. SAC Horan, his current supervisor, called him "a walking lie detector."

Satisfied that no unwelcome welcoming party awaited them, the two FBI agents walked up to the front door of Hercules's house. They positioned themselves to the right and to the left of the door frame. Agent Walker carried a black leather briefcase in his left hand and placed his right hand on the revolver in the holster on his right hip. Agent Clyde knocked twice on the door with his left hand and stood back, his right gun hand also ready for action. Hercules opened the door and invited the two men into his home for what he thought was their first visit.

What Hercules did not know was that Walker and Clyde had conducted a warrantless search of his abode before the FBI offered him a counterintelligence position. Unbeknownst to either Walker or Clyde, an FBI black-bag team had illegally tapped Hercules's telephone for one entire month prior to their search of his premises. The tap had converted Hercules's phone into a listening device as well as a telephone bug. Yet a third group of FBI agents opened, read, and resealed mail sent to Hercules's address to assure that he was "clean." After reviewing the final report summarizing the findings of this intense vetting process, the head of the FBI's Office of Internal Security concluded that Hercules Boulanger was "as unsullied as my parish priest."

Pointing at Coleman, Clyde asked Hercules in a menacing tone, "Who, might I ask, is that?"

Hercules responded, "Why, he is my nephew, Coleman Braxton. Don't tell me you can't see the family resemblance."

Clyde, unsmiling, replied, "Nope. Mr. Braxton is handsome and you are, well… Not!"

Hercules responded, "I am delighted that your eyesight appears to be improving. I stood in the firing position adjacent to yours during your last attempt at pistol qualification and I must say that based upon your performance, I was concerned about your vision."

"Ouch!" said Clyde. "I guess we had better get down to business before I have to use your bathroom, given the size of my prostate gland."

Hercules laughed and then said, "No comment!"

Pointing at the two white men in dark blue three-button suits and dark gray fedoras, Hercules announced, "Agents Louis Clyde and Clarence Walker are members of FBI counterintelligence. I want you to tell them, as precisely as you can, in your own words, what happened today at Howard University. When you are asked questions by either Mr. Clyde or Mr. Walker, answer truthfully to the best of your knowledge. If you do not know the answer to a question, do not speculate. Just let them know when you do not know for certain the answer to a question. OK?"

Nervously, Coleman said, "OK, Uncle Hercules."

The four men sat around Hercules's dining room table. Coleman, at the head of the table, had Agent Clyde to his right and Agent Walker to his left. Hercules positioned himself at the opposite end of the table from his nephew. A modest three-bulb lighting fixture dimly lit the table.

Coleman's recitation of the facts regarding his recent experience at Howard University lasted ten uninterrupted minutes. The two white men and Uncle Hercules listened to him intently. One of the white men, Clyde, took copious notes. After apologizing profusely for all the "trouble" he was causing, Coleman stopped talking.

Clarence surprised Coleman by placing his right hand on the young man's outstretched left hand. "Now, now, Mr. Braxton, you have caused no trouble at all. You are in no trouble at all. In fact, by courageously coming forward as soon as you have, I can assure you that you have earned the admiration of everyone seated at this table."

Both Hercules and Agent Clyde nodded in affirmation.

Coleman smiled sheepishly.

Walker removed his hand from Coleman's and resumed his remarks. "Mr. Braxton, would you mind me asking you a few questions?"

"Why, no, not at all," replied Coleman earnestly.

Opening his briefcase, Walker retrieved a 7 x 5-inch black-and-white photograph and placed it in front of Coleman. Coleman examined the photo and saw two middle-aged Asian men and four young Negro males in their early twenties standing together in what appeared to be a meeting hall.

"Do you recognize any of the individuals in this photograph?" asked Walker.

Pointing to one of the Asian men in the picture, Coleman said nervously, "That's Katsuie! I do not recognize anyone else."

"Are you certain, Mr. Braxton?"

"Yessir." Pointing again at Katsuie in the photo, Coleman stated, "That is Katsuie. No doubt about it."

"OK. Now, Mr. Braxton, does your high school friend, Mr. Junius Jordan Johnson, know anything about your uncle, Hercules Boulanger, or your relationship with him?"

Surprised by this question from Walker, Coleman replied, "I don't discuss my uncle with no one! Sorry, Uncle Hercules, but nobody I know would associate with me if they knew my uncle—the man I look up to most—was an FBI agent." Suddenly, Coleman raised his voice and said, *"Oh my God*!!" He then broke down, sobbing. "Sweet Jesus, if Katsuie finds out that I was here talking to you, he will have me killed!"

Walker responded to Braxton's panic with a soothing voice. "Coleman… May I call you Coleman?"

Braxton nodded his head up and down.

"Coleman, I understand how you feel. We have been tracking Katsuie and his followers for quite some time now. As you can see, we have pictures of him. We also have movies of him, voice recordings of him, letters written by him, and letters written to him. I agree with you that Katsuie is a dangerous man. His followers are dangerous folks. But you are not alone, and you need not be terrified of him and his gang. Coleman, understand this: Your war-hero uncle, the FBI, and the United States of America are all on your side. We will watch over you and protect you. Now, to determine precisely how to protect you, I really need for you to think calmly and carefully before answering my question. Does Junius or any of your friends know anything about your uncle Boulanger?"

Walker's voice and demeanor steadied Coleman. He reflected deeply and methodically—like an engineer would—before responding. "I have told no one about Herc. My mom, Uncle Hercules's sister, passed when I was in junior high school. She could not have known about Herc and the FBI, and I do not recall her ever saying anything about her brother to anyone. Herc never visited us in Baltimore. As far as my dad is concerned, let's just say that family never meant much to him. Certainly he never spoke with any of my friends because I never invited anyone to our apartment. Who in their right mind would want to expose their pals to a drug addict? Also, Dad had his own issues with the police, so he and I never discussed Uncle Herc. I have no brothers or sisters, so nothing there either. I think that it is accurate to say that my relationship with Hercules and his very existence are not known to anybody but you, me, and Herc."

Walker smiled. "Now, Coleman, how would you like to partner up with your uncle and us to shut down Katsuie and his co-conspirators?"

DOUBLE AGENT AJAX

Stunned, Coleman looked plaintively across the table at his uncle. Somewhat surprised that Agent Walker would pitch his nephew after just one conversation, Hercules broke the silence and asked Walker, "Now, just what have you got in mind, Clarence? What exactly do you want this inexperienced young college man to do for us? Are you authorized to put him on the FBI payroll? How much are you going to pay him? How will we protect him if he is in the field working with us?"

Exuding self-assurance, Clarence replied, "Hercules, this is a unique opportunity for us to infiltrate Katsuie's espionage network. Katsuie has been in circulation, recruiting Fifth Columnists to subvert our nation's security for over a decade. Coleman's engineering background makes him invaluable to Katsuie, his masters in Tokyo, and the thugs in the Japanese embassy in Washington. Through the tasks they assign Coleman, we can ascertain what the Japanese lack in terms of military systems and technology. Through Coleman, we could potentially lead the Japanese down unproductive research paths. Through Coleman, we will map out the membership and coordinates of Katsuie's agent army inside the US. Simply put, Coleman is a game-changer for us. I do have the authority to bring Coleman on board. I can commit that the US government will pay for the remainder of his undergraduate school expenses—tuition, room and board, books—plus a stipend of $100 a month. Should Coleman desire to attend graduate school, the US government will also cover his tuition, room and board, books, and continue the stipend through the completion of a PhD—hopefully in engineering. Finally, we will cover Coleman with a blanket of protection. You, Hercules, will be responsible for organizing and directing a detail that will keep Coleman safe. Anything else you want to know?"

Coleman and Hercules locked eyes. Hercules turned once again to Walker and said, "I need to take a short walk with my nephew."

Walker replied, "Fine with us, Hercules."

Coleman and his uncle strolled down U Street in the darkness toward Lincoln Road.

"Coleman, what's on your mind, son?"

"Uncle Hercules, my head is spinning. Just a short time ago, I came to you feeling alone, guilty, scared, wanting to buy a gun, run away, and hide. Now I have some silver-tongued white man telling me that the fate of the United States rests on my colored shoulders and that I should go into the Japanese dragon's den and spy for the FBI. Herc, what on earth am I getting into here? Do you truly trust these white motherfuckers? Uh, sorry for the rough language."

Hercules stopped at the corner of U Street and Lincoln Road and said, "Coleman, do you honestly think that I would work with people like Clarence Walker and Louis Clyde if I did not trust them? Clarence just complimented you. He put his career on the line for you. You are being asked, not ordered, to defend your country against a foreign enemy who has invaded your homeland. More than that, you are going to be well compensated for serving your nation. And even more than that, Clarence Walker and the FBI will allow your uncle—me!—to protect you while you do your duty. Coleman, I saw a lot of conscripted colored boys get cut down like wheat being harvested in a field during the Great War. They got paid next to nothing for their sacrifice. Those who survived combat came home to a country that, in general, did not appreciate them or even acknowledge their gallantry. But that did not matter much to them because they knew they were heroes and that the day would come when their country would recognize them as such. This is your chance to be a hero, Coleman Braxton. You find your courage and you tell Clarence and Louis that you will do whatever it takes to bring Katsuie and his bums down."

Solemnly, Coleman said to Hercules, "But how can I betray my friends, my classmates? Won't I be helping these white men to kill or injure them, or lock them up for a long time? Won't I be a sellout, a traitor, a Judas?"

Hercules looked his nephew square in the eyes and in a sonorous, somber voice that barely cloaked his rising rage said, "Coleman Braxton, you cannot betray traitors! You cannot sell out individuals who are determined to sell out your country. You cannot become a Judas by handing over Japanese spies to the FBI and the Department of Justice. Japanese spies are not our Lord Jesus Christ and the United States is certainly not pagan Rome. I am not saying the US today deserves us colored men giving our last ounce of devotion to it. I am saying that one day, America will acknowledge and respect our commitment to it. And that day will come a lot sooner when young, educated men like you stand tall and serve their nation with everything they have got. Do not let me or yourself down, Coleman. Do it!"

Coleman nodded, shook his uncle's hand, hugged him, and said, "Herc, I am ready!"

Walker and Clyde welcomed Coleman to the team with handshakes and pats on the back. Sitting down once again at Boulanger's dining room table, Clyde provided detailed guidance to Coleman.

"Your code name is 'AJAX.' Assume from now on that the Japanese and their henchmen are watching every move you make. We, your uncle especially, will see to it that any Japanese agents watching you are being watched by us at all times. Resume your normal daily routine at Howard University. When Katsuie signals you, follow his instructions to the letter. Your uncle and his team will be close by, monitoring events."

Coleman asked, "How do I get in touch with Hercules or with the FBI?"

Walker responded, "Is there a mailbox near your dormitory?"

Coleman replied, "Yes, right in front of the building."

Walker said, "If you absolutely must communicate with us, use this piece of chalk and stealthily put a 2-inch vertical line on the lower left side of the back of the mailbox that is in front of your dormitory. We will erase the chalk line to let you know that we got your signal. Within 24 hours of your signal, your uncle will contact you. He may be disguised. He may be off campus when you see him. Whenever Hercules appears, he—not you—will initiate the conversation. If, however, you see either Clyde or me instead of your uncle, follow us at a distance of ten yards. We will make evasive maneuvers to identify and brush off anyone tailing you. This may take a while. Be nonchalant. Eventually, we will find a place to meet with you. I must stress that you will significantly reduce the likelihood of being uncovered by Katsuie by minimizing contact. OK?"

Ajax nodded in the affirmative.

Walker continued. "Do you use a particular pay phone on or near campus?"

Ajax: "Yes, there is a pay phone on College Street."

Walker: "OK. Assume that whatever you say on that phone will be monitored by us, even if you have dialed no one."

Ajax, wide-eyed, said, "You can do that?"

Walker: "Yes. And a lot more. This is part of our home field advantage, you might say."

Ajax laughed for the first time that day.

Walker then advised Ajax to return to campus and reminded him never to discuss this meeting or anything that he learned at the meeting with anyone. "The most challenging part of a counterintelligence agent's life is strictly maintaining the vow of silence about the work they do. To be a star in this business, no one, other than fellow agents, should ever know that you were ever in the business!"

Ajax hugged Hercules and walked back to his dormitory. He slept soundly.

After Ajax exited, Walker asked Boulanger, "Do you think he can handle this mission?"

Hercules replied, "Clarence, I think he can. But if he cannot, the Japanese will kill him."

Walker looked at Hercules and calmly inquired, "Doesn't that bother you?"

Hercules: "Nope. I have done a lot of killing. I have seen a lot of killing. And I have witnessed a lot of other things people do to each other that are worse than killing. Nothin' in the way of murder and mayhem troubles me anymore."

Shortly thereafter, as Clyde and Walker headed back to the Department of Justice Building at the corner of 10th and Constitution Avenues, Clyde blurted out, "Hercules is certainly cold-blooded. I am glad that he is on our side."

Walker agreed. "Louis, I do not know where such men come from. We will need him and many more like him if we are to beat the Japs."

Clyde concurred. "Yep. Never thought I would respect a colored man other than Joe Louis until I met Herc."

Walker could not resist ribbing Clyde. "You know, you are beginning to sound like Eleanor Roosevelt."

Clyde laughed so hard that tears came out of his clear blue eyes.

Hercules went into his basement after both agents had left and practiced stabbing a heavy bag suspended by linked chains from the ceiling with his recently sharpened World War I trench knife.

6

A BRIEF RETURN TO THE PRESENT: FRIDAY, OCTOBER 13, 1939; QUANTICO

Precisely halfway through the course, Martin admitted to himself that this new fraternity appealed to him. Trimmer, tougher, lethal, and alert to even the smallest visual and audible details of his surroundings, Martin felt as dangerous as a wolf. Martin, Gareth, and Murph (William Murphy's new nickname) had established their dominance over every other team in every aspect of the curriculum. Their recent performance in a four-hour test tailing an experienced and elusive target in Washington, DC, greatly impressed the referees grading the exercise. Not once did the Baltimore team lose contact with the target, who admitted during the debriefing session that he could not identify any of his trackers. Every other team had been "made" and shaken off by the target within the first 30 minutes of the exercise.

At this point in the FBI training program, "the Baltimore Trio" yearned to be put into action. Their FBI and ONI overseers were equally determined, however, to keep them corralled for another four weeks.

After dinner at 7 PM, Martin, Gareth, and Murph were summoned to the office of the Marine Corps Base Commander at Quantico. Special Agent Horan and Captain McLaughlin greeted them. Horan spoke first.

"Gentlemen, your outstanding performance up to this point entitles you to a little late-night entertainment in Washington, DC. We have some civilian clothes for you. Get dressed and let's get going. We have to get you back here in time for your physical training class tomorrow morning."

Then Captain McLaughlin addressed the Baltimore Trio. "What we are going to share with you tonight is classified top secret. Divulging any aspect of tonight's treat to anyone now, or in the future, will result in your immediate dismissal from the program, a brief trial of sorts, a guilty verdict, and a long, lonely, and uncomfortable stay in a small cell at a secret prison located in Cuba. If you do not agree to or are offended by these terms and conditions, it is time for you to go back to whatever it was you were doing before you commenced this program."

Murph spoke first. "I am all in." Gareth and Martin nodded their agreement, but that was not enough for McLaughlin.

"Detective Messenger and Lieutenant JG Victor, I did not hear your consent."

Gareth stood at attention and said, "I am all in, Sir!" Martin did the same.

"OK, gents. Let's saddle up," Horan said impatiently.

And off they went.

At 9 PM, the five men were seated in a conference room near FBI Director J. Edgar Hoover's office. An agent entered the room, and without introducing himself, launched into his presentation. "A reliable source within the DC diplomatic community has informed us that Japanese naval intelligence is assembling a squad of agents to penetrate at least one radio company in Baltimore in order to extract top-secret information and technology critical to America's defense. We want to begin briefing you now so that you can hit the ground running after you graduate from the Quantico program."

Gareth interrupted. "Why wait? Why not let us loose now?"

Horan responded, "Because you are not ready to go head-to-head with Captain Saigo Masuji and his band of merry men!"

Gareth persisted. "You mean to tell me that we can't run circles around a Jap in Baltimore? C'mon—the area of operations is Baltimore, not Tokyo."

Horan admonished Gareth. "I know that you think that you are hot stuff. By Baltimore standards, I suppose that you are. But we are dealing with an adversary unlike the riffraff you club with the handle of an *espantoon* on the streets of Baltimore. Watch this little surveillance film of Captain Masuji, a highly decorated IJN officer from an old samurai family presently serving as a naval attaché at the Japanese embassy in Washington, DC. This footage was taken in Baltimore early on Sunday morning, October 8th."

The unidentified FBI agent set up a screen and wheeled out a movie projector. He turned off the lights and turned on the film. What the audience saw was Captain Masuji dressed as a common merchant seaman walking down the ramp of a Japanese cargo ship docked off Thames Street in Baltimore. Gareth, Martin, and Murph could clearly observe that as the Indian summer sun was beginning to rise, Masuji was walking north on South Broadway. From film spliced from footage shot by another camera positioned ahead of and to left of the target under surveillance, they could see no pedestrians present, just Masuji, moving confidently in the center of the sidewalk. As the Japanese Captain neared the Baltimore Gunsmith Company, a favorite haunt of Gareth's—a large figure exploded out of an arched alcove with an object that looked like a large claw hammer raised high in his right hand. The Japanese officer stepped quickly toward the attacker, looping his right arm through the attacker's left arm and over the charging man's left shoulder. Pivoting to the left on the balls of his feet and putting all of his weight into his right arm, Masuji drove the assailant's head straight into the pavement. Looking around quickly and seeing no witnesses, Masuji then dragged the lifeless body back into the alcove.

As the lights came on, Gareth gasped. "That was the felon the BCPD, newspapers and radio announcers nicknamed 'The Hammerhead Mugger.' He turned up dead in the back lot of the gun shop on South Broadway just before I left for Quantico. So that was how the bastard bought it! I'll be damned. I thought Hammerhead got himself drunk on the loading dock behind the store, tripped, fell and accidentally broke his neck on the paved surface below. I must confess, the Hammerhead Mugger banged so many Baltimoreans in the brains with his mallet before relieving them of their wallets that I thought his passing was a blessing. I suspect that the police department did not devote a lot of resources or exert a lot of effort investigating the case. You know, the view would have been that this was just another daily example of 'Baltimore Logic' in operation."

Horan picked up the conversation. "Yes, just as Masuji figured. Apparently 'Etajima Logic' is not all that different from Baltimore Logic. In any event, our samurai spy pulled the unconscious body clear through the alcove to the small loading dock adjacent to the back of the gun store. Then the good Captain took the bottle of liquor that Gareth's friend, Hammerhead, had in his pants pocket and poured the booze down the dying man's throat to make it look as though the street criminal had been intoxicated before he took a header from the loading dock into some of Baltimore's finest concrete. So, Gareth, tell me—what have you just learned?"

Gareth: "Well, Special Agent in Charge Horan, I have learned four things: First, we have the Jap embassy and its top personnel under some very extensive technical surveillance. Second, Captain Masuji is well-trained in aikido. Third, Captain Masuji knows how to improvise under pressure. And fourth, Captain Masuji knows how to disguise himself and blend in, even in East Baltimore, where I do not believe any Japanese people reside. I still believe, nonetheless, that I can take old Saigo out *mano-a-mano* and look forward to ending his career as a spy. Now, I have a question for you, Special Agent in Charge Horan. Do you know that covering up a homicide, even a homicide of one of Baltimore's most wanted violent felons, might be considered by some to be a crime?"

Horan smiled and replied, "Now, Gareth, let's not get bogged down with minor details that are irrelevant to a counterespionage investigation involving serious matters of national security."

Gareth, recognizing that he had won a point with Horan, ended the exchange by saying, "Yessir, no further questions," and saluted smartly.

At this juncture, Captain McLaughlin assumed control of the briefing. "Now that we all understand that Marquess of Queensberry Rules and possibly the Maryland Criminal Code do not apply to our counterespionage operations against the Empire of Japan, let me show you Masuji's industrial target, according to our latest intelligence."

The unidentified FBI agent then handed out folders to Messenger, Murphy, and Victor labeled Top Secret in bright red ink. Inside the folder was a photograph of a two-story brick building with the words Bendix Radio Corp embedded in the brick along the top of the structure.

Victor spoke up. "That company is on East Fort Avenue, near Fort McHenry and the Locust Point docks."

"Right," said McLaughlin. "For the moment, Bendix appears to be Captain Masuji's primary target."

Martin raised his left eyebrow and said to McLaughlin, "Now, how do you know that fact, Sir?"

Captain McLaughlin glared at Victor and replied, "Pass the Quantico course and maybe I will tell you. Demonstrate to me that you really want to beat these Nip invaders and I might even teach you how to ascertain such information."

"Roger that, Sir," said Lieutenant JG Martin Victor, who was now beginning to understand that this was not a drill. This was a war without mercy being fought in the streets of American cities, Baltimore included.

"Why would Masuji be strolling up South Broadway, mugging for your cameras, if he is interested in Bendix, which is located further south on the other side of Baltimore's harbor?" asked Gareth.

McLaughlin shook his head and smirked. "He had a personal matter that required urgent attention. The good Captain was on his way to an appointment with Martin's landlord at 14 South Broadway."

Martin blurted out, "Dr. Basswood? Does this Jap spy have syphilis, gonorrhea, or both?"

"We do not know, but perhaps you can find out. Can you recruit the good Johns Hopkins urologist to our cause," shot back McLaughlin.

Martin smiled at just how small the world was and that all roads apparently led to Baltimore. "Well, Captain, I think I know just how to recruit Dr. Henry Basswood."

McLaughlin asked, "Care to tell us how, Lieutenant?"

Martin replied, "Captain Masuji is masquerading as a lowly Jap merchant sailor. Dr. Basswood absolutely hates the Imperial Japanese Navy. When he finds out from me that Saigo Masuji is a Japanese naval officer, Hippocratic Oath or not, Henry will want to hurt him real bad. Captain McLaughlin, do you know if Masuji served at Tsushima in 1905?"

McLaughlin responded, "Why, yes. Masuji was an ensign serving on Admiral Togo's battleship, *Mikasa*."

"Well, Captain, I can guarantee you that Dr. Henry Basswood will do whatever we ask him to do, as long as it will cause grievous harm to IJN Captain Masuji," Martin said, banging his fist on the table.

Gareth chimed in. "How can you be so sure that this Board Certified 'dick doctor' hates the Japs so much that he will work with us to deep-six Masuji, Martin?"

Cracking his knuckles, Martin said, "That's easy, Dr. Henry Basswood is a Jew who immigrated to the US from Tsarist Russia with his mother. His father, Avram Kotzebue, went down with most of the crew on the Russian battleship *Suvorov* during the Battle of Tsushima. The Imperial Jap Navy killed Basswood's dad when he was just a little lad! Dr. Basswood has a photo of his late father in a Tsarist Navy uniform prominently displayed in his private office. Each morning when he says his morning prayers, he looks at the photograph of the father he never really got to know. Dr. Henry Basswood wants Japan crushed in Old Testament terms. He will see himself acting as an instrument of divine retribution by working with us."

Gareth: "Marty, do not take this too personally, but you Jews are just plain crazy."

Martin: "No offense taken, Gareth."

Horan turned to Murphy. "You have been mighty quiet, Murph. What is on your mind?"

Murphy furrowed his forehead. "While I do find Martin's references to the Old Testament and Hebrew psychology somewhat interesting, I would appreciate getting some additional background facts about our Japanese adversaries and a more precise definition of our mission. For example: How many agents does Masuji have on his team? Are his agents all Japs, or have some Americans been recruited? How are they equipped? How well have they been trained? Have they executed any previous operations from which we might get a better idea of their tactics, strengths, and weaknesses? What are our objectives as far as Masuji is concerned? Do we want to embarrass the Japs by catching their naval attaché 'yellow-handed' in the act of espionage on US soil? Do we want to kill Captain Masuji right now, or wait a little while before doing him in? Do we want to get him to kill himself? Do we want to neutralize his entire team? What does Bendix have that is so important to the Japs and to us? Do we want to feed the Japs false information from Bendix? Does Bendix have any idea that they are being targeted? Has anyone done an industrial security survey at Bendix?"

Horan replied, "Well, *boyo*, you appear to have a lot on your mind. Let Captain McLaughlin finish his briefing now, unless Rabbi Victor has some additional Hebraic observations to add to his previous sermon."

Martin did not appreciate these *goyim* ganging up on him, but he laughed along with them anyway. The words of warning from his elder brother echoed in his mind: *Martin, these Gentiles with whom you serve will never accept you or treat you as an equal, no matter what you do for them. You could find a cure for cancer or heart disease and they will still consider you to be a "Yid" or a "Kike."*

Nonetheless, Martin yearned for their approval and every one of them knew it. If McLaughlin wanted Victor to enter the boxing ring to fight Joe Louis, all the Captain would have to do is put his arm around Martin's shoulder and suggest that such a match would please him, and would also be good for the US Navy. Manipulating Martin was that easy.

Captain McLaughlin proceeded to answer some of Murphy's questions. "With the exception of one senior Bendix executive who graduated from the US Naval Academy and retired as a Rear Admiral, no one at Bendix has any idea that the company has become the target of Japanese espionage. At this point, the less the company knows about our activities, the better. Your first assignment and cover for this mission will be to conduct a routine industrial security survey at Bendix. Be very thorough. Be collegial. Gain the confidence of Bendix management. The senior executives with whom you will be working closely know that each of you have top-secret clearances and that your job is to identify every security vulnerability at Bendix. They will brief you on their most sensitive programs. You will use your knowledge of the Jap interest in Bendix to craft the advice you provide to Bendix management, but you will couch your concerns and advice in terms of hypothetical threats to the security of their facilities, personnel, information, and technical data, etc. I repeat, Bendix does not and should not have any idea that they have been specifically targeted by the Empire of Japan. We will read Bendix bosses into the program when it becomes appropriate for us to do so. Got it?"

"We got it!" replied the Baltimore Trio in unison.

"Now here is your top-secret treat for tonight. The United States Navy and Army have figured out how to use radio waves to locate and determine the range of objects moving in the air, on the land and on the sea. These radio-wave devices operate day or night, and in any kind of weather. The Japs do not fathom how far along we are in designing and building these radio-wave devices, which can be mounted on our ships and ground stations. They have built their fleet around their primitive, close-quarter night-fighting skills, for example. If we can keep them ignorant about these new technological devices, we hope to have the winning edge over the little pricks in the coming Pacific war. Let them use their searchlights and optical devices to aim and fire their guns and launch their torpedoes. We will use advanced electrical technology to find them long before they can find us, target them long before they can effectively target us, and put our ordnance on their ships long before they can strike our warships. So, Agent Murphy, we do not want Masuji dead. We want him dumb for as long as possible. We want him to focus all his attention on Bendix and to tell his superiors in Tokyo that there is nothing significant at Bendix or in the US regarding radio-wave devices for the IJN to worry about for the foreseeable future."

Martin exclaimed, "We should give Masuji the code name 'Sicinnus,' after the Greek slave who tricked Xerxes into Themistocles's trap at the Battle of Salamis."

Messenger convulsed with laughter. "Martin Victor, a product of Saint John's College, not City College."

McLaughlin did not smile. "OK, Lieutenant Victor. If that code name makes you happy, I can go along with it. Now, gentlemen, we ought to get you back to Quantico. Not a word of this meeting to anyone. This briefing never transpired. Do not discuss the subject among yourselves until we are back again together in DC for another strategy and tactics session. Any questions? None. Good. Go back to your barracks. Perfect your firearms, close-quarter combat, surveillance, and tracking skills. As you have seen, if we end up having a problem with Captain Masuji, he will kill anyone who gets in his way. Make no mistake about it—we do not want you to die for America. We want you to be invisible as you find ingenious ways to keep Masuji in the dark. However, should it come to pass that you get into a street fight with the Captain, kill him. Dismissed."

No one talked on the trip back to Quantico. Gareth choreographed in his mind the techniques he would use to beat Captain Masuji to a bloody pulp. Martin thought of questions he wanted answered by knowledgeable engineers regarding the classified radio-wave devices. Martin could visualize the 16-inch guns on US Navy battleships devastating a Japanese fleet with pinpoint accuracy in the dead of night, and perhaps even Navy aircraft using the devices to locate and strike Japanese vessels far away from US bases and task forces. Murphy remained troubled over the paucity of tactical information about his adversaries and pondered alternative plans to achieve the objective of denying the Japanese access to the new technology.

McLaughlin and Horan did not accompany the Baltimore Trio to their waiting vehicle. "Quite a sharp, aggressive bunch you have there, Horan," observed a pleased Captain McLaughlin.

"Yes, they are progressing about as well as we could unreasonably expect. We will need to prepare a complete briefing package for them in four weeks when they graduate Quantico. I think we can trust them to go along with the liberties we take regarding the Fourth Amendment of the Constitution and the Federal Communications Act of 1934," replied Horan.

McLaughlin laughed. "If Detective Messenger can go along with our national security exception to laws prohibiting obstruction of justice, I think he and the rest of them will accept without question the fruits of our exotic surveillance techniques."

Horan snorted. "Admiral, we certainly know how to pick them!"

"That's Captain, Horan!" barked McLaughlin.

Undeterred, Horan replied, "Not for long. When war comes, it's warriors like you—not sissy desk jockeys and careerists—who will be given the command authority to fight and win it."

McLaughlin: "I appreciate your confidence, but let's not get ahead of ourselves. My rank of Captain will have to do for now."

7

ANOTHER LOOK BACK IN TIME: TUESDAY MORNING, MAY 30, 1939; MEMORIAL DAY

On May 23, Coleman, Junius, Jefferson Daniels, and George Jones each received their scented faux love letters from Katsuie. Coleman and Junius were instructed to meet Katsuie on Memorial Day, May 30, at noon in front of the Lincoln Memorial. They would blend in well with the large crowd of foreign tourists and American Negroes admiring the massive monument to the martyred sixteenth President of the United States: a Greek temple 99 feet tall, facing a beautiful rectangular reflecting pool with a perimeter of over 0.8 of a mile. Daniels and Jones were directed to convene separately with Katsuie later that night at a safe house near the Japanese embassy.

Coleman and Junius stood together in front of the 175-ton statue of President Lincoln awaiting Katsuie's arrival. Hercules, dressed as a Catholic priest, and his team discreetly dispersed themselves among the milling throng. Katsuie, dressed in a blue and white Joseph Haspel seersucker suit and white Panama hat had been surveilling the area since 10 AM. He and his group of watchers failed to identify Boulanger and his four disguised men—a painter, a photographer, a National Park Service Ranger, and a groundskeeper.

The Imperial Agent concluded that the coast was clear for him to approach Coleman and Junius to conduct his spy business.

Coleman observed Katsuie first and tapped Junius on the shoulder as the smartly dressed spy climbed up the steps to meet them. The three men shook hands, and then walked down the eighty-seven steps to the reflecting pool, where they commenced their stroll: Junius to Katsuie's right side and Coleman on Katsuie's left.

Katsuie spoke in hushed tones. "Mr. Braxton, when we reach the end of the reflecting pool, please continue walking straight to the Washington Monument. Move slowly and stop several times to tie your shoes, sit on a bench, sit on the lawn, and then make a U-turn as if you intend to return to the Lincoln Memorial. The purpose of this exercise is to see if you are being followed. We will meet you at the Washington Monument in 45 minutes. Mr. Johnson, listen closely. Please leave us now, make a left turn to exit the National Mall, and meet me at the Washington Monument in 40 minutes. Pay close attention to your surroundings to determine whether you are being followed. Be unobtrusively evasive. See you soon."

Junius peeled off to the left and walked at a brisk pace to Constitution Avenue. Crossing Constitution, he turned right and then executed a quick left onto 17th Street. As he approached Pennsylvania Avenue, Junius stopped, bent down, and appeared to tie his right shoe. He tried to memorize who was behind him.

Resuming his trek up 17th Street, Junius turned right onto Pennsylvania Avenue. He walked past the White House and then stopped at the corner of 15th Street and Pennsylvania Avenue, where he took a mental photograph of everyone behind him. Picking up his pace as he walked down 15th Street, Junius made a left turn onto Constitution Avenue and then executed another left turn up 14th Street. Halfway up 14th Street, Junius turned to see who was behind him, and there she was: the same shapely Negro woman in a red dress who had been standing in front of the White House. He figured she must have been tailing him. Undaunted, Junius walked directly toward her. She stepped aside to avoid a collision. He then walked slowly down 14th street to Independence Avenue and cut across the lawn to reach the Washington Monument. Junius scanned the scene around him. The woman in the red dress was nowhere to be seen and he did not detect anything or anyone unusual around him. Katsuie then appeared and asked if he enjoyed his tour of DC.

Nervously, Junius replied, "Mr. Katsuie, I was followed by a Negro woman in a red dress near the White House. I think I lost her, but you might want to disappear right now, just in case."

Katsuie smiled. "Congratulations, Mr. Johnson. She is on our side. Perhaps you would like to meet her in the future?"

Relieved and proud of his accomplishment, Junius answered, "Oh, I sure would. I may have frightened her by my actions. I want to apologize to her."

"Mr. Johnson, you need not apologize to her at all. In this business, you do what you must do in order to accomplish your mission. I can assure you that the lovely young lady in the red dress understands this rule and admires your innate resourcefulness. I believe that you two will enjoy working with each other. Now, where is Mr. Braxton?"

Coleman had deviated from his instructions. He walked past the Washington Monument to the US Capitol and then backtracked to the Washington Monument. During his excursion, Coleman stopped to tie his shoes, turned around a few times, and even sat on the lawn between the Capitol and the monument to observe each of the people around him. He detected no surveillance. He had hoped to see Uncle Hercules, but he had not. As Coleman approached the meeting place, he saw Katsuie and Junius. The Imperial Agent was the first to speak.

"Mr. Braxton, where have you been? You are two minutes late."

"Mr. Katsuie, I walked up to the Capitol and then doubled back. I was not followed," said Coleman meekly.

"Mr. Braxton, you must obey my orders precisely and without question. You exposed yourself, my team members tailing you, and the mission unnecessarily. This is very important for your safety and for the success of our future missions. You were under surveillance by three tails who were looking for any FBI agents who might be following you. Here are photographs of your minders for this operation."

Katsuie showed Coleman mugshots of two Negro men and one Negro woman. The photos of the frowning, thick-necked men resembled the images on Most Wanted posters he had seen on the walls of post offices. The woman looked like a very cold and cruel Hattie McDaniel. As he studied the menacing faces in the pictures, fear rose within Coleman. He struggled to maintain his composure.

"Mr. Katsuie, this will not happen again. I thought I could better smoke out people following me by drawing them out over a longer distance. I will not disobey your orders ever again. I will follow your directions explicitly."

The Imperial Agent wrapped his cold, bony hand around Coleman's elbow and said, "Good. You do not get a second chance in this business. Mistakes, insubordination, and carelessness can get you and your companions incarcerated or killed and your mission compromised."

Walking toward Constitution Avenue, Katsuie spoke a few more sentences before taking his leave and getting into the backseat of a waiting taxicab. "Gentlemen, on Saturday, June 10th at 4 AM, you will be picked up in front of Mr. Braxton's dormitory by the same taxicab and driver you see before us. He will drive evasively. Ultimately, he will deposit you inside the garage in the rear of the embassy of the Empire of Japan. Your next class will last until 4 AM Monday, June 12th. One taxi will take Mr. Braxton back to his dormitory. Another taxi will deposit Mr. Johnson at the bus station for his trip back to Baltimore. Mr. Johnson, please apply for a teaching position in the Baltimore City Public School System and accept any job offered to you. Mr. Braxton, enroll in a summer engineering course at Howard University in a technical field of interest to you, preferably in electrical or mechanical engineering. We will cover all your costs and procure for you a night-shift maintenance job at the Shoreham Hotel. Study the floorplan of that hotel and its security systems carefully. Do not discuss today's operation, or our future plans, with anyone."

The two young spies in training replied, "Yes, Sir!"

Katsuie's taxi then sped off.

Coleman and Junius shook hands and went their separate ways.

And two opposing teams of watchers—one Japanese, the other American—returned to their respective rally points to debrief their day's mission and plan their next steps.

5 PM, MAY 31, 1939; THE NAVY DEPARTMENT BUILDING

Captain McLaughlin, SAC Horan, Agent Walker, and Agent Boulanger sat around a small conference room table drinking coffee produced from South American beans roasted in the Navy's huge ovens in Brooklyn, New York, and shipped to the Navy Department Building commissary in 20-lb. tins. Hercules enjoyed being served strong, black coffee by a US Navy Captain. McLaughlin knew that he could not offend the FBI by being discourteous to a Negro agent, so he graciously asked whether Hercules wanted cream and sugar. Shaking his head, Hercules smiled and said, "No, Sir, Captain McLaughlin, this is Just fine! Reminds me of Paris!"

McLaughlin nodded his head and said, "Now that is quite a compliment, Hercules! After the Armistice, I sailed my destroyer and crew into the harbor at Cherbourg. We took a train to Paris and had a truly memorable time. Great coffee, great wine, great cuisine, great cigars, great women. Nothing like winning a war!"

Boulanger agreed. "Sir, you are one hundred percent right!"

At this point, Horan figured that he had prevailed upon Captain McLaughlin's goodwill enough. "Let's map out our operating plan before World War II commences, OK?"

"Fine with me," said McLaughlin.

Horan, sounding like a football coach, said, "Hercules, we identified five Japanese watchers today. Clearly Coleman is under surveillance. How will you debrief him without the Nips knowing?"

"Agent Horan, I arranged with my nephew to take confession tomorrow morning with me posing as '*Frère Honoré*' at the old Saint Augustine's Catholic Church at 15th and L Streets. The priest there, Father Sykes, knows me well as he takes my confession regularly. He knows how to keep his mouth shut. Father Sykes also allows me to wear vestments and take 'confession' from my Confidential Informants from time to time. My team has the church and Coleman under surveillance. We have the situation covered. Please keep me informed of the chatter from the technical measures you FBI and ONI guys have in place at Katsuie's haunts, the Jap embassy, and elsewhere. If my nephew's cover gets blown, I would prefer to rescue him before the Japanese filet him and toss the chum in the Potomac."

Horan interjected. "Captain McLaughlin and I will give you all the backup you require."

McLaughlin added, "OK, go take confession. When can we reconvene?"

Hercules: "How about noon on June 1st?"

Horan, Walker, and McLaughlin nodded their assent.

McLaughlin ended the conversation. "Horan, I suppose that you will identify the members of Katsuie's crew and have additional information for us on June 1st?"

Horan: "There will be no holding back of any information by either ONI or the FBI on this operation. My understanding is that Director Hoover and ONI Director, Rear Admiral Anderson, have agreed on absolute full disclosure."

"Correct," responded McLaughlin. "Let's support and protect our mole, AJAX, and sink these Jap spies."

Horan could not resist. "Aye aye, Cap'n!"

And off they went into the night.

7 AM, JUNE 1, 1939; SAINT AUGUSTINE'S CATHOLIC CHURCH

Departing Howard University, Coleman traveled an evasive route he designed to identify any tails following him. He leisurely walked past the Howard Theatre located on T Street, and then continued south to the intersection of Florida Avenue and Rhode Island Avenue. Turning right on S Street, he walked to 13th Street and turned right again. Coleman picked up his pace as he strolled past Duke Ellington's two former homes on 13th Street. Coleman stopped to hail a cab in front of the Whitelaw Hotel at T Street and 13th Street. He instructed the driver to let him out at Thomas Circle Park and 14th Street. Walking down 14th Street to L Street and making a right turn, Coleman arrived at the front door of Saint Augustine's at 6:59 AM. He had observed no one during his journey. Looking up at the church's large rose window briefly, he whispered to himself, "Here goes!"

Coleman saw Uncle Hercules, dressed in a Catholic priest's vestments, enter a confession booth. He followed "*Frère Honoré*" into the confessional, heard the little door slide open, got on his knees, and said, "Forgive me, Father, for I have sinned."

"You have not sinned, my nephew. Not at all!" growled the voice on the other side of the wooden wall. "What facts do you need to report to me?" Coleman thoroughly briefed Hercules on every detail of the Memorial Day meeting with Katsuie and Junius.

"Excellent, my nephew. You have performed well. Exceptionally well. Create a mental map of the Japanese embassy during your visit." Hercules then passed ten $5 bills to Coleman. "Go, my son. Your next confession will be at 6 AM on Wednesday, June 14th, here at Saint Augustine's. Should you in any way feel troubled or sense the forces of darkness about you, go to any phone booth and dial this number anytime, day or night." Coleman took the slip of paper passed through the little wooden door. "Memorize this number and destroy the paper on which it is written. Leave through the rear exit of

Saint Augustine's after I leave the confessional. The Lord and his angels will always be with you."

"I love you, Uncle Hercules," whispered Coleman.

"And I love you and will protect you," said Hercules.

And that was that.

NOON, JUNE 1, 1939; THE NAVY DEPARTMENT BUILDING

Hercules summarized his morning meeting with AJAX and provided carbon copies of his typed report to both Horan and McLaughlin. "Initially, I had my doubts about my nephew's ability to handle this mission. He now appears to be shaping up. Nonetheless, I worry that our youth are not as tough as my generation was when we entered the Great War. These kids today are just too damned soft."

Horan counseled Hercules, "Keep watch over AJAX. Build him up each time you take his 'confession.' Keep your bond tight with him. The Japs appear to be teaching Coleman the rudiments of spy craft. Judging by the route he took to the church before meeting with you, he is already using their training against them. Having an asset inside the Jap embassy is quite a coup. We would certainly appreciate your nephew's getting us a detailed floorplan of the embassy."

Hercules asked, "Agent Horan, anything new with Katsuie?"

Horan: "Katsuie returned to New York City after his evening interlude with the other two Howard University students. We suspect that he is grooming them for an operation in New York, as that is their hometown. Katsuie's contacts with radical Negro groups in New York keep him busy, as well as the NYC FBI Field Office."

McLaughlin interjected. "Horan, let's discuss alternative methods of accessing information from the Japanese. That naval attaché at the embassy, Captain Masuji, interests us a lot. We suspect that he is deeply involved with

Katsuie and other troublemakers. We want to dig a little deeper into his activities. He has an apartment in the Alban Towers. Any chance your technical types could tap his phone line, bug his rooms, intercept his cables, open his mail, open his safe, see if he has got any weapons, follow him around, see whom he meets, and photograph him?"

Horan whistled. "You think we should commit those kinds of resources and expose ourselves to that much legal and diplomatic risk for a naval attaché?"

"Yes, I do," replied McLaughlin. "I have observed him at embassy parties, diplomatic gatherings, and even played poker with him and the Japanese Army attaché once at the home of the British naval attaché in DC. Masuji is the pick of their litter. We need to put him under close surveillance for a while and see more clearly what the eight-fingered spy is up to."

Horan: "I will run this up my chain of command and get back to you."

McLaughlin: "OK. Be advised that Masuji will be out of his apartment on the night of June sixth for another card game—this time at the Japanese Army attaché's apartment."

Horan: "And how do you know this?"

McLaughlin: "Because I have been invited to attend. I lose to them, so they always invite me back."

Hercules asked, "Does the Navy reimburse your losses?"

McLaughlin: "You know, that is a good idea. I am going to submit an expense report and see if the Rear Admiral will sign off on it."

Hercules: "Always trying to offer a helping hand to a fellow underpaid federal employee."

Horan: "All right, I will get on it right away. Let's meet again on June 15th. Captain McLaughlin can tell us how much money he lost to his Japanese friends. Hercules can update us on Coleman and the Katsuie conspiracy. Hopefully I will have a little more information from FBI technical sources on Captain Masuji."

The three men shook hands and went off to make their daily rounds.

7 AM WEDNESDAY, JUNE 14; SAINT AUGUSTINE'S CATHOLIC CHURCH

Following a modified version of his previous June 1 route plan, Coleman arrived at the confessional precisely at 7 AM, convinced that no one had him under surveillance. He was wrong. Fortunately for Coleman, but rather unfortunately for an individual later identified as Mr. Ralph Lester of New York City, Hercules's team detected a bicycle-mounted newspaper delivery-man with what appeared to be papers rolled up in his shoulder bag following Coleman. The bicycle rider trailed behind Coleman from 4th Street and Bryant Street all the way to Florida and Rhode Island Avenues, delivering no newspapers. After Coleman made his right turn on to S Street and the "newsie" continued tailing him, one of Hercules's men—driving what appeared to be a DC Metro Police radio car—moved to intercept the bicyclist. The deliveryman stopped, produced a Colt .38-caliber revolver from his delivery bag, fired four rounds in rapid succession at the patrol car, and then furiously pedaled away. Transmitting on the proper DC Metro Police frequency, Hercules's man broadcast the correct WMPD radio code number for "shots fired at a patrol officer," as well as a very precise physical description of the assailant, the assailant's bicycle, the assailant's clothing, and the assailant's direction of travel. In less than thirty seconds following the emergency broadcast, an alert, very real DC Metro Police officer driving a very real DC Metro patrol car saw the gun-toting bicyclist. The bicyclist saw the police car too and at Florida and 8th Streets, the Metro officer's windshield was shattered by two rounds fired by the fleeing newsie. Unintimidated, the officer drove his patrol car full speed into the gunman, crushing him and his bicycle into the intersection of Florida and 8th Streets. The "officer" who first engaged the subject was never identified. No identification could be found on the body of the gunman. An FBI check of the deceased's fingerprints, however, positively identified him as Mr. Ralph Lester, aka Omar Muhammad, a resident of New York City, a member of the Moorish Freedom Movement of Harlem and a career criminal with a history of violent felony convictions and prison terms in New Jersey and New York. No one claimed the body of Mr. Lester. At public expense, his remains were interred in an unmarked grave in DC.

Neither *Frère Honoré* nor Coleman were aware of the excitement transpiring on the nearby streets of the nation's capital. Coleman related the following information from his sojourn within the embassy of the Empire of Japan to his uncle.

"The same cab driver who picked up Katsuie on Memorial Day took Junius and me to the embassy. The driver's photo license on the car's sun visor indicated that the cabby's name was 'Omar Muhammad.' He did not utter a single word when he drove us to the embassy. No 'hello,' no 'goodbye,' no 'nice weather.' The man said nothing during one hour of evasive driving through DC, Virginia, and Maryland. He paid close attention to the rearview mirror, delivered us to the covered rear entrance of the embassy at 6 AM, and just took off. Muhammad is cold, no doubt about it."

Coleman continued. "A short, clean-shaven Japanese man—maybe in his mid-thirties, wearing a three-piece dark blue suit—greeted us at the back door and escorted us down a winding metal staircase to the basement of the embassy. Though polite, this man never told us his name. None of the trainers ever told us their names. They listen well. They teach well. But they engage in no conversation you would call social or friendly. None of the trainers wore wedding rings.

"We walked a few paces after we got to the bottom of the staircase and were ushered into a well-lit, windowless room on the right-hand side of the corridor. There were two wooden tables in the room. Each table had a stack of documents and engineering drawings and a small metal camera. The camera measured maybe three inches long, an inch wide, and half an inch deep. The camera weighed perhaps a quarter of a pound and had no manufacturer's name on it. Our trainers referred to them as 'Minox cameras.' Our 'greeter' posted me in front of one table and a separate trainer positioned Junius at the other table. They taught us how to operate the device, emphasizing that the correct shooting distance for documents is 18 inches. An 18-inch chain is attached to the Minox, so getting the correct distance from the device to the document is not all that difficult. We practiced photographing the documents on the tables until 6 PM. We would shoot two rolls of film and then the trainers would take the exposed film to the technicians in the basement development shop. The techs would bring the finished photographs to us and instruct us how to improve our picture taking. By dinnertime, we were pros. No kidding!"

Coleman cleared his throat and resumed.

"After dinner, our hosts showed us excellent training films on detecting surveillance, evading a tail, how to leave a signal on a mailbox or lamppost, and how to make a 'dead drop.' We went to bed at midnight in a windowless room down the hall from where we learned how to handle the Minox cameras. The bedroom contained two cots, a bathroom, and a shower. Junius and I talked before sacking out. He was proud of himself. He had never used a camera before and now considered himself ready to work for *Life Magazine*. We ate an early breakfast in a kitchen in the basement on Sunday morning. At about 6:30 AM, the greeter and Junius's trainer from the day before escorted us to a gym, also located in the basement. They dressed us up in Japanese fighting suits called 'GI's' and introduced us to two tough Japs who taught us how to disable an attacker by smashing his windpipe, crushing his nuts, or dislocating a joint or two. The trainers were clear that violence is an absolute last resort and emphasized that we are to avoid trouble by blending in to the urban landscape and being invisible. After lunch, we saw a movie and had a slide lecture on how to map the interiors of offices for later exploitation by teams of burglars. They also showed us how to map manufacturing plants for subsequent use by teams of saboteurs. We have a checklist to complete for each reconnaissance mission. For example, the Japs want to know the number of armed guards; the precise location of guard posts; the changing of the guard procedures; explosive materials on site, like propane tanks, gasoline tanks, ammunition lockers, the number or entrances to the site, the nearest police stations, and Army or Navy bases. Here is a copy of the entire form we are required to complete for each mission. The greeter then reviewed examples of reports, maps, photos, and movies from previous recon missions that targeted the Consolidated Aircraft plant in California, the Pratt and Whitney aircraft engine factory in Connecticut, and the home office of a US government official in DC who frequently leaves sensitive materials on his desk. Uncle Hercules, it is incredible how much access the Japanese have to our secrets."

Hercules took a moment to step outside the confessional to see whether anyone was nearby. Satisfying himself that no one else was present, Hercules said, "Continue, my son."

Coleman replied, "The greeter ended our weekend session by telling us that Japan expects Junius and me to work together in Baltimore and DC. However, he did not tell us exactly what we would be doing for them in Baltimore and DC. Our next training session will be held on the July 4th weekend. An agent the greeter called 'your controller' will pick us up in Baltimore and take us to a site near Elkridge, Maryland. The greeter did not tell us what we would be doing on Saturday, July 1st, thru Monday, July 3rd, but advised us to wear hiking boots, long-sleeved shirts, and sturdy pants. Lastly, he handed each of us $100. Herc, these guys pay well, don't they? Junius thanked the greeter profusely for the training and the money and told him that he was eager to help Japan win a war against America. Uncle Hercules, I think Junius has lost his mind. Ever since Katsuie's little talk, it is like some demon took over Junius's soul."

After Coleman completed his monologue, *Frère Honoré* once again stepped out of his little wooden room to scan Saint Augustine's for the presence of any innocent or not-so-innocent bystanders. He concluded that the church remained vacant. Relieved, Hercules commenced a mild interrogation of his nephew.

"That was quite a weekend you had, Coleman. How do you feel about what you saw, what you heard, what you did, and what the Japs expect of you?"

Coleman thought carefully about how to answer a question concerning his feelings. He had expected Uncle Hercules to grill him about missing details from the events at the embassy. Having composed his thoughts, Coleman replied, "I am losing my fear of the Japanese and the thugs who work for them. My self-control and composure are much improved. I simply play the role of a diligent, motivated student committed to Japan's goal of bringing down the white oppressor. I let Junius take the lead in all things so I look like a follower, not a leader."

Hercules then turned up the heat on his nephew and asked, "Don't you feel bad betraying your friend, Junius? You know, Junius might well go to prison, or suffer an even worse penalty for his conduct. Will you be able to testify against Junius in a federal criminal trial with his innocent, weeping parents looking on? How will you feel being called a Judas by everyone at Howard University and Frederick Douglass High School? How will you feel when former friends shun you and say you sold out poor, misguided Junius for a few pieces of the white man's silver?"

Coleman recalled his previous conversation with Hercules on this very subject. However, his uncle's brutally direct questions compelled him to search deeply into his troubled soul and find an authentic, personal answer. "I am committed to bringing down these foreign spies and the American traitors who support them. The Japanese are clever. They totally control my friend Junius now, but he wants to be controlled by them. Long before the first meeting with Katsuie, Junius hated his status as a second-class citizen in the country of his birth. Katsuie may have lit the match, but Junius chose to be a stick of dynamite. Junius is a free man, an educated man, and he has made a choice to commit treason and acts of violence against his fellow citizens, both colored and Caucasian."

Hercules probed further into Coleman and his rhetoric. "So you don't think you're a second-class citizen in America? You think you're special because you're helping the white man fight the yellow or light brown man? You don't think that after the FBI is through with you that they won't send you back to some Negro ghetto where your future will be limited by your skin color? Coleman, are you foolin' yourself, or are you just tryin' to fool me?"

Now angered, Coleman lashed out at his uncle. "Hercules, I could have just kept my colored mouth shut and not told you anything about all this Katsuie stuff. I could have told those two white FBI agents that I would do nothing more than tell them about the first meeting with Katsuie. I could have said 'no' to joining you and the FBI in this fight. But I did not say no. I said I would help you and I fully intend to go all the way to stop these monsters from conquering the United States. You are my hero, Uncle Hercules. For three decades you have risked your life defending this country and its Constitution. That alone is good enough reason for me to do the same. But since you raised this issue, why do you risk everything for the white man?"

In his low gravelly voice, Boulanger said, "Coleman, I know that I am equal to or better than any white man in America. I know that most Americans view me as inherently inferior. However, I know damn well that the Japs, and certainly the Nazi Germans, consider me subhuman and will treat me far worse than I am treated today if, God forbid, they beat the US in a war. Just look at the murderous way the Japanese treat the Chinese — 'yellow' people, I might add. You really think that the same Japanese who routinely bomb and bayonet Chinese civilians will treat American Negroes right? And the Nazis—just look at the way they hate and abuse white Jews. You really think that they are going to give us colored people a fair shake? I know exactly what they think of us and what they will do to us if they take over. We will be in much worse shape than we have ever been here. Responsible white people in the American government understand that they cannot win a war against Japan and Germany and Italy and Russia without us Negroes. Coleman, they do know this. When they see us in action and see that we helped save this country, they will recognize how unjust it is to continue denying us the full measure of rights we are entitled to as US citizens. I truly believe this.

"Coleman, I know now that your heart is pure and your mind is straight. Things are going to get a lot more dangerous as you burrow deeper into the

Japanese spy network. Use the training and skills they give you against them. Stick with me and you will get through this. I am proud of you, Coleman."

Coleman told his uncle confessor that he would always do what was necessary to make Uncle Hercules proud of him. Hercules arranged to debrief Coleman after his Elkridge, Maryland, training session on July 6 at Saint Augustine's at 6 AM, unless some unforeseen emergency arose.

Unbeknownst to both uncle and nephew, the unforeseen emergency had already arisen.

CODE RED: 10 AM, JUNE 14; DEPARTMENT OF JUSTICE BUILDING AT 10TH AND CONSTITUTION AVENUES

Hercules had just put on his suit, tie, and shoulder-holstered Smith and Wesson Model 19 .357 Magnum when his friend and former chaplain of the 369th Regiment, Father Sykes, entered the Saint Augustine's robing room. "Hercules, a white man dressed in a blue pinstriped suit, red tie, white shirt and gray felt hat wants to talk to you. He looks to me to be an FBI agent. Should I tell him you are not here?"

"No. I will go out and meet him."

Father Sykes smiled broadly, showing his perfect set of white teeth. "So, you are not in any trouble, *mon ami*?"

Hercules replied, "*Cent percent non!* Not yet Not to my knowledge at least, *mon cher Prêtre* Sykes."

The two wartime comrades hugged, kissed each other on both cheeks, and wagged their fingers at each other while saying simultaneously, "Not a word of this to anyone!" The laughter of the two men could be heard outside the robing room by Agent Clarence Walker. When Walker saw Hercules he exclaimed, "You won't be laughing when you hear the latest news!"

Hercules put his finger to his lips and said, "Let's roll, Clarence. Tell me in the car."

In front of the church, Agent Clyde had his car engine running, his left hand on the steering wheel, his foot on the clutch, and his right hand on the gear shift. Hercules got in the back seat, Walker in the front. Clyde peeled out, burning rubber.

"What's going on, gents?" Hercules said in his best theatrical *sang froid* manner.

Walker replied, "The *merde* has hit the proverbial fan, my friend. A Katsuie tail following your nephew had to be scraped off the intersection of Florida and 8th Streets with a putty knife after he shot out the windows of FBI Agent Callaghan's fake Metro PD patrol car, and later fired a few more rounds at a genuine Metro PD cop responding to Callaghan's radio call of 'shots fired at an officer.' The responding Metro PD officer handled the situation with the right level of aggression and ran over the shooter. Regrettably, the officer's nice new patrol car will take quite a while to clean, what with all the squashed gunman's body fluids embedded on the vehicle's grille, hood, tires, and windshield. In any event, it won't take long for the Japanese to realize that something untoward happened to their guy tailing Coleman. Katsuie will probably want to question AJAX harshly to see if a mole has somehow gotten into his Howard University crew. We will have to create an airtight cover story exonerating your nephew that he can repeat under torture by the Japs. We have got to get Coleman off the streets, briefed on his cover story, and put back at Howard University before dinnertime tonight."

Hercules knew that there was no way the FBI would ever consider pulling their asset, his nephew, out of this situation. They, and he, were fully prepared to risk Coleman's life to keep the newly minted FBI mole in the game.

"All right, then. The postman will deliver mail a little early to Coleman's dorm. Get me home so I can change."

Hercules got out of the moving FBI car as it pulled up to his house. Carrying his Catholic vestments, he walked quickly to his door, unlocked it, and raced to the closet in his bedroom. There, he hung his *Frère Honoré* garb up and pulled out yet another costume—a US Postal Service uniform.

After changing into his USPS outfit, he picked up a mail bag, slung it over his shoulder, and placed a mailman's cap on his head. Hercules locked the front door to his home and sauntered to the waiting FBI car.

"Howard University, please," he said to Agent Clyde as if he were directing a cab driver. A few blocks before Coleman's dorm, Hercules exited the vehicle and walked casually to the brick building. As good fortune would have it, he saw Coleman standing alone in the vestibule. Mincing no words, Hercules told his nephew, "Take a cab immediately to 10th and Constitution Avenues. I will be waiting out front for you."

Surprised by the appearance of this apparition, Coleman nodded, went to the street, and hailed a taxi. Hercules waited for him to leave the building and then walked out the back exit. He moved quickly to Clyde's FBI car and they ran red lights all the way to the Department of Justice Building. As soon as Coleman paid his driver and got out of the cab, Hercules greeted his nephew and escorted him into an elevator going to the fourth floor. They walked into an empty office where Walker briefed Coleman about what had occurred at 14th and Q Streets.

Coleman asked, "Who was the guy doing the shooting?"

Walker responded, "We do not know yet. According to the Metro PD, he had no identification on him."

Coleman inquired, "Do you have a photo of the gunman?"

Walker picked up a telephone, dialed an internal FBI lab number, and asked whether the shooter had been identified yet, and whether the lab had a photo of the deceased.

"Well, send the photo up to my office right away. Now!"

Within a minute a man knocked on the door, entered, and handed a file folder with a photo in it to Walker. Clarence pulled the photograph out of the folder and put it in front of Coleman.

"That is Omar Muhammad," Coleman said, looking directly at Hercules. "Katsuie will be furious. This is his number one thug, his chauffeur, his bodyguard."

Hercules laughed and said to Coleman, "Poor Kimura—all alone in DC with no one to protect his sorry little ass. Coleman, let me tell you what will happen and how we are going to deal with it. First, Katsuie will hear from the Japanese embassy that this jerk, Muhammad, is no more. Second, Katsuie will want to talk to you about where you were when old Omar bought the farm. I have a story for you to tell him, and no matter what he or any of his boys ask you or say to you or do to you, you just repeat the fucking story! They may yell at you. They may tell you that you are lying. They may even slap that pretty face of yours to pressure you into confessing that you are lying to them. Ignore that shit! Just hold fast to the story I tell you. As long as you make yourself believe this story and repeat it under duress, the Japs will ultimately believe it too. Do you get this, man?"

Coleman realized that his uncle meant business in a life-and-death kind of way. He squared his shoulders and said, "Just tell me the fucking story I have to repeat, Hercules!"

Smiling, Hercules laid out the cover story that he had somehow concocted in less than one hour. "Here it is, Coleman. You were at the dentist's office for a routine dental exam when all this business went down. The dentist's name is Dr. Roscoe Woodford. His office is located at 3rd and U Streets. You have seen him professionally once before, one visit during your junior year at Howard University to treat a toothache. You found Dr. Woodford's name in the DC phone book. You wanted to see a colored dentist because you know that most white dentists would not allow you to sit in their waiting room with their white clientele. So you found a Negro dentist who trained at Howard University. You liked him. He told you that annual appointments are important and he said he would provide this service to you for free until you got a good job as an engineer and could pay your own way. Now, Coleman, I am going to call Roscoe Woodford, my regimental dentist during World War I, and you and I are going to visit him. I will do ALL the talking. Roscoe and I will create a file verifying all the details of your cover story. The Japs will steal this file, conclude that you are clean, and then look somewhere else for a mole in their bullshit organization. OK?"

What else could Coleman say other than "OK" back to his genius uncle? Even the white FBI agents were shaking their heads in amazement at their associate's adroitness. Hercules left the room. Ten minutes later he returned and said, "Saddle up" to his nephew. Hercules looked at his partners and gave them their instructions.

"Clarence and Louis, you shadow Coleman all the way to the dentist's office. I will get there on my own. Keep an eye out for tails. Have the rest of the team work on a schedule for clandestinely keeping Coleman under surveillance. Soon the Japs will take Coleman for a little ride to ask him some questions. Follow them. Hopefully we will uncover the location of one of their safe houses in DC or Maryland. Let me know as soon as they return Coleman to his dorm so the 'mailman' can debrief him."

Clyde and Walker nodded. And off they all went.

NOON, JUNE 14; THE DISTRICT OF COLUMBIA, LEDROIT PARK OFFICE OF ROSCOE WOODFORD, DDS

Hercules and Coleman entered Dr. Woodford's office together.

Dr. Woodford greeted Hercules and Coleman with a wave of his exquisitely manicured hand as they entered his office. In the honey-smooth voice of a man who could have been a professional singer, Roscoe spoke. "We won't see anybody here for another two hours, Hercules. What can I do for you and your friend here?"

Hercules got right to the point. "Roscoe, this here is my nephew, Coleman Braxton. As you and I briefly discussed, Coleman needs a medical history with you that goes back at least a year. You need to have in your files and your sign-in book out front that you performed an urgent or emergency dental examination on him last year around this time. Furthermore, your files and sign-in book must reflect that you conducted a routine dental exam on Coleman this morning at 7 AM, that he required no fillings, and you cleaned his teeth. Your next routine follow-up with Coleman will be in a year. Now, I predict that soon, certainly within 48 hours or so, a colored man or woman whom you have never seen before will come to your office to make an appointment with you. The person will be friendly and tell you that Coleman Braxton recommended you to them as a fine dentist. You will say great things about Coleman, such as he is a bright engineering student at Howard University and that any friend of Coleman's is welcome as a patient of yours, as long as they pay for your services promptly. They will ask to see you as soon as possible and you will accommodate them. They will be casing your office and they, or someone with whom they are affiliated, will surreptitiously enter your office late at night and search your files for evidence that Coleman Braxton is and has been your patient. As long as your files reflect the existence of your professional relationship with Coleman, that will be that. You will not see them again. Any information you can get from the person you examine will be much appreciated. You OK with all of this, buddy?"

Dr. Woodford looked at Coleman and said, "Son, why don't you go next door and sit in my luxurious dentist chair? I want to see if your mouth is as messed up as your life."

Both Hercules and Coleman burst into laughter. Hercules looked at his nephew and said, "See? I told you, he ain't much of a dentist, but he is one true friend."

Roscoe replied, "Coleman, I am a much better dentist than your murdering uncle gives me credit for."

Hercules corrected his friend, saying, "Roscoe, I am a killer, not a murderer. And as I recall, I terminated a young German wearing a *Stahlhelm* before he could stick you with the bayonet he had fixed to his Mauser rifle. I didn't hear you complain about my killin' that kraut back then."

Roscoe fired back. "I never complained nor will I ever complain about your role as an angel of death. I just overreacted to your questioning my competence as a medical professional."

Hercules apologized to Woodford. "Coleman, Dr. Woodford here is a credit to our race. He graduated second in his class at Howard University Dental School. He is so excellent, I even pay him in cash for his first-rate but outrageously overpriced professional services. Now, Dr. Woodford, please examine Coleman and create records for him that will withstand scrutiny by unscrupulous individuals. Oh, and Coleman and I cannot be linked in any way by your documents, or in conversations you may have with anyone."

Roscoe Woodford thoroughly examined Coleman. He took dental X-rays and documented his prior and current appointments with Mr. Coleman Braxton. He also altered his year-old sign-in sheet to reflect that Coleman had appeared as a walk-in emergency case. As Hercules and his nephew prepared to leave Dr. Woodford's office, the good doctor shook hands with Coleman and said, "You do whatever your uncle tells you to do. There is no better man on the face of this earth. I have no idea what is going on here, but I know it is serious, and I will pray that God and Hercules will lead you safely through the 'valley of death,' just as they both did for me in 1918."

Coleman's eyes teared up. He dried them. And he and his uncle went in different directions after they exited the building.

10 AM FRIDAY, JUNE 16, 1939; THE EMPIRE INQUIRES

Coleman received an unannounced visit from the attractive young woman in the red dress who had tailed Junius on Memorial Day. As Coleman walked from class back to his dormitory, she approached him and said sweetly, "Hi, Coleman. Mr. Katsuie has asked me to talk to you. Would you mind walking around this impressive campus with me?"

Coleman replied, "Sure, Miss… I did not get your name?"

The woman responded, "Oh, you can call me Lucretia or Lucy, whatever you like."

Coleman said, "OK, Lucretia, how is Mr. Katsuie?"

Lucretia: "He is fine, but he needs to know precisely where you were on Wednesday morning, June 14th."

Coleman pretended to be surprised. "Why? Is something wrong? How can I help?"

Lucretia gently took Coleman's hand and said, "Nothing is wrong. Mr. Katsuie is conducting a routine security check on his DC contacts. This sort of thing happens from time to time. As you know, we have powerful, unscrupulous enemies—like the FBI, for example—so to protect ourselves from J. Edgar Hoover and people he pays to spy on us, we randomly audit certain aspects of each of our agents' lives. I know that you are new to all of this and it sounds troubling, but over time you will see that being careful helps us stay free and clear of trouble from the 'Feds.'"

Coleman pretended to accept her comforting words and her soft hand as sufficient for him to tell her his whereabouts on Wednesday the 14th of June. "Lucretia, I had an early morning dentist appointment on Wednesday. Thank goodness I got away with just a cleaning. No cavities, no fillings. I really do not like sitting in a dentist's chair knowing that he is looking for ways to make money in my mouth and hurting me at the same time."

Lucretia nodded her head and said, "I understand completely. Coleman, what is your dentist's name?"

Coleman responded, "Dr. Roscoe Woodford."

Lucretia replied, "And where is his office located?"

Coleman: "Not far from here, actually. LeDroit Park, on the corner of 3rd and U Streets."

Lucretia turned and smiled at Coleman. "Thank you. I apologize for interrupting your day. That is all I need to know for now. If Mr. Katsuie requires any additional information, I will get back to you."

Lucretia then went her way and Coleman went his.

The "mailman" was waiting for Coleman at his dormitory. Without a word, Coleman knew it was time to make a pilgrimage to Saint Augustine's Church to confess his sins. Once inside the church he "confessed" earnestly to Frère Honoré.

A squad of experienced FBI watchers now patrolled the area surrounding the church, looking for minions of the Empire of Japan. Another group of FBI agents kept a close watch on Coleman's dormitory to see if any of Katsuie's operatives paid Ajax a visit. Phone taps and listening devices, previously installed by FBI and ONI technical experts at the Japanese embassy; the Japanese consulate in New York City; the various Japanese military attachés' apartments at the Alban Towers located at 3700 Massachusetts Avenue, NW, in DC; as well as Katsuie's residence were being monitored for chatter. If Coleman's name came up in conversation, the FBI and ONI agents were to be advised immediately. All mail and cables sent to the Japanese embassy and its spies and spymasters were similarly being covered by the FBI and ONI. If the FBI-ONI mole's name was mentioned, or in any way implicated in the text of any intercepted transmission or document, the joint FBI-ONI team was to be notified without delay. The Attorney General and his top deputies were aware of the blanket surveillance of suspected Japanese, German, Italian, and Soviet facilities and personnel. Despite some concerns about statutes and prior Supreme Court precedents questioning such Executive Branch conduct, the top management of the Department of Justice reasoned that the approaching war, the President's more than tacit approval of the monitoring, and the need to protect the US from the malign influence of foreign totalitarian governments fully justified the FBI, ONI, MID (Military Intelligence Division of the US Army), Treasury Department, and Federal Communications Commission's aggressive actions.

10 AM MONDAY, JUNE 19, 1939; THE DISTRICT OF COLUMBIA, LEDROIT PARK OFFICE OF ROSCOE WOODFORD, DDS

A voluptuous woman in a red dress entered Dr. Woodford's office. Roscoe Woodford's outward demeanor did not betray his intense interest in her anatomy as he introduced himself. "I am Dr. Woodford. How may I be of assistance to you?"

Replying coquettishly, the Josephine Baker look-alike purred, "I recently moved to DC from Chicago and I am establishing relationships with medical professionals here. A friend of mine, Mr. Coleman Braxton, told me that you are an excellent dentist. So, here I am."

Roscoe Woodford thought, *Damn! Why do I have to fear such a fine-looking female specimen?*

Woodford said out loud, however, "I will have to thank young Mr. Braxton for his advertising! In Washington, DC, Howard University's brilliant engineering students like Coleman Braxton are a source of enormous pride for our community. But enough about Coleman. When would you like an appointment, Miss...?"

"Lucretia Haines. Would right now be a problem?"

Roscoe again thought, *Oh, I would like to do a thorough examination of you RIGHT now, darlin'!*

But Dr. Woodford said, "You are in luck, Miss Haines. Please complete this brief form and I will examine your teeth and gums, take a few pictures, and clean your teeth. Normally I insist on payment on the day services are rendered, but as you are new in town and were referred by one of my reliable patients, I will send you a bill for five dollars for the services I render today."

Lucretia blinked her eyes at Roscoe and said, "Oh, I have no problem paying you in cash right now. You are so sweet to interrupt your day for me."

Again, Roscoe thought, *You have no concept how sweet I am. What a pity I can't service this magnificent filly properly in 369th Regimental style.*

But Dr. Woodford said, "I think that you and I are going to get along just fine."

After she completed the form, the good doctor examined the patient and was impressed by the excellent condition of Lucretia's teeth and gums. Roscoe wished he could get to know so much more about other parts of her body. *Oh, well*, he thought. *C'est la guerre!*

Lucretia sashayed out of Dr. Woodford's office, never to be seen by him again. However, she would visit the dentist's office late that night with one of Katsuie's "black-bag job" specialists to compare the written facts from the records in Dr. Woodford's files to the tales told by the dentist and his patient, Coleman Braxton, aka Ajax.

Hercules's team photographed and recorded the not-so-surreptitious break-in. Lucretia Haines's fingerprints were lifted off her patient information form and her true identity, Lucy Smith of New York City, was determined by the FBI lab. Lucy's burglary partner took a train the next morning from Union Station to Trenton, New Jersey, where he boarded a bus to New York City. FBI agents followed the subject to an apartment in Harlem, where his fingerprints and other items were used to confirm his identity as Ahmad Izz-Al-Din, aka Jordan Pride, formerly a resident of the British-controlled island of Jamaica. Every facet of Katsuie's network was now being examined under the FBI's very powerful microscope.

By June 23, *Frère Honoré* could confirm to Coleman in the confessional that Katsuie had concluded from Lucretia's and Ahmad's prompt investigation that Coleman had nothing to do with the events at the intersection of Florida and 8th Streets. Based upon his thorough review, the Imperial Agent decided that Omar Muhammad had acted rashly and brought about his own demise. The Code Red was now over for the time being.

Hercules counseled Coleman to go about his normal daily routine, pursue his studies, and socialize with his summer-session classmates. "Coleman, no need to worry. We have you covered. Wherever you may be—even in Elkridge, Maryland—I got my eyes on you!"

8

JULY 1, 1939; A TRIP TO ELKRIDGE, MARYLAND: THE PATRIOT OUTDOOR SPORTSMAN'S CLUB

Coleman and Junius received instructions from Katsuie via perfume-scented letters to spend the Independence Day holiday together in Baltimore. When asked by Junius if Coleman could spend the July 4th holiday weekend at their home, Junius's parents answered that they would be delighted to provide accommodations for their son's engineering-student friend. To Isaiah and Frances, their son—who would soon be teaching history at Frederick Douglass High School—could do no wrong. The Johnsons dreamed of their son getting married, having children, and becoming the principal of Douglass High. Associating with an engineer from Howard University fit in perfectly with their vision of their son's bright future.

These great expectations Isaiah and Frances envisioned for their Junius appeared to be approaching fulfillment soon when Dr. Ralph Ames, a prominent practicing physician in Baltimore, called Johnson's home to invite Junius and Coleman to join him for a holiday get-together at the Patriot Outdoor Sportsman's Club in Elkridge, Maryland. Frances, flustered that neither her son nor her husband were home to take this important call, expressed her considerable pleasure that a pillar of the Baltimore medical community would invite her child to socialize with the top tier of Baltimore's Negro society.

Dr. Ames replied in his mellifluous Bahamian Island voice, "Mrs. Johnson, the honor is all mine. We want to groom the next generation of educated professionals to serve as positive role models for our community here in Baltimore. You and your husband have raised Junius to be the upright young man that he is, not I. Please advise your son and his friend, Coleman, that I will pick them up at your home at 8 AM on Saturday morning, July 2nd. I promise to return them back to you Saturday night so that you can all go to Saint Paul's Methodist Church together on Sunday morning."

Beaming, Frances replied, "You are so considerate, Dr. Ames. Thank you, and I will pass on your message to Junius as soon as I see him."

"No problem, Mrs. Johnson. You be well."

Coleman passed this information to his uncle. Dr. Ames then became the subject of an intense federal investigation. Hercules's FBI profile of Ralph Ames noted that in 1915, he had traveled to Tennessee from his home in the Bahamas to attend Meharry Medical College. After graduating first in his class at Meharry, Ames could not find a single non-segregated hospital that would admit him as a resident. Undeterred by bigotry, he moved to Baltimore in 1922 to continue his advanced medical training at the Negro-owned and -operated Provident Hospital and Free Dispensary. He treasured his relationship with Provident and continued to treat patients and train interns in Emergency Medicine even after going into private practice. The doctor lived alone in his three-story home and medical office on North Carrolton Avenue overlooking Lafayette Park, not far from the colored branch of the YMCA. Ames had no criminal record—not even a parking ticket—no civil complaints had ever been lodged against him, and he had no apparent professional or financial problems or irregularities. The man was a ghost as far as FBI records were concerned.

Yet, Hercules thought, *this guy is part of a Japanese spy ring. We have got to get to the bottom of all this*!

At 8 AM on July 2, Junius and Coleman stood in front of the Johnsons' house as Dr. Ames pulled up in his exquisitely polished, dark blue 1939 Buick Roadmaster 80 sedan. Dr. Ames exited his automobile, firmly shook hands with his two new acolytes, and bade Coleman to sit in the Buick's front seat and Junius to sit in the rear passenger seat. Isaiah and Frances waved to their son and Coleman as Ames drove off toward US 1.

Dr. Ames wasted no time getting down to spy business. "Gentlemen, I have received many positive reports from Mr. Katsuie about your diligence, calmness under pressure, attention to detail, alertness to surveillance, sobriety, and talent for saying as little as possible when questioned. Today you will get a little exposure to the use of firearms. Have either of you ever fired a pistol, shotgun, or rifle?"

"No," said Coleman.

"Me neither," said Junius.

"Good," replied Ames. "I won't have to undo any flawed practices imparted to you by some YMCA summer camp counselor. I want to accustom you to operating and cleaning a .38-caliber revolver and a 12-gauge over/under shotgun. Most of the members of the Patriots Club are doctors, dentists, lawyers, businessmen, and educators who shoot trap and skeet with 12-gauge shotguns. Many also possess and practice with revolvers, so we will blend in well. At the end of today, I will advise the club president, Dr. Jonathan Dixon, that you have demonstrated your ability to handle firearms safely and proficiently. He will invite you to participate in our Independence Day Trap-Shooting Competition on Monday at 10 AM. You WILL accept the invitation graciously. On Monday, there will be two women's teams competing against each other and two men's teams doing likewise. Since you both are novices, you will be put on opposite teams. At the end of the meet, the top male and female shooters will be announced and the club will donate a lot of money to Provident Hospital and Free Dispensary to help fund the treatment of Negro children from poor families. The *Baltimore Afro-American* newspaper will publish a story about this eleemosynary event in its July 5th edition. Any questions?"

"No, Sir," said Junius, with Coleman nodding his head in agreement.

"Good. Enjoy yourselves today and Monday. The food will be delicious, the conversation interesting, and the shooting fun. Just a few do's and don'ts: First, do not use any foul language at the club, even if you hear off color words coming from a member or two! Second, do not initiate or respond to any advances by women or young ladies at the club. Fathers, mothers, husbands, boyfriends, and brothers will be watching you closely for any act of impropriety. Be polite and respectful to the ladies at all times. Finally, **NO** consumption of alcohol or any other intoxicants, and no cigarettes. This is a proper gun club—not a bar, not a bowling alley, not a brothel, and not a pool hall. Are we clear?"

"Yes, Sir," said Coleman. This time, Junius nodded his head in agreement.

Dr. Ames turned right off Washington Boulevard, drove up a poorly paved country road, and then turned right on to a winding gravel driveway thickly bordered on both sides by oak trees. There were no other cars present. Ames turned off the car engine and announced, "Let's get to work on this gorgeous sunny day."

The good doctor opened the trunk of his car and handed three dozen rolled-up targets and a gun cleaning kit to Junius. Ames then handed a canvas bag containing twelve 50-round boxes of .38-caliber ammunition to Coleman. The doctor carried his black leather medical bag. The trio walked 25 yards up an incline and past a one-story cinderblock structure painted gray. In the center of the building was a metal front door, painted rust red, covered by an awning resting on two wooden stanchions that were painted gray. On either side of the front door were two double sash windows.

Dr. Ames pointed at the building and spoke. "There is a bathroom and sink in the clubhouse, as well as a refrigerator, some tables, chairs, and cabinets."

Walking down a small hill, Coleman noticed a large pond off to the right with an aluminum rowboat resting on a tiny sandy beach. Ames observed Coleman surveilling the waterfront.

"Mr. Braxton, we stocked that little pond with fish, but the snapping turtles, herons, mallards, and egrets seem to eat them all up before we can catch them! More important, do not go swimming in that water. Contrary to popular opinion about the absence of *Agkistrodon piscivorus* in the state of Maryland, I have seen a cottonmouth or two swimming around in our little pond here. I would not want to waste what little anti-venom I have in the clubhouse refrigerator on a non-dues-paying visitor to the club who gets himself bit after I told him to stay out of the water!"

Coleman smiled as he thought to himself, *This guy sounds like Uncle Hercules.*

Dr. Ames asked Coleman, "Now what is so amusing about toxic snake bites?"

"Not a thing, Dr. Ames," Coleman answered contritely.

"Um! Um! Um! What kind of person has Katsuie sent to me for firearms training?" complained Ralph.

Twenty-five yards from the pond stood the target range. The firing positions for pistol, shotgun, and rifle all pointed away from the water and toward a 20-foot high berm designed to absorb pistol and rifle bullets, as well as shotgun slugs, passing through targets. A trap-shooting range, also facing away from the pond, had been constructed 20 yards to the right of the target range. Ames set up a man-sized silhouette target ten yards from the firing line. He opened up his large black leather medical bag and gave each of his students a set of earplugs and a pair of yellow shooting glasses. Ralph then pulled out a Colt Official Police .38 Special revolver with a four-inch barrel from his bag, opened its cylinder, and positioned the weapon on the firing position podium with the barrel pointing toward the target. "This is the Lord's Gun Gospel According to His Loyal Servant, Dr. Ralph Ames: Never point a gun at a man unless you intend to shoot him. Never shoot a man farther than ten yards away from you. When you shoot a man, aim to kill him. You always aim for the center of mass—the man's chest. This revolver has six rounds in it. If you have to shoot a man, put all six in him—it'll do him good! Any questions?"

Both Coleman and Junius shook their heads no.

"I like you two. You do not waste my time by being disagreeable or stupid. Let's gather around as I demonstrate how to load, aim, and fire this fine gun. I am right-handed. I hold the revolver with the cylinder open in my left hand and load six .38 Special rounds. Always keep the barrel pointed at the target. Let's give the target a name. Junius, you got a name for this target?"

"J. Edgar Hoover," replied Junius instantaneously.

"Going right to the top, are you, Mr. Johnson? Going right to the top! J. Edgar it is until club members show up, then we will just call what we are shooting at 'a target.' Remember, right now, all of these prosperous club members believe in America, believe in FDR, believe in justice, believe in J. Edgar Hoover. Never let on what the three of us are all about because if you do, these God-fearing folks will hand you and me over to J. Edgar Hoover in a heartbeat! The members must think that you believe just the way they do. They must think that you want to rise within the refined, second-class colored society that's been doled out to us by first-class white people. Got it?"

Coleman and Junius nodded in the affirmative.

"Now, where was I? Oh, I remember. Now close the loaded cylinder and face J. Edgar with your feet spread a little bit more than shoulder width apart. Raise the revolver in your dominant hand and point it at J. Edgar's chest. Keep your arm straight out, with just the slightest bend in your elbow. Look down the gun sight. Keep the front blade of the gun sight even and level with the notch in the rear of the weapon. You want J. Edgar's heart right in the center of this sight picture. Once you have got your sight picture, squeeze the trigger straight back and fire. Keep firing five more times, always maintaining the front blade level even and level with the notch in the rear of the gun and always aimed at the center of J. Edgar's chest. Now watch."

Dr. Ames emptied the revolver into the center of the silhouette in under five seconds. Opening the cylinder, the good doctor ejected the spent casings, placed the weapon on the podium, and signaled Coleman and Junius to inspect the target.

"In my professional opinion, he looks deceased," announced Ames. "You agree?"

Both trainees nodded their heads yes.

"Now, Junius, you try."

And so the pistol practice went from 9:30 AM until 1 PM when Patriot Club members began to arrive. Dr. Ames retrieved the targets and placed them and the 600 spent .38 Special casings in Coleman's canvas bag. Ralph tucked his Colt into his medical bag. After walking back to the parked Buick and depositing the canvas and medical bags in its trunk, Dr. Ames led his two trainees to the clubhouse, where they scrubbed their hands carefully to remove the lead and gunpowder residue on their hands before eating the peanut butter and jelly sandwiches prepared by the fastidious doctor. While in the clubhouse, Dr. Ames introduced Junius and Coleman to half a dozen impressive men who appeared interested in making the two young men's acquaintance.

"These fine fellows are my guests," Ames said to his fellow Patriot Outdoor Sportsman's Club members. "Mr. Junius Johnson here just graduated from Morgan and will be teaching history at Frederick Douglass High School in the fall. Smart and ambitious as he is, I predict that he will get his PhD and become School Superintendent of Baltimore City Public Schools one day. And this here is Mr. Coleman Braxton. He too graduated from Douglass. He earned a BS in engineering at Howard University and is now pursuing an MS in engineering, also at Howard. There is no telling how far this man will go. Maybe he will invent a replacement for the vacuum tube, or something else extraordinary to benefit mankind!"

Both J3 and Coleman were slightly embarrassed by Dr. Ames's effusive praise, but his endorsement had the desired positive effect on the attitude of Patriots Club members—all part of Baltimore's "talented tenth"—toward the two young strangers in their midst.

After lunch, Dr. Ames retrieved his over/under 12-gauge shotgun from the trunk of his car. Coleman and Junius each carried a canvas bag containing 125 rounds of trap-shooting ammunition. Ralph then escorted Junius and Coleman to the trap-shooting range and conveyed the fundamentals of the sport to them. After walking his two students to the trap house and demonstrating how to move from one of the four trap stations to the next after taking each shot, Ames calmly opined that, "The key to trap shooting is minimalist action. Hold the gun with your right elbow out like a wing so it will remain tight to your cheek. Do not try to guess whether the target will go left, center, or right. Just keep your gun positioned well over the trap house, raise your eyebrows to let light into your eyes, and call 'Pull!' to launch the target. See the target clearly. Then shoot the target. That is all you have to do—nothing fancy. Got it?"

Junius and Coleman said, "Yes." They observed Dr. Ames effortlessly blast ten targets from the sky. Then they practiced under his careful supervision for the rest of the day. The trainees fired from each of the four firing positions located 16 yards behind the trap house. Throughout the long, hot afternoon, Dr. Ames provided steady, constructive guidance to Coleman and Junius as they shot a total of 125 12-guage shells each. Both young men agreed that the physician marksman was a superb teacher and they were confident that they would not embarrass their esteemed mentor, Dr. Ralph Ames, when it came time for them to compete.

As they packed up the shotguns, Ames informed them, "Gentlemen, you passed. I will speak to the club president and testify that in my opinion, you guys are fit and capable to compete on par with the Patriot Club's nearsighted geezers on Monday. Dr. Dixon will, of course, do whatever I ask him to do."

Dr. Ames drove his tired students, their ears still ringing from all the gunfire, back to Junius's house that evening. He reminded them that he would pick them up at 8 AM on Monday.

"Remember, you two, talk to Mr. and Mrs. Johnson about the nice, dignified men you met today. Do not go on about revolvers and shotguns, J. Edgar Hoover silhouette targets, and blasting objects traveling at high rates of speed in three different directions. Act and talk civilized to these civilians. Play the game. Our day will come. For the time being, however, you have to blend in."

Frances prepared dinner for Coleman and Junius soon after they arrived home. She sat quietly at the table as they ate, eager to learn about their experiences that day with a personage as august as Dr. Ralph Ames. The two spies in training recognized that they would have to feed Mrs. Johnson the fairy tale she wanted to hear about her son and her son's best friend hobnobbing with Baltimore's Negro elite. Avoiding any discussion of handguns, Junius and Coleman portrayed their experience in Elkridge as an outdoor Aristotelian educational experience conducted by the wise and worldly Dr. Ames, who provided his novitiates invaluable lessons about the importance of ethics and natural science to one's life. The ruse worked perfectly and a very pleased Frances slept soundly that night. Junius and AJAX too slept soundly. They accompanied Frances and Isaiah to St. Paul's Methodist Church on Sunday and behaved as if they did not have a care in the world.

But cares they did have.

MONDAY, JULY 3, 1939

Dr. Ames arrived to pick up AJAX and J3 at 8 AM. Smiling and exuding a regal air, Ralph charmed Frances off her feet.

"And how are you on this fine day, Mrs. Johnson? You don't mind if I take Junius and Coleman to meet some of my friends at the Patriot Outdoor Sportsman's Club, do you?"

With her head pointed slightly down, Frances replied, "Well, of course not, Dr. Ames. We are so honored that you have taken such an interest in our son and his best friend!"

Feigning humility with all of the polish of a British nobleman, Dr. Ames put his hand over his heart and said, "Mrs. Johnson, it is I who should be thanking you for sharing these two gentlemen with me on this national holiday. I promise to return them to you this evening, safe and sound!"

This was just too much for Frances. She curtsied, took Ames's right hand in both of her hands, and kissed his wrist.

Junius and Coleman stood, stunned by this heartfelt display of gratitude to a man preparing them for prison, or possibly death.

Unfazed by the irony of the situation, Dr. Ames told Frances, "You are far too kind, Mrs. Johnson. You have a good day with your husband and we will return this evening around 9 PM."

The three spies drove to Elkridge.

"So, did you gunslingers sleep soundly last night?" inquired Ames.

"Yessir, we did!" replied Junius. "We are ready."

"Good! Just relax and you will both do fine today. The club president was delighted by my report about your impressive trap-shooting progress yesterday. I did not mention the handgun training, so when he talks to you, emphasize how much you want to improve your trap-shooting skills and how honored you are to meet the members of the Patriots Club. Remember, these obsequious Uncle Toms only associate with people who think and act as they do. Give 'em what they want. They will fall all over themselves being good to you. Just wait and see! Blend in."

Dr. Ames parked his car at the end of the gravel driveway. As they got out of the Buick, Dr. Jonathan Dixon, the club president, greeted them warmly.

"So, you must be the two stars that Ralph told me about last night!" He thrust his hand directly at Coleman and said, "Dr. Jonathan Dixon, pleasure to meet you!"

Coleman grasped Dixon's hand, smiled broadly, and said, "Coleman Braxton. The pleasure is all mine!"

Turning, Dixon shook Junius's hand and the young man replied, "Junius Johnson. Delighted to meet you!"

"Well, aren't we a fine quartet?" announced Dr. Dixon. "I have mixed some excellent lemonade for us up at the clubhouse. Let's refresh ourselves and I will review with you the plan for today's competition."

As Dr. Dixon poured the drinks, he explained that he wanted Coleman on his team and that Junius would be on Dr. Ames's team. "You see, Ralph is the second best shot in this club. I am number one. Since I studied engineering at Howard before entering medical school, I figured I would put a guy who knows how to use a slide rule in my group."

Ames spoke up at this point. "Dr. Dixon, today may well be the day you become the second best shot in this club. Come on, Junius, let's practice a little before the crowd shows up for the tournament."

"Fine with me, Dr. Ames. Fine with me!" Dixon laughed. "Coleman, I brought my three favorite 12-gauge over/under shotguns. I want you to pick the one that suits you best."

Coleman followed Dr. Dixon to the back of the clubhouse, where he observed three shotguns that were neatly arrayed atop a felt-covered wooden table. Handing one of the weapons to Coleman, Jonathan Dixon announced, "Mr. Braxton, this is a Beretta S.03 Super Tiro. I bought it in 1937 when the missus and I visited Italy. Put it to your shoulder and see how it feels."

Turning to face the woods behind the clubhouse, Coleman opened the shotgun to examine the barrels and assure himself that it was unloaded. He smoothly brought the Beretta to his shoulder and chin. He followed the same procedure for Dr. Dixon's Browning Superposed and a German-manufactured Merkel 200E.

"So, Coleman, which one will it be?"

"Dr. Dixon, the Beretta," replied Coleman confidently.

"Coleman Braxton, you have superb taste!" said a pleased Jonathan.

Concerned, Coleman responded, "Dr. Dixon, if this is your favorite, I have no problem using the Browning."

A gruff Dr. Dixon admonished Coleman. "Mr. Braxton, when I make an offer and you accept it, I stand by our deal! What kind of man do you think I am?"

Embarrassed at his misstep, Coleman looked Dr. Dixon in the eye and said, "Absolutely no disrespect intended, Sir. My uncle taught me at a young age to be considerate of others and never to take advantage of people who treat you right."

"You mean your uncle Hercules Boulanger, Mr. Braxton?" said a serious Dr. Dixon.

Looking around to assure that no one else was in earshot, the FBI mole replied, "Yes. But Dr. Dixon, we must not talk about him. Not here. Not with Junius and Dr. Ames around. Not with anyone around."

Dr. Dixon imitated Hercules's gravelly voice. "OK, Coleman. No need to worry. We have you covered. Hercules and a few of his men have been here in camouflage outfits since before dawn, being bitten by mosquitoes, no doubt. They have binoculars and have us under constant surveillance. Just relax and help our team beat the pants off Ralph Ames."

Shaking his head from side to side, Coleman said, "Dr. Dixon, I never knew that Baltimore had so many interesting people!"

Dixon replied, "You do not know the half of it, Coleman. Now let's police up these shotguns. Fire off a box of shells or two and get dialed-in before the tournament begins. I intend to score higher than Ames and for our team to prevail!"

And off they went.

The rules for the annual Patriot Outdoor Sportsman's Club Independence Day Trap-Shooting Competition were simple. Each of the two competing teams consisted of six men. There would be five rounds of shooting. A round consisted of each of the twelve competitors firing his 12-gauge shotgun in sequence from four separate stations positioned in an arc located 16 yards behind the trap bunker. The bunker contained the mechanical device that launched the clay pigeon targets. Thus, a competitor's combined score over five rounds could range from twenty to zero, and a team's combined score could range from 120 to zero. The shooter with the highest score would win a trophy. The losing team would pay for the day's refreshments, and the Patriot Outdoor Sportsman's Club would contribute $240 to fund the care of indigent patients seeking medical attention at the Provident Hospital and Free Dispensary.

The competition commenced at 11 AM with the families of the Patriot Outdoor Sportsman's Club members looking on. Dr. Ralph Ames had the honor of being the first to fire, followed by Dr. Jonathan Dixon. From that point forward, a member of Ames's team would be followed by a member of Dixon's team until Round Two commenced, and then the entire sequential process would be repeated. By noon, the oppressive Maryland heat and humidity were challenging the skill and endurance of every one of the competitors. Coleman marveled at the poise and performances of both Dr. Ames and Dr. Dixon. These men were more than twice his age. *How do they move so effortlessly, so gracefully, and shoot so accurately?* he thought.

In less than three hours, the event concluded. Dr. Dixon shot 19 clay pigeons out of 20 and achieved his objective of out-performing Dr. Ames, who blasted 18 out of 20 targets. To Dr. Dixon's delight, his team bested Dr. Ames's team too. Coleman and Junius each scored a respectable 15 out of 20 and were heartily congratulated by their respective teammates.

Ralph Ames offered a lemonade toast to his two acolytes and graciously presented Jonathan Dixon with the top trap shooter trophy, saying, "Dr. Jonathan Dixon, an outstanding physician and psychiatrist as well as a founding member of the Patriot Outdoor Sportsman's Club, most assuredly merits this honor today. We men of medicine all know Dr. Dixon as a man possessed of a powerful super-ego, which guides his every action, feeling, and thought. What a pleasure it is for me to confer this trophy on you, my dear friend and esteemed colleague." Smiling broadly, Dr. Dixon shook Dr. Ames's hand firmly. Judith, Jonathan Dixon's devoted wife, then hugged and kissed her husband to the cheers of the crowd.

The shooting over, the barbecue began. Junius and Coleman followed to the letter Dr. Ames's rules of gun club etiquette, impressing all in attendance. A few of the members offered to introduce Junius and Coleman to their daughters, all of whom were students at either Howard University or Morgan State. Junius and Coleman, smiling nervously, thanked them and demurred ever so politely by suggesting that any such contacts should be routed through their sponsor, Dr. Ames.

By 8 PM, Ralph Ames gathered up his two trainees and indicated that it was time to depart for Baltimore. Coleman and Jonathan Dixon, who had studiously socialized with everyone at the barbecue but each other, shook hands and exchanged warm, but perfunctory, farewells.

"Dr. Ames," Dr. Dixon intoned, "thank you for introducing us to Mr. Johnson and Mr. Braxton. I know that you will mentor them and make them a credit to our community."

Dr. Ames replied, "Jonathan, I will, of course, keep these men on the straight and narrow. Congratulations again on your individual performance and your team's performance today. What a pleasure it is to be a member of this great institution."

And with that insincerity concluded, the two Japanese spies and one FBI mole drove back to Baltimore.

Ralph Ames cleared his throat and addressed Junius and Coleman. "Your performance these last few days far exceeded my expectations. Skill-wise, you know how to handle firearms effectively and safely. Interpersonally, you have overcome the skepticism Baltimore's elite colored people have for outsiders and now have important entrée into their society. I will coordinate dates with the parents who so generously offered up their daughters to you at the club barbecue. The only women you should be seeing are the ones I assign to you. There will be no double dating. Each of you must cultivate these virgins independently. Be perfect gentlemen with these debutantes. Impress the girls and their parents. Always seek to enhance your individual appearance and reputation. Blend in! Katsuie will finance this and all facets of your future operations in Baltimore and Washington. I am now your official controller. To the world at large, I will be your personal physician and your sponsor to organizations like the Patriot Outdoor Sportsman's Club. For the most part, I will meet with each of you separately in my office as any good doctor would do with a patient. From time to time we will travel together, but we must avoid people thinking that we are a team. In this regard, Coleman, it is clear to me that Jonathan Dixon has taken a real liking to you. He and his wife have no children and you have an excellent opportunity to take advantage of their strong desire to have a son. I have no doubt that Dixon will approach you to have dinner, and I encourage you to maintain contact with him and his loudmouth wife. He is highly regarded and he will tell you things that I need to know. I expect a verbal report from you soon after any encounter you have with the shrink. Any questions? None. Good. I will contact you about dates with Negro debs. Finally, while I anticipate that Katsuie will have an additional training activity for you, there is no doubt in my mind that you have made the varsity team. Congratulations!"

Dr. Ames parked his Buick perfectly parallel to the curb in front of Junius's home. The three men exited the vehicle and Ames shook hands, first with Coleman and then with Junius. They thanked Ames for the wonderful weekend. Frances and Isaiah greeted them at the front door of their home. Their casual debriefing of the two young men's experiences that day provided pleasant confirmation to Frances and Isaiah that their son and his best friend were on the up escalator into Baltimore's high society.

More sober and serious debriefings would occur in the coming days, however, for Junius and Coleman.

9 AM, JULY 4, 1939; BALTIMORE OFFICE OF DR. JONATHAN DIXON

A dapper Hercules Boulanger, wearing a gray-striped seersucker suit, sunglasses, and beige Panama straw fedora opened the gate to the colorful and fragrant garden. The garden path led to the side entrance of Dr. and Mrs. Dixons' single-family house on Montebello Terrace in Morgan Park, a neighborhood renowned for its large number of Negro scholars and successful professionals. To maintain his patients' privacy and provide them with a pleasant environment, Jonathan Dixon tended this flowers meticulously. Hercules knew this place and Dr. Jonathan Dixon well. The trauma of his World War I combat experiences initially led him to the tent of Dr. Dixon, his regiment's Chief Medical Officer and psychiatrist. A few salutary sessions with Dixon put Hercules's train back on the track. He so valued his psychotherapist that Jonathan was the only American whom Hercules invited to attend his wedding to Genevieve in 1919. Shortly thereafter, Dixon left France to rejoin Judith and resume his medical practice in Baltimore.

Hercules's loss of his beloved Genevieve, his difficult rise within the District of Columbia Metropolitan Police Department, and his lack of interest in any aspect of life other than police work brought Hercules back to Dr. Dixon for psychiatric care. For years, the two men went to great lengths to keep their complex personal and professional relationship private. And so far, not even the FBI knew anything about a Dr. Jonathan Dixon treating Hercules.

The two war comrades embraced and kissed each other on both cheeks. "*Comme dans l'Armée Française.*" Dixon sat down behind his large, polished teak wood desk devoid of paper, pens, or any objects. Hercules spoke first.

"Jonathan, I regret dragging you into this sordid situation. But as I told you on Friday, I need you. America needs you. Your pal, Dr. Ralph Ames, serves the Empire of Japan. We have identified his Japanese handler and some, but not all, of the members of his spy cell. The Treasury Department has traced significant sums of money flowing from Japanese sources to Ames.

However, we have not yet ascertained the cell's objectives or operational plans. Clearly, Ames and his handler are preparing Coleman Braxton and Junius Johnson to function as their street agents in Baltimore, and probably DC. Fortunately, Coleman chose to remain loyal to the United States and is operating as our double agent. Based on what you have observed so far, what is your impression of Coleman? Do you think he can handle the mission for which he volunteered? Is he psychologically fit for service?"

Lighting his pipe, Dr. Dixon took a few puffs of his favorite aromatic blend of tobacco and replied, "Hercules, I do not know much about the profession of spying. I do not know what the job requirements are. However, I have observed that Coleman is a quick learner under pressure. He is careful, particularly regarding the handling of weapons. He is circumspect when conversing with people. He is situationally aware. The young man is intelligent, no doubt about that, and he loves and profoundly respects you. Based on my extensive experience during World War I, it is my opinion that Coleman could have handled the rigors of frontline combat in Europe. If trench and maneuver warfare are equivalent to the spy games you are playing with Ames and the Japanese, then your nephew should serve you well."

Hercules leaned forward in his chair and spoke. "I am relieved to hear this from you, Jonathan. What Coleman is doing is every bit as dangerous as what you and I were doing in Europe not too long ago."

"Now, Hercules, be precise. I never got close to killing Germans the way you did. All I did was treat what was left of our soldiers after the shooting, stabbing, strangling, and clubbing stopped. I was never in danger. You, my dear friend, were," added Dr. Dixon.

"Doc, I am not going to debate this subject with you. You know full well, however, that you were the one who kept our unit combat effective. But enough of all that!" Hercules could not tolerate such a superb saintly man like Dixon minimizing himself.

Dr. Dixon pointed his pipe stem at Hercules. "And how are you holding up? Doesn't this daily diet of duplicity and danger get to you?"

"Me? I am doing the Lord's work, Jonathan. I would prefer taking down white Nazis, Fascists, and Communists, not colored traitors. But I must play the hand I get dealt. I go where the law, evidence, and sound professional judgment lead me. In this regard, I have one final question for you today. Do you suspect that anyone else in the Patriot Club might be a member or a secret supporter of Ames's espionage conspiracy?"

Dixon leaned back in his swivel chair, briefly looked up at the ceiling, blew a sweet smoke ring, and then opened the drawer in the teak credenza behind him. He retrieved the club membership roster and, one-by-one, went through every name. After analyzing the final name on the list, he looked directly at Hercules and rendered his opinion.

"Hercules, the only rotten apple in the Patriots Club is Ames. He is the only member I know—and I know them all well—who openly ridicules colored people like Marian Anderson, Joe Louis, Cab Calloway, Dr. Solomon Fuller, and George Washington Carver as lackeys of the white man. That fool Ames sees no difference between Eleanor Roosevelt and the Imperial Wizard of the Ku Klux Klan, James Colescott. He is your man, Hercules. Focus on him. If anybody seems to me to be getting close to Dr. Ames, I will let you know."

"Fair enough, Doc. Now I got to get back to DC. You take care, and this conversation never happened. Remember, Dr. Ames will demand that Coleman report to him about any interaction he has with you. Old Ralph does not like you and will be suspicious, as well as envious, of your relationship with his prized agent. Keep the theme of your relationship simple, believable, and nonthreatening to Ralph. Coleman is like the son you and Judith never had. Period."

Dixon got up, walked around his desk, and shook hands with Boulanger. "*Mon frère*, whatever you need, whenever you need it. I am ready to help at all times!"

"Comforting to know, Doc. Comforting to know."

4 PM, JULY 4, 1939; THE DEPARTMENT OF JUSTICE BUILDING, 10TH AND CONSTITUTION AVENUES

Hercules and agents Walker and Clyde met to review and analyze the facts pouring in from their expanding investigation into a previously unknown Japanese spy recruitment and training effort targeting the Baltimore-Washington area.

Walker briefed Hercules on the surveillance net now cast over Dr. Ralph Ames. "The FBI office in Baltimore has assigned two agents to cover Ames. Calls to the good doctor's office phone and home phone are being recorded. We have listening and recording devices planted in rooms throughout his home and office, too. His mail is being identified by the US Post Office Department and provided to the FBI for special handling. After the correspondence is reviewed, it is delivered to either Ames's home or office address, whichever is appropriate. Similarly, any RCA or Western Union cables transmitted by or to Dr. Ames will be examined by us before being delivered to its intended recipient. His savings and checking accounts are being examined by Treasury Department agents and we will be alerted when 'Honest Ralph' gets some yen from his pals in Tokyo."

After taking a sip from his cup of coffee, Walker continued. "We have learned from these surveillance efforts that Katsuie has arranged to meet Dr. Ames—get this!—at the Lord Baltimore Hotel on the evening of July 14th when the Patriot Outdoor Sportsman's Club will have their summer dinner for members. Katsuie has a room reservation at the Lord Baltimore for the night of the dinner. Apparently, he will be meeting with Walters Art Gallery personnel during the afternoon of July 14th, for reasons we have not yet established."

Hercules could not resist inquiring how the FBI got all those surveillance warrants so quickly. He also expressed mild surprise that RCA and Western Union cables could be surveilled at all under the provisions of the Communications Act of 1934. Walker, serious as ever, responded that the highest level at the Justice Department had concluded that warrants were not required where the President has determined that the conduct of foreign agents operating inside the US or US territories poses a grave and imminent threat to national security.

Walker ended his response to Hercules by saying, "This is a counterespionage campaign being fought on our soil, not the prelude to a mere criminal prosecution. If Justice decides to change its approach and prosecute individuals for violations of federal statutes, no evidence from these intrusions will be used in a court. Does this bother you, Hercules?"

Steely-eyed, Hercules answered, "Not at all. If the President, the Attorney General, and FBI Director Hoover all say that what we are doing and the way we are doing it are legally OK, then I salute smartly and follow their legitimate orders to the very best of my ability!"

"Good to know, Hercules," replied an equally stern Walker.

Hercules then asked, "Don't you think we need more manpower for this matter?"

Walker: "Excellent observation. I have alerted my superior, Horan, and the ONI Counterintelligence Officer, Captain McLaughlin, to the reasonably foreseeable requirement for more trained counterintelligence agents on the ground in Baltimore and DC. They are working the problem. I believe that we will get a plus up of skilled personnel assigned to our investigation by late fall. In the meantime, we must make do with what we have."

Hercules: "Of course. Just like we always do in wartime."

Walker: "I like your perspective, Hercules."

Hercules then said he had to don his priestly vestments to meet and debrief his mole, Coleman, at Saint Augustine's Church.

And off he went.

8 PM, JULY 4; SAINT AUGUSTINE'S CATHOLIC CHURCH

Coleman entered the confessional. *Frère Honoré* listened intently to the tone of his penitent's voice as well as to the substance of Coleman's plea.

Calmly, Coleman stated, "Father, Dr. Ames passed a handwritten note to me when we shook hands and parted on the night of July 3rd. I do not know whether Junius got a similar note, but my slip of paper instructs me to go onboard a Japanese ship called the *Yamagiri Maru* on Saturday July 15th at 10 AM. It will be docked at Locust Point Pier 6."

Hercules asked in response, "Is that all that is written on the note?"

Coleman: "No. I was ordered to commit the contents of the note to memory and burn the paper after reading."

Hercules: "And did you do as you were instructed?"

Coleman: "Of course not. I put the note in an envelope and will slide it through to your side of the stall now."

Hercules: "Good, my son. Very good. I will investigate this Japanese ship situation. Follow Ames's instructions. Be alert. We will have you covered, just as we did at Elkridge. Do you have any additional news to relate?"

Coleman's inflection became grave as he told Hercules, "Dr. Ames reviles Dr. Dixon and wants me to report on any conversation I have with Jonathan immediately. Ralph has a lot of contempt for colored people who do not support Japan over America. Ames sees the Japanese as a role model for US Negroes and all brown people in Africa, Asia, and India in their struggle to bring down 'the Nordics,' as he calls white folks. He sounds a lot like that professor who lives in Morgan Park who visited Japan not too long ago—totally taking the side of Japan against the United States and Great Britain. Ames is as dangerous and devious as he is charming. I think he fears being unmasked by a skilled psychoanalyst like Dr. Dixon."

Hercules then asked, "And Junius? What are your thoughts about your friend?"

"He will do anything Ames tells him to do. And I mean *anything*!" replied Coleman.

Hercules studied his nephew's face as best he could through the confessional screen. "Coleman, what you are doing is both right and important. We must protect decent people like Dr. and Mrs. Dixon, Frances and Isaiah Johnson, as well as the rest of our nation, from foreign and domestic enemies like Katsuie and Ames. Continue doing what you are doing just the way you have been doing it, Coleman. Keep alert. Stay smart. Maintain your composure. I have been in far worse situations than this one and I know that you and I will come out all right."

Coleman confidently added, "I agree with you, Uncle Hercules. I will see this thing through to the end."

"Bless you, my son!" flowed like honey from *Frère Honoré* lips. Coleman slipped the paper to Boulanger and left the confessional. Soon thereafter, Hercules watched his mole fade into the darkness of Saint Augustine's Church and into the street beyond.

The Yamagiri Maru, thought Hercules. *Why set up a meeting with Coleman and possibly Junius on a Jap merchant ship docked in Baltimore harbor? Perhaps a new conspirator will show his face and we will better understand what is going on here. The ONI and the FBI are going to love this. I know I do.*

Hercules changed out of his vestments, left through the church's basement, and avoided streetlights while walking to his parked car. He then drove home to commemorate the twentieth anniversary of the passing of Genevieve. After opening a bottle of champagne, Hercules poured two glasses, then raised his and quoted the poet, Paul Verlaine: "*Il pleure dans mon coeur...* [It rains in my heart...]

"*Chéri*, my love for you will never end. I do not know when we will be reunited, but I hope that soon we will walk hand-in-hand in heavenly fields of lavender, together eternally." Hercules took but one sip from the glass and went to bed.

9

FRIDAY AND SATURDAY, JULY 14 AND 15, 1939; BALTIMORE

Kimura Katsuie, suitcase in hand, trudged slowly up the stairs from the railroad track platform to the exquisite interior of Baltimore's beaux arts–style Pennsylvania Station. Diminutive, soft-spoken, and unobtrusively sophisticated, Katsuie scrupulously hid his devotion to nurturing a Negro Fifth Column within the United States to support Japan in beating bestial white America in the coming war in the Pacific Ocean.

Without pausing to scan his surroundings, Katsuie shuffled to the front door of the train station and promptly entered a taxi idling by the curb just a few feet away. In perfect unaccented English, he asked the driver to take him to the Walters Art Gallery located at 600 North Charles Street, just one mile south of Pennsylvania Station. Eagerly awaiting the arrival of the Imperial Agent were representatives of the Baltimore City Public Schools, the Enoch Pratt Free Library, Goucher College, the Maryland Institute, the Peale Museum, the Walters Art Gallery, and the cultural attaché of the embassy of the Empire of Japan. After a brief round of introductions and an imperfectly performed tea ceremony by the head of the Walter's Oriental art collection, the group formalized a plan for conducting an exhibition and essay competition for Baltimore City public schoolchildren in March of 1940 with the theme of "Martial Art of the Samurai: Japanese Arms and Armor 1156 to 1868." The winners of the competition would be chosen by an independent panel of local university professors of art and English. The prizes—watches, radios, cameras, fountain pens, and books on Japanese art and painting equipment—would be formally presented to the students by officials from the Japanese embassy. The news media, politicians, and deans from preeminent academic institutions, such as Johns Hopkins University and Kyoto University, would be invited to celebrate this peaceful cultural event at the Walters Art Gallery with the budding Baltimore scholars. With deep bows and broad smiles, the group participants dispersed after the meeting. All seemed right and hopeful in Baltimore despite the daily drumbeat of dire news about the Imperial Japanese Army running amok in China and the prospects for the United States getting drawn into another global war.

The sanguine Mr. Katsuie never noticed the two FBI agents who shadowed him from New York City to Baltimore. He missed identifying the FBI agents in and around the Walters Art Gallery who observed his every move. Later in the day when he arrived at the Lord Baltimore Hotel, he failed to detect the tap on his phone and the "spike mic" listening device that used the radiator in his room to surreptitiously collect and transmit even faint sounds emanating from his secluded suite on the southeast corner of the building's seventeenth floor. The Imperial Japanese Agent never suspected that the rooms flanking his were occupied by FBI agents operating the bugs, the phonograph recording devices, and the movie cameras capturing his movements and conversations during his brief sojourn at the Lord Baltimore Hotel. And it never occurred to Katsuie that the gray-haired bellhop who carried his suitcase, polished his shoes, and even procured the services of a statuesque Caucasian prostitute for him to savor late that night was FBI Agent Hercules Boulanger.

Dashing Dr. Ralph Ames, smartly attired in a tuxedo, arrived at the Lord Baltimore an hour before the Patriot Outdoor Sportsman's Club dinner began.

As previously planned, Katsuie greeted Ames in the hotel lobby with a bow, then swiftly escorted him to the elevator and led him to his suite.

"Showtime!" announced Agent Walker to the combined Baltimore-Washington team formed to monitor and ultimately take down these two key espionage conspirators.

Dr. Ames initiated the conversation. "Welcome to Baltimore, Mr. Katsuie. I wish that I could spend a night in this fine suite in this fine hotel. But being a Negro, I cannot."

"Dr. Ames, with your help the Empire of Japan will force the arrogant Caucasians who presently rule America to atone for the sinful indignities and injustices that they inflict daily on their nonwhite citizens. The cadres of agents you and I are creating are indispensable to the grand strategy of fracturing the United States from within so that it will crumble when Imperial Japan strikes decisively from without. Let us concentrate on our mission. What is your assessment of the two young men you will bring aboard the *Yamagiri Maru* tomorrow morning?"

Ames succinctly and precisely presented the strengths and weaknesses of Junius and Coleman. "Intellectually, Coleman Braxton far surpasses Junius Johnson. Braxton is a quick study perfectionist who hates to make mistakes. Johnson, however, is more motivated to wage war than Braxton. Junius will never question an order. Coleman will. Junius will act without hesitation. Coleman appears prone to overanalyzing situations. Braxton and Johnson's friendship since childhood binds them together tightly. Given their complementary natures and skills, they will make a formidable team."

Katsuie pulled a Parliament cigarette from his silver art deco cigarette case. Leisurely, he lit the Parliament, puffed on it, and put it in a black Bakelite holder. "I sense you have some hesitation about Mr. Braxton. Tell me what troubles you about him."

Dr. Ames replied, "He seems too independent to me, too remote. It is like he is standing outside of our movement looking in and studying what is going on. Coleman does not exude enthusiasm or total commitment to our cause. I must admit to you, however, that his close relationship with Dr. Jonathan Dixon—a man satisfied with being subservient to white men—may be unfairly skewing my assessment of Coleman. My dislike of Dixon and all that he represents is so intense that perhaps I am suspicious of Coleman just for associating with that Uncle Tom–shrink."

Katsuie: "Dr. Ames, Coleman knows much about our organization at this point. He will soon know much more about our operational methods and objectives after our meeting tomorrow aboard the *Yamagiri Maru*. Should we put Mr. Braxton under increased surveillance? Should we arrange an unfortunate, fatal accident for him? What do you recommend that we do?"

Ralph: "Mr. Katsuie, I think we need to watch him closely following the briefing tomorrow. Have Coleman tailed by one of your most skilled and accomplished operators. Let us see where he goes and with whom he meets. If he does nothing out of the ordinary, then my suspicions are the product of my biases, and therefore unfounded. However, if he does something unusual… If he attempts to contact or actually contacts the FBI, local police, or people we suspect as being involved in law enforcement, then Coleman must be eliminated forthwith and a replacement partner found for Mr. Johnson."

"I agree with your plan, Dr. Ames. I appreciate your candor. I hope that your concerns are not warranted, but I have known you long enough to give great weight to your judgment and intuition about people. Now I will take you downstairs on the elevator. Enjoy your evening. I will dine alone in my room tonight and meet you tomorrow at 8:30 AM at Locust Point Pier 6."

An ashen Agent Walker looked at his men and said, "Now you understand why we need to keep these monsters under persistent surveillance. They will kill Coleman if he does anything remotely suspicious to their paranoid minds. Clyde, find Hercules. In the little time we have left before Coleman boards that ship, Hercules has to get his nephew to go totally silent until we determine that it is safe to renew our communications with him."

To avoid any possible encounter with Katsuie, Agent Lewis Clyde hustled down seventeen floors of stairs instead of taking the elevator. He then proceeded down one additional flight of stairs to the basement of the hotel. There, in a room where guests' shoes were polished, sat Hercules talking quietly to an attractive blonde woman who, in Clyde's professional judgment, must have been a high-priced prostitute.

Hercules stood up slowly when he saw Clyde, looked at the blonde, and said, "Miss Smith, I think our little talk here is now over. Please go see the gentleman on the seventeenth floor at 9 PM, and I look forward to conversing with you Saturday afternoon. Now I must speak to my manager, Mr. Jones, here. Is that all right with you?"

Miss Smith nodded and walked up the one flight of stairs from which Clyde had just descended. She entered the lobby and shortly thereafter ordered herself a drink at the hotel's bar.

Agent Clyde briefed Hercules. "Well, Lewis, I cannot say that I am surprised by Dr. Ames's antenna picking up on Coleman's 'frequency' and wondering whether it's a signal of betrayal or just noise. Don't worry. I will alert my nephew and he will handle the situation appropriately."

Clyde shrugged his shoulders and he thought, *Doesn't anything bother this man?*

Truth be told, nothing perturbed Hercules Boulanger. World War I and the loss of Genevieve had seen to that.

By Friday afternoon, Coleman had positioned himself at Dr. Dixon's house in advance of the *Yamagiri Maru* meeting. Coleman had initially asked Dr. Ames if he could stay at his home the night of July 14, but Ames had demurred for unstated reasons. By chance, Dr. Dixon invited Coleman to spend the weekend July 14 and 15 with him and his wife. They wanted Coleman to have dinner at their home on Saturday evening in order to introduce him to Dr. Dixon's niece, a Morgan State College graduate who would be entering Howard University Law School in September. Coleman cleared these arrangements with Hercules, as well as Dr. Ames. Coleman promised Ralph that he would provide him with a full report of his stay at the home of the man Ames hated.

Hercules called Dixon's home phone, and fortunately, Dr. Dixon picked up. "Hi, Jonathan. May I speak with Coleman, please?"

"Of course, Hercules. You know, I was just on my way out the door to attend a party at the Lord Baltimore Hotel. My wife is out with a few of her friends for the evening, so you can speak openly with Coleman."

With that, Dr. Dixon handed the phone to Coleman and Hercules explained the new and evolving situation to him. He concluded his remarks by saying, "Coleman, this will be easy. Just be yourself. Do not try to contact me or anyone other than Ralph and Junius. You know that we will be watching over you. Prepare a full report of your weekend with the Dixons' for Dr. Ames. If you hear any juicy gossip from Mrs. Dixon, pass it on to Ames. Make it clear that you listened carefully to your hosts' conversations and spoke very little yourself. If the Dixons ask where you were on Saturday morning and afternoon, tell them you visited Junius. Go straight back to your dormitory after you leave Baltimore on Sunday. From then on pursue your normal routine. Go to class. Complete your schoolwork in the Howard University library. Go to the gym. Do the little job that the Japs arranged for you at the Shoreham Hotel. Do not make any new friends. Do not go to any new places. Do not try to shake the tail that is following you. This surveillance by the Japanese will all blow over in two weeks, I estimate. When the coast is clear, I will contact you. I repeat, no matter what, do not break your cover! Do you have any questions?"

"No questions, Uncle Hercules. I understand. Thanks for the warning and the instructions. Take care of yourself!"

Hercules laughed at the thought of his nephew telling him to be careful and hung up the phone. Hercules said to himself, "Maybe there is some hope for this boy to become a real man!"

In his suite at the Lord Baltimore, Kimura Katsuie made a brief telephone call to a number in New York City. He hung up the phone after three rings. His signal alerted the operator at the Japanese consulate in New York monitoring a bank of phones assigned to individual Japanese operatives that Imperial Agent Katsuie needed backup at the location from which he dialed. The consulate logbook entry for Katsuie for July 14 provided the operator with his address in Baltimore. The consulate operator then called his counterpart at the Japanese embassy in Washington, DC, and informed him that Kimura Katsuie needed prompt assistance at the Lord Baltimore Hotel. Within an hour of receiving the alert, the embassy dispatched a formidable Imperial Japanese Navy Lieutenant named Kato Yukinaga—currently studying English at Georgetown University—to travel to Baltimore and do whatever was required by the Imperial agent.

A kimono-clad Katsuie treated himself to a sumptuous lamb chop dinner accompanied by a bottle of champagne. At 9 PM—as his aged, but worldly procurer promised—Miss Smith knocked on his door. Katsuie could not have been more pleased by what he saw and soon felt. Smith, blonde, buxom, and ten inches taller than the 5-foot-tall Katsuie, bent forward, put her arms around the Japanese spy's shoulders, and kissed him passionately on his neck. By 11 PM, the Imperial agent had sated himself, if not Miss Smith, by attempting numerous positions popularized in shunga art prints. Smith, however, had been quite pleased at receiving $75 from Katsuie for her services. The "talkie" movie produced by the amused FBI agents monitoring events on the seventeenth floor that night became a counterespionage romantic farce film classic.

At 11:30 PM, the hotel front desk rang Katsuie's room to inform him that a motorcycle messenger from Washington, DC, had arrived with a message for him. The irritated desk clerk told Katsuie that the "large Asian man" insisted on hand delivering the message to the addressee only and inquired whether it would be OK for the hotel bellhop to escort the fellow to his room.

"Fine. Fine with me. Have the bellhop bring him up," said Katsuie, impressed by the efficiency of the Japanese spy communication system operating in the US.

Hercules led the muscular military man to the Imperial Agent's room. Katsuie gave Hercules $25 and thanked him profusely for this superb service.

Hercules smiled, bowed low, and asked Katsuie if he wanted him to wait outside his door until it was time to shepherd the messenger down the elevator to the lobby.

"Sure. This may take 30 minutes. Do you mind?" said a polite and deferential Imperial agent.

"No, Suh. No problem at all," replied an equally polite and deferential FBI agent Hercules Boulanger.

Once the door to the suite closed, Katsuie issued orders to Lieutenant Yukinaga. "Go directly to the *Yamagiri Maru* freighter docked at Pier 6 on Locust Point. You will see on your street map of Baltimore that Locust Point is to the south of this hotel, near Fort McHenry. The ship's Captain will be expecting you and will provide you with suitable accommodations for the night. Your mission is to maintain close surveillance of a Mr. Coleman Braxton for ten days following the briefing that I and others will give to Mr. Braxton and his partner, Mr. Junius Johnson, tomorrow at 10 AM aboard the *Yamagiri Maru*. You will attend this briefing. You will shake hands with Messrs. Braxton and Johnson and remain totally silent for the duration of the meeting. The briefing will end by 1 PM. Mr. Braxton will be spending Saturday night at the Montebello Terrace home of a Dr. Jonathan Dixon in North Baltimore. On Sunday, Braxton will return to his dormitory at Howard University in Washington, DC. He will probably take a Greyhound Bus from Baltimore to DC. Tail him, or have him tailed. Maintain a detailed log of all observations of Coleman Braxton. We want to know where he goes and what he does. Get photographs of the people with whom he converses. Feel at complete liberty to requisition any technical, photographic, and secretarial personnel from the embassy you need to support you in this surveillance effort. Use the *Yamagiri Maru's* secure communication system to transmit your manpower requests to the embassy. No one on the ship or at the embassy will deny any request for assistance you make. Your mission is that important. I will visit you at the embassy on July 26th to review your complete report. This Coleman Braxton may be a US spy in our midst. Be discreet. Be stealthy.

Be ninja. Be thorough. Most important, however, is for you to be objective. Your report will provide the basis for our decision to take or not take severe action against Mr. Braxton. Do you understand?"

The Lieutenant grunted, "*Hai!*" and bowed slightly forward.

Katsuie opened the door for the messenger to leave. Hercules walked the hulking Lieutenant to the elevator, rode down seventeen uncomfortable floors with him, and watched carefully as the "messenger" roared south mounted on a cream and black Harley-Davidson EL Knucklehead motorcycle. *Now that is one badass Jap*! thought Hercules. "In a fight, I would need to shoot that young samurai two or three times in the heart with a .357 Magnum at a range of not less than seven yards if I didn't want Coleman to collect on my life insurance policy," muttered Hercules as he headed to his "office" in the hotel basement to meet with Walker and Clyde.

As they sipped hot black coffee from the Lord Baltimore Hotel's fine china cups, Walker advised Hercules and Clyde that his top-level contacts at the Federal Communications Commission in DC and its Fourth Radio District station at Fort McHenry would issue orders to monitor all known Japanese Navy radio frequencies and intercept all messages transmitted from or to the *Yamagiri Maru*. The FCC listening stations at Fort McHenry (Baltimore) and Laurel (Maryland) had tape and phonograph recording devices ready to document the contents of these intercepted transmissions. Navy codebreakers and linguists in Washington, DC, had been assigned to produce English language texts of any intercepted Japanese transmissions as soon as possible for the FBI and ONI agents working this counterespionage case.

Walker then announced, "Unfortunately, we have not found a way to bug the cabins within the *Yamagiri Maru*. We will have to wait until we can safely debrief AJAX, pick up loose chatter from Dr. Ames and Katsuie, and acquire little nuggets from the Japanese embassy in order to develop a complete understanding of tomorrow's meeting at Locust Point. In the meantime, we have identified the motorcycle-riding gorilla our friends on Massachusetts Avenue sent to surveil Coleman. Lieutenant Kato Yukinaga was born in Tokyo, the sole son of a powerful Yakuza boss. Yukinaga graduated in the top ten percent of his class at Etajima, distinguishing himself as the Captain of Etajima's aikido, kendo, wrestling, and weightlifting teams. Kato is the son of a professional killer and is a highly skilled killer in his own right. We are cleared to dispose of him if he tries to harm Coleman or gets aggressive with any of our agents. You guys have any questions or anything to add to this conversation?"

Hercules inquired, "Can I keep the $25 tip Katsuie gave me tonight?"

Walker, smiling, said, "No, Hercules. Put the money in an FBI evidence envelope. Seal the envelope. Label the envelope and make certain that the envelope is deposited correctly as part of the case record."

"Damn," replied Hercules. "I wanted to buy some US savings bonds for my nephew!"

"No one is preventing you from doing so, Hercules," said a still-smiling Walker.

"Good point, as always, Agent Walker. Fine point, Sir," said a totally disingenuous Hercules.

Clyde then spoke up. "Who gets to follow Katsuie after the meeting?"

Walker responded that if the Imperial Agent returned to New York City by train or bus, he would be covered by agents from the New York Field Office. If Katsuie remained at the Lord Baltimore, Hercules would babysit him. If Katsuie goes to DC, Clyde will tail him. Walker added that the FBI Field Office in Baltimore retained coverage of Dr. Ames.

"As for Kato Yukinaga, we have a special team dedicated to him. I would not want to be Yukinaga's life or travel insurance carrier," Walker said solemnly.

And with that, the team dispersed to their respective posts for the night.

Hercules called Miss Smith before shutting down for his typical four hours of sleep. "I apologize for calling so late, Miss Smith, but I wanted to hear with my own ears that you were not treated roughly by the man on the seventeenth floor."

Smith laughed out loud. "Mr. Attucks, if all of my clients were as negligibly endowed, gentle, and generous as that little fella, I could probably work until I was sixty and retire to Roland Park. He was a perfect gentleman. I thank you for your concern. If I can ever help you out again, just call me."

"Miss Smith, you are at the top of my list. One last question—did the 'little fella' ask how you came to know me or how I got to know you?"

"No. He did not ask me any questions at all. From the moment he first saw me until the time I left his room, all he could say was things like, 'You are beautiful. You are a goddess. I love you.' Like I said, he was a perfect gentleman."

Hercules then asked, "Now think hard. Did he indicate where he would be traveling to next?"

"You know, now that I think of it, he told me he would be going to DC on Sunday afternoon."

"Very good, Miss Smith. Excellent. Did he want you to accompany him to DC?"

"No. He did not make such a request. He did say he would have you call me the next time he was in Baltimore, however."

Hercules then said, "Miss Smith, thank you so much. Please have a good night and enjoy the rest of your weekend."

"You too, Mr. Attucks."

And that was that.

JULY 15, 1939; PIER 6, LOCUST POINT, BALTIMORE

Agent Walker left nothing to chance. By 5 AM on Saturday, July 15, he had unmarked two-man radio cars stationed near three intersections: Nicholson and Hull Streets, Andre Street and Fort Avenue near Latrobe Park, and Key

Highway and Fort Avenue—key land choke points should events become violent at Locust Point Pier 6. Walker even encouraged the Office of Naval Intelligence to have a 1,300-ton displacement *Farragut* class destroyer positioned on the Patapsco River south of Fort McHenry just in case the *Yamagiri Maru*, for whatever reason, attempted to flee Baltimore harbor. Walker and Clyde manned a command, control, and communications center at the FCC's Fort McHenry station. Hercules remained by his phone in the basement of the Lord Baltimore Hotel, ready to respond to any unforeseen contingency that might arise. He respected Walker's professionalism and concern for Coleman's safety. Nonetheless, Hercules knew full well that his nephew could not truly be protected from Yukinaga, a human weapon aimed at him at close range.

"*C'est la guerre*," Hercules said out loud. He then returned to reading *The Baltimore Sun* and enjoying his favorite brand of coffee—A&P's Eight O'Clock, roasted in Maryland since 1859. He mused to himself, "Sometimes I just cannot believe that these white people pay me overtime for doing just what I like to do. What a country!"

At 10 AM, Katsuie, Dr. Ames, and ship Captain Oda Kenshin welcomed Coleman Braxton and Junius Johnson aboard the *Yamagiri Maru*. The two young men were escorted to the Captain's quarters, where IJN Intelligence Officer Lieutenant Commander Takeo Ezima and Lieutenant Kato Yukinaga greeted them with frighteningly firm handshakes. Katsuie formally introduced each of the meeting participants and requested that they take a seat around the Captain's large wooden table. He then explained the purpose of the brief meeting.

"The Imperial Japanese Navy exercises ultimate control over all Japanese vessels, commercial as well as military, wherever they may be worldwide. For example, Captain Kenshin and his crew are loading scrap metal here at Locust Point onto the 7,800-ton *Yamagiri Maru* pursuant to a commercial contract with a US metals broker. The metal will be used to manufacture naval warships in Japan. Captain Kenshin is a graduate of the Japanese Naval

Academy in Etajima, Japan. He serves in the IJN reserve and his duty to the Emperor and the IJN supersedes his responsibility to the owner of the *Yamagiri Maru*, who pays his salary. The crew of this ship is composed exclusively of Japanese citizens. They too understand that their first and foremost duty is to Emperor Hirohito and his Imperial Navy. My point to you is that every Japanese ship and every Japanese crew in an American port can be directed by a coded radio transmission to operate as a naval unit in US territory at any time. As agents of Japan, Mr. Braxton and Mr. Johnson, any Japanese ship in Baltimore harbor or Philadelphia Harbor or New York Harbor or Boston Harbor, or wherever, will provide you support, protection, and even transportation to Japan from the US should you require it. Your *Baltimore Sun* newspaper lists each day the Japanese ships arriving in port and leaving Baltimore harbor. Pay close attention to this information daily. Additionally, you may receive a communication from me or someone designated by me to report to a specific Japanese vessel to receive instructions, training, or equipment. Please do so as requested. I know that what we are asking you requires a considerable amount of trust in the Empire of Japan. Understand please that you are important human assets to us and we will do what is necessary to protect and support you. Is this clear? Do you have any questions?"

Junius spoke directly to Katsuie. "Mr. Katsuie, so far, Coleman and I have done nothing to serve the cause. I appreciate all this attention and care from you and Japan, but we need a mission. Give us something significant to do!"

Katsuie's face glowed with the warmth of a loving grandfather gazing upon his grandson as he walked around the table to where Junius sat. Putting his frail hand on Junius's shoulder, he said, "Junius, your spirit moves all of us in this room. We too are eager to bring down the tyranny of FDR and the government of the United States. However, we must await the orders of our Emperor, who commands the Imperial Japanese Army and Navy, before taking specific actions. I believe that soon, you and Coleman will be given an important mission and your warrior spirits will be engaged against the oppressors of brown and yellow peoples around the world."

Junius thanked the Imperial agent and repeated his eagerness to become operational.

Katsuie returned to his position at the head of the table and looked Coleman. "And you, Mr. Braxton… Do you have any questions or concerns?"

"No, Sir. I, like Junius, will follow whatever orders are given to me. I am an engineer. Give me a problem and I will find the best or optimal technical solution to solve it. If Junius and I require more training to perform future missions, we are ready to study and practice. We are the youngest people in this room and have much to learn. But like my friend Junius, I am eager to accomplish a mission that will advance the cause of our people and Japan."

Katsuie, smiling, walked to where Coleman was seated, looked at each person around the table, lingering just a little bit longer as he gazed at Kato. Katsuie then placed his hand on Coleman's shoulder and announced, "Thank you Mr. Braxton. We know that you and Mr. Johnson are truly committed to Japan's strategic goal of defeating the racist regime running the United States in a war and replacing it with a just and tolerant government. Let us continue with our briefing."

Stone-faced, Lieutenant Yukinaga understood the Imperial agent's signal that he trusted Coleman Braxton. Nonetheless, Kato Yukinaga's counterespionage training made him a total skeptic. He thought, *If Katsuie is wrong and Coleman turns out to be an FBI mole, the damage the traitor could do to the Emperor and Japan would be significant.* Kato resolved to do all that was necessary to unmask Coleman if, in fact, he was a mole.

Lieutenant Commander Ezima spent one hour reminding Junius and Coleman that they must always be aware of their surroundings and sensitive to being tailed.

"Vary the routes you take. Always double back, even when going to class, to work, to the movies, to a restaurant, or on a date. Do not leave through the same door you entered. If you are traveling south, go north or east or west first. Randomly stop to drink a cup of coffee. Vary your modes of travel. Cease walking and hop on a bus or hail a cab. Suddenly leave a bus or a taxi and commence walking. Be unpredictable. If you see the same people or person after you have changed direction, routes, or mode of travel, you are being followed. Shake them off before you proceed. Take your time. Arrive late. If necessary, do not meet your contact or complete your mission. Note well who is following you. Do you see vehicles with unusual antennae more frequently as you move about? Memorize the license plates and the type of vehicle bearing those plates. Keep a record of these sightings and compare them with future suspicious encounters. Never lead the FBI, military intelligence, or naval intelligence to your fellow agents. If you are stopped or arrested, say nothing. Insist upon calling a lawyer. No matter what the police or FBI tell you or promise you, say nothing. If they beat you, say nothing. If they threaten your family, say nothing. I will give each of you the name and number of a lawyer in Baltimore and a lawyer in DC. These lawyers will not ask you any questions. They will use every legal device to protect you from devious government agents. Let the lawyers do their jobs. Your job is to remain totally silent. Once you start talking to the FBI, you are finished and we are finished. Remember, we will find a way to rescue you. We have a system in the United States that has functioned well since 1920. Follow our rules and the probability of your operating effectively and safely will be very high. Any questions?"

Both Junius and Coleman said, "No."

Ezima then concluded with one more warning. "Mr. Braxton and Mr. Johnson, this honorable and important work may, at some point, become a heavy psychological burden for you. Never unburden yourself by discussing these matters to your family members, friends, teachers, religious figures, physicians, or lovers. Trust no one, only us, to help you cope with any emotional difficulties you may experience in the future. Even our finest agents have had moments of doubt, distress, and fear. There is no sin in this. Do not be embarrassed to share your darkest thoughts with us. We have all been there ourselves and will guide you back to the light. Do you understand?"

Junius and Coleman both replied, "Yes."

Next, Captain Kenshin took the two young men on a tour of the ship. He showed them where weapons, ammunition, and explosives were concealed. He showed them the wireless system and explained that the Japanese diplomatic and naval codes were "invulnerable" to cracking. Finally, he showed them the secret ship compartments designed to hide and exfiltrate Japanese agents such as themselves should the need ever arise.

At 1 PM, the meeting ended. Dr. Ames drove Coleman to Dr. Dixon's home. During the brief drive to Morgan Park, Ralph learned that Coleman would be taking the earliest train to DC from Pennsylvania Station on Sunday morning. Ames called this information in to the Japanese embassy so Kato could arrange proper coverage of Coleman's movements. Junius took a bus home to spend the evening with his parents. A taxi drove Katsuie to Penn Station, where he boarded a train for DC. A local FBI agent and Lewis Clyde followed three automobiles behind the Imperial Agent's taxi in an old unwashed coupe painted an "un-FBI" light green. Clyde boarded Katsuie's train undetected. Lieutenant Yukinaga fired up his Harley-Davidson and raced to the Japanese embassy to brief the team of watchers that he had requested in a short, coded message that he sent at 3 AM Saturday morning from the *Yamagiri Maru*'s very-high-frequency radio. Before he crossed the border between Maryland and DC, Kato Yukinaga's efficiency apartment at the Alban Towers had received some FBI electrical surveillance "upgrades" so that Bureau people could get to know him a bit better.

Walker called Hercules at his "office" in the Lord Baltimore Hotel and told him that Yukinaga's burst radio transmission had been intercepted and decoded.

"Hercules, the Japanese Lieutenant has assembled a team to track Coleman for the next ten days." Hercules packed up, drove his car to his home in DC, and prepared to watch Yukinaga and his goons watch his nephew for the next ten days. As he showered, Hercules reflected on the quality of his work so far and muttered, "I think I deserve a raise."

Agent Walker reported the Friday and Saturday Baltimore saga to Agent Horan on Saturday at 5 PM. Horan listened intently and replied, "Clarence, there can be no doubt now, even without a detailed debrief of Coleman, that the Japs are using their merchant ships as espionage bases in American harbors. They are operating well inside our perimeter. I would appreciate a written report on Monday morning. We need to alert our ONI contact, Captain McLaughlin, about this situation immediately. I will call him after I speak to my boss, the Assistant Director. The AD will no doubt ask Director Hoover whether this matter should be an agenda item for the Interdepartmental Intelligence Conference meeting he will be leading this week. Additionally, I will contact our Special Agent in Charge of the Baltimore FBI office and suggest that we have a confidential meeting to inform the Baltimore City Police Department Commissioner, or his designee, that he has a complex espionage situation requiring BCPD, the FBI, and ONI to collaborate and coordinate on a whole new level. Clarence, let me know what additional resources we need to take the initiative away from the Japanese and eliminate this threat to our national security root and branch. Agent Walker, this Hercules fellow of yours appears to have talent. We need him. I will see to it that he gets an award and a significant bump in his salary. Keep him happy."

Walker agreed totally.

And that was that.

10

SATURDAY, JULY 15, 1939; DINNER WITH DR. AND MRS. DIXON AND THEIR NIECE, LUCILLE

Dr. Ames deposited Coleman at the curb of Dr. Dixon's house and sped off to avoid having to engage in any meaningless banter with a man for whom he harbored so much contempt. Before exiting the car, Coleman covered a subtle detail with Ralph. "Thank you for the lift, Dr. Ames. If Dixon asks how it came to pass that you drove me to his place after I told him I was meeting Junius and never mentioned your name, what story should I use?"

"Good point, Coleman. Tell Dr. Dixon that you saw me driving past Junius's house and waved. I stopped and asked how you two guys were doing. You mentioned that you were in town to meet Jonathan's niece for dinner at Dr. Dixon's home in Morgan Park and I insisted on saving you the time and carfare associated with taking public transportation to northeast Baltimore. That should pacify the psychiatrist."

"OK, Dr. Ames," replied Coleman. "That is a solid cover story."

"Coleman, send me a little note summarizing what is going on with the doctor and his wife. I want details. Any marital discord, any financial problems, any excessive drinking—I want to know about it. OK?"

"You got it, Doc. I will write the report on my train ride back to DC on Sunday morning and mail it to your office address."

"Thank you. See you soon, Coleman. Excellent meeting today. You and Junius were both impressive."

As Dr. Ames departed, Coleman consciously cleared his mind of his experience on board the Japanese freighter. Clearly, the very large, very silent young Japanese naval officer meant trouble, more trouble than he could handle unarmed. Fortunately, Hercules was there to deal with such a hard case. Coleman looked up at the blue sky, took in a deep breath, and thought, *I am going to take tonight off and charm Dr. Dixon's niece.*

Judith Dixon, an attractive middle-aged woman with the vocal cords and lungs of an opera soprano, greeted Coleman at the front door. "Now what are you so happy about, Mr. Braxton? You have not been misbehaving, I hope! Was that Dr. Ames who left you on the sidewalk and did not have the decency to come in and say hello to my husband and me?"

"Mrs. Dixon," Coleman exclaimed, "which question do you want me to answer first?"

"Oh, any one of them, or none of them! Dr. Dixon constantly counsels me to restrain myself from meddling in other people's affairs and interrogating them as if I were a Baltimore City Police Detective. But I tell him that I am 'Pure Baltimore.' When I like someone, I just want to know everything about them. And I also want them to know that I truly do care about them. Coleman, I like you. Dr. Dixon likes you. Why shouldn't I let you know how we feel?"

"Mrs. Dixon, now that is a question I want to answer!" Coleman replied as warmly as a son would to his mother. "From the very first, Dr. Dixon and you made me feel like I mattered. You cannot imagine the impact you have had on me in such a short period of time. I see the considerate and respectful way you and Dr. Dixon are with each other. You two are beautiful people and I appreciate you welcoming me—a total stranger—into your lives."

With tears in her eyes, Judith Dixon hugged Coleman and could not stop herself from saying, "Coleman, you are no stranger. God sent you to us. You are his gift to us."

Stunned, Coleman returned the hug and said softly, "Mrs. Dixon, you are God's gift to me!"

Dr. Jonathan Dixon witnessed this tender event from the living room couch and shook his head slowly. He thought, *How strange the world is that a rogue like Ralph Ames could bring such joy into Judith's life, into my life. Maybe there is a God after all!*

Jonathan rustled the *Baltimore Afro-American* newspaper and called out, "Judith, is young Mr. Braxton here?"

"Why, yes he is, Jonathan. Why don't you put down that worthless journal and greet our guest?"

With that command, Dr. Dixon joined his wife and "son" in the doorway, shook Coleman's hand, and said, "Why don't we let this gentleman go upstairs, take a shower, and get ready for dinner with our Lucille? She should be arriving in about half an hour."

Coleman followed Dr. Dixon's suggestion and prepared himself to entertain Jonathan's niece. He joined the Dixons downstairs seconds before Lucille rang the bell to the front door.

Coleman never anticipated Lucille. Darker in complexion than her uncle Jonathan, the form-fitting emerald-green sleeveless dress she wore revealed the taut body of the Morgan State track star that she was. But it was her clear, unblinking eyes and radiant voice that transfixed him. *No jury would ever decide against one of her clients*, he thought. *They would be afraid to cross her and be in love with her at the same time.*

Coleman reflexively grasped Lucille's outstretched hand as she said, "So, you are Coleman Braxton, the brilliant Howard University engineer that

Uncle Jonathan and Aunt Judith have not stopped talking about. It is a pleasure to meet you."

"The pleasure is all mine," replied Coleman awkwardly. "The Dixons may have exaggerated slightly about my IQ."

"We most certainly did not!" interjected Dr. Dixon.

"For once, I agree with Jonathan!" followed Judith in rapid succession.

"Well, there you have it, Coleman. Both Dr. and Mrs. Dixon cannot be wrong!" concluded Lucille.

"It's three against one. Who am I to dispute this verdict?" conceded Coleman.

All four laughed and they continued laughing through dinner, dessert, and a walk around Morgan Park. Lucille took Coleman's hand as they walked in front of Judith and Jonathan. "My parents will be picking me up soon in their new car. They want to impress you. They are desperate to marry me off."

"Lucille, you are far more impressive than any manufactured product. I hope that you will not object to my calling you in two weeks to arrange a date," Coleman responded nervously.

"Two weeks! How could you stand to be away from me for two weeks?" Lucille retorted.

"It will be very difficult; however, this so-called 'brilliant engineer' has a civil engineering project that must be completed by the end of this week and a final exam a week later in his first graduate-level electrical engineering course that he wants to ace. Lucille, you are not flawed in any way. It is me and my tendency to be a perfectionist."

"All right, Coleman Braxton, but this perfectionist faux pas of yours is going to cost you!"

"Your Honor, I am prepared to pay whatever penalty you deem appropriate for any unintended harm I may have inadvertently caused you," replied Coleman spontaneously.

"You are a condemned man, Coleman. I am a very demanding woman."

"I am prepared to accept your punishment, Lucille."

The two stopped, turned, and kissed just a little too long for Dr. Dixon.

"Enough of that, you two! My brother and sister-in-law will have my hide if this sort of thing continues!"

Judith admonished Jonathan, "You old curmudgeon. Stop terrorizing these young people. Lucille and Coleman, you smooch all you want. But nothing more. This is your first date!"

The four laughed loudly. A shiny, 1939 midnight blue Chrysler Royal Windsor pulled up with Lucille's proud parents smiling through the windshield. Lucille introduced Coleman to her folks. She got into the car and they drove off.

"Nice job, Mr. Braxton," said Judith.

"Coleman, you are going to be part of our family! I can feel it," added Jonathan.

Coleman put his right arm around Judith's shoulders and his left arm around Dr. Dixon and said, "I hope so."

They walked together back to the Dixon's home. Nothing more needed to be said.

The Dixons went to bed and dreamed of attending Lucille and Coleman's wedding. Judith Dixon went an additional step further and saw herself holding the couple's first child after he became baptized.

Coleman stared at the ceiling and considered the great danger to which he was selfishly exposing the Dixons and Lucille. He whispered to himself in the dark, "Lord, what have I done? What am I doing?"

11

JULY 16, 1939, THROUGH JULY 27, 1939; YUKINAGA'S SURVEILLANCE OF AJAX AND BOULANGER'S SURVEILLANCE OF YUKINAGA: WASHINGTON WINS ONE

Lieutenant Yukinaga pushed his "scratch" embassy staff surveillance team relentlessly for ten consecutive, fruitless days and nights. The official embassy photographer produced excellent quality photographs of Coleman doing nothing at all suspicious. The student engineer diligently attended class, performed prescribed laboratory assignments, and studied in the university library when not in class or in the lab. Coleman walked alone, sat in class alone, experimented in the lab alone, and studied in the library alone. He performed his menial job at the Shoreham Hotel, signaling no one, and returned to his dormitory alone when his shift ended. Each morning he left campus to visit a café where he purchased a cup of coffee and a copy of *The Baltimore Sun*. Sharp-eyed Japanese embassy military attachés observed that by the time AJAX had finished his cup of coffee, he had circled each report in *The Baltimore Sun* newspaper of a Japanese vessel visiting, scheduled to visit, or departing Baltimore harbor. To Kato's consternation, the surveillance target did not go to movies, dances, bowling alleys, bars, concerts, museums, pay phone booths, or stores. He received no letters. He mailed no letters.

Coleman appeared to be a monk to each of the Japanese watchers, except Lieutenant Yukinaga.

Hercules and his team marveled at Coleman's professionalism and enjoyed hearing Yukinaga mumble to himself in his apartment about the waste of time and resources allocated to learning nothing about this "Negro mole." The IJN gorilla would have much preferred to torture the truth out of Coleman. Kato knew in his heart that no one, not even an engineering graduate student at Howard University, could lead such an empty life. The target had to be acting according to a clever FBI plan designed to reinforce the Imperial Agent's misplaced confidence in his ability to identify and recruit super-spies. If Kato were allowed to conduct a little "smacky-face" interrogation of Coleman or, better yet, lift a fingernail or two with a pair of pliers, he was certain that Coleman Braxton would admit being a mole. But Yukinaga knew that Katsuie would never permit the son of a Yakuza boss to employ such harsh investigative methods to confirm or refute a mere hunch of Dr. Ames's.

"Perhaps circumstances will change soon and I will be given free rein to do the necessary," Kato consoled himself.

At the embassy, before dawn on the 26th of July, a frustrated but resigned Lieutenant Yukinaga presented his detailed surveillance findings, officially clearing Coleman, to a very pleased Imperial Agent Kimura Katsuie. The FBI listening devices picked up and recorded the entire conversation between Kato and Katsuie. The Bureau translators produced a transcript for Walker, Clyde, and Boulanger to read by 11 AM. Agents Walker and Clyde were relieved to read a passage near the end of the transcript where Katsuie thanked the Lieutenant for his excellent work and then ordered him to cease all surveillance of Coleman Braxton immediately. The final words spoken to Kato by the Imperial Agent were, "Return to your language lessons at Georgetown University and enjoy your time in America."

Hercules, however, took a different view. He told Walker, "Kato Yukinaga will not just fade away. We must continue our watch on him as well as our monitoring of his apartment and telephone for a little while longer. I do not intend to resume contact with Coleman for a few more days. Let's see if our motorcyclist has an insubordinate streak in him. If King Kong Kato pursues his own investigation, we have to be prepared to handle him roughly. I doubt Katsuie or anyone at the Japanese embassy has the fortitude to control someone with Yukinaga's kind of resume."

Walker pushed back. "Hercules, you know that we have budget and manpower constraints. And from a legal perspective, we can't eliminate a citizen of the Empire of Japan—an active duty IJN officer—just because we deem him to be potentially inconvenient."

Pushing back harder, Hercules replied, "From a cost perspective, I am just asking for a few more days, a week at most, of surveilling Kato. If, based upon our observations, we conclude that he presents a clear and present threat to the security of one of our most valuable undercover assets, then we may need to act. Far be it from me to waste taxpayer dollars or behave inappropriately toward a Japanese assassin operating in our nation's capital!"

"OK, Hercules," said Walker. "I approve your request to keep watching Kato for one more week. If he becomes a genuine threat to an important asset assisting us in our ongoing investigation of Japanese espionage in the US, then come up with a plan to humiliate him publicly, embarrass the Empire of Japan, and get his own team to pull him off the field. You think you can do that?"

"Piece of cake, Agent Walker," Hercules said with a smile. "Would you mind much if I take my leave now and go down the hall to meet with the leader of the special team that has been following Yukinaga?"

Walker replied, "Keep me informed. No surprises. I do not want the first report I receive about some unfortunate fatal motorcycle accident involving a Japanese Navy language student to come to me from *The Washington Post*, WMAL, or some other public source of information. FBI management needs to be prepared to express its concern and determination to investigate thoroughly such an unfortunate incident in a convincing manner to the overwrought pencil-necks at the State Department who must respond to an angry demarche from the Empire of Japan."

Off went Hercules to brainstorm with Agent Alphonse Zangara, a legendary G-man whose no-holds-barred methods were the bane of most Department of Justice lawyers. On December 25, 1910, when he was barely three years old, Al's mother Mary, a non-swimmer, drowned herself by jumping from Bridgeport Connecticut's new Congress Street Bridge into the frigid waters of the Pequannock River. Al was then "nurtured" solely by his father, Mario, a former Barnum and Bailey Circus strongman who had abandoned his career in show business to accept a lucrative job offer from a local loan sharking entrepreneur in need of someone capable of collecting interest and principal payments due from slow-paying borrowers. By the time Al entered high school, he towered over his imposing and infamous father. Public school officials recognized that they needed a plan for controlling a local mobster's formidable ninth grade son who, in junior high school, had demonstrated adroitness in both mathematics and mayhem. The high school principal and the chairman of the math department stepped up to the challenge and devoted themselves to channeling Al into developing his quantitative skills. The football coach assisted the principal and the department chairman by imposing "the 3 No's" on Al as prerequisites for team membership: no getting into fights, no disrespecting Social Studies and English teachers, and no getting arrested.

Al responded well to this no-nonsense style of adult supervision. Despite succumbing from time to time to Mario's requests that he assist his father in the family "business," Al cleverly avoided problems with local law enforcement throughout high school and managed to win an academic scholarship to Fordham University's School of Business and Accounting. Graduating at the top of his undergraduate class in 1931, he won yet another scholarship to attend the Fordham University School of Law, where he became an editor of the *Law Review* and member of The Order of the Coif. Graduating Fordham Law in June of 1934 and confronted by a difficult job market resulting from the continuing Great Depression, Al Zangara did the unthinkable. He joined the Federal Bureau of Investigation. Within five years of becoming a lawman, the son of Mario Zangara had acquired a reputation for brilliance and ruthlessness that earned him a coveted position in counterintelligence at FBI headquarters.

Hercules tapped Zangara's office door. Seated behind his large desk, Al looked up and motioned for Boulanger to enter. Hercules approached Al cautiously. How else would anyone approach a man who stood 6 feet, 10 inches, weighed 325 pounds, and wore a pair of size 18-E wingtip shoes? "Agent Zangara, I am Agent Hercules Boulanger and I need to discuss your surveillance effort targeting IJN Lieutenant Kato Yukinaga."

Zangara stood up, walked around his desk, and shook Hercules's hand. "Pleasure to finally meet the agent who broke this case wide open! Have a seat. Has our boy Kato been misbehaving?"

"Not yet, but all of my instincts tell me that he will violate his orders and attempt to harm our mole within the next few days," replied Boulanger.

Al whistled and said, "You think that Yukinaga will really risk going after your nephew? He has no evidence upon which to justify assaulting AJAX! Kato has been told by Imperial Agent Katsuie to stand down."

Impressed by the speed with which Zangara got to the beating heart of the matter, Hercules explained, "Intelligent, highly educated, highly trained cutthroats like Imperial Japanese Navy Lieutenant Yukinaga will go to great lengths to eliminate any doubt that they have in their minds about the presence of a double agent threatening an operation. In his gut, Kato knows that my nephew Coleman is too true to be good. If I were Yukinaga, I would take a run at Coleman. You are from Bridgeport, Connecticut, Agent Zangara—wouldn't you?"

Grinning like his father did just before breaking the arm or the leg of a defaulting borrower, Al replied, "You got it, Agent Boulanger! No loose ends! So, what do you want to do about Kato and when do you want to do it? We have lots of options to consider in this regard."

Hercules confided in Zangara, "The people who control the Bureau want to avoid having to ship Lieutenant Kato Yukinaga's ashes back to Japan in an urn aboard a US cruiser, like we did recently with former Japanese Ambassador Hiroshi Saito. I have been directed to find a way to disgrace Yukinaga publicly so that his government will have to recall him back to Japan. The problem here is that there is very little time to create such an incident before Kato makes his move and compels us to put him on hold. Agent Zangara, you know him better than anyone. Does he have a vulnerability we can exploit within the next 48 hours?"

"Oh yes, he most certainly does have an Achilles' heel, Hercules! And from now on, call me Al! You want a cup of coffee? This may take a little time to choreograph correctly."

Surprised by the collegiality, Hercules shrugged his shoulders and replied, "Sure. You got any Eight O'Clock in this building?"

He was even more surprised when Al said, "Hercules, that is the only coffee to drink. I will have my secretary brew us a fresh pot! How do you take your coffee?"

"Black is all I drink." Then, feeling more comfortable, Hercules added, "Why spoil all the effort A&P puts into roasting those coffee beans just to contaminate them with milk and sugar? Never made no sense to me at all!"

"I could not agree with you more, Hercules!" With that, Zangara politely requested his secretary to prepare a fresh pot of Eight O'Clock coffee. The two agents then got down to conspiring.

"Hercules, when you were working full time for the DC Metro Police Department, did you ever have occasion to enforce the laws prohibiting crimes against nature or sodomy?"

Hercules cleared his throat. "Yes, once or twice, maybe."

Without missing a beat, Zangara asked a follow-up question. "Did you ever have to visit or raid an establishment that catered to men who engaged in these sorts of illegal acts?"

"Uh-huh," grunted Hercules.

"And do you recall the location of any of these dens of iniquity?"

"Might have been a bathhouse around 15th and G Streets, if I recall correctly."

Like a teacher talking to his favorite student, Al replied, "Hercules, you do recall correctly. Now guess who I observed meeting a man at Lafayette Park and escorting the handsome fellow to that bathhouse on two separate occasions during the past week?"

"IJN Lieutenant Kato Yukinaga!"

"Yep!" said Al.

"Agent Zangara, you are a gift to US law enforcement and counterintelligence."

"Hercules," replied Al, "I like to think so!"

At noon, the Eight O'Clock coffee arrived and the two men toasted each other. Zangara's secretary shook her head as she walked out of the Bridgeport giant's office.

"Hercules, you still got any friends working at the DC Metro Police Department?"

"A few very close amigos, Al. In fact, one or two of them are detectives working on the Vice Squad."

"Well, Hercules, how about we alert them that heinous crimes are about to be committed by as many as twenty men in a Turkish bath at 15th and G Streets tonight at around 10 PM? Your former associates will probably need a few wagons or a bus to haul these guys off to Police Court. Think they can handle this?"

Smiling, Hercules replied, "Well, yes. I believe that they have been quite effective in the past at bringing large numbers of outlaws to justice. Do you mind if I tell them that they should claim total credit for this raid and never mention the involvement of federal agents in this matter?"

"I do not mind at all, my good man! Don't you think this is what close cooperation between the FBI and local law enforcement is all about?" replied Al sarcastically.

"Agent Zangara, perhaps some *Washington Post* reporters and photographers would appreciate this kind of story to grace the front page of their fine newspaper tomorrow morning. Imagine how interested *The Post's* subscribers will be when they read about a well-put-together Japanese naval officer getting involved in such exotic goings-on in the nation's capital!"

"Hercules, as long as the Fourth Estate has no idea of our involvement, it's OK with me. Now let's get Walker's blessing and get rolling on this."

And off the two crime-fighting cavaliers went to impress their management with their creativity and alacrity. Zangara's secretary resumed shaking her head as the FBI agent, son of a Bridgeport mobster, and the only Negro FBI agent she had ever seen walked side by side to the office of Clarence Walker.

Walker gave a green light to the plan and alerted the Assistant Director responsible for counterespionage matters. Hercules got his buddies on DC Metro Vice spun up and they offered the story to their favorite reporter and photographer at *The Washington Post*. Zangara's special squad reported to him at 9 PM that Kato had hooked up with a well-dressed man at Lafayette Park and that the two were headed to 15th and G Streets. Hercules radioed the news to DC Metro Vice and they gave the couple 30 minutes to get to know each other before hitting the bathhouse doors hard, screaming, "RAID! HANDS UP!" while plastering police raid warning posters all over the place.

Kato was caught in flagrante delicto, arrested, put in handcuffs, and paraded before the flashing camera of *The Washington Post* photographer. Twelve men were arraigned before the Police Court judge, who set bail for each of them at a startling $500 (the equivalent of approximately $9,000 in 2019). Lieutenant Yukinaga was permitted one phone call.

The Japanese embassy immediately dispatched their high-priced US criminal lawyer and an embassy counselor to bail out the ill-starred language student who had been charged with sodomy and the standard offense of "resisting arrest." The new Japanese ambassador, a mild man even by polite diplomatic standards, hit the roof when advised by the embassy staff that the morning edition of the July 27 *Washington Post* would publish a detailed account of the "Turkish Bath Bust" accompanied by an embarrassingly clear photograph of a shirtless, handcuffed Lieutenant Yukinaga flanked by two unsmiling DC Metro Vice Squad detectives.

"I want this *baka*, this fool, out of the United States as soon as US law permits. I want Kato Yukinaga to suffer severe consequences for his humiliating Japan," raged the ambassador to his counselor. "Keep him in the embassy basement so he cannot get into any additional difficulties. Clean out his apartment. Make certain that his rent has been fully paid. And get him to sign the title to that motorcycle of his so we can sell it and use the proceeds to pay for some of his legal expenses. Now I must prepare a cable for the Foreign Minister, reporting this disgraceful news, and groveling before him for allowing such a dreadful calamity to occur on my watch."

The 78-rpm record of these remarks produced from FBI recording devices connected to the bugs within the Japanese embassy became yet another counterintelligence romantic comedy classic added to the secret files of "The Bureau."

Late in the afternoon of July 27, Walker accompanied Zangara and Hercules to the office of the Assistant Director of the FBI responsible for counterintelligence. The AD, a Certified Public Accountant as well as an honor graduate of Georgetown Law School, shook the hands of both men and conveyed FBI Director Hoover's deepest admiration for their outstanding performance.

"Few people will ever know about your brilliant achievement, but J. Edgar Hoover will personally inform the President of your exploits tomorrow morning in the Oval Office. Gentlemen, you have brought honor to the FBI and protected the vital security interests of our nation. Keep up the superb work. Agents like you will help us defeat our Japanese, German, Italian, and Russian enemies. Now get back to work."

Once out of the Assistant Director's office, Walker handed each of them a Robert Burns DeLuxe Clear Havana cigar and announced, "I trust that your future accomplishments will justify more of these coming your way!"

Zangara replied, "No matches? How do you expect us to ignite these beauties?"

Walker responded, "Al, I can't do everything for you!"

At which point Hercules added, "I've got my World War I trench lighter, Al. I can, and I will, take care of you."

Al and Hercules went out of the Department of Justice Building into the hot DC early evening air. They lit their cigars with Hercules's lighter, blew blue smoke into the sky, and reveled in their victory over the Empire of Japan.

Al turned to Hercules and said, "Let's grind some more of these bastards into the pavement."

"You got a deal, Al. I will debrief Coleman and afterward, we can use his information to assist us in planning our next op. I guess you should go home to your wife and kids now."

"Home? Hercules, I live alone. I need no wife. I need no children. My mother was a suicide. I can't have anything to do with my father. I have no brothers or sisters. The FBI is everything to me. So, you go talk to your nephew and I am going back to my office to review today's reports and come up with some ideas for future skullduggery we can visit upon our friends on Massachusetts Avenue."

"You know, Al, I used to think I was the only person living alone who was not at all lonely. Nice to know that I am not the only alone person who is not lonely," mused Hercules.

"You are no Sigmund Freud either," opined Zangara.

Hercules departed to put a signal on the mailbox near Coleman's dormitory.

6 PM, JULY 28, 1939; SAINT AUGUSTINE'S CHURCH

Coleman entered the confessional. *Frère Honoré* slid the door uncovering the screen and said, "Welcome, my son."

Coleman: "Uncle, I must say that what you did to Kato Yukinaga was a fine piece of police work. The *Washington Post* front-page story amused me more than any comic strip I have ever read. You took a dangerous man off the streets in the most embarrassing way."

A deadpan Hercules replied, "I had nothing to do with it. The DC Metro Vice Squad did it all. They deserve your praise and applause, not little old me."

"You are one humble FBI man, Uncle Herc," said a sincerely grateful and relieved Coleman Braxton.

Hercules then reminded his nephew that they had work to do and that the FBI needed a detailed report of what transpired on the *Yamagiri Maru*. After reviewing the facts with Hercules, Coleman pushed a typed, six-page single-spaced report to his uncle through the narrow space on the floor between the conjoined booths.

Hercules then informed his nephew, "Coleman, you have been cleared by the Japs to continue functioning as their agent. However, Dr. Ames will still suspect you, so be careful around him. Katsuie trusts and apparently likes you. He should be assigning a mission to you soon. Once we determine what kind of information Katsuie and his bosses want, we will provide you with relevant but misleading data and fabricated supporting documentation to hand to them. Your work product will make Katsuie and Ames look good to their masters. Of course, it will take the Japanese years to figure out that they have been had. Hopefully by then we will have won the war against the US started by the Japanese Empire. So prepare yourself, Coleman. You have a long road ahead of you. Any questions or concerns?"

Coleman asked the question foremost on his mind. "Will you be able to protect Dr. and Mrs. Dixon and their niece, Lucille, from Ames and the Japanese?"

"Of course, Coleman," replied Hercules. "I have been indebted to Dr. Dixon and his family since World War I. You must understand by now that I never abandon or let down a comrade!"

"No disrespect intended, Uncle Hercules, but I think I am in love with Lucille. Is it safe for her to get close to me?" asked a concerned Coleman.

"Coleman, there ain't nothin' at all safe in this world at this time. Despite it all, however, you have got the right to lead your life. You can court this lady. Just remember, Ames will be watching. Katsuie will be watching. Keep your mouth shut tight about me and about this business! If you want to keep Lucille safe, you ought NEVER to disclose to her anything about what we are doing. Even if you marry her, never say nothin'. Even if you stay married forty years, you never say nothin'. Even if you have children and grandchildren, you never say nothin'! You go to the grave with this part of your life kept secret! Do you understand?

"Yessir, I do."

"All right, then. Signal me when Katsuie comes out of his little rat-hole and communicates with you," ordered Boulanger. "Now, I am going to leave this booth and make sure the coast is clear. Hope to see you soon, nephew."

"Uncle Herc, I know that I am repeating myself and I know that you have already committed to protecting the Dixons and Lucille, but please do all you can to keep them from harm. I could never forgive myself if their involvement with me caused them to be harmed."

"Coleman, do not repeat yourself and stop worrying. When you worry, you make mistakes. When you make mistakes, you and the people depending on you will likely get hurt. Stay focused on accomplishing the details and objectives of your mission. Leave all other matters to me. Period."

Frère Honoré walked slowly to the robing room. Coleman headed to Howard University.

While uncle and nephew were talking surreptitiously in a confessional, another step toward war in the Pacific had been taken. The US State Department notified the Japanese Foreign Ministry of America's intention to terminate the 1911 Treaty of Commerce and Navigation between the two nations within six months.

8 AM, AUGUST 2, 1939; THE DEPARTMENT OF JUSTICE BUILDING, 10TH AND CONSTITUTION AVENUES

Horan, along with agents Walker, Clyde, Boulanger, and Zangara, convened to discuss Coleman's *Yamagiri Maru* memo and Hercules's subsequent debrief of his nephew at the Saint Augustine's Catholic Church. Walker began the proceedings by informing the group that DC prosecutors had acceded to the Japanese embassy's spurious claim of diplomatic immunity for Kato in exchange for two official written commitments: (1) that the "errant diplomat would be immediately repatriated to Japan accompanied by Japanese guards," and (2) that the "errant diplomat would never again be assigned by the Government of Japan to serve in any official or nonofficial capacity in the United States, or in any US territories."

Hercules advised them that Coleman had not yet been activated by Katsuie for a mission. Zangara reported that the Office of Naval Intelligence had intercepted a coded message sent from a Japanese technical intelligence officer to Captain Saigo Masuji, an IJN attaché at the embassy, instructing him to launch an all-out investigation of US radio-wave technology for detecting and tracking ships and airplanes. Listening devices within the embassy picked up Masuji ordering someone to get US lawyers to search patents filed having to do with said technology.

Zangara added, "We are waiting to learn which academic institutions, corporations, and individuals Masuji targets. We should know in a week or so where he will concentrate his spying efforts. So far, Katsuie, Ames, Johnson, and our mole, Coleman Braxton, do not appear to be involved in this radio-wave business."

Walker concluded the meeting by asking who wanted to accompany him to Baltimore to meet with one of the fourteen direct reports to the Chief Inspector of the Baltimore Police Department and inform him of the Japanese espionage activities in his fair city. Irritated, Walker commented, "The Baltimore City Police Commissioner considered the meeting so insignificant that he delegated responsibility for attending it to a direct report of his direct report, the Chief Inspector."

Hercules declined the offer, saying, "Whatever message you want this mid-level Baltimore police bureaucrat to transmit up his indifferent chain of command will not get listened to at all if I accompany you. Any positive relationship you want to establish with this guy will never get off the ground with me in the room. The BCPD waited until 1938 to hire its first four colored policemen. Not one of them is in uniform. All four of the Negro officers are plain clothes! The BCPD Commissioner is a strict, no-nonsense, former judge who was appointed by the governor of Maryland in 1938 to clean up a scandal-ridden police department. By most accounts, the Commissioner is an incorruptible, disciplined executive doing precisely what he was hired by the governor to do. However, no one could reform the entire BCPD in just one year. The guy you will see may well be a holdover from the 'old BCPD' and resent what little change the Commissioner has instituted regarding the complexion of the police department. I think you should appear with just the Special Agent in Charge of the Baltimore FBI office. Make the BCPD Captain or Lieutenant or Inspector feel important. Get him firmly on our side. Isn't that all you really want from this first meeting?"

Walker attempted to take the edge off this unusual outburst. "Now, Hercules, while I do not intend to argue with you about your opinion of the BCPD, I trust that you do not view me or anyone on this team as harboring any prejudice against you. Everyone in this room, as well as the Assistant

Director, admires you and recognizes that your contributions to date have been invaluable to our success. If you have any concerns about us, let's clear the air now."

Hercules calmed himself before speaking. "Clarence, I have no problem with this team. I am committed to this team. I want to ruin the Japanese and the traitors who assist them. I am simply being brutally realistic about when I can add to our team's performance and when I cannot. In this instance, my best judgment says that I should remain here with Clyde and Zangara working on the case."

Clyde and Zangara nodded their heads in agreement.

"OK, fellows. I will see you tomorrow evening and report on my meeting with some individual who indirectly reports to the Baltimore City Police Commissioner."

2 PM, AUGUST 2, 1939; OFFICE OF THE HEAD OF THE DETECTIVE DIVISION, BALTIMORE CITY POLICE DEPARTMENT HQ, FALLSWAY AND LAFAYETTE STREETS

Agent Walker and the Senior Agent in Charge of the Baltimore FBI office met with BCPD Captain Giles Renaud. Affable, ambitious, and whip-smart, Renaud's intuition told him that working with the FBI to counter espionage activities occurring in Baltimore would likely advance his career. With his disarming charm, Renaud motioned to his visitors to sit around his conference table and said, "Gentlemen, what can I do for you?"

Dispensing with all preliminaries, the FBI SAC let Walker take the lead.

"Sir, a joint FBI and Office of Naval Intelligence investigation has uncovered evidence indicating that agents of the Empire of Japan are operating in the City of Baltimore, particularly in the harbor area. Weapons training in Elkridge, Maryland, and at least one clandestine meeting aboard a Japanese merchant vessel docked at Locust Point occurred during the month of July. The precise objectives of these Japanese agents have not yet been ascertained;

however, we anticipate learning more about their intentions within the next two weeks."

The head of detectives looked at Walker. "So what do you want from me?"

Walker cleared his throat. "Investigations such as these require close cooperation between local, state, and federal police agencies, as well as the ONI and MID. We would appreciate your assigning one of your most competent detectives to work with us on this matter and subsequent counterespionage cases. To prepare him for this work, the FBI has created an intensive eight-week program at Quantico, Virginia, where he will train as a member of a team of FBI, ONI, and MID agents responsible for investigating espionage and sabotage cases in the Baltimore area. The cost of this training will be covered entirely by the federal government."

The Captain allowed an uncomfortable period of silence to follow before responding to Walker's proffer. "I accept your offer to train one of my detectives—cost free to the City of Baltimore—subject to the caveat that whomever I designate will continue to report to me. I will remain at the top of his chain of command. Additionally, any federal agents other than FBI agents who will be operating in my city must be identified to me and cleared by me personally. I am quite confident that I speak for the Commissioner when I tell you that we do not want our city turning into a Wild West town with armed men, over whom we have little control, conducting raids and getting involved in gun battles in the City of Baltimore. As you no doubt know, the BCPD is run by a man who is a firm believer in discipline and order. Can you, Director Hoover, and the leadership of ONI and MID live with these conditions?"

Walker did not hesitate replying to Renaud's question. "Yes, Captain. Your conditions are reasonable and acceptable to us. We will make your conditions explicit to all course trainees. Should you have any issues or questions with our counterespionage activities in Baltimore, here is my card and phone number. Feel free to call me collect. Also, we would appreciate the opportunity to keep you briefed on investigations in Baltimore at times and places convenient for you."

Renaud replied, "That is acceptable to me, Agent Walker. When do you need my detective for your training course?"

"Our next counterespionage course commences September 16th."

"Agent Walker, the Baltimore City Police Department Detective optimal for your purposes is Special Squad Detective Lieutenant Gareth Messenger. Messenger knows Baltimore as well as anyone in the department. He has served with distinction in the central, southern, southwestern, and eastern police districts, where the harbor and most of the city's defense businesses are situated. Detective Lieutenant Messenger attended Baltimore City College High School, my alma mater, where students learn that success in life is earned and victories are won by self-reliant individuals who commit to doing more than that which is required of them and to improving themselves each and every day. You might have to rein him in every now and then, but Gareth Messenger is, as you will see, the right man for this job. Any other requests or information for me, Agent Walker?"

"No, Captain. We greatly appreciate your thoughtful contribution to our effort to defend our national security," Walker said earnestly.

Captain Renaud replied, "Remember, discipline and order at all times in my city, Agent Walker."

"Absolutely," answered Walker. "Discipline and order."

As Agent Walker and the SAC for Baltimore walked west on Lexington Street to the new, eleven-room suite of FBI offices at the 200 Court Square Building, Walker turned and pointed to the BCPD HQ and said, "Renaud is a hard-charger. With his support, we are going to crush any and all Nazi, Jap, and Communist spies in this town!"

Shortly after the meeting, Renaud briefed his boss, the Chief Inspector.

"I received troubling news from the FBI that Baltimore has become a target for Japanese espionage. I have accepted their generous offer to train one of our detectives on how to conduct state-of-the-art counterespionage investigations. Our detective will remain under my command, but will be seconded to a team of FBI, Office of Naval Intelligence, and Military Intelligence Division agents who will operate in Baltimore to contain and extinguish the threat. The Detective Lieutenant I have selected is Gareth Messenger. He is 'Pure Baltimore' and will keep us informed of his team's activities. The federal government understands too that discharging firearms in Baltimore must be kept to an absolute minimum. In this regard, would you mind directing your State Police Sergeant contact to test the firearm skills of any non-FBI agents who want to carry weapons in Baltimore and sign off on their pistol permits? I want these *federales* to understand that we have a serious interest in their behaving with great discipline and restraint. Finally, do you want to advise the Commissioner about this matter or just hold it close?"

The Chief Inspector approved Renaud's decisions and agreed to his request regarding State Police Sergeant Alexander Ioffe. He concluded the conversation by saying that he would personally advise the Commissioner. "Captain Renaud, keep me informed of significant events concerning this counterespionage situation. It's probably best if we have these conversations face-to-face in secure facilities, such as your office or mine. Other than Sergeant Ioffe and Detective Lieutenant Messenger, let us maintain this information under a close hold, or 'absolute need to know' basis. The FBI will freeze us out of their activities if they conclude that we cannot keep counterintelligence matters off the front page of *The Baltimore Sun*."

Renaud replied, "Chief Inspector, I agree with you totally."

And that was that.

9 AM SATURDAY, AUGUST 19, 1939; HOME AND OFFICE OF DR. RALPH AMES

In response to Benkei's August 14 cable to activate his two Baltimore agents for a mission, Kimura Katsuie directed Dr. Ames to arrange a weekend meeting with Coleman and Junius at the doctor's North Carrolton Avenue home. Ames contacted Coleman on August 16, providing the date, time, and location of the get-together, but not its purpose. Coleman promptly signaled

Boulanger and reported the details to him. Hercules, feigning ignorance of the information contained in telephonic, postal, and cable communications contemporaneously intercepted by the FBI-ONI surveillance blanket covering Masuji, Katsuie, and Ames, thanked his nephew for relaying the facts to him in a timely fashion. Cautious and thorough as ever, Walker ordered FBI technicians to swiftly and discreetly check the surveillance devices they had previously installed in Ralph Ames's home and add a few more for good measure. Walker wanted every word spoken by the spies recorded clearly.

Katsuie arrived at Ames's office on Friday afternoon after the doctor's final appointment. Contrary to Benkei's directive, the Imperial Agent informed Ames of all the details contained in the secret August 14 cable concerning Masuji's order to activate the two new agents. The FBI technicians monitoring the Katsuie-Ames conversation were astounded by the boldness of the Japanese espionage operation. Hercules, Walker, Clyde, and Zangara, however, were elated. Their adversary's amateurish tradecraft handed American counterintelligence a front-row seat ticket to a live performance of a key espionage conspiracy planning session.

"It really doesn't get much better than this," marveled Al Zangara. "We are inside their communication and decision loops. We know where the Japanese spies are going, and why, long before they commence their operation. It is just unbelievable!"

Walker warned Zangara, "Al, do not get overconfident. These are highly motivated fanatics. Until they are in custody or in coffins, operatives like Masuji, Katsuie, and Ames can inflict a lot of damage."

Zangara replied, "Point taken."

Al silently resolved that from then on, he would keep a tight lid on comments he uttered when working around Walker.

At 9 AM, Junius and Coleman arrived at Ames's home. Ralph opened the door and ebulliently welcomed them. "Great to see you! Come on in. Why don't we join Mr. Katsuie here in my living room and enjoy the view of Lafayette Park?"

The Imperial agent stood, bowed slightly, and greeted them with, "Pleasure to see you both."

As they took seats, Ames asked, "You two men want some coffee?"

"We sure do," replied Junius. Dr. Ames brought each of his spies a cup of freshly brewed coffee. Then they conspired.

Katsuie initiated the conversation. "Coleman and Junius, we have an important mission for you. This operation demands much skill and patience. Phase 1 requires that Coleman obtain a job at the Bendix Radio plant near Fort McHenry. Due to the growing demand for its military products, Bendix is hiring engineers, office staff, and workers of all kinds. There are advertisements for new employees placed by Bendix in *The Baltimore Sun* several times each week. Coleman, you should examine these ads and apply for any job that is available. Of course, we would be delighted if you obtained an engineering position. However, to the best of our knowledge, Bendix has hired no Negro electrical or mechanical engineers, so we cannot realistically expect that you would be considered for such a position initially. A successful infiltration demands patience. So get a job, any job, at Bendix. Once hired, devote yourself to developing a solid reputation as a diligent worker with a pleasant personality who consistently strives for excellence and is always helpful to and considerate of fellow employees. We know that moving upward in the Bendix organization will take time. Do not become frustrated. As more important positions become available, apply for them. We assess that your excellent people skills, positive attitude, and intellect will be recognized by management. We are confident that you will win promotions, acquire knowledge, and ultimately obtain access to secret programs at Bendix."

Katsuie then paused, looked into Coleman's eyes, and asked, "Do you have any questions for me at this point?"

In a serious voice, Coleman replied, "Mr. Katsuie, I agree with you that once I get my foot in the door at Bendix—or any other enterprise, for that matter—my work ethic and personality should lead to advancement. I will do all that I can to overcome Baltimore's barriers blocking Negroes from getting white men's jobs, but it will take time. I trust that your bosses are prepared to be as patient as you say they are."

Katsuie, smiling serenely, answered, "We Japanese are a very patient people, Coleman. You will see."

Following up, Coleman then focused on logistics and mechanics. "Mr. Katsuie, I am living in DC. Why would Bendix hire me for a job in Baltimore?"

The Imperial agent came prepared for this question. "Dr. Ames will rent a room to you on the third floor of this building, which he owns, and provide you with superb recommendations as your landlord who knows you well. You will make it clear to Bendix job interviewers that you need gainful employment now in order to generate savings necessary for you to finance your future master of science degree in engineering at Howard University."

Coleman replied, "Understood, Mr. Katsuie. Dr. Ames, are you OK with this?"

Ralph smiled and said, "Coleman, it gets a little lonely in this house. I could use the company. Do you play chess by any chance?"

"No, Dr. Ames, but I am eager to learn from you."

Clearly pleased, Ralph Ames responded, "Coleman, we will get along just fine."

Katsuie then turned to Junius. "You will be teaching at Frederick Douglass High School full time soon. Be a model teacher. Cultivate your professional relationships carefully. Earn the admiration and support of the school principal, your department chairman, your fellow teachers, your students and, most important, your students' parents. You must be perceived as a proficient educator of young people and a positive role model who is above suspicion. Maintain your close, friendly relationship with Coleman. Your operational responsibilities will increase significantly when we progress to Phase 2. We know, Junius, that you are eager to accomplish important goals. You will have to be patient. I can assure you that in time, your deeds will inflict great damage to the Caucasians who presently dominate the United States, and will immeasurably advance the cause of America's oppressed colored peoples. I cannot tell you today precisely what we have in mind, but do not doubt that you and Coleman are now involved in a very important mission. Junius, do you have any questions?"

"Will there be any more opportunities for me to train or improve my skills while I wait?" asked Junius anxiously.

"Dr. Ames and I will see to it that you maintain and enhance your surveillance techniques, weapons handling, and martial arts skills. It goes without saying, of course, that you should not discuss your training activities with anyone or display your talents to anyone, even your parents. To be effective, you must appear nonthreatening, noncontroversial, invisible. Learn from the unfortunate example of the recently disgraced Lieutenant Kato Yukinaga. I am certain that you read about him in the newspaper and heard about him on the radio. Yukinaga, an officer with great promise, did not exercise restraint over his passions and became a dishonorably visible celebrity. He ruined any chance of serving his Emperor as an agent operating inside the United States. Junius and Coleman, think before you act. Do not take unnecessary risks that might lead to your covers being compromised. The successful agent's identity will never be recorded in history. Your adversary should know nothing about you, your missions, and the damage you do to him. Are we clear on this?"

"Yes, Sir," replied Junius and AJAX in unison.

The FBI-ONI surveillance team smiled in total agreement with the advice of the Imperial agent.

8 AM, AUGUST 22, 1939; NAVY DEPARTMENT BUILDING, ALL HANDS LONG-RANGE PLANNING SESSION

Captain McLaughlin chaired the joint ONI-FBI counterintelligence meeting concerning the Japanese espionage activities targeting radio-wave technology and devices for use in locating and tracking ships and aircraft. In attendance were FBI agents Horan, Walker, Clyde, Zangara and Hercules. At McLaughlin's request, Walker summarized the key events to date and provided brief biographies of the conspirators involved in the matter.

Captain McLaughlin then explained the Navy's position regarding goals and next steps.

"For the time being, we have got to keep the Japanese spies focused on Bendix and away from firms where significant radio-wave device work is presently being conducted, particularly RCA, Westinghouse, Western Electric, Sperry, Philco, and, of course, the Naval Research Lab. In time, Bendix will become a producer of these devices for the Navy and the Army, but not for at least a year and a half to two years. We must make Masuji's decision to focus his resources solely on Bendix appear to be correct. The Captain's spy inside Bendix will purloin authentic-looking data and documents regarding radio-wave devices and courier them to the Japanese embassy via another member of Masuji's spy network. Bogus documents and data will be crafted to deceive the Imperial Japanese Navy into thinking that US progress in this field is limited and our interest muted. We want the people funding military technology development teams in Tokyo to prioritize their spending on programs other than those involving radio waves. We will also engineer documents specifying approaches to radio-wave devices that we know do not work, thereby encouraging the IJN to waste precious time and resources on producing deficient equipment. Hopefully, the Japanese will get frustrated and just give up on developing the technology. However, if they persist, by the time their engineers figure out that they need to pursue alternative technical paths, our Navy will have an insurmountable lead over the IJN in fielding this revolutionary equipment on our bases, ships, and aircraft."

Horan then asked, "How do you intend to get Boulanger's nephew into Bendix? According to *The Baltimore Sun*, the company's hiring practices would not meet with Eleanor Roosevelt's approval."

McLaughlin glowered at Horan for making a negative gratuitous remark involving the wife of the Commander-in-Chief. "The FBI's record regarding job opportunities for Negroes is no better than Bendix's at this point in time,

Agent Horan," he replied icily. "In any event, my personal contact at Bendix will assist us in placing Hercules's nephew in the company's Fort Avenue facility. He needs a driver at the present time and no one at the company will be suspicious if he hires Coleman to be his chauffeur. Our cooperating Bendix executive will give Coleman excellent performance reviews and see to it that he receives training in electrical engineering. After a reasonable amount of time, Coleman will earn promotions to positions providing him with access to areas within the company that will excite Masuji and keep him concentrating on Bendix. The longer we can string the Japs along with fictitious programs from their source within Bendix, the better."

Walker then asked, "Who will produce the fictitious information we feed Masuji?"

Captain McLaughlin then announced, "I have a clever technical expert at the Naval Research Lab in Anacostia who will create plausible data and documents that will at first confuse the Japanese, and then ultimately convince them that they have nothing to concern themselves with regarding US Navy radio-wave devices. Keep in mind that the Imperial Japanese Navy prides itself on its night-fighting capabilities. The last thing they would want to do is invest significant resources to develop, manufacture, install, and maintain complicated electrical equipment that can help them see and fight in the dark. Such equipment will require training their sailors to do what the IJN thinks it already does better than any other navy in the world. We will tailor our information to reinforce the IJN's and Masuji's preexisting biases."

Hercules spoke up. "Captain, you sure have a lot of friends in interesting places!"

"Yes, I do, Agent Boulanger, and I am delighted that you appreciate that fact," replied a dour McLaughlin.

Horan decided that it was time to end the meeting. "How about we all get back to work and review our progress together on Friday the 26th?"

McLaughlin: "One last thing. I read your report of Agent Walker's meeting with the Baltimore Police Captain of Detectives. I am going to mobilize a US Naval Reserve officer born and raised in Baltimore who graduated in the same high school class as the detective lieutenant the BCPD intends to send to the FBI counterintelligence course. This naval officer's undergraduate major involved the history of ancient Greece and Rome and his naval service and training is predominately technical in nature. He is presently pursuing a degree in law, which should satisfy the Baltimore Police Captain's concern about armed, out-of-control federal agents causing chaos in his fair city."

Walker asked, "Any more detail you can provide me about this guy? I would like to check him out before you give him a job offer."

A stern Captain McLaughlin replied, "You do not tell me who to bring on board my ship, Walker! However, you and your snoops can go check out Reserve Lieutenant Junior Grade Martin Victor, who has resided at 14 South Broadway in Baltimore for the past six years. He is a graduate of Saint John's College in Annapolis and teaches history at his alma mater, Baltimore City College High School. He is about to complete his law degree at the University of Maryland Law School's evening division. Lieutenant JG Victor is a proficient radio officer and a skilled boxer who trains twice a week with boxing coach Jacob Epstein at the Young Men's Hebrew Association on Madison Avenue in Baltimore. Lieutenant JG Victor has never been arrested, and his US Navy medical records indicate that his health is excellent. He has no tattoos and has never contracted a venereal disease. Now, if you come up with some disturbing facts about Lieutenant JG Victor that might alter my assessment of his suitability for this Baltimore espionage matter, you had better tell me long before I order him on September 13th to quit work, quit law school, leave his lady friend, leave home, and attend your FBI counter-espionage program at Quantico that commences on September 16th."

Walker, mildly embarrassed, replied wanly, "Aye aye, Captain. If you would not mind, I would appreciate reviewing ONI's file on your Lieutenant JG Victor."

Captain McLaughlin nodded his head and handed Martin's personnel folder to Walker. "Don't you or any of your men spill any coffee on this, Agent Walker!"

"Thank you. We will maintain its pristine condition, Captain McLaughlin."

Late that night, alone together in Zangara's office, Hercules and Al Zangara reveled at Walker's dressing-down by Captain McLaughlin. "Now that was a textbook ass whupping," averred Hercules.

"No doubt about it," opined Zangara. "Captain M crucified Walker over questioning his hiring of a Jewish Naval Reserve officer to serve as an ONI agent! Priceless, Hercules. What a country!"

And that was that.

12

COLEMAN BRAXTON GETS A JOB AT BENDIX

On August 24, 1939, after checking *The Baltimore Sun* reports on ship traffic in Baltimore harbor, Coleman turned to the classified "Help Wanted, Male" section. And there it was: Bendix Radio Corporation at 920 Fort Avenue in Baltimore needed an executive chauffeur. Applicants for the position had to have at least a high school degree, were required to work weekends, wear a suit and tie, and have experience driving in the District of Columbia. Lastly, no mailed-in applications would be accepted. Applicants had to appear for an interview at the Fort Avenue facility at 9 AM on Tuesday, August 29.

During "confession" at Saint Augustine's Church on the previous Monday evening, August 21, *Frère Honoré* mentioned to Coleman that a Bendix classified help wanted advertisement for an executive chauffeur would be published shortly and that he should call Dr. Ames as soon as he saw the ad in *The Baltimore Sun*. "Coleman, tell the doctor about the ad and protest that college graduates do not become chauffeurs. He will argue with you. You can push back, but ultimately you must appear to submit sullenly to his authority."

"Herc, who is this executive who needs a chauffeur?"

Hercules explained. "Coleman, he is part of our team. You can trust him one hundred percent. When we have completed our mission, you will get an engineering position at Bendix, if you want one. This is how the system works. You do excellent work for an executive—the higher up the exec is, the better. A teacher-student bond will develop between the two of you and then you have someone with clout who will support your promotion up the organizational ladder. Just be the organized, reserved gentleman engineer that you are. Everything will work out fine."

"Uncle Herc, how will I communicate with you if I am living under Dr. Ames's roof? You know he wants me as his disciple."

To Hercules, Coleman appeared to be nervous to the point where he could not see his way clearly out of a simple problem. Hercules, a man who had lived by his wits, courage, and cool ferocity, found this recurrent weakness in his nephew troubling.

"Coleman, whatever you want me to know, just tell your new boss at Bendix. You will see him every day. Without exposing yourself or me, you will be able to get messages to me quickly. This Bendix job solves your communication problem. No more Saint Augustine's Church confessions at all hours of the day and night, my good man!"

His tension overcome, Coleman apologized, yet again, to his uncle for getting carried away with himself. Hercules, who hated apologies and apologizing, took this opportunity to counsel his nephew. "Coleman Braxton, when you start to get those feelings of fear, guilt, and panic, calm yourself down. You are an educated problem solver. Jesus, you know all that statistics, calculus, physics, and engineering stuff. You can think and analyze your way out of anything. Emotions are your enemy. Control them! Your mind, man— that is what will save you every single time. And a little initiative don't hurt none neither, Coleman."

Coleman stepped outside the confessional and shook his uncle's hand and said, "I got to go find the suit I wear to funerals. I got a job interview with a powerful white man in Baltimore!!"

"Bless you, my son," said a clearly pleased *Frère Honoré*.

9 AM, AUGUST 29, 1939; BENDIX RADIO BUILDING AT 920 EAST FORT AVENUE, BALTIMORE

The unsmiling, armed uniformed guard posted at the front door of the defense firm on 920 Fort Avenue said to Coleman, "State your business. Why are you here?"

Coleman handed the classified ad to the guard, cleared his throat, and said, "Suh, I am here to apply for the job in this ad."

The guard read the text and said, "Well, it does not say 'Whites Only.' Wait here. I am going to find the person who placed this ad."

And off he went. Several minutes passed before the guard returned and growled, "Come with me." Coleman felt lost walking past the maze of offices and wondered how he would ever find his way back to the front door. Finally, the guard stopped in front of a large office with a row of windows facing Fort Avenue and announced, "Dr. Crowe, here is your applicant."

Richard Crowe, a Class of 1910 US Naval Academy graduate with a PhD in electrical engineering from MIT, did not rise from his desk. He looked at Coleman and said, "Enter." Crowe then looked at the guard and said, "You can close the door when you leave the room."

After the door shut, Richard Crowe, a Texan from the Hill Country town of New Braunfels, got up, walked around his desk, and shook hands with Coleman. "Have a seat. Mind if I examine your resume?"

Coleman handed the document to Crowe and sat down. Dr. Crowe, still standing, read the document and said, "Is everything on this piece of paper accurate?"

Coleman replied, "Yes, Sir!"

"You sure of this?" said Dr. Crowe.

"Yes, one hundred percent sure!" responded AJAX.

Grinning, the bespectacled balding man said, "So why would a man working on a graduate degree in engineering in DC want to become a chauffeur in Baltimore?"

A skeptical Coleman answered, "You know, Dr. Crowe, a lot of people have asked me that question recently. My answer to them is that I need money to pay for graduate school. Bendix is an engineering company. I will be working for a Bendix executive with a company car who has a big office with windows facing Fort Avenue. I think I can work my way up here into a real engineering job once my boss and the folks around him see how capable I am. Baltimore is my hometown. Rent is reasonable here. Should I go on?"

Laughing, Dr. Crowe answered, "No. Tell me why you are really here, son."

"My FBI agent uncle told me that I could trust you, so I will. I am here to stop the Japs from stealing US military secrets!"

This time, a severe Dr. Crowe replied, "That is correct. You, the FBI, the US Navy, and I are going to squash this spy network like a bug! However, today I must interview every applicant and then select you. All Bendix salaries are set by the company's personnel department and accountants. The annual salary for a beginning executive chauffeur is $1,379, a little less than a high school teacher's pay. We will improve on this number as your responsibilities and time of service increase. I understand that you are interested in an engineering job. May I ask what kind of engineering interests you?"

Coleman had not anticipated this question, but after a moment's reflection, he said, "Electrical engineering."

Crowe replied, "Great field. Bendix Radio is all about electrical engineering. I will see to it that you get to take some of the in-house courses on radio engineering that we offer to ambitious employees. For now, however, be a team player. For example, if I ask you to drive another manager somewhere, just do it with no questions asked. If an employee, guard, or manager, or even an executive, says unpleasant things to you, pay it no mind. Be polite and let me know the name of the person and what they said or did. When I commanded a submarine-hunting destroyer during World War I, Negro sailors were restricted in military occupation specialties and not treated with a great deal of respect. Over time, I improved the atmosphere on my ship, and our overall performance protecting convoys improved. Your primary mission is to maintain your cover and help to destroy the Jap spy network targeting Bendix. Do not let anything get in the way of that objective. If you have to put up with some crap, just know that I will fix the person creating the problem. Your job is to get along with everyone at Bendix, no matter what. Is this OK with you?"

Coleman nodded his head and said, "Yes, Sir!"

"OK, then. You will get a call at the Baltimore phone number you put on your employment form tomorrow afternoon. You will be told that you have a job offer with the salary I quoted to you. You will be delighted! And from now on, unless I tell you otherwise, I expect to see you at work at precisely 8:30 AM, dressed in a suit, a starched white shirt, a tie, and polished shoes, starting on August 31st. I want to see my face reflected in the toe area of your shoes. This may be Bendix, but my heart is US Navy. As long as I am your manager, you may be employed by Bendix, but your heart belongs to the US Navy too. As time goes by, you will understand what this means. I think we ought to take a little drive to DC to see some of your 'friends' on Friday, September 1st. Does this work for you?"

Coleman nodded his head and shook Dr. Crowe's hand.

An avuncular Crowe said, "Mr. Braxton, SMILE! This is going to be fun. Trust me!"

The guard escorted AJAX to the street without saying a word. Coleman could not believe that he looked forward to becoming a chauffeur! He knew that he would have to say, "I do not know, but I think I did OK in the interview" to Dr. Ames that evening when asked, "Did you get the job?" But more importantly, Coleman now understood that Uncle Hercules's team was his family now and that this team and this family had to win at all costs.

There is no second place in the spy game; just first place and dead, he thought.

SEPTEMBER 1, 1939; BALTIMORE AND DC

At 8:30 AM, Coleman and Dr. Crowe departed the Bendix Radio parking lot in the executive's exquisite royal blue Chrysler Imperial Custom sedan. Crowe sat in the front seat, near Coleman, rather than far away in the rear seat of a vehicle with a 144-inch wheelbase. The Imperial Custom's Fluid Drive transmission impressed Coleman, as it required no shifting of gears unless he wanted to exceed 60 miles per hour in standard overdrive.

"What do you think of this machine?" Dr. Crowe asked Coleman.

"Sir, it is a beauty! This vehicle deserves to be washed and polished and have its interior cleaned every day. I read the owner's manual cover to cover last night. One day, I intend to own a Chrysler Imperial myself," gushed Coleman.

"A wise choice, son. A very wise choice. I saw this car on Young & Newton's dealership on Keswick Road near where I live and I bought it right on the spot. Aside from the car's technical advances, its sleek dashboard controls, royal blue paint finish, and contrasting red Chrysler badges just grabbed me. Mrs. Crowe thinks that I ought to see a psychiatrist, but she has been wrong once or twice before since I first met her. Our two sons are naval officers steaming around the Pacific Ocean, one on a heavy cruiser and one on an aircraft carrier. If they were here, they would approve of this automobile. I just know it. In any event, I am glad you approve."

As Coleman drove, Dr. Crowe read *The Baltimore Sun*. The headline disturbed him:

NAZI ARMY INVADES POLAND
VICTORY OR DEATH FOR ME—HITLER

"Coleman, the US cannot stay out of this war much longer. We cannot sit by and let the Germans, Japanese, Italians, and Russians take over the world," said Crowe grimly.

"You sound just like my uncle, Dr. Crowe," replied Coleman.

"You mean FBI Agent Hercules Boulanger?" said Crowe to the utter astonishment of his young driver.

"You know him?" inquired Coleman.

"I know of him, Coleman. Captain McLaughlin briefed me about your uncle. He sounds like a real asset for our team," replied Crowe.

"Dr. Crowe, he is the best man I have ever met. Whenever I have a decision to make, I always ask myself, 'What would Hercules do?' or 'What would Hercules think?' or 'Would Uncle Hercules approve?'" added Coleman.

Crowe looked at Coleman and said, "You are very fortunate to have such a role model. I ask the same questions of myself as you do, I just insert the word 'Dad' where you put the name 'Hercules.' My late dad ran a ranch in Texas. When I was foolish enough to ask his opinion about doing something he would say to me, 'Well, boy, what should the best version of you do to get this thing done right?' And then I would just do what I thought he would do. It was that simple."

Dr. Crowe then opened his briefcase, placed the newspaper in it, and retrieved a Bendix file folder filled with documents. He read and annotated each and every page in the file by the time his Imperial arrived at a parking area reserved for dignitaries near the Navy Department Building. Dr. Crowe said, "We can park here, Coleman." As they got out of the car and walked toward one of the ugly temporary buildings erected during World War I, Crowe chuckled. "You are going to find this interesting."

At the guard station near the front entrance, Dr. Crowe flashed an identification badge to a Marine sergeant carrying a holstered .45-caliber semi-automatic pistol. Dr. Crowe announced, "We are here to see Captain McLaughlin."

The guard examined his clipboard and replied, "Thank you, Dr. Crowe. I need some identification for your guest." Coleman produced his Maryland driver's license. The guard wrote down the name and number in his logbook and handed Coleman an ID card with red stripes.

"Clip this to your lapel," instructed the Marine. "Miss Catharine Saint Armand will escort you to the Captain's office." A tall woman in a gray suit appeared and they followed her up a flight of stairs and down a long corridor. After a few left and right turns, they arrived at a door with no number.

Miss Saint Armand rapped on the door and from the inside, Coleman heard a gruff voice say, "Enter."

Inside the room, Coleman saw a distinguished-looking man in a blue uniform, Hercules, Walker, and another FBI agent—judging by his clothing—sitting around a long wooden table.

Captain McLaughlin rose from his chair, strode over to Coleman, shook his hand, and said, "Welcome to the Office of Naval Intelligence. My name is Captain Charles McLaughlin. I believe you know Agents Boulanger and Walker." Pointing at Zangara, the Captain said, "This is FBI Agent Alphonse Zangara, the latest addition to our team."

Zangara got up from his chair, took one giant step forward, and shook Coleman's hand. Astounded by Al's size and speed, Coleman could barely get out the words, "Pleased to meet you!" as his hand disappeared into the immense paw at the end of Agent Zangara's very long arm.

McLaughlin returned to his conference table and signaled for everyone to be seated.

"Gentlemen, the purpose of this meeting is to establish security guidelines and set a few future milestones. Mr. Coleman Braxton, code named AJAX, is key to this operation. He will be the conduit through which we pass worthless information to the Japanese network. We know from recent experience that the Japanese and their US agents put surveillance on AJAX to assure themselves that he is not a mole inside their organization. To limit their ability to penetrate our communication channel with our agent, henceforth, all communication to and from AJAX must travel exclusively through Dr. Crowe, my close friend and classmate in the US Naval Academy Class of 1910. Richard's brain has always been far more impressive than his body, which is why he is a big-shot Bendix executive with a chauffeur-driven 1939

Chrysler Imperial Custom sedan. He owns a home in Baltimore's prestigious Roland Park neighborhood, as well as another, more modest abode on
Varnum Street in northeast DC, where he stays when Bendix needs him to
manage sensitive government procurement issues. Richard's basement office
in the Varnum Street residence contains a Mosler Model 125 S safe. We may
use this office and safe in a few months to lure, distract, delay, and confuse
our Japanese embassy friends and their US agents."

McLaughlin paused and studied the faces of the men around the table.
"Any questions?"

Hercules, as always, could not resist asking an impertinent question. "Is
Crowe on retainer to the US government, or is this just a one-time favor to
you?"

McLaughlin responded, "Hercules, Dr. Crowe is doing us a favor, and
doing his patriotic duty for his country. Does any of this concern or upset
you?"

Hercules, sensing an evasion of some sort, pressed impertinently on.
"Why, no, but I want to say here and now that I admire Dr. Crowe for being
such a good friend and such a good patriot, for working two tough jobs, and
for taking no money from the government while working on one of his two
tough jobs."

Dr. Crowe then spoke up. "Agent Boulanger, thank you. I deeply appreciate your commendation."

Zangara then asked Captain McLaughlin how he wanted the FBI to
communicate with Dr. Crowe. "Should we contact Dr. Crowe through you,
Captain McLaughlin, and avoid any direct FBI-to-Crowe communication?"

"Good question, Agent Zangara. The general rule should be for the FBI
to use me as the communication channel to Dr. Crowe. However, in an
emergency involving the physical security of Dr. Crowe or AJAX, when you
cannot get me or the new ONI officer I am bringing on board in November,
you FBI agents do what you deem appropriate. We know that the opposing

team plays rough. I would rather take the small risk of somehow showing our hand than have Crowe or AJAX become casualties. Does this work for you?"

Walker jumped in. "Speaking for the FBI, we accept this approach. We should discuss any adjustments to our communication system in the future if events warrant."

McLaughlin agreed that the FBI and ONI work should closely together on these complicated matters.

Captain McLaughlin continued. "AJAX, has Dr. Ames given you any idea what he and Katsuie want you to take out of Bendix?"

Coleman responded, "No, Sir. They want me to get in good with my boss and all the Bendix employees. They want to see me get a promotion into a position of trust where I can get access to secrets. But they have not told me what secrets they want me to get access to."

McLaughlin then asked, "Did Dr. Ames inquire about Dr. Crowe and what he does at Bendix?"

Coleman thought for a moment and replied, "Dr. Ames asked to see Dr. Crowe's business card. He told me that he liked that Dr. Crowe had a PhD in electrical engineering from MIT, that his title was Senior Vice President, and that Dr. Crowe appeared to be involved in government contracts."

McLaughlin followed up. "Any other questions or requests that you gather additional information at Bendix?"

"No, Sir," said Coleman.

McLaughlin then provided some guidance to Coleman. "Sooner or later, Ames and Katsuie are going to get restless and push you to get information about Bendix programs, people, military contracts, etc. Tell Dr. Crowe exactly what they say they want you to get and we will provide you with something appropriate to give to them. Never give Ames or Katsuie anything that Dr. Crowe has not personally cleared for release. For example, if they ask you to describe the physical layout of Bendix Radio or ask for a map of the facility or a personnel directory, we will give you a specially prepared version of the documents to give to them. Do not call Dr. Crowe from Dr. Ames's house. Try to communicate face-to-face with Dr. Crowe inside the walls of Bendix Radio as much as possible. We want to control the process of releasing information to the Japanese. Are we clear? Any questions?"

Coleman replied that he understood, and that communicating with and working with Dr. Crowe was proving smooth and efficient.

"Good to hear this, Coleman. OK, gentlemen, unless you have other topics to discuss, I suggest that we return to our respective places of employment to monitor and control events as they arise. And if I may, I need a word with Dr. Crowe."

Everyone but McLaughlin and Crowe filed out of the office and the Captain closed the door.

Dr. Crowe quietly addressed the Captain. "You were right about Hercules Boulanger. He is clever and he knows we are withholding information from him."

McLaughlin replied, "Richard, absolutely no one in the FBI—and certainly not AJAX—can ever know who you really are. Your wife, Bendix, the Congress…even the President does not know that you continue to serve as a Rear Admiral in the US Navy. The Chief of Naval Operations and the head of ONI are adamant that your double life remain top secret. You are involved in some of our most important long-term, clandestine operations on account of your ability to move about in financial, industrial, technological, political, academic, and diplomatic circles undetected and unsuspected. I know that you like this Coleman Braxton kid and his uncle and feel uncomfortable dissembling and deceiving them. I respect them too for the risks that they are taking to defeat this menace. Nonetheless, this is the nature of our business. We must compartmentalize each operation and maintain covers. Are we OK?"

Rear Admiral Richard Crowe smiled, shrugged his shoulders, and said, "Of course we are OK!"

And that was that!

Driving back to the Department of Justice, Hercules asked Walker, "You ever heard of this Crowe fellow before?"

Walker replied, "Cannot say that I have. What's bothering you about him?"

Hercules responded, "I am not bothered by him, just curious about him. He is solid, smart, and smooth. Crowe is no amateur doing a favor for his old school buddy, Charles McLaughlin. Look, Richard Crowe has Coleman completely engaged and positive. I do not doubt that Crowe is committed to winning this battle in our war with the Japs—I just don't like when people on my team do not level completely with me about themselves."

Walker hammered back at Hercules, "So let me get this straight. You know that Crowe is more than capable of performing his role in this case. You just do not like that he failed to tell you his life history! Come on, Hercules. Let's just play the hand we have been dealt by ONI. Of course ONI personnel will never tell us everything about themselves. But as far as this investigation goes, McLaughlin's pulling Crowe out of a hat helps us immeasurably. They are not holding back on relevant information or resources. ONI is even adding a new agent whom we will train and indoctrinate at Quantico. Most importantly, you can be confident that ONI is looking out for Coleman. McLaughlin told us so in today's meeting. Hercules, Crowe is not a problem for you, or any of us. Do you copy?"

"Yes. You just beat this puppy to death, Clarence," Boulanger replied morosely.

Walker, however, was not finished. "In the interest of openness, Hercules, there is a secret that Al and I have to share with you at this point. But I cannot have you anxious that we are keeping you in the dark when I do not tell you everything right away. Do you appreciate that operational security sometimes demands that even essential facts do not get communicated to all team members simultaneously?"

Now this got Hercules's blood up. "Clarence, where are you going with this riddling of yours? Just tell me what you think I need to know now and then we can discuss whether I think you should have told me about it sooner."

Zangara intervened. "No offense intended, but you two are beginning to sound like elementary school students bickering with each other. Knock it off, fellas! Now, Hercules, just before you and Coleman reported the Katsuie-Howard University recruiting connection to FBI counterintelligence, I recruited a deep cover agent working inside the Japanese embassy. Her name is Kinuyo Hara and she is Captain Masuji's secretary. Contrary to FBI policy, Kinuyo and I are romantically involved. Only Agents Walker and Horan know about this extraordinarily valuable and vulnerable Confidential Informant. No one else at the Bureau is even aware that we have a CI inside the Japanese embassy. We intend to keep it that way until the time comes when we provide her with asylum in the US. Furthermore, we have not told ONI about Miss Hara, and we do not intend to ever tell them about her, either. Sometimes we just have to limit knowledge about the existence of an undercover agent, particularly one operating next door to her most likely potential executioner. Masuji will filet her slowly in the embassy basement if he finds out about her involvement with me. Hercules, until it became clear that Coleman would add value to our little war with the Japanese embassy-sponsored espionage ring, we had to keep you out of the loop. Do you now understand that in the counterintelligence world, there is no rule requiring full disclosure of all the facts even among members of the same team? Do you appreciate that we had valid reasons for keeping the fact about this CI, who is also my lover, operating inside the Japanese embassy under wraps?"

A solitary tear rolled down from Hercules's eye. He hated that tear: *la larme pour Geneviève*. But there it was. "Do you love this woman, Al?"

"I do, Hercules. I do very much," whispered Zangara.

"Well, Al, I confess that I have acted like a fool. Let me know what you want me to do to protect this Miss Hara. One day you will have to tell me how you met. One day I hope to attend your wedding."

"Hercules, you will be my best man!"

And that was that.

8 PM THURSDAY, SEPTEMBER 21, 1939; DR. AMES'S HOUSE, BALTIMORE

For four weeks, Dr. Ames imposed little on Coleman. Both men met early in the morning to have breakfast and superficial conversation with each other in Dr. Ames's well-stocked kitchen before separately rushing off to work. Both men worked late hours and saw little of each other at night. This period of relatively quiet solitude for Coleman ended on Wednesday morning when Dr. Ames said, "Coleman, why don't we have dinner together here in my dining room at 8 PM on Thursday night? I will cook us up some steaks and we can have a leisurely discussion about what is going on in your busy life."

Coleman nonchalantly replied, "Thank you. That is a welcome idea. I should be finished at work by six thirty tomorrow. I will come right home and we can talk, just the two of us."

Pleased with Coleman's cooperativeness, Dr. Ames added, "Coleman, what flavor ice cream should we have for dessert? I like any flavor as long as its ice cream!"

Coleman took little time responding, "How about Hendler's chocolate?"

Ralph Ames slapped his thigh and said, "My favorite. Best ice cream in the world. We are going to have a terrific dinner."

The previously bored FBI electrical surveillance team was bored no longer. The wires between Baltimore and Washington and the FBI and ONI crackled with the report that Ames was about to issue an order to AJAX. When Coleman dutifully reported the news to Dr. Crowe that morning, the executive replied, "I am surprised that they waited this long to put the move on you. Ames will ask you a lot of questions about me—what I do each day, to whom do I report, where do I go, do you attend meetings with me, how do I maintain my records, do I talk openly about specific topics, is there a safe in my office, what kind of safe is it, do I ever ask you to file documents for me, do I take work documents home with me, where do I live, have I ever let you in my house…etc. Coleman, he will be all over you. The good news is that for the most part, you can tell him the truth. For example, I have never let you in my house. As Ames has observed, our routine is that you drive me to Ames's house after work and I drive home. He knows that I pick you up at 8 AM the next day and you drive me to Bendix. Dr. Ames probably thinks my wife and I do not want a Negro near our house. As you know now, I do not want Ames or the Japanese to invade my home because they think that I do work there and maintain important files in my house. It is important for them to know that I never take my briefcase home, nor do any work at home. I do all my work at Bendix. If I work late into the night, Ames knows that you remain with me until I have completed my work. As for discussions about projects in which I am engaged, tell him that there is an airplane radio communication system for the British military that occupies a lot of my time. If he asks about my government contract and government relations activities, just say that you drive me to the Navy Department Building and carry my briefcases for me while I go from office to office. Mention that you sit in the waiting room of each office I visit while I conduct my business behind closed doors with the men inside each of the offices. Tell him that I am meticulous about documents. There is only one document on my desk at a time. I keep most files in a locked cabinet and some red-bordered documents in a Mosler safe, drilled and cemented into the floor of my office at Bendix. This will fascinate him and he will encourage you to think about ways to gain access to the safe. Finally, when he asks about our relationship, tell him the truth. We have an excellent working relationship. I have enrolled you in Bendix engineering classes and you are the first Negro ever to have been admitted. By the way, the reports that I have received from the instructors are that you are doing well. How do you think you are doing?"

Coleman replied, "Dr. Crowe, I look forward to work each day. Even the guards treat me respectfully now. I think they like the way I wash and polish your car most every day and that I do not put on any airs just because I wear a suit and study engineering. As for the in-house Bendix electrical engineering courses I am taking, the quality of instruction here from Johns Hopkins- and MIT-trained instructors significantly surpasses the quality of education I received at Howard University. My background skills in applied mathematics and physics need improvement; however, I am catching up by studying the books you have given me and solving the problems at the end of each chapter. I have always enjoyed solving math problems. When I get stuck, I look at the answer book and I see how to solve the problem. There is nothing here so far that I cannot master."

Dr. Crowe, smiling, said, "You have the right stuff, Coleman. Keep at it. If you have a question or get stuck, you should talk to the instructors. Never let the embarrassment of not understanding something right away prevent you from asking questions that will help you learn."

"Understood," answered Coleman.

Crowe then said, "I have to call Captain McLaughlin and alert him to your upcoming inquisition. Then we need to drive out to Towson to inspect the plans Bendix has to build a new, state-of-the-art engineering and manufacturing facility out there."

Dr. Crowe then closed his office door and Coleman went out to the parking lot to wash and polish the magnificent Chrysler Imperial.

DINNER WITH DR. AMES

At 7:45 PM, Dr. Ames watched as Coleman exited from the Imperial Custom's driver's seat, walked around to the right front passenger door, and opened it for Dr. Crowe to alight. Ralph shook his head in mild disgust as Coleman then followed behind Crowe and held the driver's door open as the middle-aged executive slid behind the wheel of his cherished Chrysler. Coleman then carefully closed the door and stood at attention as Richard Crowe drove off to dine with his wife, Wilhelmina, at their stately home on Beechdale Road in Roland Park.

As Coleman entered Ames's house, the sweet aroma of sizzling porterhouse steaks greeted him.

"Coleman Braxton, you are about to experience a gastronomic delight!" announced a beaming Ralph Ames. "Go wash your hands and let's get to work!"

Coleman did not bother to walk up to his room on the third floor. He removed his jacket, untied his tie, loosened his collar, rolled up his shirt-sleeves, and availed himself of the facilities in the first-floor guest bathroom. His ablutions completed, he walked to the exquisite mahogany dining room table and sat down. Coleman noted that Dr. Ames had removed the table leaves so that he could sit across from Coleman and observe his facial expressions closely.

Ralph asked Coleman if he would like a drink. "Just water, thanks, Dr. Ames," replied the wary FBI mole.

"Please, call me Ralph when just the two of us are together, Coleman. We do not have to hide anything from anybody within these walls." The laughter emanating from the FBI surveillance hide could not have been more uproarious.

Ames poured himself a glass of Merlot and reveled in its taste and body. He then served the steak. Coleman cut into the rare piece of meat, took a bite, and rolled his eyes. "Ralph, this is THE best steak I have ever tasted!"

"Not too rare for you?" asked a delighted Dr. Ames.

"No, Sir! It is perfect."

"Sure you don't want a glass of this French wine? It goes perfect with the steak."

"No, Ralph, I avoid alcohol. Just does not agree with me. Baltimore water suits me fine."

"Suit yourself, Coleman. Far be it from me to promote unhealthy practices!"

Both Coleman and Ralph laughed at this remark.

At this point Dr. Ames asked, "So, how was work today?"

"Ralph, we drove out to Towson and toured the twenty-eight-acre site where the new Bendix engineering and manufacturing building will be located. The entire place will be air conditioned. Can you imagine the electric bill for such a luxury?"

"No, I cannot, Coleman. It will be good for the working people, particularly when the heat and humidity of a Baltimore summer makes life miserable. Everybody will want to be at work rather than at home, so I suppose makes a lot of good business sense. What will be produced there?"

Coleman rattled off a list of products, none of them of any interest to Ames. After listening patiently, Ames asked, "Coleman, have you heard or read anything about a defense program at Bendix to locate and track ships or airplanes with radio waves?"

Coleman paused to search his memory and then replied, "No. I have heard about and seen radio direction finders and radio communication products at Bendix, but nothing like a radio locating and tracking device. Is there a name for such a thing?"

"No, Coleman, not that I am aware of. The Japanese suspect that Bendix has a secret program with either the Navy or the Army, or maybe both branches of the military, to produce such a product. This kind of radio-wave device is on the top of Katsuie's list of things for you to look into. Do not display your interest in radio-wave location and tracking devices when you are at work. Keep your eyes and ears open, however."

Coleman, looking pensive, said, "OK, Ralph. I will receive, not transmit."

"You got it, Coleman! Now eat some more of the steak before it loses its flavor."

After the main course, Coleman got up and collected Dr. Ames's plate, put it on top of his, and walked to the sink. He washed the dishes carefully, dried them with a cloth, and placed them neatly on the draining board.

"Coleman, you are the most orderly, responsible dinner guest a host could possibly have!" joked Ames.

"Ralph, I am just trying to move the process forward so I can get a bowl of that Hendler's ice cream!" replied a genuinely eager Coleman. "I might not drink French wine, but I do enjoy Baltimore vintage ice cream."

Dr. Ames hit the table with his hand and repeated, "Baltimore vintage ice cream! I am going to use that one, if you do not mind!"

"Ralph, you can use that and any line as long as you feed me steak and ice cream every month or so!" quipped Coleman.

"You know, Coleman, this is the first time you have displayed a sense of humor in my presence. Keep it up! In my line of work, I see a lot of pain and sorrow. I need a relief from it all every now and then. Yesterday, for example, a three-year-old child got away from his parents, ran right into a trolley, and got mutilated. There was absolutely nothing I could do for the poor little fellow. His mother and father were beyond any consolation from either me or the reverend on call at the hospital to handle such tragic events. You probably have wondered why I am not married, why I never married, and why I never will marry. Here is why: Life is as fleeting as it is precious. Every married woman wants a child. It is in their nature. They cannot comprehend what will happen to their child after they get pregnant and give birth—all the accidents, all the physical injuries, all the illnesses, all the psychological damage that results from being mistreated by a society that hates them. No, they ignore all that. They just want to carry that baby and love it and protect it. I cannot participate in that female fantasy. I will work night and day to save my patients' lives at the Provident, but I do not want to create those fragile, ephemeral lives. You must think I am crazy talking so much and holding up the serving of Baltimore's vintage Hendler's chocolate ice cream to you."

Coleman reflected on how limited his understanding of people was. There are "N" dimensions to each person, he concluded. *Dr. Ames is as troubled and complicated a soul as God ever put on this earth. This sensitive healer refuses to love and reproduce. He can be so charming, generous, and kind toward me. Yet this same man hates white people, despises decent members of his own race like Dr. Dixon, and supports an invasion and violent overthrow of the US government by foreign dictators.*

After ruminating about Ralph, Coleman spoke. "Dr. Ames, you are not at all crazy. However, I do want that Hendler's ice cream as soon as possible."

Ralph hit the table again with his hand and laughed until tears came from his eyes. "Coleman, you are an excellent dinner and houseguest!"

With that, they finished off a container of chocolate ice cream and consumed cups of Baltimore's other after-dinner favorite—Eight O'Clock coffee.

Coleman carried the dessert dinnerware to the sink, then scrubbed and dried each piece until they all sparkled. After completing his chores, he asked Dr. Ames, "Have you seen Junius recently? I have tried to get together with him for the last two weekends, but he says he is too busy with work to go out. This does not seem right. Is he OK? Is he mad at me for some reason?"

Ralph replied, "Coleman, I spoke with Junius recently. He told me that teaching at a public high school involves quite a bit more effort and time than he ever thought possible. Each day, five days a week, Douglass High School has him teaching three different history courses to five classes of the lowest performing and most incorrigible students attending the school. To complicate matters further, his colleagues, including the chairman of his department, are not being at all collegial. Each week he must prepare new lesson plans and home assignments from scratch for each one of the three different courses he teaches because his fellow faculty members refuse to share any of their plans or materials with him. On top of this, he must prepare quizzes and tests for his one hundred and forty 'scholars' and grade them, as well as check the nightly homework he assigns. According to Junius, this kind of hazing for new teachers is the accepted method for weeding out weaklings! Coleman, Professor Darwin would be proud of Douglass High School! In any event, this is a long way of saying to you that Junius is swamped with work and that he is not angry with you at all.

"Another thing may limit your contact with Junius. Once he adjusts to his new work environment, Mr. Katsuie plans to enhance Junius's surveillance and countersurveillance skills. Without getting into too much detail, the plan is for Junius to go to DC on a Saturday morning and follow a specific Japanese embassy employee straight through to Sunday afternoon. To make things interesting, an embassy security officer or two will attempt to tail Junius at the same time. Junius will have to identify and shake the people following him at the same time he is tailing his target. Repeated practice like this over weekends and holidays should sharpen our tired teacher, don't you think?"

Coleman thanked Ralph. "Well, that makes me feel better. When you see Junius, tell him I said 'hello' and that I hope that we will be able to get together soon."

Dr. Ames replied, "Coleman, Junius will always be one of your very closest friends. Work may sometimes get in the way of your socializing, but your friendship will endure."

"Thanks, Ralph. I think everything is straight in the kitchen and dining room. I am going to get a little rest. If I hear or see anything about radio-wave location and tracking devices, I will get back to you when I come home after work. Thanks again for the great dinner and interesting conversation."

"The pleasure was all mine, Coleman. Sleep tight."

And that was clearly **NOT** that!

Alarms went off immediately when Walker learned that Junius would be in DC surveilling Japanese embassy staff. Agent Zangara's "off-the-books contacts" with Miss Hara would now have to be far more carefully planned and orchestrated to avoid detection and certain death at the hands or direction of Captain Masuji. Coleman's skillful manipulation of Dr. Ames during dinner, however, did not go unnoticed. Coleman gave away little and managed to get an ocean of useful information and insight into the mind and vulnerabilities of Ralph Ames. In the words of Hercules Boulanger, "My nephew might not get himself killed if he continues to develop like this."

Finally, the radio-wave device cat was out of the bag and bogus documents would have to be prepared by Captain McLaughlin's experts at the Naval Research Lab for delivery to Dr. Ames by Coleman.

13

FRIDAY, NOVEMBER 10, 1939: GRADUATION DAY AT QUANTICO

Unable to attend the counterintelligence program graduation ceremony due to a last-minute meeting called by the President, the FBI Director dispatched as his representative the Assistant Director who headed the Bureau's General Intelligence Division. The Assistant Director, an unabashedly patriotic man who had risen rapidly since joining the FBI in 1930, delivered an eloquently emotional speech spiced with colorful law enforcement lingo from the FBI's American Gangster Era that began in 1924 and ended in 1938. The focus now, however, was on national security. The Assistant Director brought everyone to their feet cheering when he concluded his speech by stating:

> Foreign enemies of the United States are presently operating inside our borders, attempting to subvert our ability and willingness to defend our nation and our Constitution. These satanic servants of dictators are being aided and abetted by American Fifth Columnists. Your sacred mission—the mission for which this school has impeccably prepared you—is to root out these malefactors and bring their sordid careers to a swift and just end. Men, report now

to your respective posts. And may God preserve and protect you as you defend the United States of America.

Before presenting each graduate with an official FBI diploma signed by J. Edgar Hoover, the Assistant Director announced that the award for the team with the highest combined score for all course subjects—physical fitness, hand-to-hand combat, weapons handling, surveillance and countersurveillance, industrial security assessment, US internal security laws pertaining to espionage and sabotage, and mission planning—went to Gareth Messenger, William Murphy, and Martin Victor, Team Baltimore. Speaking extemporaneously, the Assistant Director added, "It is a distinct honor and rare privilege for me today to bestow upon Martin Victor membership in the FBI Possible Club for his perfect score in our pistol marksmanship course. I feel sorry for any spies who are unfortunate enough to be assigned Baltimore as a city in which to operate. They have no idea what will be coming right at them!"

Martin felt his heart bursting with pride as a photograph was taken of him shaking hands with the Assistant Director and receiving his diploma, Team Award certificate, and Possible Club membership card and certificate. He was fighting fit and razor sharp mentally. Team Baltimore believed themselves to be invincible. They were ready to play Saint George to the Japanese dragon. But above all else, Martin wanted Gertrude Kowalska. He had little time—three days to be precise—before his team had to report to DC for an in-depth briefing regarding the Japanese espionage effort targeting Baltimore. Following the briefing, the team had to create a detailed plan for conducting an industrial security assessment at Bendix Radio Corp. commencing Monday, November 20. Time was tight.

Before Gareth, Murph, and Martin took the train to Baltimore, they met with Captain McLaughlin, Special Agent Horan, and Special Agent Walker. McLaughlin addressed them.

"Gentlemen, Horan, Walker, and I picked you to be Team Baltimore. You have vindicated our judgment. You have done yourselves proud. However, school is over. Now you must defeat the most talented and motivated bunch of murderers and thieves that we as a nation have ever encountered. Never forget, there is no second place in this business. You either win or you are disgraced…and likely dead or disabled. You have three days to make your wives, families, and girlfriends miserable. See you at 10:00 hours at the Department of Justice on November 14th.

"DISMISSED!"

The final act at Quantico came when Martin Victor received a dark gray Stetson fedora as a combined graduation and Possible Club membership gift. "Martin, it takes a lot to surprise experienced FBI counterintelligence agents, but you managed to do it!" said Special Agent Horan as he handed Martin the box containing the hat. "Not one of us took you for a gunslinger. How wrong we were! We hope that you never have to demonstrate your proficiency out on the street. Nonetheless, knowing what you are capable of gives us comfort that our wives and families will not likely collect on our life insurance policies."

Martin thanked them and put the fedora on his head. "It matches my suit, white shirt, and wingtips perfectly. I will wear it with pride and always be reminded of the outstanding group of men with whom I work."

Gareth, in jest, asked, "How come I did not get a fedora?"

Walker responded, "Stetson doesn't make a hat big enough to fit your size head!"

Gareth quipped, "In that case, you are all forgiven."

1:30 PM FRIDAY, NOVEMBER 10, 1939; 14 SOUTH BROADWAY, BALTIMORE

Martin, dressed in a suit, white shirt, tie, wingtips, and Stetson fedora, rang the bell to Dr. and Mrs. Basswood's home. Grace Basswood opened the front door and said, "Well, aren't you something?" Then she called out, "Henry, come out and look who is here!"

Irritated by Grace's bellowing in her distinctive western Maryland dialect of English, Dr. Basswood opened the door to his office with an angry look on his face. The scowl brightened noticeably and immediately when he saw Martin.

"Looks to me like somebody got you into good physical shape, my boy. May we assume by that suitcase in your hand that you are back to stay?"

Martin smiled and said, "If you two will still have me, the answer is yes!"

Dr. Basswood shook Martin's hardened hand, and said, "As long as you pay your rent on time, you have got a deal!" Martin and Harry laughed. Grace did not laugh. She did, however, nod her head in approval.

Grace announced somewhat sarcastically, "We have kept your apartment nice and clean while you were away training for the Olympics. I must go to the butcher store now to buy a chicken for Shabbos dinner tonight. I know that you probably will be running off with that odd brother of yours this evening. Let us know when just the three of us can have lunch or dinner together and hear about your recent adventures."

Martin had anticipated this request and responded, "How about Sunday for lunch, say around 1 PM? Does that work for you?"

Grace Basswood replied, "Yes, indeed. How about cold cuts from Attman's Delicatessen on Lombard Street? I will pick up some rye bread, fresh mustard, pastrami, corned beef, sliced turkey breast, lettuce, and tomatoes, and we can have an indoor picnic!"

Martin, appreciating the generous offer, replied, "Perfect, but the cold cuts are on me. I am earning a decent wage now and I insist. No debating this point, Mrs. Basswood!"

Grace looked at Henry, then looked at Martin and grumbled, "Well, I don't like it a bit, but I will not argue with you…" and then she poked Martin on the chest four times, once for each of the words "…JUST THIS ONE TIME!"

"All right then, Grace, the three of us will have an indoor picnic this Sunday."

Grace then got her pocketbook and exited the house to go "food shopping" as she liked to call it.

After she closed the door, Lieutenant JG Martin Victor, US Navy Office of Naval Intelligence, asked Dr. Basswood, "Henry, do you have a minute? I would like to speak with you privately in your office with no one around to listen in."

Without a word, Henry let Martin enter his office. He closed the door and the two men sat facing each other.

"Dr. Basswood, I am now speaking to you in my official capacity as an officer in the US Navy. Everything we talk about today and from now on must remain strictly confidential. You cannot talk about this with anyone, not even Grace or your rabbi. Do you agree to these terms?"

"Yes, Martin. Now get on with it," replied Dr. Basswood as if he were discussing surgical techniques with Dr. Osler at Johns Hopkins Hospital.

Martin launched into his carefully prepared remarks. "On Sunday, October 8th, a Japanese seaman visited your office. Do you recall this?"

"Martin, I am forbidden from providing information about my patients without their written approval. All of this information is doctor-patient privileged information."

"I understand your obligations, Henry. Let me continue." Martin opened the briefcase that he had been carrying and retrieved a file folder from which he withdrew a photograph of Captain Masuji decked out in his IJN dress uniform festooned with medals. He was standing at attention and saluting another Japanese officer.

"As you can see, Henry, the pinky and ring fingers of this heavily decorated Imperial Japanese Navy officer's right hand are both missing. These appendages were severed during the Battle of Tsushima in 1905 when this naval officer served under the command of Admiral Togo on the Japanese battleship *Mikasa*. The name of this officer is Captain Saigo Masuji and he is presently serving as a naval attaché at the embassy of the Empire of Japan on Massachusetts Avenue in Washington, DC. He has never been married and has a well-deserved reputation for seducing other men's wives. Captain Masuji is also a spy currently running a ring of espionage agents infiltrating advanced technology companies in Baltimore that engineer and manufacture advanced defense products for the US Navy. Masuji's mission is to have his agents steal data, documents, and working models of classified American weapons, which he sends to Japan to be reverse engineered and incorporated into the IJN fleet. Knowledge of these secret programs also helps the IJN to improve their tactics against US Navy warships. It should come as no surprise to you that the strategic goal of the Imperial Japanese Navy is to defeat the US Navy in the coming war at the time and place of their choosing. This espionage effort by Captain Masuji is key to Japan achieving its objective. Am I being clear, Dr. Basswood?"

"Perfectly clear, Martin," replied an agitated Henry Basswood, who then raised his voice. "That son-of-a-bitch has lied to me repeatedly, Martin. He hid his identity, his place of employment, his address, his marital status, and his level of sexual activity in the United States."

Opening the uppermost desk drawer on the right side of his desk, Henry produced a loaded nickel-plated .38-caliber Colt Official Police revolver with a 6-inch barrel. He released the pistol's cylinder, counted six rounds of ammunition, and clicked the cylinder back into the revolver's frame. Placing the weapon on the top of his desk, Henry announced coldly, "I am going to kill him!"

Realizing that he had overcome Henry's reticence to breach his confidential relationship with his patient, Martin replied, "Now, Dr. Basswood, it is too early to turn this guy's lights out. We need to keep him around for a while so that we can identify and round up his entire gang. If you kill him, not only will you go to prison for the rest of your life, or possibly be executed for committing first-degree murder, we will lose the possibility of destroying, root and branch, a Japanese espionage network operating in Baltimore and elsewhere in America. How about you help us accomplish this goal before he has an unfortunate automobile accident or gets perforated by a US law enforcement 'firing squad' when he resists arrest? If you do it my way, Dr. Basswood, you and I can have it all—the Jap espionage conspiracy totally foiled and a dead Jap naval officer—with neither of us having to spend any time behind bars."

Henry put his revolver back in his desk, took off his glasses, and transfixed Lieutenant JG Victor with his cold blue eyes. "Martin, do you promise me that this Masuji will never return to Japan alive?"

"You have my word, Dr. Basswood. When this operation is over, only Masuji's ashes, neatly packed in an urn, will return to Japan."

His lust for Masuji's blood temporarily deferred, Henry said, "Martin, tell me what you want me to do."

"Dr. Basswood, let's save that conversation for a walk on Sunday morning. I have an urgent matter that needs tending to on Howard Street." Using Henry's Hebrew name, Martin said, "*Gut Shabbos, Chaim.*"

And Henry replied, "*Gut Shabbos, Moshe.*"

Martin walked up the stairs to his third-floor apartment and washed his face and hands. He combed his hair, poured some Old Spice aftershave on his hands from its distinctive buoy-shaped bottle, and rubbed the heavily scented lotion onto his face. Martin recalled his brother Milton started using Old Spice when it first came on the market in 1938. Soon thereafter, Martin began anointing his face and neck with the same brand of aftershave following the adage *If it is good enough for Milton, it is good enough for Martin.*

He walked down the stairs to catch a cab. Henry stopped him briefly and said, "Masuji's fake name is Miyamoto Ijuin. He has an appointment scheduled in my office for a Neosalvarsan and bismuth treatment for his syphilis at 6:30 AM on Monday, November 13th. You might not want to be here when he arrives."

"Thanks, Henry. I will not be here, but the FBI, the ONI and the Baltimore City Police Department will be. You will not see them, but they will be here."

And off Martin went to North Howard Street.

3 PM FRIDAY, NOVEMBER 10, 1939; 106 NORTH HOWARD STREET, BALTIMORE

Carefully inspecting the Sun Radio Company's shelves of vacuum tubes to assure herself that boxes of RCA diodes had not been incorrectly mixed with boxes of RCA triodes, and determining how many of these electrical devices needed to be reordered from the manufacturer, Gertrude did not notice that her *kochanie* had entered the store. Martin walked up to the counter, cleared his throat, and asked, "Excuse me, Miss Kowalska. Do you by any chance have any RCA 56 five-pin triodes in stock?"

Dropping her clipboard, she ran to her man and embraced him in a manner so intimate that Shalom Cohen, the store owner, exclaimed, "Miss Kowalska, this is a place of business!"

Gertrude paid no heed to Shalom this one time. As Martin lifted her off the floor, she smothered him with kisses that covered his lips and cheeks with an extraordinary amount of Elizabeth Arden red lipstick.

"Gertrude," Martin whispered, "I think we have upset Mr. Cohen quite enough today. Let's go out to dinner after you finish work. I can afford to pay for us to have a meal at a real restaurant now. I am earning $4,000 a year! I will return at 6 PM."

Blushing, Miss Kowalska nodded her head, whispered, "Yes" and squeezed Martin's hands sighing, "My *kochanie*!"

Martin looked at the owner of Sun Radio, shrugged his shoulders and, for reasons he never could quite explain to himself, said, "*Gut Shabbos* to you, Mr. Cohen!"

Shalom Cohen looked at Gertrude for a long while. He spoke not a word. In his life he had never seen such spontaneous, explosive passion. For a moment, he grieved that no woman had ever expressed her feelings so intensely for him. But as he pondered what he had witnessed, he grieved for Gertrude and thought to himself, *A candle can burn for a long time before it consumes both the wick and the wax. Gertrude and that young man are more like a stick of TNT. The fuse is lit, burns quickly, and explodes, leaving nothing but wreckage.* Unsatisfied with this superficial model of intimate human behavior, Shalom wracked his brain and his heart in an effort to comprehend the scene he had witnessed in his store. Shortly before closing, the shopkeeper-inventor finally understood, saying to himself, "Men and women are not candles or matches or chemical explosives or machines. The love that Gertrude feels for that man transcends rationality. How does one explain such ethereal beauty? Who am I to pass a harsh judgment on such natural magnificence?"

Shalom approached his employee, took her hands in his, and through his tears said, "Gertrude, it is all right. It is good. It is beautiful. You have a wonderful weekend. I will see you on Monday."

For Shalom, Gertrude and Martin it truly would be a sweet and "*Gut Shabbos.*"

3:30 PM FRIDAY, NOVEMBER 10, 1939; THE EQUITABLE BUILDING, OFFICE NO. 336

Seated behind his desk, the tattered cuffs of his worn-out white shirtsleeves rolled up over his thick wrists, Milton Victor studied, with great intensity, the deposition of a crooked plaintiff's prevaricating "expert witness." Without knocking on the door, Martin casually walked into his older brother's office, disrupting the Maestro of Cross-Examination's concentration. "Vacation over already?" mocked Milton as he eyed his trimmed-down, muscled-up kid brother. As Martin drew closer, Milton could not miss the bright red lipstick smears on the "vacationer's" face, neck, and collar. "Now let me guess, Martin: Either you visited a bordello on Baltimore Street OR Mom kissed you goodbye before you decided to interrupt me while I struggle to earn an honest living. Since our mother is deceased, it must be the former. Am I correct in my analysis?"

Grinning, Martin responded, "You are such a regular Bertrand Russell, Milton!"

Milton walked to his brother and hugged his hardened body. "Martin, it looks like they almost made a real man out of you."

"Milton, I won first prize in a massive shooting contest!"

"Real rounds of ammunition or BB's, Martin?"

"Only .357 Magnum and standard .38 Special rounds, Milton."

"Yay for you, Martin!"

"No need to minimize my achievement, big brother. I practiced really hard to be selected outstanding gunman."

"The rabbi at the Lloyd Street Synagogue will be awfully proud of you!"

Milton's sarcastic remark made Martin double over with laughter.

"Will you be off to some unknown location soon, Martin?" inquired Milton seriously.

"I will be stationed in Baltimore for a while, Milton. I do not know precisely for how long, but you will be relieved to hear that I am earning enough money to treat you to a dinner at Haussner's on Monday night."

Milton elevated his eyebrows. "Well, this will be a real first! Offer accepted! Meet me here at 6 PM on Monday and we will drive to our favorite haunt." Martin nodded and Milton continued. "Now, was it Vivian Leigh or some other dignified lady who marked you up like that?"

"Milton, it was not Vivian Leigh. You know that I prefer 'Pure Baltimore' women, not British women!"

"There has never been a pure woman from Baltimore and you know that!" opined Milton.

"If you promise not to overreact, Milton, I will tell you her name and a little bit about her. If you keep your promise not to overreact, I will introduce you to her."

"*Gevalt*, Martin, she's not a member of our faith, is she?"

"No, she is not Jewish. But her family's geographic origins are quite close to our family's."

"She is Polish!" replied an astonished Milton Victor. "Martin, you never consider the consequences of your deeds, do you?"

"Let us just say that I tend to follow the logic of my heart, Milton."

"Since you compared me to Bertrand Russell, let me advise you that mankind reasons with its brain. Mankind commits folly when it follows its heart."

"You may have a good point there, Bertrand, but there you have it."

"Martin, what is your *ksiezniczka's* name?"

"Gertrude Kowalska. And you are correct, she is a princess."

"Of course she is, Martin. I would appreciate meeting this Gertrude of yours, and I promise to conduct myself in a thoroughly dignified manner. But let me caution you: NEVER bring her near Henry and Grace! Those two will "sit *shiva*" for you if you do. I am accustomed to your Bohemian behavior, and as your big brother, I will never abandon you, despite your irrational conduct. However, I am the only person you know who will be tolerant of this romantic excess. Everyone else, especially her family, will want your scalp for crossing the line separating red and white from blue and white. Do you understand? Do you copy?"

"Roger that, Milton. Gertrude and I both know that this situation is fraught with the kind of danger for which Baltimore is renowned. We have been secretive and will continue to conduct our relationship covertly. But you know and we know that sooner or later, these sorts of things get uncovered and we will have to deal with the consequences. Milton, I know that I cause you a mountain of grief. It is not intentional. I am just different."

"Martin, you are more than different," replied Milton. "You are eccentric. But I respect you for it. And now that you are a gunslinger, perhaps you can handle Gertrude's father, brothers, uncles, nephews, and a mob of anti-Semitic Polish Patterson Park peasants. I must get back to work. See you at Haussner's at 6 PM on Monday. And bring your Princess Gertrude with you."

"Yes, Sir!" replied Martin.

After Martin departed for North Howard Street, Milton shook his head and said, "What is wrong with that boy?" Then he laughed to himself and returned to engineering a devastating cross-examination of a lying expert witness.

6:30 PM FRIDAY, NOVEMBER 10, 1939; MILLER BROTHERS RESTAURANT, 119 WEST FAYETTE STREET, BALTIMORE

Gertrude and Martin walked arm-in-arm into Miller Brothers, a restaurant famous for its diverse clientele of local political bosses, movie stars like Basil Rathbone and Peter Lorre, and even FBI Director J. Edgar Hoover when the horses were running at Pimlico Race Course. Unaccustomed to restaurant dining at this level and somewhat intimidated by the boisterous crowd, Gertrude stayed close to her man. Seated at a table for two, they studied the menu, emblazoned with an art deco lobster and two mutually supportive phrases: "The Place to Eat" and "Nationally Famous." Gertrude whispered to Martin, "Let's save some money and order the Single Portion Served for Two of Prime Rib cooked medium rare, broiled potatoes, and creamed spinach."

Martin looked lovingly into Gertrude's eyes and replied, "If that is what you want and the way in which you want it, fine with me!"

Never breaking contact with Martin—either optically or manually—Gertrude responded, "*Kochanie,* you are all I want!"

Instantly tumescent, Martin decided not to say, "*Gut Shabbos*" and instead whispered, "Gert, you are my one true love." In fact, Gertrude Kowalska was the first woman—and the last—he would ever love.

"What would you like to drink before dinner?" Martin asked Gertrude.

"You mean alcohol, Martin?"

"Yes, I mean alcohol," replied an amused Martin.

"How about a lime daiquiri on the rocks, *Kochanie*?"

"Now you are talking, Gertrude!"

When the waiter appeared, Martin ordered two lime daiquiris on the rocks. After the two mixed drinks were placed on their table, the two lovers toasted each other and ordered their meal.

"So, Martin, can you tell me anything about what you have been up to the last eight weeks?" Gertrude asked somewhat forcefully.

With aplomb, US Navy Lieutenant JG Martin Victor lied to his love. "First, the Navy has stiffened its physical fitness requirements for officers, so they worked us hard every day to improve our strength, agility, and endurance."

Interrupting, Gertrude commented, "Boy, I'll say!! You are as hard as a rock, Martin. Nobody in their right mind should mess with you!"

Keeping his deceptive emphasis on physical fitness going, Martin replied, "You would not believe the Marine Corps Drill Instructor that we had. In under an hour, he could do 100 push-ups, 100 sit-ups, 100 jumping jacks, 100 squat thrusts, and 30 pull-ups, one after the other, and then run five miles! He never let up! The man was relentless! There is no one tougher than a United States Marine Corps Drill Instructor."

"Oh my!" exclaimed Gertrude. "How were you able to keep up with them?"

"You had no choice," Martin replied. "You cannot say no to a drill sergeant. At first, he motivated us by simply terrifying each one of us. Then he got inside your mind so that you motivated yourself. You do not want to let the DI and the rest of your training platoon down by quitting, slacking off, or even underperforming. Finally, you become just like your drill sergeant, deriding people who are weak, timid, fearful, or uncombative. The system works."

"Remind me not to join either the Marines or the Navy, Martin!" said Gertrude playfully. "What else did you accomplish?"

"I learned about the latest secure radio- and telephone-communication techniques. I cannot say more than this, but we worked day and night mastering highly technical stuff."

To Martin's relief, Gertrude had heard enough about the previous eight weeks. "Martin, I missed you so very much. I feared that you might not ever come back to me. I hate to ask you this, but what happens next? Will the Navy take you away from me again soon?"

"For the time being, I will be working in Baltimore most of the time, with sporadic temporary assignments in Washington. My commanding officer has said nothing about future postings and I am not about to ask him," cautioned Lieutenant JG Martin Victor.

"OK. Let's talk about us, Martin."

"Not so fast, Gertrude. What have you been doing while I was away? Have you been dating other guys?" said Martin, toying with Gert.

"Martin, you may be in great shape, but I will whack you with a two-by-four that has been soaked in oil for saying such things to me. I have one man in my life and you are IT! Don't you play with me, Lieutenant Victor. You do and you will find out how tough a Polish Baltimore woman can be!"

"OK. I surrender. Let's talk about us. I have another surprise for you."

"What's that?" said an excited Gertrude Kowalska.

"My brother Milton wants to take you and me out to dinner on Monday evening. Milton wants to meet you!" announced Martin.

Concerned, Gertrude asked, "Is that a wise thing? I mean, you know... We have been pretty careful about keeping our relationship confidential."

"Gertrude, we are going to have to bring Milton into our little private world. He raised me. He has always looked after me. He is a good man. He will never let either you or me down," replied Martin.

"If you say so, Martin. I regret that I cannot make a similar statement to you about anyone in my family. They do not have anything nice to say about your people. My parents and siblings frighten and embarrass me. But facts are facts, and they cannot be ignored or wished away. *Kochanie*, here is one more fact: You are more important to me than they are. I can live with their rejection. I cannot live without you."

"Whatever comes, my love, we will remain together," replied an equally honest Martin. "The waiter is coming. Let's eat!"

The graduates of Patterson Park High School and Baltimore City College High School shared their Single Portion of Prime Rib for Two together at Miller Brothers, thinking only of each other and not at all about the hateful and dangerous world in which they lived.

SATURDAY, NOVEMBER 11, 1939; "I'D LIKE TO INTRODUCE YOU TO SERGEANT ALEXANDER IOFFE OF THE MARYLAND STATE POLICE"

At 5:45 AM, Henry and Martin briefly bantered and enjoyed a cup of coffee in the Basswood's spartan kitchen. Dr. Basswood, attired in a simple Joseph A. Banks suit, would soon walk alone to the Lloyd Street Synagogue—as he did every Saturday—to pray from 7 AM until 12:30 PM. Henry carried a 36-inch-long cane when he strolled the streets of Baltimore. The handle of the cane, if pulled from the wooden shaft, would separate and a 20-inch-long blade of sharp surgical steel firmly affixed to the handle would then be ready for Henry to perform surgery on a mugger. Dr. Basswood once told Martin, "I do not administer anesthesia to such patients under such conditions."

After synagogue, Dr. Basswood would return home, typically arriving at 1 PM. Grace would have a large lunch prepared for the two of them. Henry would inevitably interrupt the peace of the Sabbath by describing to Grace the numerous factual and logical flaws contained in the rabbi's sermon.

"Grace, do not let that man give the eulogy at my funeral. I would rather there be a bagpipe played or automobile horns blown than have my few friends be subjected to the irritating sounds that come from that fool's mouth."

Exasperated, Grace would typically reply, "Henry, I want you to carefully climb down from the worn-out saddle on that high horse you are riding. You might be wrong, Dr. Basswood. I do not know enough to have an informed judgment about anything you are lecturing about. The rabbi is not here to defend himself and challenge your arguments. I cannot make any sense of most of what you are saying, either. So, give me some peace on this *Shabbos*. Talk about something noncontroversial, like Hitler and the Nazis or Emperor Hirohito and his samurai monkeys!"

Henry would then submissively smile at Grace's invective and confess to maybe having been a little harsh in his assessment of the rabbi. After lunch, "The Bickersons"—as they affectionately called themselves—would walk up North Broadway to visit the 10.5 foot tall, 2,000 pound Carrara Marble statue of *Christ the Consolator* standing with outstretched arms under the dome of the Johns Hopkins Hospital Administration Building.

"Well, he is still here!" Henry would say, shaking his head.

And Grace, recalling all the abuse she endured as a Jew growing up in Hagerstown, Maryland, would reply, "Maybe Baltimore will have an earthquake this week!"

The two would then turn their backs on Christ and walk home to 14 South Broadway, where they would take a nap together. After sunset, their friends, mostly Jewish physicians practicing at Johns Hopkins Hospital, would meet at the Basswoods's home to gossip and listen to *War News, Lowell Thomas, Amos and Andy*, and *Evening Music Melodies* on the radio while drinking tea through sugar cubes held between their front teeth and eating pastries. The night would end with the doctors extinguishing their cigarettes or cigars in a sculpture of an erect three-inch circumcised penis with Hitler's face making up its glans, corona, and frenulum. A short shaft descended from Hitler's head into an ashtray consisting of two scrotal indentations at its base. Dr. Basswood, a self-taught sculptor, created the masterpiece after Hitler became German Chancellor in 1933.

At 6 AM on Saturday, November 11, 1939, BCPD Lieutenant Gareth Messenger met Martin in front of 14 South Broadway. Gareth patted him on the back and said, "My boss wants you to meet Sergeant Alexander Ioffe of the Maryland State Police. The deal is that Alex decides whether you get a permit to carry a pistol in Maryland or not. Ioffe is the one lawman that everyone who matters in this state trusts. The governor, the mayor of Baltimore, the Speaker of Maryland's House of Delegates, the Maryland State Senate president, judges, and every man who wears a badge and carries a gun revere this Jewish refugee from Ukraine. Have you ever met Alexander Ioffe?"

Martin shook his head "no." "I have heard some of the legends about him from my boxing coach at the YMHA, but I have never met him. The coach told me that Ioffe was the youngest of a dozen children and that his family immigrated from Odessa to Baltimore after the Kishinev Massacre in 1903."

Messenger exclaimed, "Odessa? The WHAT massacre?"

Patiently, Martin explained to Gareth. "Odessa is a city in Ukraine which was once a part of Tsarist Russia. Today, the Soviet Union controls Odessa and Ukraine. Kishinev is a tiny town in Bessarabia, which too was once a part of Tsarist Russia and is now a part of the Soviet Union. Kishinev is about 100 miles from Odessa. In 1903, a *pogrom*—an anti-Jewish riot—killed some four dozen Jews in Kishinev. Hundreds of Jewish women were raped. It was a real horror show. In any event, this violence motivated many Jews from the region encompassing Kishinev and Odessa (as well as other parts of Tsarist Russia) to come to America. My boxing coach said Ioffe is so incredibly tough because he came from that blood-soaked region."

Gareth cautioned Martin, "Look, do not offend this guy. I have never met him either. He is just another one of those tough-guy lawmen the public, the papers, and the politicians thrive on. You and I have a mission requiring that you be armed. Focus on the mission and not Jewish history, OK? Ioffe just needs to observe firsthand that you know how to use a pistol safely, responsibly, and accurately."

"I have got it, Gareth. I can handle this."

Gareth said, "Good. I will drive us to the Pikesville Armory where we will meet Ioffe at 7 AM. It is entirely his show from then on."

"Got it," replied Martin.

Although a mere 5 feet, 6 inches in height, Sergeant Alexander Ioffe exuded an unusual mixture of bonhomie and intimidation. Dressed in a freshly pressed Maryland State Police khaki uniform with three orange stripes above the elbow on each sleeve, a shiny black leather Sam Browne belt around his waist and shoulder, and a gold badge over his heart, Ioffe stood akimbo in the armory driveway. Sporting a street fighter smirk, the Maryland State Police Sergeant barked, "Which one of you two is Martin Victor?"

Raising his right hand, Martin simply said, "I am."

"So, Victor, what kind of handgun do you prefer?" I have an M1911A1 Colt, a Colt Shooting Master .38 Special, a 3.5-inch barrel Smith & Wesson .357 Magnum, a—"

Martin interrupted Ioffe's shopping list and said, "The Smith & Wesson .357 Magnum will suit me just fine."

Ioffe smiled knowingly like James Cagney's character "Brick" Davis in the movie "G-Men." "I figured you would select the revolver you had been using at the FBI Academy for the past couple of months. Wise choice, Victor. Do me a favor, fella—use only .38 Special ammunition, not .357 Magnum rounds, inside the City of Baltimore. If, God forbid, you must shoot someone in Baltimore, I want you to plug that specific someone and not a few additional innocent people standing behind the guy farther down the street. Magnum bullets, as opposed to .38 Specials, have a nasty habit of going through a criminal and causing collateral damage, particularly in a dense urban environment. Out in the country, I do not mind if you load .357's, but in the City of Baltimore, put good old .38 Specials in the cylinder. OK?"

"Roger that, Sergeant Ioffe!" replied Martin.

"You Navy guys crack me up. 'Roger that!' Victor, did you really become a member of the FBI Possible Club?"

"Yes, I did, Sergeant Ioffe. I have a certificate signed by J. Edgar Hoover and a Possible Club membership card attesting to that fact," said Martin proudly.

"Martin, you can call me Alex from now on. Let's go inside the armory. I want to see what you got."

After Martin fired fifty-four rounds of rapid-fire bullseyes at targets that Alex placed 25 feet downrange, Sergeant Ioffe announced, "Martin, it's a real pleasure to have a member of 'The Tribe' on the team fighting these Nazi and Jap bastards." Handing Martin the pistol carry permit that he had prepared prior to the qualification session, Alex said, "If I can be of any assistance to you, here is my State Police phone number, my home phone number, and my home address off Park Heights Avenue, near Pimlico Race Course. I hope to see you again soon, *boychik*."

The two men shook hands and Ioffe joked to Martin, "Eight more and we will have a *minyan*!"

Martin responded, "*Baruch Hashem*, Alex!" Both men laughed together. Gareth appeared dumbfounded.

As they walked to Gareth's automobile, Messenger said, "Marty, what is it with you Jews? You and Ioffe do not know each other. You have never met before. Yet Ioffe sized you up accurately in an instant and treated you like a brother."

Martin explained, "Gareth, you remember what I told you about Kishinev? Alex and I have that in common. You know, when people call me a 'kike' behind my back? Alex and I have that in common. And do you remember how you felt when the *Hindenburg* dirigible airship exploded in New Jersey in May of 1937?"

Gareth answered, "I felt bad when I heard the live radio broadcast of the event. The photographs of all those people burning to death as the *Hindenburg* went down sickened me."

"Well, Gareth, both Alex and I felt like dancing in the street when those Nazis got incinerated and their swastika-emblazoned balloon burned to ashes on the tarmac at Lakehurst, New Jersey. Alex and I have that in common, too. The hatred much of the world harbors toward Jews binds Alex and me together as tightly as protons, neutrons, and electrons in an atom."

Gareth ran his hand through his hair and said, "Martin, you Jews are crazy!"

"Yes, we are, Gareth. Yes, we are. Would you mind stopping by Mateuz Piwnik's gun shop?"

Gareth lit up at the thought of visiting his friend Mateuz, one of the few true weapons experts in Maryland. "Next stop, 218 South Broadway!"

A sign with the image of a large blue and white revolver and the words "Baltimore Gunsmith Co." in bright red letters underneath hung high over the entrance to Mr. Piwnik's store.

"Welcome, Gareth," said Mateuz. "Who is your friend?"

"We work together, Mr. Piwnik. Martin is OK!" replied Gareth.

"If Martin is OK with you, then he is OK with me! Is Martin OK with anyone else, Gareth?"

"Yes. He is OK with Sergeant Alexander Ioffe too!" answered Gareth.

"So this Martin is one hundred percent OK," concluded Mateuz.

"Yes, he is. One hundred percent OK. He is even OK with the G-men in the Court Square Building," added Gareth.

"So this Martin is Revolver Royalty, is he not?" Piwnik asked proudly.

"You are correct, Mr. Piwnik. Martin is most definitely Revolver Royalty. He is a member of Mr. Hoover's Possible Club."

"So this Martin friend of yours is the Crown Prince of Revolvers!"

"Precisely." Gareth beamed.

Turning to Martin, Mr. Piwnik asked, "Crown Prince Martin, what can I do for you today?"

Martin started to say "Mr. Piw—"

Mateuz interrupted and said, "Crown Prince Martin, please call me Mateuz."

"Mateuz, I would like to purchase a Smith & Wesson .357 Magnum with a 3.5-inch barrel, a Jordan quick draw holster, one box of .38 Special ammunition, one box of .357 Magnum ammunition, and a cleaning kit for the weapon."

"And Crown Prince Martin, do you have a permit to carry this magnificent device?"

Martin handed Mateuz Piwnik his recently acquired permit signed by none other than Alexander Ioffe.

"Excellent. I will return momentarily," said Mateuz.

The gunsmith placed the Smith & Wesson box on the counter farthest from the front entrance to his shop. He opened the box and extracted Martin's blue metal beauty. "Try it, Crown Prince Martin," said Mateuz.

Martin opened the cylinder to verify that its six chambers were empty. He pointed the Magnum toward the back of the store and dry fired it.

"Crown Prince Martin, I sense that the trigger mechanism needs some refinement. Would you object to my working on your Smith & Wesson this afternoon? You may pick it up early this evening."

"You are the expert, Mateuz. Tell me what time would be best for you."

"I think 5 PM would be best, Crown Prince Martin," said the gunsmith. "May I show you the holster?"

"Yes," replied Martin. A few test draws confirmed that this rig worked well for the newly crowned Crown Prince of Revolvers.

"Mateuz, what do I owe you?"

"Crown Prince Martin, it is I who owe you for your service. Sixty dollars for everything."

Martin replied, "Mateuz, that is just the price of the pistol. Surely the price should be greater."

"Yes, it should be greater, but this is for you Crown Prince Martin," proclaimed the gunsmith.

"I am honored. Thank you, Mateuz. See you at 5 PM." The gunsmith nodded in the affirmative.

Gareth and Martin left the store. "Thank you, Gareth. Look at all we have accomplished and its just 11 AM. How would you like to be treated to a milkshake at Flaum's on Baltimore and Wolfe Streets?"

"I cannot say no to a free milkshake."

When the two counterintelligence agents entered the soda shop and stood at the counter, the owner called out, "*Maishe*! How the devil are you?"

"I am just fine. Meet my good friend, Baltimore City Police Department Lieutenant Gareth Messenger."

"Lieutenant Messenger, your friend made the finest milkshakes and ice cream sodas ever produced in this shop. I miss him! Now what can I do for you?"

Gareth replied, "I would really appreciate your permitting *Maishe* to make vanilla milkshakes for the three of us. Treat is on me!"

The soda shop owner responded, "You have a deal, Lieutenant Messenger!"

Martin walked behind the counter, donning an apron and a white cap with a flourish. After scrubbing his hands like a surgeon, Martin whipped up the best tasting vanilla milkshake Gareth had ever tasted. "*Maishe*, you have talent!" pronounced Gareth. The three men toasted each other. Gareth paid, but left no tip!

"See you at the train station early Tuesday morning, *Maishe*," joked Gareth. "What does *Maishe* mean, Martin?"

"It means *Moses* or *Moshe*. It is my Hebrew name, Gareth. It's like an endearing nickname."

"I will never understand you people, pal," answered Gareth.

And off both agents went with plenty of daylight left in Baltimore. Martin met Gertrude at the Baltimore Municipal Airport in Dundalk where they watched a massive Pan Am transoceanic seaplane take off for London. "I would not want to get near Europe right now. Would you, Martin?"

"I am perfectly happy here in Dundalk with you, Gert," replied Martin as he held her near. The two walked to the bus stop and went to the Stanley Theatre on Howard Street to see *Jamaica Inn*, a new Alfred Hitchcock film starring Charles Laughton and Maureen O'Hara. The despicable criminal conduct of Charles Laughton's character, Sir Humphrey Pengallan, infuriated Gertrude. Despite the well-deserved death of Pengallan at the conclusion of the film, Gertrude continued to rail that evildoers should be executed publicly so that decent people and victims of horrible crimes can see that there is justice and retribution in the world.

Martin knew better than to attempt to reason with Gertrude regarding matters where she perceived individuals were "clearly" wrong and "clearly" guilty of committing a "clearly" serious crime. *She is one tough, but adorable nut*, he would sometimes think. Other times he would shudder at her inability to appreciate the Bill of Rights, the presumption of innocence, and the rules of criminal procedure. *God help any innocent defendant if Gert is on the jury deciding his case. There is no "beyond a reasonable doubt" standard for her. If you are accused, she thinks you must be guilty.*

But that was Gertrude Kowalska—a strong, opinionated, passionate, straightforward woman with no guile. And Martin loved her for it.

After enjoying the movie, they each ate a hamburger at a restaurant near the theater. Martin looked at his watch and realized that he had 15 minutes to get to Mateuz's gun shop.

"Gert, I have to meet a man about a business matter this evening at 5 PM. It is important that I arrive on time. I know that you have family obligations on Sunday, so we will get together Monday evening. I will pick you up at Sun Radio at 5:30, OK?"

Gertrude replied, "Of course it is OK, Martin. I understand that you must do what you must do. However, you must understand that I feel good only when I am with you. I have surrendered my heart to you. Never forget this. For me, there is only you. Never take this love of mine for granted."

Gertrude's candor about her feelings for Martin consistently overwhelmed him. In the Victor family, expressions of affection, love, passion, and tenderness did not occur often, if at all. Martin kissed Gert and the two went their separate ways—Gertrude to her parents' house in Patterson Park and Martin to the Baltimore Gunsmith Co. on South Broadway.

At 5 PM sharp, Martin entered Mateuz's shop and was handed his .357 Magnum with its trigger action significantly improved. After checking the cylinder, Martin dry fired the weapon and smiled. The reduced pressure required to actuate the trigger increased the Smith & Wesson's rate of fire.

"Excellent work, Mateuz. Thank you."

"Crown Prince, please come and visit me whenever you have the time."

"Will do, Mateuz," answered Martin. He walked up the street to 14 South Broadway, climbed three flights of stairs, unlocked the door to his apartment, and hid the weapon, ammunition, cleaning equipment, and holster in a locked desk drawer. While not foolproof, this method of securing the pistol would have to do for now. Most of the time he would be carrying the revolver, and practically no one ever climbed the stairs up to his third-floor apartment.

Martin then stripped to his shorts, shadowboxed in front of the mirror for 20 minutes, took a bath, and thought about Gertrude. He could hear the revelers below in Henry and Grace's apartment. Filled with energy, Martin dressed, walked down the stairs, and took a long, soul-searching walk. By the time he returned, the cigars and cigarettes had been extinguished in Henry Basswood's sculpture and the partygoers gone. All was silent. Martin walked up the three flights of stairs. He knew what he had to do. He then fell soundly asleep.

SUNDAY, NOVEMBER 12, 1939; 14 SOUTH BROADWAY, BALTIMORE

After their cup of coffee together at 6 AM, Henry said to Martin, "Let's take a walk to Thames Street and see what public health threats the tides have brought into the harbor."

"You are the expert in such matters," replied Martin.

The streets were vacant. It was a good time to talk. Henry spoke first. "Martin, let me provide you with a few details regarding this Jap's syphilis. When he first came to my office, he had a chancre sore on his penis. This indicated to me that his infection was in the primary stage, that is, within twenty-one days of contact with a syphilitic. I drew fluid from the chancre, examined some of the fluid with a dark field microscope, and observed corkscrew-shaped *Treponema pallidum*, the bacteria causing syphilis. Your Captain Masuji told me that this was the first time he had been infected with any venereal disease. Based upon my examination of him, I saw no evidence to conclude otherwise. He agreed to undergo ten weekly intravenous treatments with Compound 914—Neosalvarsan—in combination with injections of small doses of bismuth. At the time he told me that his ship was undergoing some repairs and would not depart the Port of Baltimore until December 11th. Masuji had his fifth injection in my office at 7 AM on Sunday, November 5th. Beginning with his second treatment, I have tested his Wasserman reaction before administering the Neosalvarsan and bismuth and it has remained consistently negative. While this serological test has no value as proof of infectiousness, given that his infection was in the primary stage and was being treated promptly, Masuji himself is likely not infectious at the present time. Of course, current medical science indicates that eighteen months of continuous treatment are required to be confident of a cure of syphilis. In any event, Masuji's tenth injection and final treatment will be administered by me in my office at 7 AM on Sunday, December 10th. To date, Masuji has tolerated the treatment well and experienced no headaches, dizziness, vomiting, insomnia, skin rashes, or fever."

Martin inquired, "Did Masuji indicate to you who infected him?"

Henry replied, "He clearly lied to me on this point. Masuji said that prior to his merchant vessel arriving in Baltimore, the ship had docked in New York to collect scrap metal. He admitted to frequenting a few bordellos during the week or so that he spent in New York, and had no idea which prostitute infected him. In consideration of the new information you have provided to me regarding his authentic identity, someone likely infected him with syphilis in Washington, DC. That individual may not be receiving treatment and infecting additional individuals. If possible, you ought to find out who transmitted the bacteria to Masuji and verify that he or she is getting proper treatment at the present time."

Martin agreed to pass this information and recommendation up his chain of command. "Henry, continue to treat Masuji and let me know whether he reschedules any future appointments."

Dr. Basswood replied, "I will do so. I trust that this information is useful."

Martin replied, "More than I can tell you, Henry. Just keep your relationship with him on track. Now, let's walk back to 14 South Broadway so I can relate the substance of our discussion to my commanding officer. After I have accomplished this task, I will have an unrelated sensitive question to ask you."

"Ask away when you are ready, Martin," replied Henry.

A SUNDAY MORNING CALL TO CAPTAIN MCLAUGHLIN

Lieutenant JG Martin Victor dialed Captain McLaughlin through the ONI emergency contact switchboard at 7:15 AM. An irritated Charles McLaughlin returned the call to Martin ten minutes later. "Victor, do you know any Latin?"

"Yes, Sir, Captain McLaughlin," replied Martin.

"Then you know what *coitus interruptus* means?" growled the Captain.

"Yes, Sir, Captain McLaughlin," replied Martin.

"Then you know whatever you are calling me about had better be vital to our nation's security!" barked McLaughlin as he looked lasciviously at a naked Catharine lying on top of his bed, shaking her head and smiling at him. The sunlight through the window of his bedroom illuminated her magnificent right breast's areola and nipple.

My God, what a woman! he thought as he heard Martin say, "Sir, I just completed interviewing Dr. Basswood and have obtained actionable information concerning Sicinnus."

"You mean Masuji, Victor?"

"Yes, Sir," replied Victor.

"Well, go on then, Lieutenant," replied a less angry McLaughlin.

Martin related all of Dr. Basswood's medical details about Masuji to the Captain.

"Thank you, Victor. I will contact Walker and arrange a full complement of agents to cover our Japanese friend. Do you think the good doctor would permit us to install a hook switch bypass and turn his office telephone into a bugging device?" inquired McLaughlin.

"As long as the device is removed after Masuji departs, I think Henry will go along with it."

McLaughlin: "OK. Make the deal with the doctor and one of the Baltimore FBI agents will stop by to install the thing. Martin, sleep somewhere other than in Dr. Basswood's house tonight. I do not want any screwups with Sicinnus on Monday."

Martin: "Got it. Please ask Special Agent Walker to arrange for one of the Baltimore FBI office agents to pick me up in a radio-equipped car at 3454 Auchentroly Terrace well in advance of the syphilitic's arrival at 14 South Broadway on Monday morning."

"Any other orders for me, Lieutenant?" snarled McLaughlin.

"Sir, I said 'Please,'" quipped Martin.

"You are a regular officer and a gentleman, Victor!" came McLaughlin's retort. "Write up your report of your conversation with Dr. Basswood and submit it immediately."

"Yes, Sir, Captain."

McLaughlin concluded, "I will ask Walker to get your partner Detective Lieutenant Messenger in on the Monday morning show at Dr. Basswood's office."

"Excellent," replied Martin.

And that was that.

MARTIN VICTOR'S OFFICIAL AND UNOFFICIAL CONVERSATION WITH DR. BASSWOOD

Martin rejoined Dr. Basswood in his office. "Henry, my commanding officer thanks you for your assistance. We have one additional favor to ask of you. Would you mind if we temporarily install a device that will allow us to listen to Captain Masuji's conversation with you in your office tomorrow? The device will be removed shortly after he leaves your office."

Henry rubbed his forehead with the thumb and forefinger of his right hand for two seconds while he thought, *Masuji poses a threat to anyone with whom he comes into contact. He has to be stopped.* Dr. Basswood replied, "Martin, I will permit this narrowly restricted intrusion to assist you and the government in bringing down this Japanese spy."

"Good," said Martin. "I will spend tonight at my brother's place to avoid an inadvertent meeting with Masuji."

Martin then proceeded to execute the plan he devised during his walk the night before. "Henry, as I mentioned before, I have an unrelated question to discuss with you."

Dr. Basswood wondered what could possibly be next on his spy "son's" Sunday surprise list. "Go on, Martin."

"Henry, I want to propose marriage to a woman not of our faith, but on the condition that she converts to Judaism before our wedding. Her family will likely disown her, but I believe she is prepared to endure the loss. Which rabbi in Baltimore do you think would assist us in the conversion process so that she will embrace our faith fully, respectfully, and joyfully?"

Totally taken aback, Henry fired off difficult questions at Martin. "Is this woman pregnant?"

"No, Henry. We have not even had intimate relations."

"How long have you known this woman?"

"Two years. I first met her when I purchased some shortwave radio equipment at the store where she works. I then saw her at Carlin's Park, asked her to dance, and we have been dating surreptitiously since then."

"Why marry now? Look at the perilous business in which you are involved. Anything could happen to you. Also, the US will soon be involved in a war. You will certainly serve and see combat. Whether you will survive is not that certain. Don't you think that now might not be the best time to embark on marriage and potentially have children?"

"Henry, you have just stated some of the reasons why I think that now IS the time for us to get married. I love this woman. I want to have a family. I want to defend not just my nation, but also my wife and my children. How can I permit the threat of a Hitler or Hirohito to prevent the establishment of another Jewish family?"

Henry, a decisive surgeon accustomed to making difficult decisions under pressure, determined that his renter was right. "Well, Martin, there is only one rabbi in Baltimore for the job—Rabbi Meir Elkanan. He is a *Litvak* scholar who does not say stupid things in Hebrew, Yiddish, German, Lithuanian, Russian, French, or even in English. He loves America. He is an ardent Zionist. He has never married. He has devoted his life to the Jewish people. He can even carry a tune. If this woman agrees to your terms and conditions, Grace and I will introduce you both to Meir. If this woman's family tosses her out into the street, we have an apartment for her here. One final point: You must promise not to engage in sexual relations with her in this house before you are married, Martin."

Martin heard Henry's caveat forbidding premarital sex at 14 South Broadway and realized that the urological surgeon had issued a license for Gertrude and him to consummate their relationship anywhere else. Martin replied, "Henry, thank you. You have my word that we will conduct ourselves strictly in accord with your condition."

Dr. Basswood put his hand on Martin's shoulder and said, "This has been quite an invigorating morning, don't you think?"

Martin responded, "And it is not yet over, Henry. A technician will arrive before lunch to install the device we discussed. Please remember, Grace can know nothing of this Masuji business."

"Martin, if this conversion and marriage business develops, Grace will have many other things on her mind. Your woman will get a PhD in Judaism from Grace, as well as a PhD from Rabbi Elkanan. Poor girl."

At 11 AM, an agent from the Baltimore FBI office called Martin and advised him that he would arrive at 11:30 AM with the device. Henry and Martin greeted him in front of Henry's office, and by noon, the agent had installed the hook switch bypass. Before departing, the FBI agent said to Martin, "I will pick you up at 3454 Auchentroly Terrace at 5 AM. I drive a dark blue Chevrolet sedan, Maryland license plate number 414-967. See you in the morning."

And that was that.

Lunch was uneventful, except for Grace asking who came to the office at 11:30 AM on a Sunday morning.

"One of Martin's new associates, Grace. Martin is bringing us a new class of patient."

"You mean decent people without venereal disease, Henry?" Grace said, frowning.

"Precisely that, dear," Henry replied, smiling.

Martin thought to himself, *Ah, The Bickersons!*

After lunch and a walk with the Basswoods, Martin called his brother and asked if he could spend the night.

"The Basswoods throw you out?" Milton asked.

"No, Milton. For reasons we will not get into, I need to spend Sunday night with you, my dear brother."

Milton: "So they did throw you out. Should I evict my tenants in the apartment downstairs?"

Martin: "No, let your tenants remain for the time being. Are they tenants at will?"

Milton: "With a ne'er-do-well brother like you, of course they are tenants at will! I never know when I will have to bail you out. I am prepared at all times to protect you. Will you need a lift to work on Monday morning?"

Martin: "Nope. A colleague will be picking me up at 5 AM. Thank you for your generous offer, however."

Milton: "Isn't that a little early for you? You need your beauty rest!"

Martin: "I will go to bed early to preserve my good looks, Milton."

Milton: "Always thinking about yourself, Martin. I thought we would stay up and converse with each other."

"I never liked those kinds of tennis shoes, Milt," Martin quipped.

Milton: "You are a goof. You know that, Martin?"

Martin: "Runs in the family, I think!"

Milton: "Enough of this banter. When will you be arriving?"

Martin: "I will catch a bus and be at your place by 5 PM."

Milton: "No, I will come and get you."

Martin: "You would do that for me?"

Milton: "No, I am doing it to annoy Grace Basswood. You know how much I irritate her."

Martin: "And you call me a goof!"

Milton laughed. "You got me there, Martin. See you soon."

Martin kept his promise to Sergeant Ioffe and loaded his revolver with six rounds of .38 SPL ammunition, not .357 Magnums. He then threaded onto the belt holding up his suit trousers a leather strip with six loops. Into each loop Martin inserted one round of .38 SPL ammo. Then he tossed a final six rounds in his right front pants pocket. Martin inserted the revolver in his new holster and put on his suit jacket. He practiced quick draw techniques in front of the full-length mirror affixed to his apartment's closet door. Brushing his suit jacket back and crouching ever so slightly, he produced the weapon quickly, smoothly, and parallel to the ground. *Let 'em come!* he thought. *I will shoot their hearts out.*

Lastly, Martin put a change of underwear and socks, as well as his Dopp kit, in an overnight bag. He was ready to go.

Milton parked his DeSoto perpendicular to the sidewalk in front of 14 South Broadway. He laughed to himself as he rang the doorbell and imagined how disappointed Grace Basswood would be to see him. Milton was right. Grace opened the door, made eye contact, frowned deeply, and executed an about-face. "Martin is upstairs."

"Nice seeing you, Grace!" Milton replied.

Milton walked two stairs at a time to the third floor and tapped on his brother's door. Martin opened the door and Milton observed the bulge on the lower right side of his brother's suit jacket.

"Are you licensed to carry that cannon, Martin?" he asked.

"You want to see my permit, Milton?"

"Yes. I am not going to transport a potential felon in my DeSoto," Milton said seriously.

Martin produced the permit. Milton read it carefully and shrugged his shoulders. "What is this world coming to?" He sighed.

The two brothers walked down the stairs and drove to Druid Hill Park. As they drove, Martin asked, "You ever hear of a Rabbi Meir Elkanan?"

"Yes. He officiates at a synagogue near Eutaw Place. I have heard a few of the eulogies he has delivered. Elkanan appears to be a thoughtful fellow. But that is all I know about him. Why do you ask?"

Martin then related his conversion conversation with Dr. Basswood to Milton. "Martin, I thought I told you NOT to discuss such matters with the Basswoods," growled Milton.

"I took the initiative, and Henry was very supportive," replied Martin.

A frustrated Milton explained to his younger brother, "But what about Grace? If she disapproves, you will be out on the street in no time! Henry will not stand up to her in your defense, I can assure you of that!"

"Stop worrying, brother. It will all work out," Martin asserted confidently.

"Sure, Martin. Everything will work out just fine! You are carrying a loaded weapon to work. You can't sleep in your own apartment on a Sunday night. You are planning to marry someone who will be cast out of her hateful family and community for simply dating you. You are first in line to go to war with the murderous Nazis and Japs. Everything is just fine, fella!"

"Like I said, Milton—nothing here that we cannot handle!" Martin said with an insouciant grin.

Milton terminated the conversation by saying, "God help me, Martin."

14

5 AM MONDAY, NOVEMBER 13, 1939; 3454 AUCHENTROLY TERRACE, BALTIMORE

FBI Agent Donald Foster stopped his radio-equipped company car in front of Milton Victor's two-apartment townhouse. Martin opened the right front passenger door and sat down. "Good morning, Agent Foster," Martin said perfunctorily.

"You too, Lieutenant Victor," said a jovial Foster. Trying to make conversation, Foster asked, "Agent Victor, is this really your first case?"

"Yes. Does that bother you?" asked Martin.

"It should, but it does not. I am delighted to be doing something other than investigating bank robberies and Migratory Bird Act violations."

"I hear you," replied Martin. "What could be more satisfying than defending our country against espionage?"

Foster nodded his head. "Totally agree with you. Now, where do you want to roost while this Jap spy visits his dick doctor?"

"How about the loading dock in back of the Baltimore gunsmith shop at 218 South Broadway?"

"OK. Do you think the store owner will mind?" asked Agent Foster.

"Nope. He and I are friends. I will introduce you to him."

Mateuz was entering the back door to his shop when Martin and Agent Foster drove into the parking area. "Greetings, Crown Prince!" Mateuz said as he waved at Martin. "Who is your *kolega?*"

Martin responded, "Mateuz, meet FBI Agent Donald Foster. Do you mind if we stay here for about 2.5 hours?"

Mateuz replied, "Of course not. Mr. Foster, would you like to come in and examine my merchandise? Crown Prince Martin has spent all of his money with me already. But you, Mr. Foster—I have not had the pleasure of doing business with you yet."

Foster followed Mateuz into the store. Martin stood by the car door and listened to the radio chatter. Everyone on the team appeared to be in place. Gareth was on the roof of the Cluster Theatre at 303 South Broadway with binoculars pointed toward the northwest branch of the Patapsco River. Stationed at the Broadway Market disguised as a porter, Hercules pretended to move crates of live chickens. Agent Zangara, dressed as a merchant sailor, positioned himself at the Norwegian Seamen's Church across the street from Dr. Basswood's office. Agent Murphy, parked in an alley near Baltimore Street and South Broadway, waited while his passenger, Agent Walker, purchased cigarettes and coffee from the drugstore on the southwest corner of the intersection.

Captain Masuji, dressed as a simple Japanese merchant seaman, casually walked north on South Broadway, scanning the area for anything appearing out of the ordinary. All seemed in order as he rang the bell at 14 South Broadway. Dr. Basswood ushered his patient into the examination and procedure room adjacent to his office. There Henry drew blood to test for a Wasserman reaction. Next, Henry had Masuji lie on his back and he carefully administered the "wonder drugs" bismuth and Neosalvarsan into his patient. By 8 AM, the treatment had been completed. Soon thereafter, the Japanese spy entered the part of the office where Dr. Basswood took patients' medical histories to confirm his next appointment scheduled for Sunday, November 19, at 6:30 AM.

Benkei sat facing Henry and said, "Dr. Basswood, thank you again for seeing me so early in the morning. I do not wish to have my shipmates become aware of this personal embarrassment. They assume that I am taking a morning constitutional, as few local enterprises are selling their goods and services at this hour. Again, thank you."

Dr. Basswood replied, "Mr. Ijuin, my profession demands that I do all I can to restore my patients back to health. If I can minimize your embarrassment and promote your willingness to receive treatment for your condition by seeing you early in the morning, then so be it. How are you feeling right now?"

"I feel quite good, Doctor."

"Are you experiencing any dizziness?"

"No, Doctor."

"Any nausea or stomach upset?"

"No, Doctor."

"Have you had any difficulty sleeping?"

"No, Doctor."

"Have you developed any skin rashes since I last saw you?"

"No, Doctor."

"Any bouts of fever?"

"No, Doctor."

"Mr. Ijuin, I am delighted at the way in which you have tolerated these treatments. I again caution you to avoid sexual contact with other individuals."

"I understand, Doctor, and I will comply with your instructions," replied Masuji, feigning contrition.

"Very good. I will see you this coming Sunday at 6:30 AM."

Captain Masuji exited 14 South Broadway and walked north three blocks to Orleans Street, where he hailed a taxi and requested the driver to take him to Pennsylvania Station. He boarded the first train to the District of Columbia.

And that was that.

10 AM SICINNUS TEAM MEETING, FBI OFFICE, COURT HOUSE SQUARE, BALTIMORE

As soon as Agent Foster and Martin received the all-clear message from Walker over their car radio, they paid a visit to Dr. Basswood. While Foster removed the hook switch bypass device from Dr. Basswood's office, Martin debriefed Henry.

"He acted exactly the way he always has since I first met him. The only difference in today's conversation was his use of the word 'embarrassment.' Previously Masuji said only that he wanted to keep this matter private. Also, I intentionally left a *Baltimore Sun* in plain view for him to see. The article should have inflamed him, as it was all about *Generalissimo* Chiang Kai Shek announcing that Japan was losing the war and how foolish Japanese leaders were. However, Masuji said nothing to me about the article."

Martin cautioned Henry, "We appreciate your effort to get Masuji to talk; however, keep your dealings with him just the way they have been all along. Any deviation from the established routine might set off a warning buzzer in his mind. He knows his business well and is sensitive to breaks in established patterns."

Henry vowed to Martin that he would not freelance again. Foster and Martin then headed to the meeting in the FBI office downtown. As they entered the Court Square Building lobby, Martin saw Gareth waiting for the elevator.

"How was your morning, Gareth?" Martin asked.

"Let's just say that Mrs. Messenger, who has been missing me terribly for the past eight weeks, was not at all happy to have me leave her side at 4 AM.

One day you are going to have to apologize to Brigid for this inconvenience, Martin."

"If it will make your life easier, Gareth, I will gladly do it!" replied Martin.

Inside the office conference room, Agent Walker briefly introduced Martin, Gareth, and Agent Foster to Hercules and Al Zangara. "Baltimore City Police Detective Lieutenant Gareth Messenger and US Navy Lieutenant JG Martin Victor are the two new members of our task force. Along with Agent Murphy, Gareth and Martin distinguished themselves as the top team at the Counterintelligence Academy the FBI runs at Quantico. Agent Donald Foster has been detailed to assist us in any actions limited geographically to the City of Baltimore."

Following this introduction, Martin disclosed Dr. Basswood's observation regarding Masuji's novel use of the word "embarrassment," and Walker, Hercules, Murphy, Messenger, and Zangara agreed that this might indicate that Masuji had an exploitable vulnerability. Walker added, "We have had eyes on Masuji each time he visits Baltimore. He travels from DC to Baltimore alone. He spends the night before each of his appointments with Dr. Basswood aboard a Japanese merchant vessel docked in Baltimore harbor. He does not leave the ship until the morning of each appointment. Without any backup, Masuji walks by himself to 14 South Broadway, taking a circuitous route from the Japanese vessel to Basswood's office, presumably to detect any surveillance. After each appointment, he takes a taxi to Penn Station, purchases a *Baltimore Sun* newspaper, and boards a train back to DC. He sits alone on the train reading his copy of *The Baltimore Sun* and returns to his apartment at Alban Towers to shower and to change his clothes. Masuji then goes back to the Japanese embassy to work. Based on these observations and information obtained from other technical sources, no one at the embassy appears to have any idea about Captain Saigo Masuji's medical issue, or his weekly jaunts to Baltimore to visit Dr. Basswood. Clearly, he wants this part of his life in America 'off the books.'"

Hercules spoke up. "Masuji is not a complete loner. We need to find out who infected Masuji. He did not get venereal disease from sitting on a toilet seat at the Japanese embassy. Maybe he got dosed while seducing someone in our government who has access to sensitive, defense-related information. Perhaps he targeted a naïve infected secretary working for an executive in a defense company in order to get access to secret weapons program information from her. My point is that there may be a piece of this conspiracy puzzle that we have missed."

Walker decided to think out loud. "Hercules, I agree with you. Based upon the medical evidence we have collected so far, Masuji contracted syphilis from somebody twenty-one days or so before he first visited Dr. Basswood. Your hunch is worth pursuing. Martin, after our 10 AM meeting tomorrow, review all of the Navy's observations of Masuji for the entire month of September, through October 4th. Captain McLaughlin indicated to us previously that he encounters our diseased Jap spy at various DC social engagements. Perhaps he recalls a woman or a man who seemed physically attracted to Masuji, or vice versa. Murphy, look through our FBI surveillance library on old syphilitic Saigo, please. See if anything intimate pops up. Messenger, you can assist Murphy."

Walker continued. "Oh, Gareth and Martin, from Tuesday through Friday you get to room together, at government expense, in a quaint little hotel near the Department of Justice Building. You can even expense your meals. You cannot, however, charge any booze you consume to Uncle Sam. It will be just like old times for you two. Murphy, since you are a graduate of Calvert Hall and have seniority, you get to room alone. OK, except for Zangara and Hercules, you are all dismissed."

Walker closed the conference room door. "Zangara, without exposing your Confidential Informant to any undue risk, see if she has any idea who Masuji dates or has as a dance partner. Hercules, provide whatever backup Alphonse needs to protect his CI. I am going to call McLaughlin and get him ready for Martin's request tomorrow to access ONI intel files on Masuji's social escapades."

AGENT WILLIAM MURPHY FINDS A PHOTO

Murphy searched through the FBI's files on Captain Masuji. The transcripts of his office and apartment telephone conversations provided no hint of his having an intimate relationship with anyone. The same was true of his mail and cable traffic. The Captain appeared to be succinct and formal in his communications. Continuing his search through the Masuji files, Murph opened a file folder containing an 8 x 11.5-inch envelope labeled "August 24, 1939, Japanese embassy military and naval attachés dinner party—Carlton Hotel photographs." The envelope contained twelve 8 x 10-inch images of the party attendees posing at their elegantly prepared dining tables. In each photo, five men, mostly of Japanese origin, were standing directly behind a seated woman. Most of the women in the pictures were Japanese. The unsmiling Japanese men were standing at attention with their arms stiffly at their sides. The unsmiling Japanese women sat with perfect posture, hands folded on the table in front of them and staring blankly into the camera. However, in the photograph of Table No. 6, Murphy observed a smiling Captain Masuji, immaculately attired in his IJN uniform, standing behind an attractive Caucasian woman in a sleeveless black dress. Masuji's three-fingered hand rested on the young woman's shoulder. Leaning back in her chair, Masuji's "date" had bent the elbow of her arm and placed her hand provocatively on top of the Captain's claw.

"Well, what have we here?" said a satisfied Agent Murphy. He put on his suit jacket and took the photo down the hall to the office of Special Agent Walker.

"Murph, we have to identify this woman." Walker dialed Zangara and said tersely, "Come to my office. Bring Hercules with you." Walker showed the photograph to Alphonse and Hercules. "Murphy found this in our Masuji surveillance files. The photo was taken at the Carlton Hotel on August 24th, 1939. That woman looks awfully friendly to our Jap Captain, doesn't she?"

Hercules replied, "Yep. Problem for Saigo is she may be friendly to a whole lot of men a whole lot of the time!"

Zangara guffawed and Walker continued. "Either of you ever seen her before?" Hercules and Zangara shook their heads. "Well, gents, we have got to identify and locate this person." Walker looked at Alphonse and Hercules. "Any ideas how we find her?"

Zangara spoke first. "Well, based upon my limited knowledge of such women, I would go to the Carlton Hotel Bar tonight and see if this is where she does business…if you get my drift."

Hercules, not to be outdone, added, "Yeah, why don't we have Murph here take his candid photo and go to the Carlton Hotel Bar? He might just see her and find out more about her and her clients."

Murphy ended the conversation. "I think I am going to go have a drink and dinner tonight by myself at the Carlton Hotel. I will report my findings to you tomorrow. Thank you for your attention, insights, and direction."

With that, Murph returned to his office, got his coat and hat, and walked to the Carlton Hotel at 923 16th Street, NW, just two blocks north of the White House. Built in 1926 by Washington, DC, developer Harry Wardman, the Carlton's beautifully executed beaux arts architecture pleased even the dour Agent Murphy.

Sitting down at the bar, Murph ordered a scotch on the rocks from a portly, red-faced bartender with a waxed handlebar moustache. "Any particular brand of scotch, my good man?"

Murphy replied, "Johnnie Walker Red."

"On its way," responded the bartender. Delivering the drink, the bartender also delivered the benediction. "*Sláinte!* Alfred O'Reilly at you service, Sir." Murphy raised his glass toward Alfred and forced a smile. Upon completing his libation, O'Reilly inquired whether Murph desired another drink.

"No, Alfred. I need some dinner first."

"Would you prefer to have dinner at the bar, or at a table?"

"Here at the bar will be just fine."

Alfred produced a menu for Murphy. Skimming the document, the FBI agent ordered a steak, medium rare, and a hearts of lettuce salad with Russian dressing.

"On its way," replied O'Reilly. Analyzing the minimum number of words exchanged so far, Murphy concluded that the bartender was a man who observed a lot and said little, unless someone engaged him in conversation.

The perfectly prepared steak pleased Murphy. He preferred to eat alone. He preferred to do most things alone. Idle chatter irritated him. Ciara, Murphy's wife, understood her husband well and she scrupulously maintained a home environment designed to protect Murphy's need for solitude. She never invited people into their home when William was present. The radio remained off until William left the premises. Their three sons—all choir boys—kept quiet when he was home. William Jr., Seamus, and Liam knew not to have their school friends socialize at their house. Murphy loved his wife and children in his limited way. His family loved him too, despite his remoteness. They demonstrated their love by avoiding him as much as possible.

His plate clean, Alfred asked Murphy if he wanted coffee. O'Reilly could tell from Murphy's trim physique that this man did not eat dessert. "Mr. O'Reilly, black coffee, please."

"On its way," replied the bartender.

When the coffee arrived, Murphy asked, "Do you have a moment?"

This confirmed O'Reilly's hypothesis that he had been serving an FBI agent. "Delighted, mister…"

"Murphy," said William, discreetly showing Alfred his badge. Placing the photo on the counter, he asked, "Have you ever seen this person?"

O'Reilly nodded his head in the affirmative and replied, "That is Miss Elizabeth Robertson. She visits the hotel from time to time to attend parties hosted by foreign embassies. I have seen her recently at affairs sponsored by the Germans, Japanese, and even the Russians. She works at the State Department, don't you know! I have heard that she is a terrific golfer and has quite a reputation at both the Kenwood Golf and Country Club and the Beaver Dam Country Club."

Murphy removed the photo and said, "Thank you, Mr. O'Reilly. Have a good evening."

Agent Murphy returned to Special Agent Walker's office immediately and brought him the news. "Clarence, we have her name. We have her place of work. We know that she plays golf at courses frequented by Japanese and German diplomats. This is a potential new axis of Masuji espionage activity. I want to construct a more complete profile of Miss Elizabeth Robertson and present it to the team tomorrow."

Walker admonished Murphy. "It is 8 PM. Just how do you intend to construct such a detailed profile for tomorrow?"

"I know a person at the State Department who will assist us. She will be discreet, and no one over at State will know that she helped us. May I make the call?"

Walker looked up at the ceiling. "Sure, Murph. Get to it."

An hour later, Murphy's contact brought him Robertson's personnel folder. While his friend waited, he read the file and took notes. In one hour he had summarized the folder's contents. His contact returned to her office on the State Department's Far East Desk and returned the file to its precise location. No FBI or State Department log entries were created regarding the removal or replacement of Robertson's personnel file. No bureaucratic trail had been left. It was as if nothing had happened.

Murphy gleaned a lot from the file. An only child, Elizabeth Robertson grew up in Clay County, Tennessee. Both of her parents could trace their family trees back to the early families who settled in Tennessee after the French and Indian Wars. Her father was president of The Agrarian Bank of Tennessee. Her mother taught at a local elementary school. Elizabeth attended the women's high school branch of the prestigious Ward-Belmont School in Nashville favored by the aristocratic families of middle Tennessee. She graduated cum laude from Smith College in 1931 with a major in economics and a minor in East Asian history. Miss Robertson then spent two years studying Japanese language, culture, and history at Kyoto University. Her sterling academic record, understanding of global economics, passable proficiency in the Japanese language, and scintillating social skills made her a natural candidate for the Department of State. The fact that her father contributed significantly to the Democratic Party and that President Franklin D. Roosevelt's Secretary of State since 1933 also came from a famous Tennessee family did not count against her getting hired at the Department of State either. Elizabeth worked in the Economic Analysis section of the State Department that focused on relations with the Empire of Japan. Her personnel record appeared to be unblemished.

So much for the veracity of Department of State personnel folders, thought Murphy.

MONDAY, NOVEMBER 13; BALTIMORE, GERTRUDE MEETS MILTON VICTOR

After the meeting in the Baltimore FBI office, Martin returned to his apartment at 14 South Broadway, packed his suitcase for his upcoming excursion to DC, and prepared himself to introduce Gertrude to Milton. He showered and put on a fresh new white shirt to wear with the suit, tie, and shoes he had worn that day. Arriving at Sun Radio by taxi, he entered the store and waved his right hand at Shalom Cohen. Gertrude came out of the store washroom looking vibrant. No one looking at her would have guessed that she had worked a full day, skipping lunch so that she could leave a little early with Martin.

"See you tomorrow morning, Mr. Cohen," Gertrude said sweetly.

"Have a good evening, you two," Shalom replied enthusiastically.

The couple briefly walked hand-in-hand on Howard Street before hailing a cab and heading to Haussner's. Waiting for them in the rear of the restaurant sat Milton Victor, nursing a Manhattan.

Milton rose from the table, smiled broadly, greeted Gertrude with a handshake, and pulled a chair out for her to sit upon. "Miss Kowalska, you are every bit as lovely as Martin said you were. And, as you no doubt know, Martin exaggerates a lot."

Returning Milton's smile, Gertrude said, "Please call me Gertrude, Milton. Your brother led me to believe that you were a one-hundred-per-cent-serious lawyer who eats people alive in a courtroom. Instead, here you are a proper and polite gentleman."

Milton, still smiling, quipped, "As I said, Martin exaggerates a lot."

The three laughed and Milton asked, "What would you like to drink, Gertrude?"

"A lime daiquiri on the rocks, please."

Milton shook his head. "Just like my brother." He then ordered two daiquiris.

Milton commenced his jocular cross-examination. "What does an attractive woman like you see in Martin?"

Gertrude turned slightly, put her left hand on top of Milton's right hand, and replied, "Everything, Milton. I see my everything in your brother."

It took a lot to astound Milton Victor. But he had to admit that Gertrude Kowalska had managed to stun him…briefly. "Well, Gertrude, my brother is a lucky man. A very lucky man."

Martin sat in utter silence. The daiquiris were brought to the table. Milton raised his glass and said, "To Gertrude and Martin!"

Gertrude added, "*Na zdrowie!*", clinking her glass with Milton's and then Martin's.

Milton looked at his brother and repeated, "You are a lucky man, Martin. A very lucky man."

The dinner cemented a relationship that would endure forever.

9:45 AM, NOVEMBER 14, 1939; THE DEPARTMENT OF JUSTICE

Before the official Sicinnus Team assembled, Agent Walker advised Hercules and Zangara of Murphy's report concerning Captain Masuji's possible penetration of both Miss Robertson and the US State Department.

"Alphonse, in view of this change of circumstances, show the photo of Miss Robertson to your Japanese embassy CI. Perhaps Miss Hara has information about Masuji's 'professional' relationship with Robertson. I want to know what a member of one of Tennessee's First Families is giving Masuji, other than syphilis."

Zangara advised that he had a rendezvous with his CI scheduled for Sunday morning on November 19. Masuji would be receiving his seventh treatment from Dr. Basswood in Baltimore at that time. On the 18th of November, Hercules would commence tailing Hara to determine whether she was under surveillance by any Japanese agents. Hercules would continue this countersurveillance effort until Hara returned to her apartment on Sunday night.

Walker reminded Zangara to have the Baltimore FBI office alert him immediately if Junius Johnson boarded a bus to DC. "If Johnson's training mission is to follow Miss Hara, should we call off the meeting with her? Or should Johnson have an accident?" asked Hercules.

"In the unlikely event that Junius Johnson does tail our CI, call off the meeting. Let Johnson convince himself and others that Hara is not a security risk for Masuji," replied Walker. "Reschedule the get-together for as soon after Johnson leaves DC as possible."

At 10 AM, Gareth, Murphy, and Martin joined the meeting in Walker's office. Walker brought the team up-to-date on Miss Robertson, a new espionage suspect.

"Martin, call McLaughlin and see what you can find at ONI on Masuji and this Robertson woman. Your planning for the Bendix Industrial Security Review will have to begin tomorrow morning. Gareth, you and Murphy should continue mining our resources here for facts about Robertson. I am going to visit a friend who is a member of Kenwood Country Club and an avid golfer to get some more background detail on Elizabeth Robertson. Let's get together here at 6 PM to review our respective findings."

Martin called McLaughlin's office and was ordered to see the Captain at 11 AM.

"I heard about this State Department woman from Walker," the crusty Captain announced to his subordinate. "I have never heard of her." Martin then showed McLaughlin a copy of Elizabeth Robertson's photo. The Captain examined it closely. "I have never seen her." Pointing to two boxes filled with files sitting atop a table in his office, McLaughlin informed Martin, "Everything ONI has on Masuji is in those boxes. Go through them and see if there is any link to Robertson."

"Yes, Sir." Martin had learned to enjoy reading chronologically arranged sets of documents from his litigator brother. Milton often said, "Master the documents. Master the case." After a few hours, Martin learned a few new facts about Saigo Masuji. The IJN Captain kept an eight-shot, box-magazine, 8mm Nambu Type 14 semi-automatic pistol on a shelf next to his bed. According to the ONI agent who surreptitiously entered the Japanese naval attaché's apartment, the weapon was clean and oiled. "No match for me and my S&W," muttered Martin. Other than a sword called a *kyū guntō* from the Russo-Japanese War, several razor-sharp *kunai* throwing knives, a golf bag containing fourteen new Wilson golf clubs, and an eight-tube RCA T-80 tabletop AM/shortwave radio receiver, the Captain did not have any additional significant material possessions. Masuji had never married and maintained no contacts with family members residing in Japan. In reverse order of importance, his hobbies were aikido, ballroom dancing, golf, and loose women. Two recent photos in one file folder were relevant to the team's effort. The label on one photo dated May 1, 1939, taken at the Kenwood Golf and Country Club, clearly stated that Masuji had played in a mixed Scottish foursome tournament with Elizabeth Robertson as his partner. In the photograph, the two of them were raising the trophy they had won high into the air. According to the label on the picture, the two unsmiling opponents they had defeated in the competition were a Nazi Army attaché named Major Joachim Lansdorff and an extraordinarily healthy-looking blonde woman who looked like a Third Reich Aryan poster girl. Her name was Ulrike Koch. Miss Koch's position at the German embassy was Assistant to the Deputy Chief of the Press Section. *So much for the invincible master race,* thought Martin. In a second photo, dated July 8, 1939, Captain Masuji posed again with Major Lansdorff at the Kenwood Club, which hosted the Japanese Ambassador's Trophy event. "Looks like Major Joachim Lansdorff needs to be added to our list," Martin said out loud. "An early Chanukah gift! Finally I get to hunt a genuine German Nazi target!"

Before returning to 10th and Constitution Avenue, Martin reported his findings to Captain McLaughlin. "I guess I missed that one photo of Miss Robertson, Lieutenant JG Victor. I need to get back to sea. These DC desk jobs dull your senses! Where would you want to serve when the war comes, Victor?"

Martin thought quickly. "Whatever ship you are commanding, Captain, that is where I want to be!"

McLaughlin looked into Martin's eyes. "I will remember what you have just said. I want to command what will ultimately be BB57, the battleship *South Dakota*. Its keel was just laid down in New York on May 7th. Imagine entering Tokyo Bay on that warship and observing the Emperor of Japan sign the articles of surrender on its deck! You want to be there with me, Martin?"

"Sir, YES, SIR! Sounds just like Lysander sailing into Piraeus and bringing down the Athenian Navy once and for all! Let's finish off Masuji and then steam west, Captain!"

"Keep me apprised of what our FBI friends are up to, Victor. Remember, the US Navy's interests come first."

"Aye aye, Captain!" Martin saluted crisply and walked to the Department of Justice.

McLaughlin called the Rear Admiral commanding the ONI and quickly briefed him on the Masuji matter. At the end of the conversation, the Rear Admiral asked McLaughlin, "How is Lieutenant JG Victor handling his new assignment?"

McLaughlin responded, "Sir, we have a warrior here who wants to win some medals. He is ready to shoot his way into Tokyo Bay with me."

"Good. You don't mind if I join you and Victor when the time comes?" said the Rear Admiral.

"You can put your flag on my BB anytime, Sir!" replied Captain Charles McLaughlin.

"Keep me informed, Captain!"

"Aye aye, Sir!"

And that was that.

Murph and Gareth searched through the boxes of files amassed by the FBI regarding the embassy of the Empire of Japan and Masuji. They found no linkage between Masuji and Robertson. Furthermore, the official FBI file on Masuji's spying activities contained nothing connecting him to either Major Lansdorff or Ulrike Koch.

Walker, on the other hand, had a productive private luncheon exchange with Edwin Coar, his source at the Kenwood Golf and Country Club. A California Institute of Technology aerospace engineering PhD, Dr. Coar was the Glenn L. Martin executive overseeing the Mariner Patrol Bomber (PBM Mariner) program with the US Navy. Coar possessed an encyclopedic knowledge of his firm's aerospace engineering and manufacturing assets, capabilities, and programs. The first full-scale prototype of the PBM Mariner seaplane had flown successfully in mid-February 1939. The Navy intended the twin-engine PBM Mariner to operate as a longer range, more heavily armed, and higher gross-vehicle-weight bomber than the Consolidated PBY seaplane currently in service. In mid-October, Walker had first met Edwin Coar to arrange a time when the FBI-ONI team could conduct an Industrial Security Review of the sprawling Glenn L. Martin facility located in Middle River, Maryland, near the city of Baltimore. The two men got along well and Coar enthusiastically consented to provide full support for the team's inspection during the month of March 1940.

Seated at a corner table far from other diners in the Kenwood Golf and Country Club's restaurant, Walker quickly got to the point with Dr. Coar, a man he respected and trusted.

"Ed, I need for you to read and sign this one-page FBI secrecy agreement before we proceed. The matters we will be discussing are classified and of the utmost urgency, so they require all the strict legal formalities of a secret military development project."

Coar read the agreement and, as he signed it, said, "You know, the Glenn L. Martin Legal Department would not exactly approve of what I am doing. However, for an exigent situation of the type we have here, the lawyers will just have to forgive me."

Walker replied, "Ed, your lawyers will never be cleared to know anything we are about to discuss."

"I figured as much," responded Coar. "Now, what can I do for you?"

"Ed, we have concrete evidence that espionage agents trained and directed by the Empire of Japan have targeted a specific defense firm in the Baltimore area. While Glenn L. Martin is not the company the Japs are interested in right now, we suspect that it will be soon. During our investigation, an individual surfaced who may or may not be assisting the Empire of Japan's spies. We need to determine objectively and fairly whether this person is an enemy agent or not."

Coar then spoke. "I understand. Just because you mention a person's name to me does not mean that you have sufficient credible evidence that the individual committed a specific federal crime."

"Correct. We are investigating an individual who appears to associate frequently with foreign actors we know to be bad, but we have no evidence that this person has done anything wrong. So, with this important caveat in place I want to ask you: Do you know a Miss Elizabeth Robertson?"

"Yes," said Coar, "I do. She is an outstanding golfer. Very competitive. From time to time my wife and I have played eighteen holes of golf in club mixed foursome tournaments against her and one of her harem of male companions."

Walker then asked, "Do you know anything about any of these men of hers?"

"Yes. There is one particular foreigner whom I do not like. He asked far too many questions about my work, and when I deflected his inquiries, he attempted to charm my wife into making disclosures."

Walker asked, "Do you recall this man's name?"

"Oh yes. Major Joachim Lansdorff. He works at the Nazi embassy in DC on Massachusetts Avenue. He gave me his card." Coar retrieved his wallet from his front left pants pocket, opened it, and handed the card to Walker. "Here—keep it. People at this club do not know this, but my wife converted from the Jewish faith to Catholicism in order to marry me many years ago. Lansdorff said some awfully hateful and hurtful things about Jews while we were playing golf. Robertson appeared to concur with him in this regard. I feared my wife might take a driver out of her bag and club the knucklehead, so I advised him to knock off the *Mein Kampf* stuff because my wife and I never mixed politics with golf. He shut up after that, but after we finished playing, I made it clear to Elizabeth privately that she should be more careful about the male company she keeps."

Walker followed up. "And how did Robertson respond to your admonition?"

"I will never forget or forgive her for what she said. She told me that I needed to understand 'the Nazi point of view.' Hitler, according to her, faithfully represents the opinion of most Germans who oppose Jewish control over key economic and cultural institutions in their country."

Walker asked, "What did you say in response?"

"I said nothing to Robertson, but I told the president of the club that evening that my wife and I never wanted to participate with Elizabeth Robertson again in any Kenwood function. I told him that if I had been aware of her poor character when she applied for club membership, I would have blackballed her at that time."

Walker: "Awful, Ed, just awful. Were there any other similar incidents involving Robertson and her companions of which you are aware? Are there any other individuals you think might have knowledge of her activities and character whom I should contact?"

"I observed her playing golf with an imposing Japanese embassy guy who had only three fingers on his right hand in late spring of this year. They were competing in a mixed foursome against Major Lansdorff and some severe-looking young *fraülein*. Robertson seemed quite taken with her somewhat distinguished golf partner, particularly after she had consumed a few too many drinks. Oh, and I saw the Japanese embassy fellow playing golf with Lansdorff during the Japanese Ambassador's Trophy competition in July. That is pretty much all I know. If I hear of any other credible stories about Elizabeth Robertson from my friends, I will get back to you."

Walker told Coar not to play G-man at Kenwood or appear too overt in hunting for information. "If, in the normal course of things, someone volunteers some useful information, sure, we would like to hear about it. Ed, what you have related to me is quite helpful. What we definitely do not want to do is inadvertently tip off Robertson, Masuji, or Lansdorff that they are under surveillance."

The two friends paused to eat their club sandwiches and drink their Coca-Colas. After a little light banter, Coar said, "Clarence, I would not ever want to do your job. I am glad that there are decent people like you protecting America, but I do not want to be near these lowlifes. You know, my son joined the Reserve Officer Training Corps program at Johns Hopkins University this year. He is a physics major. The boy loves anything involving electricity. His goal in life is to get a PhD from MIT in this field and work at Bell Labs in New York City. I dread the thought of my innocent young man going to war against Nazis and Japs. But what can we do? We cannot surrender out of fear, can we?"

"No, America cannot show weakness or surrender to the likes of Hitler and Hirohito, Ed. That would be unthinkable…hateful. Keep in touch and we will be seeing you in Middle River in the beginning of March unless something unexpected happens."

Walker shook hands with Coar and the two men returned to their work.

6 PM, NOVEMBER 14, 1939;10TH AND CONSTITUTION AVENUES

Martin and Walker presented their findings to the team. Walker asked the team members for their thoughts on how to proceed. Zangara spoke.

"First, following 'Occam's Razor,' let's assume that Lansdorff, Koch, Robertson, and Masuji infected each other with syphilis, so we need not spend time searching for a fifth man or woman. Second, based upon Coar's interchange with Robertson about 'understanding' Nazi Germany and her apparent affinity for both Masuji and Lansdorff, I would say we have reason to dig a little deeper into her life to determine whether she is betraying the US to the Nazis or the Japs, or both. Third, Major Lansdorff needs a serious going-over. To date, we have not seen the Nazis and the Japanese cooperating from an operational perspective in the field of espionage. So, fourth, we need to determine whether they are working together or not. Bottom line, Elizabeth Robertson and Major Lansdorff should now be examined to determine whether either of them (or both of them) ought to be added to Masuji, Katsuie, Ames, and Junius as priority targets for us."

Walker looked around the room. "Any additional or opposing views? Any modifications to Alphonse's analysis?" He paused. "Nothing? OK, I will speak with SAC Horan and then get clearance from the Assistant Director to pursue Robertson and Lansdorff. In the meantime, Al, see what we have in our existing FBI files on 'Joey' Lansdorff. Once you have done this, follow him. Hercules, you watch Robertson. Following clearance, we will get our technical support people to cover Lansdorff and Robertson, and also recruit some additional watchers. Murphy, Gareth, and Martin, you now have until Wednesday morning at 09:00 to work out your plan for conducting the Security Review of Bendix. I will fly-speck your plan with you at that time. Afterward, we will see what else you can do to assist us here in DC. The three of you should return to Baltimore on Friday evening. Spend some time with your families and hit the ground running at Bendix at 09:00 hours on Monday, November 20th. Your host at Bendix will be one of their senior executives, a Naval Academy grad with a PhD in electrical engineering from MIT named Richard Crowe. Have a good evening."

Agent Zangara retrieved the FBI file on Major Joachim Lansdorff, one of the Third Reich embassy's Wehrmacht attachés since mid-1933. A graduate of the *Kriegsakadamie* in Berlin, Lansdorff had risen through the ranks to become a Bureau Chief within German Army Intelligence in 1931. A US State Department memo to the FBI, prepared in March 1933 reported that *Der Führer* himself had interviewed and approved Major's Lansdorff's appointment to the German embassy in DC. The *Washington Post's* society columnists frequently fawned over Lansdorff and his family. Numerous articles were published extolling the Major's knowledge of US Civil War history, his superb horsemanship and polo skills, his well-spoken, well-dressed, and well-coiffed wife, and his handsome teenage son who had attended a public high school in DC and graduated as class valedictorian in 1939. The Lansdorff family reified the Nazi *Übermensch* myth, which *The Washington Post* dutifully echoed.

"This is enough to make me want to vomit," groused Zangara as he examined the press clippings. "How could *The Post* reporters ignore the Major's openly anti-Semitic public statements about 'Jew Bankers,' 'Jew Financiers,' 'Jew political wire-pullers,' etc., and still rave about this Nazi creep?"

complained Zangara. However, it was the classified FBI and US Army military intelligence reports of Lansdorff's popularity with high-ranking US Army officers that sent Zangara into the stratosphere with rage. "How can some of our senior soldiers like this guy?!" Zangara bellowed as he pounded the table on which he was reading the documents. "Well, Sir, I am going to make it a point to bring this horseback riding kraut spy down a few pegs," resolved the ruffian from Bridgeport.

Zangara showed his typed Lansdorff report to Hercules before reviewing the document with Walker. "Al, why don't we just fix his saddle before he goes riding this weekend? Be a real shame if he had to be shipped back to the Fatherland as a quadriplegic," said Hercules.

"Why, Agent Boulanger, that would be wrong!" replied Zangara. "But between the two of us, let's keep it as an option."

Having blown off a little steam, Al submitted his report to Walker. Walker read it while Zangara stood in his office. "This should tip the balance and persuade the Assistant Director to target Lansdorff," opined Walker. "Start tracking his movements. We are going to nail this Nazi and his US accomplices."

Meanwhile, Hercules found an inconspicuous place from which he could conduct surveillance of the entrance to Elizabeth Robertson's upscale apartment building located in Northwest, DC at 1600 16th Street. From his location, he could view her apartment windows as well. Between 7 PM and 9 PM, he waited and watched. At 9 PM, a Chevrolet sedan with Maryland license plate number 418-778 pulled up to the curb across the street from the apartment house. Robertson let herself out of the car and jaywalked to the entrance of the building. The Chevrolet sped away, heading north.

"It looks like that guy will not be getting infected tonight," mused Hercules. He noted that Elizabeth's apartment lights went out at 10 PM. He waited until 11 PM and then returned to the Department of Justice Building. Zangara, working away behind his desk, waved as Hercules entered the office.

"Mind if I use your telephone, Al?"

"No problem, Hercules. Just leave ten cents on my desk."

"Al, it is a long-distance call," quipped Hercules.

"Then don't talk too long and leave a quarter. Can't you see I am working, Herc? Enough already!" growled Zangara.

Hercules called the late-night duty officer at the Baltimore FBI office. "This is Agent Hercules Boulanger. I need whatever information you can get me on the owner of a late model Chevrolet, Maryland plate number 418-778 by 8:45 AM tomorrow. Send the information by teleprinter to Agent Alphonse Zangara at Main Justice in DC."

"Roger that, Agent Boulanger. This is Agent Karl Dennis. Out."

"Hercules, leave fifty cents. That was a long call," Zangara said in a falsetto female operator's voice while pressing one side of his nose shut.

"Al, looks like Miss Robertson had a male visitor driving a Chevy with Maryland plates. My gut tells me he is from Baltimore, Maryland. I will bet you fifty cents that we have another troublemaker to add to our list."

"You have got a bet, Herc. Let's get out of here."

The two friends left the building, eager to resume their hunt early Tuesday morning.

8:30 AM WEDNESDAY, NOVEMBER 15, 1939; 10TH AND CONSTITUTION AVENUES

Boulanger received his information from Agent Dennis at 8:30 AM sharp. The vehicle's owner, Friedrich Westphal, lived alone in a row house in East Baltimore on the corner of Luzerne and Baltimore Streets. He had inherited the home from his parents.

Significantly, Agent Dennis had learned that Westphal worshiped at the Kreuzkirche Lutheran Church located near City Hall, attending the prayer services conducted exclusively in the German language. Founded in the mid-eighteenth century by German immigrants, Kreuzkirche Lutheran Church established itself over time as a center of German-American culture in Baltimore. A German-educated Lutheran cleric, who became a naturalized American citizen after World War I, led the Kreuzkirche congregation. In November of 1934, following a three-week stay in Nazi Germany, the reverend leader of the Kreuzkirche Lutheran Church raised a few eyebrows when he was quoted as saying in *The Baltimore Sun* newspaper: "Hitler has given Germany a sense of security it had not known, and there is gratitude everywhere." In the same interview, he was also reported to have said that he could not find anyone in Germany who believed that there had been actual cruelties practiced against German Jews by the Nazis, and that the discrimination against Jews living in Germany "was the same as German-Americans experienced in the United States during World War I."

In 1936, some students at the all-female Western High School in Baltimore submitted a written protest in reaction to a speech the Lutheran reverend delivered to them in which he expressed unqualified support of the Hitler regime's "work." The reports of the reverend's serial faux pas regarding Hitler and Nazi Germany, however, had no discernible impact on him or his position as leader of the Kreuzkirche Lutheran Church.

Westphal's parents, both deceased, immigrated to the United States in 1910 and became naturalized citizens in 1913, the year their only child Friedrich was born. Friedrich graduated from Baltimore's Polytechnic High School in 1930 and earned a degree in mechanical engineering from the University of Maryland in 1934. Since his graduation, Westphal had worked at the rapidly expanding Glenn L. Martin engineering and manufacturing campus in Middle River.

Dennis concluded his brief report by advising Hercules that his background check into Friedrich Westphal was continuing. In a postscript, Dennis added that the subject of his surveillance effort subscribed to the *Täglicher Baltimore Correspondent*, a daily paper published in German.

Boulanger shared the teleprinter document from with Zangara shortly before the two were to meet with Agent Walker. "Herc, you won our little wager. I owe you fifty cents. It hurts me that your doggedness and intuition have, so far, produced results superior to mine regarding this case," said Zangara somewhat dejectedly.

"Get used to it, Al. You ain't seen nothin' yet, partner! Now let's go impress Walker with our work."

Pleased with the latest Boulanger/Zangara update, Walker communicated its contents over the phone to Horan and the Assistant Director. They, in turn, gave Walker the green light to proceed with "peeling the bark off" Elizabeth Robertson, Joachim Lansdorff, and Friedrich Westphal.

"I will get Agents Karl Dennis and Donald Foster from the Baltimore FBI office added to your crew full time," Walker informed Hercules and Alphonse. "Dennis has been through the complete four-month Quantico counterintelligence course for FBI agents, and he is fluent in German. Foster worked well with Martin Victor last week, and I understand that he yearns to take a break from investigating routine federal criminal law violations in Baltimore. I will see to it that Dennis and Foster attend our meeting tomorrow morning and introduce them to the entire team. We have got to move fast. Once again, we are playing catch-up with the Japs and the Nazis in Baltimore and DC. We must regain the initiative."

To emphasize the importance of the Sicinnus Team's mission, SAC Horan led the Wednesday morning meeting with Walker, Hercules, Zangara, Clyde, Murphy, Gareth, and Martin.

"Gentlemen, our investigation of Captain Saigo Masuji and Imperial Agent Kimura Katsuie's targeting of Bendix Radio's Baltimore operations has been officially expanded to include a thorough look into the possible espionage activities of three new individuals: Major Joachim Lansdorff, a military attaché at the German embassy; a State Department officer named Miss Elizabeth Robertson; and an engineer employed at the Glenn L. Martin facility in Middle River, Maryland, named Friedrich Westphal. We have fragmentary evidence indicating that Lansdorff, Robertson, and Westphal may be operating against Glenn L. Martin. Robertson's close connections to both Lansdorff and Masuji raise the potential that Germany and Japan might be jointly targeting Glenn L. Martin. They may also be operating together against Bendix Radio. Your job is to find out definitively what each of them is up to and the extent to which German and Japanese agents under diplomatic cover are cooperating to commit acts of espionage against enterprises in the US defense industry."

Walker then issued orders. "Gareth, Martin and Murph, I have not forgotten about your site security inspection plan for Bendix and will review it with you on Thursday. Keep in mind that we do not want to miss monitoring Masuji's appointment with Dr. Basswood on Sunday morning. We will follow the same procedure as last weekend. The Baltimore FBI office will provide us with two agents—Donald Foster and Karl Dennis—for the duration of this investigation involving Bendix and Glenn L. Martin. Agent Clyde, rustle up some black-bag boys and pay Elizabeth Robertson's apartment a visit. Leave a few 'party favors' behind so we can listen to and record Elizabeth's telephone calls and other *lésions dangereuses* encounters with her suitors. I want her mail and cable traffic covered. Work out a plan for following her around town. SAC Horan has generously consented to assist you in this endeavor for this weekend. Who knows, maybe you will get a promotion if you do well! Any questions?"

Murphy, uncharacteristically, spoke up. "Sir, I think I should dine each night for the rest of this week at the Carlton Hotel Bar. My newfound friend, O'Reilly, might have some additional tidbits for me. And you never know… I might see Robertson meeting some interesting people"

Walker asked Lewis Clyde if he had a problem with Murphy surveilling Robertson in this solo manner.

Clyde responded, "Clarence, I will tell you right now, you can assign Hercules, Gareth, Murph, Martin, and Zangara to anything I am doing anytime without asking for my concurrence. Murph, I appreciate and accept your offer of assistance."

Walker ended the meeting on that positive note. "Well, that's it for now. Unless something significant occurs, we will reconvene tomorrow at 9 AM."

Clarence Walker, who on the day of his confirmation chose Bernard of Clairvaux as his personal patron saint, viewed himself as a modern Knight Templar. He was determined to rid America of evil foreign invaders. Walking past his secretary, Walker paused, said, "Good morning," and then "Please get me Edwin Coar at Glenn L. Martin on the phone."

Walker's secretary soon thereafter said, "Mr. Coar is on the line."

Clarence picked up and said sprightly, "How are you this fine morning, Ed?"

Somewhat less than sprightly, Coar replied, "You tell me, Clarence."

"Ed, we need to meet privately. Will you be in DC this week?"

"Clarence, I will be in DC tonight. I have meetings with my Navy PBM Mariner customers tomorrow."

Walker continued to push his luck and asked, "Ed, would you mind stopping by my office at 10th and Constitution Avenues for a thirty-minute conversation? Then, if you have time, you can take me to the Cosmos Club."

"Walker, how did you know that I am a member? Oh, that's right—you know everything!" replied an amused Edwin Coar.

"Not quite, Ed. But I am working on it each and every day."

"OK. How about I visit you at seven tonight?"

"Perfect, Ed. See you then. You will be glad that you did."

This last bit of insouciance by the FBI agent triggered Edwin Coar to reply, "Clarence, when was the last time you went to confession?"

"Actually, Ed, I went to confession early this morning at the Cathedral of Saint Matthew the Apostle on Rhode Island Avenue. Why do you ask?"

"I just wonder how a God-fearing fellow like yourself can tell me that I will be glad to see you when you know that I won't."

"Ed, to paraphrase my patron saint, Bernard of Clairvaux, 'Real happiness will come … in accomplishing God's will.' I assure you that both you and I will be happy, as we will be doing that which God expects us to do."

In response, Ed said, "Clarence, sometimes I think you might be a fanatic. Looking forward to seeing you this evening, Saint Bernard!"

Walker hung up the phone and gazed at the stack of cables, memos, and phone message slips on his desk. *Best job in DC*, he thought.

Suddenly, Clarence's secretary called out, "Agent Walker, it's the Baltimore SAC calling. He says it is urgent."

He picked up the phone. "Clarence, we overheard Junius Johnson being told by Dr. Ames that the two of them will drive to DC on Saturday morning. Ralph will be interviewing Howard University Medical School students interested in internships at Provident Hospital in Baltimore for most of the day while Junius practices his surveillance techniques tailing a Jap embassy employee named Hiroaki Shima."

Walker replied, "That is good news. Thank you. And thank you again for assigning Agents Dennis and Foster to this case full time. I am forever in your debt. Will I see you this Sunday after our samurai sailor boy gets his Neosalvarsan-with-a-bismuth-chaser treatment and heads back to DC?"

"No, I cannot. Our seven-year-old daughter, Constance, is scheduled to have a tonsillectomy at Johns Hopkins Hospital on Friday. My wife insists that I be a good father and spend the weekend with the kid as she convalesces."

"Your wife is right, of course. We will have plenty of opportunities to meet as this investigation progresses. I will say a prayer for your daughter's swift recovery."

"Thanks, Clarence. Bye."

Walker decided to stretch his legs and walked to Al Zangara's office. He passed on to Zangara the news about Junius's Saturday assignment. Al insisted that they stick with the preexisting plan and have Hercules follow Miss Hara. "Masuji may have another jackal in his kennel. I do not want to put our CI at risk, Clarence."

Walker pushed back. "Al, is this your best professional judgment about protecting a CI? Or are you too personally involved with Hara to assess objectively that the risks of her being uncovered this weekend have gone way down and we have higher priorities to which we should allocate our limited agent resources?"

Zangara got up from his desk. Towering over Walker, he pointed his forefinger at his boss's chest and said, "Sir, based upon our recent experience, we know that Katsuie and Masuji have a network of agents stretching from DC to New York City. Our CI works inside the Japanese embassy. She works for Masuji. I would not want to have to explain to Director Hoover that we lost an asset of unique value when we had a man as capable as Hercules available to protect her. Viewing this situation objectively, what else would you have Hercules do this weekend that is more important than covering Hara?"

Walker shrugged his shoulders. "You can sit down now, Al. No change in the plan for this weekend."

"Thank you, Sir," said Zangara. "I am confident that this is the right course of action for the Bureau."

And that was that.

6:30 PM WEDNESDAY, NOVEMBER 15, 1939; THE CARLTON HOTEL

A forlorn bartender overseeing an empty bar perked up when Agent Murphy entered and said, "The usual." Alfred O'Reilly saluted Murph with two fingers. Soon thereafter they toasted *sláinte,* clinked their communion cups of scotch, and savored the moment in this place where two troubled Gaelic men can share a mystery.

O'Reilly broke the silence. "Your lady friend created a bit of a scene here last night, *boyo.*"

Murphy replied, "I trust that she did not have to be hauled off by the local constabulary for drunk and disorderly conduct, my friend. You know you are not supposed to sell firewater to hostile Cherokee Indians who have wandered off the reservation!"

"No, Your Honor, nothing quite that dramatic transpired, but t'was a memorable event, nonetheless. Seems as though your State Department colleen is none too pleased with Mr. Hull's approvin' Mr. Roosevelt's decision to ship something called 'PBM's' to those devilish British occupiers of our beloved Eire."

Murphy asked O'Reilly, "With whom was she cavorting when this outburst occurred?"

"That, Sir, I do not know. Her male drinking partner was average in height, possessed a full head of close-cropped black hair, and dressed in a wrinkled dark suit and white shirt, with a paisley tie stained dark with residue from some long-ago meal. The lad carried a worn, light brown leather briefcase and spoke with an unmistakable Bawlmer accent. He did not fit the profile of the typical high-born State Department employees I am used to encountering in this fine establishment. Anyway, he pleaded with Miss Robertson to keep her voice down which, of course, enraged her even more—slightly inebriated as she was at the time. Mercifully, the two of them left the bar and took their argument with them. Fortunately, Elizabeth kept to her custom of leaving a respectable tip for poor old Alfred!"

At this moment, a group of men converged on the bar demanding service. Murphy thanked O'Reilly and said, "I will be having a steak and a glass of water over in that table in the back." He gestured with his right hand.

"Medium rare with hearts of lettuce salad and Russian dressing?" inquired Alfred.

"Precisely. Good of you to remember!" replied Murph.

"It's my job to recall such things. But thank ye for noticin'!"

After dinner and a cup of coffee, Murphy paid the bill and left a generous gratuity for O'Reilly.

"Will I be seeing you anytime soon, Mr. Murphy?" asked O'Reilly.

"You just never know, Mr. O'Reilly."

To this, the bartender responded, "Do not be a stranger, milord!"

And that was that.

Meanwhile, back at the Department of Justice Building, Walker was having a private chat with Edwin Coar in his office, door closed. "Ed, do you know an engineer named Friedrich Westphal?"

"I know that an individual by that name works in the PBM program group responsible for integrating the Wright 2600 engines with the plane's elegantly engineered gullwing, but I do not know him personally. Has Mr. Westphal done something wrong?"

Walker replied, "Not that we know of. We do not have conclusive evidence that he has engaged in espionage. We do know, however, that recently he met in DC with a person of interest, a US government employee whose frequent interactions with two known foreign intelligence agents—one Japanese, the other German—concern us."

"Clarence, do you want me to fire a Glenn L. Martin engineer based upon this kind of speculation?

"No, Ed. But you ought to keep an eye on your engineer and be careful about providing him access to sensitive government information. We are watching Westphal closely. Are there secret aspects of your PBM program that the US Navy and your company would not want the Nazis and the Japs to know about?"

Coar leaned forward and in a low voice said, "Not exactly. However, there is one thing nobody would want them to know about that might, in the near future, become a part of the PBM program. Clarence, this story is a little convoluted."

"I am all ears, Ed," replied Walker.

Coar continued. "The Royal Air Force and Royal Navy have expressed an interest in purchasing PBM's for anti-submarine, convoy escort, and anti-surface ship bombing missions. My understanding is that the President recently gave a green light for PBM sales to the Brits. They have already ordered San Diego-based Consolidated Aircraft's less-capable PBY seaplanes to fulfill similar mission requirements and have had one or two PBY's in service since July. Now, here is where you and I must be very careful not to damage relations with our British friends. What I am about to tell you is top secret in Great Britain. They have no idea that I am aware of an airborne radio-wave device, which they have had in development since mid-1936, that is capable of seeing and tracking enemy ships and aircraft from afar in daylight, at night, and in cloudy weather. Their wizards have test-flown this gizmo in variety of RAF aircraft. Once refined, this product could be modified for use on long-range PBM or PBY patrol bombers. This revolutionary weapon system would give the Brits and us a significant edge over the Jap and the Nazi navies!"

Walker stopped Coar at this point and asked, "How did you learn about this top-secret, non-US program? Have you told anyone other than me about it?"

"Clarence, I have told no one—not even Mr. Glenn L. Martin—about the program. You are the only person with whom I have ever discussed this subject. This potato is beyond hot. The British are in a fight to the death with Hitler and are, as a consequence, hyper security conscious. Look, I travel to London on business and do not want to get locked up in some British dungeon by blabbing about a new and magical jewel in the crown of the King of England.

"My first inkling about this British program came in mid-1938 as the result of a casual conversation I had with the Western Electric engineering sales manager responsible for setting up an increased capacity phone system that we desperately needed in Middle River. Clarence, you would not believe the growth in communication traffic Glenn L. Martin has experienced with foreign government customers in places like England and France, who are concerned about their orders for Martin's A-22 Maryland and A-30 Baltimore bombers. Simultaneously, our US government customers, as well as our suppliers of everything from aluminum to aircraft engines, drove up our demand for Western Electric equipment and AT&T service. In any event, this talkative Western Electric engineering sales manager explained that he was late for his meeting with me that day because his train from New York City to Baltimore had been delayed due to equipment trouble. He then mentioned to me that while he was in New York, a purchasing representative from a British government agency involved in aviation signed a major contract with him to purchase Western Electric's powerful Type 4304 vacuum tubes used for transmitting radio waves. The engineering sales manager was excited because, with this sale, his bonus for the year now seemed assured. That airplane people in the United Kingdom would be dabbling in advanced vacuum tubes appeared odd to me, so I asked the young man what the Brits would use the tubes for. He looked left and right and then said to me quietly that his customer indicated to him that the British government was experimenting with radio-wave devices on aircraft that would allow them to detect ships, submarines, and enemy airplanes. The kid then rolled up his sleeves and got to work on Glenn L. Martin's phone system. I have not seen or talked to him since.

"However, after that conversation, I have seen and heard about unusual antennae protruding from RAF aircraft like the Avro Anson K6260, Lockheed Hudson light bomber, and, most importantly from my perspective, the Short Sunderland flying boat patrol bomber. Clarence, I anticipate that whatever radio-detection devices the geniuses in England create, the RAF and the Royal Navy will want them installed on their patrol bomber aircraft, like Glenn L. Martin's PBM. Even before the US gets involved in this new war, I know that our own Navy and Army Air Corps will want PBM's equipped with the latest and greatest advances in targeting and sinking things like submarines and surface ships. As PBM program manager, I need to be prepared to meet my American military customers' future requirements quickly and, therefore, I keep my eyes and ears open and my mouth shut tight about sensitive matters like this one."

Hiding his astonishment at the coincidence of radio-wave detection devices surfacing at both Bendix and Glenn L. Martin, Walker attempted to reassure Coar and agreed to cooperate closely with him on defense technology issues in the future.

"First, Ed, I sincerely appreciate your being so candid with me. You are protected as an FBI Confidential Informant. Your identity and all the information that you convey will be closely held by me. Second, should the British officially read you into their secret program, call me. Third, I will alert you regarding the results of our security review of Westphal once it is completed. For the time being, since there is no secret information to protect, let him continue to do his assigned work. However, be alert to the risk that he might covertly attempt to damage equipment and aircraft, copy sensitive drawings and documents, or provide enemy agents access to your facilities. Fourth, if you have no questions, let's go to dinner at the Cosmos Club!"

7:30 PM, NOVEMBER 15, 1939; THE COSMOS CLUB, LAFAYETTE SQUARE AT 1318 H STREET, NW, WASHINGTON, DC

Edwin Coar and Clarence Walker walked to the Cosmos Club. Just south of the club stood the brightly illuminated White House. Coar remarked, "You will not see 10 Downing Street lit up like that anytime soon."

Walker agreed. "Ed, the world is a mess. And it is going to get worse before it gets better. The United States cannot sit by and let maniacs like Hitler, Stalin, Mussolini, and the Emperor of Japan take over the world. Unfortunately, but unavoidably, a lot of young American men are going to be sacrificed stopping these thugs."

Coar sadly agreed.

Walker had heard about the Cosmos Club and its elite membership. Edwin Coar earned his admission to this rarefied precinct of accomplished Americans via his personal portfolio of aeronautical patents, senior executive position at Glenn L. Martin, and connections to similarly renowned people in academia, industry, and government. As they were led to their table and seated, a formally attired waiter asked, "Dr. Coar, will you and your guest be having a drink before dinner this evening?"

"Yes. I will have a Glenlivet Single Malt Scotch Whisky, neat. Clarence, what will you be having?"

"The same," replied Walker.

"Your health!" toasted Ed and Clarence nodded.

"Dr. Coar, I have never tasted anything like this!"

"Clarence, I hope that I am not corrupting you."

"Go ahead, Ed. Try and corrupt me!"

The two laughed. "Clarence, you see that distinguished-looking fellow seated diagonally across the room from us?"

"The guy seated across from an Army Air Corps General, Ed?"

"Yes, Clarence. That is Dr. Vannevar Bush, former dean of MIT's School of Engineering. In the beginning of 1939, Dr. Bush became the president of the Carnegie Institution of Washington. He is also a member of the National Advisory Committee for Aeronautics. I know of no man in America who understands the union of the sets of technology and defense as well as Dr. Bush. The nation will know that FDR is serious about entering and winning the war when he brings Vannevar Bush into his administration in some significant scientific capacity. The newly appointed Chief of the Air Corps, General Henry H. Arnold, is seated across from Dr. Bush. If this espionage case of yours continues, I suspect that you may have the honor of meeting both of those distinguished gentlemen and patriots."

"Way above my pay grade, Ed. That is J. Edgar Hoover–level, not Clarence Walker, SAC-level."

"Don't sell yourself short, Agent Walker. You have what it takes. I am an excellent judge of such things," replied Coar confidently.

"Dr. Coar, I won't argue with you. But I am just two steps above a beat cop."

Ed shook his head and said, "When you shut down this Axis conspiracy, you will move up."

Clarence replied, "From your mouth to God's ears!"

The two men dined, skipped dessert, drank coffee, and departed. "Thanks for the treat, Ed," said Clarence as he headed back to the Department of Justice Building.

"I look forward to having a victory party here with you in the future," replied Coar. "See you soon."

And that was that.

9:30 PM, NOVEMBER 15, 1939; 10TH AND CONSTITUTION AVENUES

Gareth, Martin, and Murphy were putting the finishing touches on the Bendix Security Review Plan they would present to Walker the next morning when Clarence entered their conference room. "What have you got for me?" he asked.

Messenger replied, "Good to see you, Boss. We are ready to show you our plan now, if you have the time."

Walker, smiling, said, "Well, let's have at it."

Clarence read the document outlining the plan in 20 minutes and then proceeded to ask each one of the men insightful questions about his individual role in its implementation. Satisfied that the techniques taught at Quantico were all covered, he approved the plan, but requested that they pursue one additional area of inquiry exclusively with Richard Crowe.

"After you have performed the standard FBI review at Bendix, get him to talk about the field of radio detection, location, and tracking devices. Let's find out the full extent of his knowledge, not simply what he knows about Bendix's activities. Document his responses precisely."

Murphy then told Walker about his conversation with O'Reilly. "I bet that Friedrich Westphal was the guy in the Carlton Bar with Robertson and that the incident O'Reilly reported to me occurred on the same night Hercules observed the Maryland license plate number on Westphal's car."

"Show O'Reilly a photo of Westphal Thursday evening when you have dinner. See if your bartender can positively identify Westphal as Elizabeth's consort that evening," instructed Walker.

"OK, see you all tomorrow morning for our all hands meeting at 9 AM. Agents Dennis and Foster will be joining us," announced Clarence with a Parthian shot.

Zangara and Hercules were busy that evening surreptitiously surveilling Miss Hara from different angles to pick up any individuals or teams tailing her. From the Japanese embassy to her apartment, they detected no watchers. The two agreed to conduct the same procedure Thursday evening, Friday evening, and all day on Saturday, just to be safe.

"Al, what do you want to do if we actually detect surveillance of Hara?" Hercules asked in his gravel-voice.

Zangara responded, "Herc, we will conduct a countersurveillance protocol after Kinuyo enters her apartment, commence tracking the tracker or trackers, and determine their identity and base of operations. Our tactical decisions will have to be made with more facts. My gut instinct is always to 'disappear' these kinds of people, but hopefully, none of that kind of unpleasantness will be necessary."

Hercules pulled up the fabric from his right lower trouser leg, revealing his sheathed fighting knife. "Al, whatever way you want to resolve threats to Miss Hara is OK with me. All I ask is that we keep everybody else out of this part of our business. They are fine fellows, but a little soft and squeamish by my standards."

Al raised his right thumb up and said not another word.

9 AM, NOVEMBER 16, 1939; 10TH AND CONSTITUTION AVENUES

SAC Horan introduced Baltimore FBI Agents Karl Dennis and Donald Foster to the assembled team. Karl Dennis presented their latest findings on Friedrich Westphal.

"We have confirmed through a Confidential Informant, who himself is a member of Baltimore's tightly knit German community, that Westphal is an underground member of a small, pro-Nazi organization called the *Kriegerbund*. From a recent photo we showed him, our CI identified Friedrich Westphal attending *Kriegerbund* meetings at the *Deutsches Haus* located on the corner of Cathedral Street and Preston Avenue, not far from the Mount Royal B&O Railroad Station. Our CI also saw Friedrich stringing swastika pennants at Gwynn Oak Park on German Day in September. Based on the information to date and the sensitive nature of his job at Glenn L. Martin, we decided to visit his residence while he was working. We discovered a treasure trove of pro-Nazi periodicals, a copy of *Mein Kampf* with its many anti-Semitic references underlined, a Hitler Youth dagger, and a framed signed photograph of Adolf Hitler. We also uncovered a shortwave receiver, numerous Nazi shortwave radio listening guides from the New York City–based German Library of Information with circled program times for broadcasts by Frederick W. Kaltenbach—an expatriate American citizen shortwave radio commentator from Goebbels's *Deutsche Kurzwellensender* overseas network located near Berlin—a framed photo of Max Schmeling knocking out Joe Louis, a framed photo of Westphal standing next to Fritz Kuhn at the German-American Bund Rally at Madison Square Garden in February of this year, and an undated photo of Friedrich posing with a Springfield 30-06–caliber bolt-action rifle at Camp Nordland in Andover Township, New Jersey. We did not have time to go through his desk and filing cabinet drawers to examine his carefully catalogued correspondence. We will arrange to do so soon, at which time we will also leave a few electrical devices to help us keep better informed of his pro-Nazi activities and contacts. It is abundantly clear that Friedrich Westphal is an active Nazi sympathizer, and given his employment in a key US military aircraft company in Baltimore, persistent surveillance of him is required."

Horan thanked both Dennis and Foster for their fine work and endorsed their taking additional comprehensive surveillance measures targeting Westphal. "We need a complete map of this man's activities, contacts, co-conspirators, and operational plans, if any. I want your investigation update memos sent to Clarence Walker via secure teleprinter. I am particularly concerned that we prevent Westphal and any accomplices from committing acts of espionage against Glenn L. Martin's research, engineering, and manufacturing assets. I want no unpleasant surprises from a Nazi agent we have in our sights."

Both Baltimore agents nodded their heads in agreement. Walker thought, *Perhaps I will ask Coar to send Westphal on a business trip for a few days and give Dennis and Foster a little extra time to complete their reconnaissance mission in Westphal's home.*

Horan continued. "I understand from Clarence that there is considerable work in progress, so I will not consume any more of your time today. Unless there is a major break in the case, I expect a full review of this matter on November 30th." As he left the room, Horan added, "Oh, have a Happy Thanksgiving with your families on November 23rd."

Walker then assigned Gareth, Martin, and Murphy to report to Hercules and Zangara from Thursday through Friday early afternoon. Hercules, Gareth, and Martin teamed up to review Robertson's intercepted mail and the recordings of conversations from her apartment telephone line. Walker also assigned them to conduct a surveillance of Captain Masuji's secretary, Miss Hara.

"We have received an indication that Miss Hara may want to change sides and work for us. However, we do not know whether she is merely a Japanese 'dangle' to entrap and embarrass us or a freedom-loving Japanese national who genuinely wants to become a patriotic American citizen. We want you to follow her. See if she is being covered by a Jap counter-intel team trying to catch us making a pitch to her to become an FBI CI. Hercules will brief you on the details. He is your tactical commander for this exercise. Zangara has another job I need him to do, so he won't be joining you."

Hercules then explained that at 4 PM, they would take a break to conduct countersurveillance of Miss Hara as she walked to her Alban Towers apartment from the embassy of Japan. She routinely left the embassy at 6:30 PM.

Martin would position himself on foot, slightly above the Alban Towers Apartments at the northwest corner of Cathedral and Massachusetts Avenues. Hercules, also on foot, would be stationed just below the apartment building on the east corner of the intersection of Garfield and Massachusetts Avenues. Gareth would initiate the surveillance from his post on the east corner of the intersection of California and Massachusetts Avenues, just across the street from the embassy of Japan. When Miss Hara exited the building, he could spot anyone following her home. According to Hercules, Hara's routine for Thursday nights involved cleaning her apartment, doing laundry, dining alone, and reading until bedtime at 10 PM. She would not leave her apartment until 6:10 AM the next morning, at which time she would take the bus and ride the 1.4-mile trip down Massachusetts Avenue to the embassy of Japan. Martin would board the bus at Newport and Massachusetts Avenues, approximately 2.7 miles north of Hara's Alban Towers bus stop. He would get off the bus at Rhode Island and Massachusetts Avenues, one mile south of the embassy. Hercules and Gareth would pick up Martin when he got off the bus and the three agents would drive to the Justice Department for the morning team meeting.

On Thursday, Zangara and Murphy would analyze English translations of Lansdorff's recent mail, transcripts of his home and office phone calls, and copies of his cable traffic. Murphy would follow up with O'Reilly at the Carlton Hotel Bar in the evening and show him a photo of Westphal. They would all reconvene that night to compare notes. On Friday, each group would contribute their findings at the team meeting. Walker believed he had all of his assets allocated efficiently in both Baltimore and DC. He anticipated that useful information would soon be forthcoming.

Clarence Walker left the meeting and called Coar. "Ed, are you free to talk?"

"Yes. What can I do for you?"

Clarence asked, "Do you know if Mr. Westphal needs to travel outside the state of Maryland for a few days anytime soon?"

Ed Coar responded, "No, but I need to send someone to Curtiss-Wright in Patterson, New Jersey, for a two-day meeting next week—Monday and Tuesday—to discuss their more powerful 1,700 horsepower engine for the PBM, called the Wright R-2600-12. Westphal would be the right engineer to assign to cover the meeting. Does this suit you?"

Walker replied, "Perfect. You read my mind."

Ed: "Consider it done."

Walker then called Karl Dennis to let him know that he would have the run of Westphal's house for Monday and Tuesday. "Keep an eye on the house on Sunday just to make sure he doesn't leave a guest to look after the place while he is gone. Do your absolute best to get in and out of his home unobserved."

Dennis crisply advised Walker that he and Foster would handle all of the details and report when the Westphal black-bag job was completed.

Lewis Clyde's black-bag job on Robertson's apartment turned up only one document of interest for Hercules, Gareth, and Martin—a recent bill from a local DC physician who had been treating her with weekly injections of Neosalvarsan and bismuth for sixteen weeks.

"A man would have to be nuts to sleep with a woman other than his wife in America today!" railed Clyde to Walker. "What is this country coming to? Here is a college-educated woman who keeps a clean apartment—no piles of paper, no junk, and immaculate floors, walls, counters, cabinets, bathrooms, and closets. Shame she isn't as immaculate in her personal life!" he quipped. "Robertson says very little on the phone too. Whatever she is up to, she must be doing it in person and leaving little evidence of her activities. We will have to catch her in the actual act of committing espionage in order to put her behind bars. She is clever. I have to give her that."

Having heard enough defeatist talk, Hercules said, "Lewis, she will make mistakes. The amateur folks working with her, like Westphal, will slip up too. Everyone does. Even pros like Masuji get a little too impatient, a little too reckless, a little too eager to please their superiors, and they screw up. We just need to maintain a high level of persistent surveillance on her, Lewis. You will see. We will get her. We will nail all of them."

Lewis paused for a moment and said, "Hercules, consider me reset and ready to catch Robertson and her accomplices when they fall."

Hercules smiled. How many times had he seen good police and good soldiers demotivate themselves by thinking that their foes were ten feet tall? Hercules's experience taught him that he could defeat any adversary by outthinking, out training, outworking, and outfighting them. Walker valued Hercules's ability to motivate his teammates. After World War II ended, he wrote a letter recommending that Hercules receive an award for meritorious service. The letter read, in part, "FBI Agent Hercules Boulanger's bravery, intelligence, and never-ever-give-up attitude made him a superb role model and natural leader of his fellow FBI, ONI, and MID agents. His élan was contagious. We all became better men for having worked with him."

Like Elizabeth Robertson, Lansdorff left no clues about his activities during his office phone calls and meetings. His mail and cable traffic were also clean. Walker thought, *Clearly, surveillance of our targets will have to be run for a long period of time. They have got to be communicating with each other and with agents like Westphal. Lansdorff has got to be receiving information requests and directives from the goons in Berlin. Now that we are focused and paying attention, we will get them.*

The FBI-ONI team's countersurveillance of Miss Hara on Thursday evening detected no watchers. The few pedestrians observed along Massachusetts Avenue from the embassy to Alban Towers were walking south, while she moved at a brisk pace north. No one followed her at any point. Martin wondered out loud whether the bus ride he would be taking on Friday morning made any sense. Hercules told him in no uncertain terms to stick with the plan and keep his eyes open.

"Martin, you need practice in the art of seeing but not being seen. Buy a *Washington Post* early edition and read it while you are on the bus. Keep reading it when Hara gets on the bus; however, pay attention to anyone who puts their paper or book down to gaze at her. Watch them. Study them. Sometimes rookies, or just plain sloppy surveillance agents, let down their guard. If you suspect that you have identified a bad guy, stay on the bus and follow him or her. We will be right behind the bus if you do not get off at the Rhode Island Avenue stop."

Murphy got a hit at the Carlton Hotel Bar on Thursday evening. O'Reilly took one look at the photo of Westphal shown to him by the FBI agent and said, "That's the guy I told you about who told Robertson to pipe down the other night!"

Murphy proceeded to order and consume his usual dinner. Over a cup of coffee, he thanked O'Reilly for providing information about Robertson. Handing the bartender what appeared to be a business card, Murphy said, "Alfred, if you need to contact me about Miss Robertson's activities, call this number and identify yourself to the operator. You will be asked a few questions and I will get back to you as soon as I can. If you believe that you have something urgent requiring my immediate attention, tell the operator and either I or one of my colleagues will miraculously appear."

"No problem," replied O'Reilly. "Take care of yourself, *boyo*! I am beginnin' to take a likin' to ye."

"That makes two of us," answered Murphy. He then headed back to Walker's office to report that Westphal had indeed traveled to DC to meet with Elizabeth Robertson the previous week. As he walked, he thought, *Pays to have a friend or two in this life, Billy-boy.*

6 AM FRIDAY, NOVEMBER 17, 1939; NEWPORT AND MASSACHUSETTS AVENUES BUS STOP

Waiting for the bus to arrive, Martin Victor looked every inch the federal government bureaucrat headed for another day at the office. Dressed in a dark blue suit, white shirt, blue tie, and overcoat, he held his briefcase in his left hand and his *Washington Post* folded under his left armpit. On his right side rested his S&W .357 Magnum in its Jordan quick draw holster. Martin had not rehearsed an onboard bus shoot-out scenario at Quantico. He made a mental note to suggest a firearms training exercise for buses and trains. Martin believed he would prevail in any close-quarter gun battle; however, he also knew that there was no substitute for training under the same conditions in which you have to fight. Relaxed, yet aware of his surroundings, Martin boarded the bus.

The garrulous driver greeted him with a loud, "I ain't seen you before. You new here or sumthin'?"

Smiling, but somewhat chagrinned at being singled out so openly, Martin put a coin into the cashbox, smiled, and said, "I just got a job in DC, and today is my first day at work."

The driver continued his cross-examination. "Well, good for you. Where are you working?"

Martin decided to end this conversation. "The Federal Trade Commission."

The driver replied, "Never heard of it! Well, work hard and make the most of it, pal."

Martin thanked his inquisitor and walked to the center of the bus. Only two passengers had boarded previously, an old couple seated side by side, holding hands, heads facing forward and utterly uninterested in Martin's unwanted exchange with the bus driver. Only three new, ordinary-looking riders had boarded by the time the bus arrived at Alban Towers. Miss Hara, unsmiling, deposited a token into the coin box and sat in the row of seats immediately behind the bus driver. Next in line behind Miss Hara was an unkempt, overweight, middle-aged man perspiring profusely at the effort required for him to climb the three stairs into the bus.

Then Martin saw the tall, blonde, well-coiffed Ulrike Koch. The bus driver launched into his interrogation routine. "Well, aren't you a pretty lady. I haven't seen you on this bus before. Are you new in town?"

Visibly aghast at the *untermensch's* impertinence, Koch said not a word in reply, marched forward, and sat in the row of seats across the aisle from Martin. She had an unobstructed view of Hara seated seven rows in front of her. Martin nonchalantly read his newspaper. The headline read: **British Bombs Hit Pocket Battleship, New Jane's Manual Hints.**

Lieutenant JG Victor thought, *Now here is an interesting article!* Totally engrossed in the naval war between the Royal Navy and the *Kriegsmarine*, he appeared to pay no attention to either Hara or Koch. The ruse worked as Ulrike Koch, in her Hara surveillance report to Joachim Lansdorff, made no mention of Martin's presence on the bus. Miss Hara alighted from the bus in front of the embassy of Japan at 2516 Massachusetts Avenue. She walked briskly through the embassy's iron gate and disappeared into the building after entering the front door.

The bus continued down Massachusetts Avenue past Sheridan Circle, Dupont Circle, and Winfield Scott Circle. Martin knew that Hercules and Gareth would be fired up when he did not leave the bus at the Rhode Island Avenue stop. *Good*, he thought. *A little excitement is a great way to start the day.*

He was correct in his assessment. Hercules's blood pressure rose rapidly as he put the transmission of his car into gear and Gareth tapped his Magnum for good luck.

When the bus stopped at 1435 Massachusetts Avenue, Martin saw the swastika-emblazoned flag of the German embassy. Miss Koch exited the rear door of the bus and marched into Hitler's outpost in Washington, DC. Martin waited until the bus stopped at M Street and 13th Street before leaving the vehicle.

"Have a great day at work." blared the bus driver.

Martin waved and said, "Thanks. Today should be terrific."

Martin got in the back seat of Hercules's sedan and said, "Bingo. That Nazi *fraülein*, Ulrike Koch, was following Miss Hara."

Hercules could not resist reminding Martin that he had wanted to blow off the surveillance the day before. "Hercules, lesson learned. If you see me doing something stupid, just tell me and I will return to the straight and narrow."

Hercules nodded and Gareth said, "Well done, Martin. City forever!"

At 8:20 AM, the three smiling watchers entered Walker's office at 10th and Constitution. "What's up?" said Walker. "Hercules rarely smiles unless he has hurt someone."

Hercules announced, "U.S. Navy Lieutenant JG Martin Victor proved this morning that he is capable of accomplishing more than *polishing the handle of the big front door* and *sticking close to his desk*, as Gilbert and Sullivan would say. I do not know how he did it, but he identified Ulrike Koch, a Nazi embassy employee, tailing Miss Hara, Captain Masuji's secretary, this morning."

Walker buzzed his secretary. "Get Al Zangara in here, now."

Al lumbered into the office, saw Hercules, and grimaced. "So she is under surveillance!"

Walker ordered Zangara to close the door. Clarence then explained to Gareth and Martin that Miss Hara was an FBI Confidential Informant, probably the most important CI the FBI had at the present time.

Walker added, "We must limit the number of people, even FBI agents, who know about Hara. Do not mention anything about this to Horan, Lewis, Murphy, Dennis, or Foster."

Walker did not mention anything about the intimate relationship Hara had with Zangara to Gareth and Martin. As Walker explained to Zangara and Hercules later, "Those two Baltimoreans did not need to know that particular detail."

Walker then asked, "So, Martin, how did you know about Miss Koch?"

"Sir, I read all of the reports in all of the folders in the file cabinet reserved for this case. I saw the photos of Ulrike Koch that you examined after your conversation with Dr. Coar."

Wide-eyed, Walker asked Martin, "Did you unlock the file cabinet in order to read the folders? What other snooping have you been doing in your spare time?"

Martin shrugged his shoulders and responded, "No, Sir. The file cabinet has been unlocked for the entire time we have been working in DC. I simply familiarized myself with its contents. I like to know everything, Sir. I read Navy technical manuals on triodes, tetrodes, and pentodes for relaxation. You want to know about tube constants or dynamic transfer characteristic curves, I am your man! As a US naval officer, I have been trained to follow the principle that 'dominance demands superior knowledge.' Sir, it is what I believe and it is the way I am wired. Why would I not read relevant case files in an open file cabinet in the office in which I am working?"

Realizing that he, Horan, Murphy, and even Captain McLaughlin had severely underestimated Martin's capabilities and motivation, Walker suppressed any further desire he had to chew out Martin for not requesting permission to view the entire unlocked file cabinet. *Better to rein in a race-horse than push a mule*, Clarence thought.

"OK, Martin. Good work. Great work. Why don't you and Gareth get a cup of coffee? I need to speak to Hercules and Zangara about another matter."

After Gareth and Martin left Walker's office, Clarence closed the door, rolled his eyes, and said, "Unbelievable! What else have we missed about Martin Victor?"

Zangara laughed and replied, "Clarence, Eastern Europe, New York, New Jersey, and apparently Baltimore are full of people like Martin. The FBI, the Navy Department, and the Department of the Army underestimate and underutilize guys like Martin for the same reason we underestimate and underutilize guys like Hercules. If we are going to win the war that is coming, we are going to have to make the most of everybody and everything we have got! Now, how do you want us to deal with *Fraülein* Ulrike Koch?"

Walker replied, "You two can do whatever you deem necessary and appropriate—subject, of course, to your obeying the 'Washington Post Rule.' Keep the reputation of the FBI free from taint and tell me about anything significant that might get published in *The Post* well before the story hits the newsstands."

Hercules and Zangara walked to Al's office and closed yet another door. "Al, I am beginning to like Walker. How about if I find out Miss Koch's address and see if anything needs to be repaired where she is living? I may not make the meeting. Tell the guys I got a doctor's appointment."

Zangara patted Hercules on the back and said, "Get out of here."

15

FRAULEIN KOCH

Hercules found Miss Ulrike Koch's address—The Belvedere Apartments located at 1301 Massachusetts Avenue, NW. By 11 AM, he was knocking on the office door of the building superintendent, a retired DC Metro Police Department officer who knew Hercules from his days on the force. After Hercules showed Kevin Farley his FBI badge and credentials, the superintendent could not have been more accommodating.

"Well, Agent Boulanger, you have come quite far in our proud profession. What can I do to be of assistance to you, Sir?"

Hercules replied, "Sergeant Farley, I need to visit a Miss Ulrike Koch's apartment on the seventh floor of this beautifully maintained eight-story, 212-unit building."

Farley replied, "Agent Boulanger, the young Nazi *fraulein* has already departed for her place of employment and is not in her apartment at the present time. Is this visit of yours for unofficial official purposes?"

Hercules fixed his eyes on Farley's and said, "Oh, it's unofficially official all right. You sound as though you have had some unpleasant experiences with this young German woman."

"Yes, I have, Agent Boulanger. Many people in this building have had negative encounters with her, particularly our Hebrew residents, their guests, and our Negro maintenance workers. For a diplomat, *Fraülein* Koch can be exceedingly undiplomatic, if you get my drift!" replied Farley.

Hercules shook his head. "Let's see if we can improve the ambience at The Belvedere then."

Farley responded, "Why don't we just do that, Agent Boulanger?"

Opening the door with his gloves on, Farley admitted Hercules into Koch's National Socialist retreat. A framed photo of Ulrike in her *Bund Deutscher Mädel in der Hitler-Jugend* [BDM, or League of German Maidens] track and field uniform posing with *Reichsjugendführer* Baldur von Schirach sat prominently on a desk located a few feet to the left of the door through which Hercules and Farley had entered Koch's apartment. A swastika-encrusted Hitler Youth dual-purpose dagger/letter opener also graced the desktop. Hercules sat on the solid wooden chair facing the desk and tested each of the drawers. All three of the desk drawers were locked. Still seated, he looked up and saw an 8.5 x 11-inch black-and-white framed photograph of Adolf Hitler hanging on the wall behind the desk. A sofa was positioned against the wall to the right of the desk. In front of the sofa sat a low wooden table, on which was placed an exquisite Telefunken 965GWK shortwave radio.

Hercules got up from the chair, turned slightly, and faced left. Straight ahead he saw a small kitchenette. To the left of the kitchenette he saw the door to the sole bedroom in the apartment. He walked into the bedroom and spied a king-sized bed and a small spartan dresser with five drawers, none of which had locks. Over the dresser hung yet another copy of the same official photograph of Adolf Hitler that was mounted on the living room wall. Koch's closet contained clothing tailored to fit her athletic physique. A full-length mirror was affixed to the inside of the door separating the bedroom from the apartment's kitchen and living room.

Boulanger exited the bedroom, turned left, and examined the kitchenette. The kitchen cabinets held just one open box of oatmeal. Period. The kitchen drawers were occupied by a limited number of utensils and dinnerware. One bottle of milk adorned the interior of the refrigerator. The oven top had one pot on one of its four burners. The inside of the oven showed no sign of use.

Farley broke the silence. "Agent Boulanger, this *fraülein* keeps a very tidy household, don't you think? She must not eat very much at home. I know that she rarely entertains any guests."

Hercules replied, "Let's not jump to conclusions just yet. Before I agree with you, I want to examine the contents of her desk and dresser drawers and search for a safe or some hidden compartments. By the way, could you describe any of her visitors?"

Farley squeezed his chin with his right hand. "Hercules, she has never had a woman guest that I know of. I have seen a middle-aged German man, very military looking, visit from time to time. I heard from one of my assistants that once a big Asian man with a moustache and only three fingers on one of his hands went up to her apartment. Not one of these men ever spent the entire night with her."

Hercules showed a photo of Lansdorff and a photo of Westphal to Farley. "Ever seen either of these two gents, Kevin?"

"Hercules, the older, military looking fellow is the man I mentioned to you. I have never seen the younger guy before. You got a picture of the Asian?" said Farley with a sly smile.

"Nope. No three-fingered Asian male photos today, Kevin. Now just give me an hour to finish up here and I will be on my way."

"OK, Hercules. But please go down the stairs and out the back entrance. Neither you nor I want one of the residents to see you and call the cops," admonished Farley.

"Will do," Hercules retorted.

In less than one hour, Hercules Boulanger found no safe or hidden compartments, but he did discover all he needed to compromise Koch. Inside the desk was a black Leica IIIb 35mm camera with an Elmar lens. Ulrike had used the expensive equipment to take a superb quality 8.5 x 11-inch photo of a nude Joachim Lansdorff posing in her bedroom holding a riding crop and sporting a significant erection. In the background, Hitler's slightly out of focus portrait could be seen over Lansdorff's shoulder.

"Now this would be of great interest to Mrs. Lansdorff, and the German ambassador," said Hercules. A second 8.5 x 11-inch photo of a nude Negro male (who later turned out to be one of Farley's maintenance men) posing in Koch's bedroom, holding a riding crop, wearing a Nazi armband around his powerful-looking right bicep, and displaying an even more significant erection than Lansdorff's. This scene, with Adolf Hitler clearly visible over the black man's shoulder, would be of monumental concern to Joachim, the German ambassador, Baldur von Schirach and, no doubt, to *Der Führer* himself. From an FBI perspective, he then found the *piece de resistance*—a third bedroom photo of a nude Captain Masuji holding a riding crop in his claw with serious old Adolf in the background looking down upon the Japanese spy's erection, which was of truly biblical proportions.

Oh, man. This photo might even blow up the Anti-Comintern Pact of 1936 between Nazi Germany and Japan, thought Boulanger. One thing was clear to Hercules: Threatening to make these images public could be used effectively to persuade Miss Koch to spy for America. "Not a bad day's work!" muttered Hercules as he took Koch's negatives, locked her desk drawers, and departed unseen down the back stairs of The Belvedere Apartments.

Hercules arrived at the FBI office after the meeting ended and Gareth, Martin and Murphy had left to catch a train back to Baltimore. He joined Al in Walker's office for a private lunch consisting of peanut butter and jelly sandwiches and cartons of milk. Walker advised Hercules that he had not missed anything at the meeting.

Zangara asked, "Hercules, what did you find out about *Fraülein* Koch?"

Hercules debriefed Zangara and Walker, showing copies of the three bedroom photos that he had rushed the FBI lab to develop for Agent Walker.

"So, what is your plan, Hercules?" asked Clarence.

Hercules replied, "I think you should approach Koch with the photos tonight after she returns home from work, and give her the opportunity to join our team as a CI."

Walker interrupted Hercules. "Why me? Why tonight?"

Hercules responded, "Koch will not listen to me—for obvious reasons—and we certainly do not want her to meet Zangara because of the potential for exposing Hara as an FBI CI. In any event, I need to keep after Miss Hara from now until Sunday morning to make certain that no one else is tailing her before she meets with Al. Hara needs to tell Al what she knows about the Japanese-German connection in DC and Al needs to put gathering intelligence about such a connection on Hara's to-do list."

Walker: "Let's talk about *Fraülein* Koch."

Hercules: "I can arrange to have The Belvedere superintendent, Kevin Farley, a retired DC Metro Police Sergeant, call Koch's apartment and tell her that he has a package for her that he would like to bring up to her before he goes off shift. Farley will bring you up to her apartment. She will open the door and you can tell Ulrike you found something personal that belongs to her and hand her the photos in a sealed envelope. If she invites you in, you should ask Farley to leave. He, of course, will be waiting for you outside, just in case she gets violent. The only weapon in her apartment is a Nazi dagger. If she has another weapon, it will have to be on her person or in the bag she carries to work. If she is smart, she will thank you for the photos and ask you what you want as a reward. Then you can give her the standard pitch to become an FBI CI—protection, money, new home in the US in exchange for information. Again, if she is smart, she will ask for some time to think about the offer. You will tell her that she has until Sunday morning, when you will stop by and see her again. We will be listening to her phone conversations and following her closely for the intervening 36 hours. If she is smart, she will take the deal. If she is not smart and tells her Nazi buddies at the embassy about our approach to her, they will send her back to Germany immediately and dispose of her. Or they just might terminate her here. Clarence, I am betting she is smart and you will have a new friend. Just do not agree to be photographed by her!"

Walker thought of the numerous ways the Hercules's plan could go disastrously wrong. "You know, Hercules, your plan exposes your commanding officer to a great deal of physical and career-ending risk. I think that Al Zangara is more *Fraülein* Koch's type than I am. I approve the plan, but Al makes the pitch. Keep me informed."

Zangara asked Walker, "May I object to this decision?"

Walker: "No. You may not."

Zangara: "May I ask a question about this decision of yours?"

Walker: "No. You may not."

Zangara: "We will keep you informed, Boss."

Walker: "Thank you."

And that was that.

Hercules and Zangara strolled to Al's office and closed the door. "Christ, Hercules, for a moment I was afraid Walker would agree to confront Koch. She would try to rough him up for sure. Your plan only works if I execute it."

Hercules replied, "Al, there was no way a choir boy named Clarence was ever going to spend a Friday evening blackmailing a dangerous female Nazi spy who enjoys taking pornographic photos in her apartment. These kinds of operations are best left to risk-taking heartbreakers and life-takers like you and me who enjoy a challenge. Now, let's talk to Kevin Farley and have us some fun tonight!"

Zangara replied, "You know, Hercules, we both will have to go to Saint Augustine's to confess our sins after this."

Hercules asked, "Do you think it will help? Do you think God forgives people like us who do whatever is expedient in order to advance a cause we believe to be just?"

Zangara: "Yes, I do believe that God understands, but only if we acknowledge to him in his house that that the wrongs we commit against evildoers are necessary to prevent them from committing disproportionately greater wrongs against humanity. Neither you nor I are doing any of this skullduggery in order to become FBI Director or to enrich ourselves. Invaders bent on violent conquest like Masuji, Katsuie, Lansdorff, and Koch have got to be stopped. If we do not stop them, who will? If we do not stop them now, then when? Do American cities have to be bombed and our coastlines overrun before we take the gloves off and deal with the Nazi, Japanese, Soviet, and Fascist spies in our midst who are paving the way for attacks by enemy armies, navies, air forces, and American Fifth Columnists?"

Hercules whistled and said, "Al, I am with you. Let's head over to The Belvedere Apartments. If things go right this weekend, I will even go to Saint Augustine's with you and we can both confess our sins to Father Sykes. You may have some difficulty squeezing into the confessional, but you are used to working in tight spots."

In his office at The Belvedere, Kevin Farley stared up at Al Zangara and then down at the enormous, brightly polished wingtips he wore.

"Hercules, where did you find this one? Is he related to Primo Carnera? He looks like an enforcer for some New York City crime family. No disrespect intended, Mister…"

Hercules now spoke. "Kevin, Al here is a colleague and close, personal friend of mine. We need a little assistance from you this evening. Would you mind calling Miss Koch's apartment shortly after she arrives home from work? Tell her that a delivery person has a package for her and he insists that she sign a receipt for the parcel in his presence. Tell her that you will accompany the man to her apartment and then escort him out."

Squeezing his chin with his right hand out of nervousness and suspicion, Farley asked, "Hercules, your colleague Al is not going to hurt *Fraülein* Koch, is he?"

"God forbid!" replied Hercules. "Al is a devout Catholic from Connecticut. He graduated from several prestigious Catholic educational institutions. He goes to Mass and confession regularly. He most certainly would not harm an unarmed woman in her apartment. Al just wants to help Miss Koch improve the quality of her life here in America. Frankly, I do not foresee any problems."

Still squeezing his chin, Farley said, "OK. Do not make me regret assisting you guys!"

Zangara then interjected. "Sergeant Farley, there is nothing here that we cannot handle in a professional and pacific manner. Do not concern yourself."

Kevin looked up at Zangara. "I guess I really cannot say no, can I?"

"Actually, you cannot and you should not," replied Zangara. "I mean this sincerely, Kevin. We come in peace."

Farley surrendered, saying, "OK. She should be here around 6 PM. Why not wait in my office? Keep the door closed. I will come and get you."

At 6:10 PM, Farley opened the door to his office, looked at Hercules and Zangara, and said, "Show time!"

The three men rode the elevator to the sixth floor, where Hercules got off. He walked to the fire escape stairway door, opened it, and climbed the stairs to the seventh floor. He waited behind the fire door that opened onto the seventh floor of The Belvedere. Farley and Zangara exited the elevator when its doors opened onto the seventh floor. Farley knocked on the door. Ulrike opened the door, saw Zangara, and blurted out, "Are you here to arrest me? I have diplomatic immunity."

Zangara replied, "Miss Koch, I am not here to arrest you. I am here to return some valuable property that belongs to you. May I enter your apartment?"

"You may," she answered, "but I want Mr. Farley to come in also."

Both men walked into the apartment. "Would either of you like a drink?" she said.

"Perhaps later," replied Zangara. "In fact, I would very much like to have a drink with you in a little while.

"Miss Koch, please take this envelope and examine its contents," instructed Zangara.

She did as she was told. Her face reddened. "How did you come by these?" she inquired.

"I do not think that we need trouble ourselves with such details," said Zangara. "I want to offer you asylum in the United States, a new identity, a home wherever you would like to live in America, and a comfortable income for the rest of your life."

"In exchange for what, Mister…"

"You can call me Al. In exchange for providing me with some information about your current employer and place of work for the next twelve months or less, my government will provide you with all of the aforementioned benefits."

"Al," replied Ulrike calmly, "what would you do if I insisted on calling the ambassador right now?"

"Miss Koch, I would be very concerned for your safety. I believe that you know how very unreasonable your current employer can be regarding the issues raised by the subject matter of your artistic photographs. My government, on the other hand, is quite tolerant and will set you up with your own studio in Nevada or New Mexico, for example, so that you can forever freely express yourself artistically. Surely you recognize that your government will not be so open-minded and generous."

"Al, you are correct about my government. Are you authorized to bind your country to the deal you just offered me?" Ulrike replied earnestly.

"One hundred percent, Miss Koch. When people such as yourself take risks to assist the United States of America and the FBI, we scrupulously keep the promises we make to them. Be assured, within twelve months you will be leading a far better life than you ever imagined possible," replied Zangara just as earnestly.

"Then let us shake hands, Al," replied Koch.

"After you put that dagger you have up your left sleeve back on the desktop," directed Al.

Koch complied. The two shook hands. "Would you ever pose for the artistic genre of photographs I shoot, Al?"

"No one has ever asked me to do such a thing, Miss Koch."

"Well, consider yourself asked," Ulrike said somewhat forcefully.

"Let's talk more about your *oeuvre* over a drink," said Al.

Koch then smiled sweetly and said, "Mr. Farley, I appreciate your witnessing this event, but I believe that you ought to leave now."

Farley left without saying a word and closed the door behind himself. He walked down the hall and opened the fire door.

Hercules saw Farley squeezing his chin like a farmer milking a cow and said, "You know, Kevin, I am not a doctor, but you are going to disfigure that pretty face of yours if you keep doing that."

A mystified Farley replied, "Hercules, I served on the DC Metro Police Force for thirty years. I thought I had seen and heard just about everything a man could see and hear. Well, tonight, your pal Al proved me wrong! I just witnessed the most astonishing performance by a lawman in the history of law enforcement." Farley then described how effortlessly Zangara had turned Koch, reciting the conversation between Al and Ulrike verbatim.

Hercules's reaction: "Kevin, I bet Al would have been a Roman emperor had he lived in Italy 2,000 years ago. The man has almost every gift a mortal can be given: brains, brawn, boldness, courage, intuition, insight. He is just bigger than life. Ulrike is in for a real treat tonight that will likely last until Saturday morning! I am going home to catch a few hours of sleep. Thanks for helping us, the FBI, and America out here, buddy!"

"Hercules, I should be thanking you! This is the first meaningful thing I have done since I retired from the police department. Please tell Al what I said about him. If you two need anything else, just call me."

And that was that.

16

5 PM, NOVEMBER 17, 1939; 106 NORTH HOWARD STREET, BALTIMORE

Gertrude's eyes sparkled the moment she saw Martin's face through the glass of Sun Radio's front door. Even Shalom Cohen, whose mind was preoccupied with how he would fill the latest order he had received from the FCC Radio Intelligence Division on time, felt good that his employee was happy again.

"Gertrude," said Shalom, "why don't you let me close the store tonight? Go doll yourself up and have a night on the town with your Lieutenant Victor."

Gertrude replied, "Thank you, Mr. Cohen. Will you need me to do a few hours' work for you tomorrow morning? I know you must deliver a half-dozen units next week to your government customer and do not have time for counterwork, paperwork, bookkeeping, and housekeeping."

Cohen turned to Martin and asked, "Can you survive without her from eight AM tomorrow until noon?"

Martin quipped, "Working on *Shabbos*? *Gevalt*, Mr. Cohen. I suppose there must be a national security exception somewhere in the Talmud. OK. I assure you, however, that I will darken your doorstep at noon sharp tomorrow and rescue my Gertrude!"

Shalom shook hands with Victor. "We have a deal, Martin!"

Gertrude giggled all the way to the restroom. While she "dolled herself up," Cohen put his arm around Victor's shoulder. "Martin, please marry Gertrude. Do right by her. Do you have any idea how in love she is with you? Do have any idea how fine a person she is?"

Martin whispered, "Do not worry. I am working on this issue and hope to have it resolved this coming week. Do you know Rabbi Elkanan?"

Cohen: "Of course. He is a celebrity in the Baltimore Jewish community. Meir stands on the correct side of every important issue and seems to find a principled Jewish justification for each public position he champions. I joined his Eutaw Place Synagogue because of the way he stood up to a few members of the local rabbinate who criticized Henrietta Szold on the issue of Zionism and the reestablishment of a Jewish State in the Holy Land. Here was a valorous Jewish woman who moved to the Middle East in order to rebuild a Jewish homeland and rescue European Jews from that son-of-a-bitch Hitler, yet some yellow-bellied Jews living safe and secure in Baltimore refused to support her good works! Despicable!"

Martin asked, "Do you think he would agree to convert Gertrude to Judaism?"

Cohen: "Does Gertrude want to convert? Her family will most certainly disown her, and her brothers will probably come after you with baseball bats and brass knuckles."

Martin: "I need to discuss this subject with her, but I think at the end of the day she will do so willingly."

Cohen: "Then Rabbi Elkanan will do it. Let me know if you want me to speak with Meir."

Martin: "OK. I will keep you informed. And do not worry about her brothers' baseball bats or brass knuckles. I earned an advanced degree in hand-to-hand combat at Quantico."

Cohen: "I bet you did. You know, I was a Military Police Officer in Europe during the Great War. I may be forty-five years old, Martin, but I can still handle myself in a scrap!"

Martin: "I have no doubt about your self-defense capabilities, Mr. Cohen. I deeply appreciate your willingness to provide assistance to me in the event hostilities break out. Hopefully, it won't come to that."

Gertrude appeared, the sensual scent of Emeraude perfume following her like a floral breeze. "Mr. Cohen," Gertrude announced, "Martin and I have to go!"

Gertrude and Martin had agreed that Martin would reserve a room for the night at the Lord Baltimore Hotel. This would be a first for both Baltimoreans. Gertrude's cover story for the evening involved some lying, if necessary, by her friend Basia, who had recently rented an apartment near her place of employment, the Glenn L. Martin plant in Middle River. If questioned by Gertrude's parents, Basia would testify that she needed a little assistance from Gertrude setting up her new apartment. Both of Gertrude's parents liked Basia and viewed her as a good girl, so their Eastern European–virtue alarm bells did not ring when they were informed by their daughter of her plans to spend Friday night in Middle River.

Gertrude and Martin walked hand-in-hand down Howard Street, made a left turn down Baltimore Street, and arrived at the Lord Baltimore in under ten minutes. They said little to each other, a rarity. The elevator took them to the fifth floor and Room 517.

As soon as Martin closed and locked the door, Gertrude hugged and kissed him. She undid his shirt and unbuckled his belt. He fumbled with removing her clothing, but before too long, the two lovers were naked on the bed. Martin had no difficulty entering Gertrude. She gasped and grabbed his buttocks, pulling him fully inside her. Losing all control, Martin ejaculated. She let out a deep sigh and would not release her ferocious grip on him.

Martin felt certain he would faint. But he did not. Every drop of him settled inside her. She wept. He wept.

Given the point in time of Gertrude's menstrual cycle, they knew the likely consequences of what they had just done and were happy that they had done it. Martin whispered, "My God, Gertrude, the way I love you."

Gertrude could barely manage to say, "Oh, Martin. Oh, Martin." Yet she maintained her hold on him.

And that was that.

Lost in time and lost in their embrace, Gertrude slowly moved her hands up Martin's back to his neck and said, "Let's take a shower together."

Lieutenant JG Victor had heard of such things from a heavily tattooed Chief Petty Officer who had served many years in the Asiatic Fleet in China. The thought never occurred to Martin that an East Baltimore woman—or any woman, for that matter—would ever want to take a shower with him! Martin knew, however, that Gertrude meant business. He held her hand as they went into the bathroom. She adjusted the water temperature and stepped into the shower first. Her natural beauty captivated him. He took the bar of Ivory Soap so generously provided by the management of the Lord Baltimore Hotel and gently lathered her every line and every curve. Gertrude reciprocated, and when gliding the soap bar over Martin's firmly erect penis, said, "My *kochanie*, you are perfect."

Confused and embarrassed, Martin said not a word. He just embraced Gertrude as she guided him into her once again. And once again he exploded inside her as she rhythmically repeated the words, "*Ko-chan-ie, Ko-chan-ie, my ko-chan-ie.*"

"Gertrude," Martin said softly, "I am beginning to think that you like me!"

She burst into laughter. "You, Martin Victor, are a very funny man!"

"And you, Gertrude Kowalska, are my everything!"

Gertrude replied, "And never forget that I am."

"I will not, Gertrude. For as long as I live, I will never forget."

They dressed. They held hands. They walked to the elevator and dined in the hotel restaurant. The toasted each other's daiquiris. Then Martin removed a small box from his left jacket pocket with his left hand and placed it in front of Gertrude. "Open it."

She did. There, glistening in the candlelight, she saw a diamond ring. Martin said, "Gertrude, will you marry me?"

She replied, "Of course. I thought that you would never ask."

Now it was Martin who laughed. "You are a very amusing goddess, Gertrude."

She replied, "And don't you ever forget that either!"

After dinner, Gertrude and Martin returned to Room 517 and made love in order to make certain—at least as certain as they could—that they would produce a child. Afterward, they showered together and made love yet again. Then they slept in each other's arms.

Before sunrise on Saturday morning, Gertrude said sadly, "Martin, you know my parents, my family, my church, my neighborhood will never accept you. They will cast me out into the street for what we have done and for what we intend to do. What about your people? Will they accept me? Will they accept our child, our children? Will your brother accept us? What about the Basswoods? What about Shalom Cohen?"

"Gertrude, they all will accept you, us, and our children with no reservations. We must speak with Rabbi Elkanan, Shalom Cohen's rabbi. He will explain what we must do so that my community will embrace us fully. Then you must decide if you are prepared to do whatever is required."

"Martin, you are all I want. Whatever I must do, I will do with a loving heart."

"Gertrude, we will do everything together with loving hearts."

And that was that.

8 AM SATURDAY, NOVEMBER 18, 1939; 14 SOUTH BROADWAY

After escorting Gertrude to Shalom Cohen's store, Martin hailed a cab and headed to the Basswoods's residence. Grace and Henry, both dressed for Sabbath services at the Lloyd Street Synagogue, were finishing breakfast at their kitchen table when Martin walked through the open door to their apartment.

Grace spoke first in her inimitable Hagerstown, Maryland, drawl. "Well, look what the cat drug in."

Henry followed up her remark with a slightly more refined, "Grace, we have to reconsider our willingness to let just about anyone wander into this place."

Martin, smelling like an Ivory Soap bar floating in a bottle of Old Spice aftershave lotion, replied, "Top of the mornin' to you two too, Dr. and Mrs. Basswood."

Grace ordered Martin to sit down and have a cup of black unsweetened Eight O'Clock coffee. As she poured the elixir into a fluted white Lenox china coffee cup, she announced, "Martin, you have to stay in good shape, so no sugar, no cream, no cake, and no *treif*."

Henry nodded in approval. "Grace is right, you know. Doesn't happen often, Martin."

Grace expressed her displeasure at this remark. "Henry, you just had to add that last sentence, didn't you? You Hopkins doctors are coldhearted men. You save the tumors you remove and throw out your patients."

Martin interjected before this conversation went off the rails. "Now, no bickering on *Shabbos, kinderlach!*"

Henry guffawed. Grace just sat stone-faced and asked, "So, Martin, why are you exposing yourself to all this Basswood discord?"

"Grace, we three need to talk a little about a very serious personal matter that has come up." Martin then reviewed his history with Gertrude Kowalska (excluding, of course, the recent events at the Lord Baltimore Hotel). He told them that Gertrude was prepared to convert to Judaism as part of her commitment to marrying him.

Martin then asked, "Grace and Henry, would you consider introducing Gertrude and me to Rabbi Meir Elkanan so that we can initiate the conversion process?"

Grace minced no words. "Martin, is this Gertrude a good girl? I cannot vouch for someone I have not met and do not know, especially to someone as refined and pure as Meir Elkanan!"

Martin took Grace's hand. "Grace, Gertrude is honest, hard-working, smart, and very strong. I would like to introduce you to her this afternoon. She has worked for Shalom Cohen on Howard Street since she graduated from high school. Cohen is the gentleman who sold you and Henry that RCA radio and phonograph apparatus sitting in your living room. He thinks the world of Gertrude. He trusts her implicitly with handling the cash and checks coming into his store each day. She does his bookkeeping and orders expensive electrical products to maintain the shop's inventory. Shalom Cohen relies on Gertrude to ensure that he complies with his contractual obligations to the US Government. In fact, he has her working this morning so he can complete an important order for the Federal Communications Commission. Shalom is a member of Rabbi Elkanan's synagogue and he has offered to introduce us to the rabbi too."

Grace frowned. "Why do you need us if you have this businessman to pave the way for you with Elkanan?"

Martin replied, "Grace, we want to be part of your family! We want you and Henry to be with us from the beginning. Rabbi Elkanan needs to know that people of the caliber of you and Henry believe in Gertrude and me. You are a member of Hadassah. You know Henrietta Szold. Henry is a member of Betar in America. Henry is on the board of the Young Men's Hebrew Association. You are pillars of the Baltimore Jewish Community."

Grace looked into Martin's eyes and said, "All right. I will meet this Gertrude Kowalska today. That is all I am agreeing to do. After I examine her soul, I will decide whether I approve of her or not, Martin."

Martin replied, "Fair enough. Henry, do you agree to this procedure?"

Henry nodded his head. "Martin, we will see you both for lunch this afternoon."

And that was that.

Martin went up to his room and called the Baltimore FBI office. After two rings he heard, "Karl Dennis, FBI. To whom am I speaking?"

"Martin Victor."

"Lieutenant Victor, good morning. What can I do for you?"

"Mind if I stop by your office? Best not to talk about business on the phone."

"Roger that, Victor. See you soon. Out!"

Martin decided to walk the one mile to the FBI office. He and Dennis reviewed the preparations for surveilling Masuji's Sunday morning visit to Dr. Basswood's office. Martin then learned that Donald Foster and Karl Dennis had organized a full-scale search of Westphal's home beginning before dawn on Monday, November 20, through the predawn hours of Tuesday, November 21. Westphal would be in New Jersey at a Glenn L. Martin vendor's plant during that time.

"We will photograph everything of interest and put a wiretap on his phone. Should be a piece of cake," said Dennis.

Martin replied, "Gareth, Murphy, and I will be working at the Bendix plant on Fort Avenue if you need some assistance."

"Thanks for the offer. See you Sunday morning, Victor. I will pick you up at your brother's place, correct?"

"Yes. He enjoys my company," Martin replied. "I am headed to his office now to irritate him."

Martin walked across the street to The Equitable Building and took the elevator to the third floor where, in Office No. 336, Milton sat hunched over his desk reviewing documents his opponent intended to get admitted into evidence in court on Monday.

"Martin," Milton said with an evil grin, "I am going to derail the plaintiff's case by convincing the judge to exclude each of these documents as irrelevant and immaterial. When I am done, the plaintiff will sue his lawyer for malpractice. Now, what do you want?"

Omitting any discussion of the events at the Lord Baltimore Hotel, Martin updated Milton on the conversion situation with Gertrude. Milton rocked back in his chair, then rocked forward, rose, and shook hands with his brother.

"Martin, congratulations. Please consider me as a candidate to be your best man."

"Milton, you have the job!"

"That, Martin, is because you do not have another friend in the world other than me!" joked Milton.

"Correct, Milton. Thank God I have always had you! Oh, can I sleep over at your house tonight?"

"Martin, what is going on at 14 South Broadway that requires you to not sleep in your apartment?"

"Milton, I cannot tell you the reason."

Milton again grinned. "Lieutenant Martin Victor, man of mystery! Now please go see Gertrude. I have got a lot of work to do."

Martin saluted and walked to 106 North Howard Street.

He stood in front of the plate glass window, staring at Gertrude as she demonstrated a black Bakelite RCA 75-X-17 Oriental Charm Art Deco AM radio to a customer. She deftly used her beautiful hands and polished red fingernails to accentuate each detail on the radio's chassis. The middle-aged woman customer turned on the radio and tuned it to her favorite frequency.

She listened to the music coming from the compact set and must have told Gertrude something like, "I love it. Put it in its box and I'll take it!" The customer hugged Gertrude after she paid for the device and left Sun Radio smiling.

Martin admired competent salespeople. He enjoyed testing their knowledge of the products they were paid to sell. Martin delighted in haggling over price and tormenting merchants by walking out of their store after he had learned everything there was to know about their merchandise. With the exception of Gertrude, Martin could walk away from anything and anybody. Martin knew from the start that he could not resist Gertrude's allure. He wanted all of her for all time. And for once, he did not bother with the cost! Whatever the cost of his love for Gertrude would be, he would gladly pay it!

Gertrude beckoned Martin to come in from the street. Martin winked at her and said, "Well, Gertrude, you hoodwinked another one!"

"Another happy customer, my *kochanie*! You know all about that, don't you?"

Martin wagged his finger at her and said nothing. Inside him, however, a cyclone of emotion swirled. *I do know all about that*, he thought. *I want to know more about that for as long as possible.* Then Martin returned to reality.

"Gertrude, the Basswoods have invited us to have lunch with them today. Grace will put you through her version of a third-degree interrogation. Just be yourself and let the chips fall where they may. One last thing: Grace never smiles. Grace never laughs. In Grace, God seems to have created a humorless individual. So do not be concerned if Grace appears to be overly serious. That is just Grace Basswood being herself."

"Martin, I am ready. We must marry soon. Twelve weeks, if possible. I have no experience with these matters, but *Kochanie*, I have a new feeling inside me. I think that you and I are no longer alone. I think that God favors us."

He squeezed her hand and replied, "You are right, Gertrude. He knows that you and I will bring good into this troubled world."

"See you on Monday, Miss Kowalska," Shalom Cohen called from his office and radio lab in the back of his store. "Behave yourself, Lieutenant Victor! Miss Kowalska is the key to the success of my enterprise!" he added as the couple departed.

Martin unlocked the front door to 14 South Broadway and held Gertrude's hand as they walked down the narrow, unlit hall leading directly into the living room of Basswood's ground-floor apartment. Grace and Henry stood up from the sofa. As the sunlight from one of the living room windows illuminated Gertrude's beautiful face and innocent smile, Grace concluded that this woman would be appropriate for her Martin.

Henry, true to his profession and his "Russian soul," wondered how pleasant it would be to give Gertrude a thorough physical exam. His words, however, betrayed none of his true thoughts. "Miss Kowalska, welcome to our home. May this be the first of many such visits!"

A tear sanctified by the sun shimmered and ran down Gertrude's right cheek. Gertrude thought she heard a voice say, "God favors you!"

Grace, Gertrude, Henry, and Martin sat down at the dining table in the Basswood living room. Dr. Basswood said a prayer over the wine and all four people around the table replied "Amen" and drank. Next, Dr. Basswood said a prayer over a round *challah* and all four people replied "Amen" and ate. The edited story of how Gertrude and Martin met and how dating evolved into courtship and courtship blossomed into a marriage proposal pleased Grace. The discussion concerning Gertrude's decision to convert to Judaism pleased Grace even more.

"Gertrude, you just let me know what I can do to be helpful. If you do not mind, Henry and I would like to accompany you and Martin on your first visit to Rabbi Elkanan. We know him quite well and we want him to know how happy we are that you and Martin will marry. Would you object if we could get the rabbi to meet with you and Martin on Sunday, either late afternoon or early evening?"

Gertrude took Grace's hand. "Mrs. Basswood, Martin and I accept your kind offer and I will try not to make a nuisance of myself in the future."

"Gertrude, please call me Grace. I doubt that you could ever be a nuisance. Martin, on the other hand…" This rare occurrence—Grace Basswood attempting to be humorous—caused everyone but Grace to laugh.

After lunch, Gertrude assisted Grace with cleaning the dishes. Henry and Martin disappeared into the living room for a chat. "Martin, your friend showed up on Friday and installed that device of his again in preparation for my Japanese patient's visit tomorrow morning. Is there anything new I need to know about?"

"Not really, Henry. I will tell you that our investigation is expanding and that your patient is in for some unpleasant surprises. So just keep your professional relationship with him on an even keel and one day soon you will see him pay dearly for his perfidy."

Henry replied, "I wish I could do more, Martin. I cannot understand why President Roosevelt is not doing all he can to help the British and the French bring down that beast Hitler!"

"Dr. Basswood, we have to trust our Commander-in-Chief, who knows a lot more than we do about the threats to our national security. From the US Navy's perspective, he is preparing our defenses wisely. The impressive growth of the US Navy under FDR should make the Nazis, the Japanese, and all the rest of the bums think long and hard about going to war with us. However, I agree with you. No amount of military buildup will deter a maniac like Hitler or a clown like Hirohito, who thinks he is a descendant of their pagan god, Amaterasu. We will have to beat both Germany and Japan decisively in a war and kill their current leaders in order to restore world peace and security. In the meantime, you and I have to do our part and follow orders from our Commander-in-Chief."

Grace and Gertrude appeared and Henry said, "Ladies, let's take a walk in the sunshine!" Henry and Martin walked together. Grace and Gertrude walked arm-in-arm together and talked continuously until they returned to 14 South Broadway. Martin shook Henry's hand and kissed Grace on the forehead. Gertrude kissed Henry briefly on the cheek and then hugged and kissed Grace.

"You sure know how to pick a wife," Grace said to an astonished Martin.

"Grace, I agree with you," replied Henry.

"And I agree with you and Grace," said Martin.

"And I agree with Grace, Henry, and Martin," said Gertrude.

And that was that.

6 PM, NOVEMBER 18, 1939; 3454 AUCHENTROLY TERRACE

Martin reviewed the edited version of recent events involving his courtship of Gertrude with his brother Milton.

Milton observed, "Martin, you certainly are building a strong defensive network around your position. Hopefully the coming assault from Miss Kowalska's family will not be able to breach your fortifications. You two are in for the shock of your lives!"

Martin replied, "Milton, you are ever the optimist."

Milton reminded Martin, "I specialize in anticipating and preparing for the worst-case scenario, Martin. What are you going to do when Mr. and Mrs. Kowalska throw their daughter into the street?"

Martin replied, "I don't know. We will cross that bridge when we come to it."

Slightly raising his voice, Milton said, "No, Martin! You are standing on that bridge right now. Didn't they teach you anything at Quantico! Jesus Christ, Martin! You must have a plan! You are hopeless. Look, when the 'Kowalska War' starts, you will move in here with me and the Basswoods will let Gertrude take over your apartment on the third floor of 14 South Broadway. That will solve her security problem and get you far enough away from

Patterson Park that we will have time to see the Kowalska clan coming for you. I will stand with you as your ready reserve."

Attempting to calm his brother, Martin said, "Milton, you are a tactical genius. But cooler heads will prevail and there will be no war."

Milton responded, "Trust me, Martin. In this town, the only cool heads in a conflict over a Polish woman marrying a Jewish man are the ones attached to the Polish and Jewish bodies in the Baltimore city morgue refrigerators. You are a classics scholar, little brother. Think Trojan War, Helen and Paris, Greeks versus Trojans, and Achilles versus Hector and you will understand the nature of the struggle to come."

Martin laughed. "*Homer*, Milton? All these years and I never knew my big brother studied ancient Greek literature. OK, let's just move on to another more pleasant topic. How is the war going in Europe?"

Milton replied, "I anticipated your short attention span too, Martin. I bought us some Hendler's vanilla ice cream and I am going to make you and me a chocolate ice cream soda!" Milton then placed his right hand on top of his upturned left hand and pulled them apart vertically, making the sound of a whirring electric motor as he executed the gesture. As always, his little brother giggled like an elementary school kid when his big brother performed his chocolate ice cream soda skit.

"A Milton Special! Now you are talking! Big brother, you are finally making some sense."

And that was that!

6 AM, SUNDAY, NOVEMBER 19, 1939, BALTIMORE HARBOR, AMERICAN SUGAR REFINERY PIER, ASAKASAN MARU

Captain Masuji thanked the Captain of the *Asakasan Maru* for his hospitality and got into the taxicab awaiting him at the American Sugar Refinery pier. "Fleet Street and South Broadway," he instructed the driver. Ten minutes later,

Masuji exited the cab. Many eyes were on Benkei as he meandered through the streets attempting to identify efforts to surveil him. He detected none. Arriving at 14 South Broadway at 7 AM, he observed Dr. Basswood in his white coat looking east toward the sun, eyes closed and taking a deep breath in through his nose.

"A beautiful morning, Dr. Basswood!" said a smiling Masuji.

"Indeed, Mr. Ijuin. A glorious morning. Please come in."

Masuji removed his sailor's pea coat and hung it on the hook in Dr. Basswood's waiting room. He then sat facing Henry and answered the doctor's list of routine questions with routine responses.

At the conclusion of the interrogation, Henry said, "Mr. Ijuin, we are nearing the end of this phase of your treatment. I trust that upon your return to Japan, you will consult your physician and continue these treatments under his care."

"I will do so, Dr. Basswood. And let me say that I will always appreciate the consideration and excellent care you have provided to me."

Henry thanked Masuji for his kind words and joked that he had no idea how he would spend his Sunday mornings after November 26. Both men chuckled insincerely as they entered the treatment room. Dr. Basswood drew blood from Masuji to test for his patient's Wasserman reaction. Henry then prepared the Neosalvarsan and bismuth and slowly injected the preparation intravenously. "I will look in on you in 15 minutes, Mr. Ijuin. Relax and think of your pleasant return home," Henry said in a friendly tone of voice. When Basswood returned, he could see that Masuji had tolerated the treatment well and announced, "You may leave now. Please do not exert yourself today. Take care and I will see you next Sunday at seven AM."

Captain Masuji put on his coat, shook Henry's hand, and walked south on South Broadway to get another look at the harbor and to verify that no one was tailing him. He walked west at the intersection of Broadway and Gough Street and then through a maze of side streets to Pratt Street. Continuing west on Pratt Street, Masuji turned south on Howard Street and entered the

Camden B&O Station to take a train back to DC. He had no inkling of the surveillance net surrounding him and did not identify FBI Agent Donald Foster, a fellow passenger on his southbound train. While Masuji was away, of course, the listening device in his apartment had been checked and contents of his apartment thoroughly examined and photographed.

Miss Hara met with Zangara on Sunday morning at an FBI safe house in Arlington, Virginia. She stated to Al that she kept no records for Masuji concerning either Glenn L. Martin or Friedrich Westphal. As far as she knew, Masuji's relationship with Joachim Lansdorff was entirely social. She had never heard of an Ulrike Koch, either.

"Our relationship with the Germans is cordial, but remote," Hara said. "I will watch for changes in this regard. I can tell you, Al, that Captain Masuji appears frustrated at the lack of progress from Katsuie's spy inside Bendix. Benkei told Katsuie this past week to get some results soon or find a new spy."

"What happens to a spy who does not produce results?" Zangara asked.

"Benkei will have him eliminated," Miss Hara replied.

"How do you know that Masuji will do such a thing to an American citizen on American soil?" asked Zangara.

"I have heard the Captain warn Katsuie, 'There must be no loose ends.' Katsuie has assassins from New York who handle the termination of potential traitors to the Empire. Whoever this failing spy is has little time before he disappears," said Miss Hara in a matter-of-fact voice.

"Have you ever heard of a Miss Elizabeth Robertson?" Al inquired.

Hara blushed. "The woman from the State Department?"

Zangara nodded yes.

Hara sighed and said, "Al, she is a dirty woman who brought great shame to Captain Masuji. I heard Benkei speaking to a Japanese merchant ship Captain about her in August, I believe. The merchant ship Captain and Captain Masuji attended Etajima together and have remained friends for many years. I overheard Benkei ask his friend if he knew of any competent doctors who treat venereal disease in Baltimore. His friend said that seamen from many nations afflicted with syphilis and gonorrhea use a doctor from Johns Hopkins whose name I do not recall. I think I heard that the doctor has an office near the harbor in Baltimore. Benkei cursed this Elizabeth Robertson as the source of his infection and said that he would gladly kill her, but her access to information in the US State Department made her too valuable to discard."

Zangara looked sternly into Kinuyo's eyes. "Why have you never told me about any of this?"

Miss Hara bowed her head and said softly, "How could I discuss such a topic with the man I love? We both know that Captain Masuji is a dangerous man, a bad man. I did not want to contaminate our relationship with talk about Benkei's vile personal life."

Zangara did not let up. "Kinuyo, I have to know every detail about Masuji. Nothing you tell me will affect our relationship. Nothing. If we are to prevent Benkei from doing evil, I must know everything he would not want me to know. Do you understand?"

Miss Hara sadly said, "I have done wrong, Al. Are you angry with me?"

"Absolutely not, Kinuyo. I am not angry with you. You have not done wrong. You are very helpful. I apologize for not being sufficiently clear about the information I need from you. If you ever have doubts about what to tell me, simply tell me about it and let me decide whether I need it or not. I need to know about Benkei's problems—all of them: personal, professional, financial, social… Everything.

"Now, let us stop talking about business."

And that was that.

8 PM, NOVEMBER 19, 1939; 10TH AND CONSTITUTION AVENUES

Zangara entered his office and saw Hercules seated comfortably behind his large desk. "Nice desk, Al. You think I will ever get a desk like this in an office like this?"

Zangara replied, "Why are you asking me questions to which you already know the answer, Hercules?"

Hercules said, "I figured that if you can be an hour late to our meeting, I can ask you uncomfortable questions. So now we are even!"

"Good, Hercules. Now that we have dispensed with irrelevant banalities, let me tell you some new news. Ulrike Koch may turn out to be as valuable a source of intelligence as Miss Hara, potentially even more valuable. Koch hates Lansdorff. In fact, she has hated the Nazi Party since she was sexually abused as a teenager by older male Nazis who administered the League of German Maidens. She told me that the League of German Maidens is really the 'League of German Mattresses.' According to Koch, Lansdorff is a crypto-bisexual spy and a member of an informal sex ring of US-based officials from the German Foreign Ministry, Abwehr, and other Nazi intelligence services, several of whom are stationed in the German consulate in New York City. A devious First Secretary in the New York German consulate living in Brooklyn named Dr. Heinz Engel may be the ringleader, but Koch is not certain of this. Be that as it may, Ulrike admitted to me that she prefers women to men. Lansdorff is aware of her tastes and uses her to generate and disseminate what the Nazi Party affectionately calls 'degenerate art' among the degenerate ring members. Think of it, Hercules—we could threaten Lansdorff with public release of this salacious material if he refuses to become an FBI asset! To avoid exposure, the odds have to be in favor of him coming to work for us."

Hercules nodded his head in agreement and said, "However, we would have to whisk Ulrike Koch away to New Mexico real fast if Joachim does not play ball with us. Walker will have to be briefed. This could cost Uncle Sam a lot of money and is way above our pay grade."

"Agreed…which leads me to Miss Hara. First she confirmed to me that it was the Southern belle, Miss Robertson, who dosed Masuji with syphilis. Second, Masuji appears to be cultivating Robertson as his agent inside the Department of State. Third, Hara is unaware of the Nazi and Japanese intelligence communities working together in the US. And fourth, apparently Masuji is getting nervous about your nephew and may have him executed if he does not produce any genuine intel soon. We need to release a bogus document to Coleman so he can placate three-fingered Benkei."

"Do we have such a document?" asked Hercules.

Zangara shook his head. "No, and we asked for one some time ago. Walker will have to shake the tree and get Captain McLaughlin to get some US Navy clerk somewhere to author a fraudulent report for us to put in Coleman's hands."

Hercules's demeanor hardened. "Let's not get my nephew killed because some guy who spends his whole life behind a desk is too lazy to type!"

"Agreed," said Al. "Let's call Walker."

They called and Clarence told Al to wait for him at FBI HQ. He did not want to discuss case matters over the phone.

At 11 PM, Walker arrived and received his briefing from Zangara and Hercules. After their report, Walker advised them, "I have a fictitious Naval Research Lab report that Captain McLaughlin recently had manufactured by his folks in Anacostia. The bogus memo appears on its face to have been prepared for the Chief of Naval Operations, Admiral Stark. It will certainly arouse Masuji's interest and divert the Imperial Japanese Navy from aggressively pursuing a program to develop radio-wave detection devices for their ships and aircraft. The fraudulent NRL document discusses a sole experimental US Navy shipboard radio-wave detection device distinctly inferior to a system the US Navy already operates on some of its capital ships. According to the phony report, the primitive device will not be tested at sea until the third quarter of 1940. The document significantly understates the budget dollars being devoted to pursue this technology and raises doubts about the need at this time for the Navy to invest its scarce resources when it has more urgent requirements for advanced torpedoes, and enhanced optical devices to improve large- and medium-caliber gun accuracy for US naval vessels. Finally, the misleading NRL report has comments appended to it from senior officers in the Navy Bureau of Engineering, the Bureau of Ships, the Bureau of Ordnance, and the Bureau of Personnel, questioning the desirability of attempting to insert a complex new technology in the fleet when the Navy already has considerable difficulty training its sailors and officers how to operate existing systems. Our Office of Naval Intelligence experts who have lived in Japan understand its culture, are fluent in Japanese, and have spent considerable time hobnobbing with IJN officers helped to polish the report's text. They conclude that the document will elevate Masuji to star status with his IJN bosses and keep the Emperor's naval brass focused on technical matters other than radio-wave detection devices.

"As for your trying to cash in on the Nazi sex shenanigans, let's wait a while and see what gold we can mine from Miss Koch before we prematurely send her into a costly retirement in America's scenic southwest. I want to commend you for your continuing excellent work. You two guys keep this level of performance up and we may have to promote the both of you. Any questions?"

Hercules asked, "Clarence, how do you intend to get this hot document to fall into Coleman's hands in a manner that appears credible to a semi-sophisticated guy like Captain Masuji?"

"Good question. Coleman will 'discover' the report in the course of performing his routine duties for Dr. Richard Crowe, his boss at Bendix. One of Crowe's responsibilities at Bendix is to keep the firm abreast of technological advances and US Navy customer requirements in the field of radio and electrical devices. This information comes from a variety of academic, industrial, and US government sources. Coleman, now a trusted associate of Dr. Crowe, will see the sensitive Navy document one night while covertly riffling through the Rear Admiral's briefcase. Using the camera provided to him at the Japanese embassy, Coleman will copy the twenty-page-long NRL report and its attachments. Coleman's pal, Junius, will pick up the film and deliver it to Masuji for processing."

"Clarence, Masuji will wonder why a disciplined former US naval officer would leave a sensitive report like that in his briefcase and not have locked it up in a safe," said a concerned Hercules.

"Not to worry, Hercules. Dr. Crowe will experience severe chest pains one morning while working at Bendix Radio Corporation in Baltimore. An ambulance will be called and Crowe will be rushed to Johns Hopkins Hospital. Coleman will seize this opportunity to search his boss's briefcase. Does that work for you?"

"Yes, Clarence—as long as an official medical file is generated at Hopkins Hospital for Dr. Crowe. I have experience in these matters. Agents working for the Japanese will verify the accuracy of the key facts in Coleman's story regarding how the document got into his hands. One of those agents would likely be Dr. Ames. Ralph will certainly find a way to access Crowe's complete medical report to determine whether he truly was brought by ambulance to Hopkins Hospital after experiencing chest pains at work. Do you have a cardiologist at Hopkins on our payroll who can perform this service?"

"Do we ever, Hercules! The cardiologist is Richard Crowe's brother, Dr. Philip Crowe. Trust me, this medical report will have every *i* dotted and every *t* crossed. Even Mrs. Crowe will not be told the truth about this 'medical emergency.' She will have to experience the trauma of thinking that her husband had a cardiovascular incident. We have to assume that whoever investigates this story will cross-check Crowe's closest personal contacts to validate the facts."

"Clarence, now that is nice work!" said Hercules.

"Why, thank you, Hercules. A compliment like that coming from you means a lot to me."

And that was that.

In Baltimore on Sunday evening, November 19, 1939, a different kind of meeting took place in Rabbi Meir Elkanan's Eutaw Place synagogue office. As promised, Dr. and Mrs. Basswood arranged an interview for Gertrude and Martin and insisted on introducing the couple to the rabbi in person. Meir Elkanan, a Talmudic scholar with degrees from the Realschule in Frankfurt, Germany, the City College of New York, and The Jewish Theological Seminary of New York, rose from his desk as the four supplicants entered his office.

Immaculately attired in a tailored blue wool suit, Rabbi Elkanan had a full head of steel-gray hair and a neatly trimmed goatee. He greeted his guests warmly in Hebrew, saying, "*Shalom. Bruchim Habaim* [Welcome. Blessed are those who come.]" He shook Henry's hand with a firm grip and then Martin's. He bowed in true European fashion to both Grace and Gertrude and bid all to be seated. Grace and Henry vouched for the excellent character of the two young people and encouraged Elkanan to accelerate the conversion process as Martin, a Lieutenant in the US Navy, had been mobilized and might be shipped out at any time, given the dangerous world situation. The rabbi thanked Grace and Henry for introducing him to Gertrude and Martin and asked whether he might meet with the couple in private. Grace and Henry got up from their seats, and as they walked out, Henry put his hand on Martin's shoulder and Grace kissed Gertrude on the top of her forehead.

Rabbi Elkanan then spoke. "I can think of no married couple in Baltimore for whom I have greater respect than Henry and Grace Basswood. They talked to me on the telephone at great length about both of you, Gertrude and Martin. Henry and Grace told me how much they approve of the two of you becoming husband and wife. Rarely have I heard the two of them agree so strongly on any subject. Based upon their recommendation, I wholeheartedly agree to guide Gertrude every step of the way during the process of conversion, and I look forward to officiating at your wedding."

Rabbi Elkanan then looked directly at Gertrude and said, "Please tell me why you want to take this bold step, which will fundamentally alter your life."

Looking at Martin and taking his hand, Gertrude turned to face Elkanan. "Rabbi, I am not an educated person the way you are. I look at the numerous books filling the shelves along the walls of your office and marvel at how different my background is from yours. So, please pardon me if I express myself awkwardly or inelegantly by your standards. First and foremost, I believe that there is only one God. This one God created mankind. He is same for both Christians and Jews. There is no separate God for Christians and separate God for Jews. There is just God. Rabbi Elkanan, you and I both know that neither of us can fool God. And as God is my witness, I love Martin and cannot conceive of my life without him. I want us to build our family on a firm foundation. There can be no such foundation without the two of us sharing the same faith. I know that my family will never accept either Martin or his brother Milton because they are Jews. We, therefore, have but one realistic option regarding our future family's faith."

Rabbi Elkanan smiled. "Thank you for your candor, Gertrude. Do you have any questions for me?"

Gertrude replied, "When can we start?"

Elkanan responded equally succinctly. "Will Monday evening at seven PM work for you?"

Gertrude: "Yes. Is there a curriculum and a reading list?"

Elkanan: "Yes, I will review all of the course details tomorrow with you and Martin. I understand that time is of the essence. Typically, the process takes eighteen weeks, but I believe we should be able to complete all that needs to be completed within twelve weeks. Will this be acceptable to you?"

Gertrude: "Yes. We will do whatever is required."

Elkanan cautioned Gertrude. "Please keep in mind that going to synagogue, prayer, and being an active member of the community is a lifetime requirement. The beauty of Judaism reveals itself in this way."

Gertrude: "Understood. Thank you, Rabbi."

Rabbi Elkanan turned to Martin. "Do you have any questions? You have been silent throughout all of this, Lieutenant."

Martin looked directly into Meir Elkanan's eyes. "Rabbi, I have avoided engaging with my faith long enough. Gertrude and I will walk across this bridge together with our heads held high."

Rabbi Elkanan walked around his desk and put his hands on top of Martin's shoulders. "Martin, Rabbi Nahman of Bratzlav wrote, 'The whole world is a narrow bridge, and the essential thing is not to fear at all.' I too will walk across this narrow bridge together with you and Gertrude, fearlessly."

And that was that.

17

8:30 AM MONDAY, NOVEMBER 20, 1939; BENDIX RADIO CORPORATION, 920 EAST FORT AVENUE, BALTIMORE, MARYLAND

Gareth introduced himself, Office of Naval Intelligence Lieutenant JG Victor and FBI Agent Murphy to the receptionist at the front entrance of the Bendix Radio plant and office building in his typical friendly fashion. "Ma'am, we are here to see Dr. Richard Crowe. He is expecting us."

In a clear and strong voice, the receptionist replied, "Gentlemen, before I go calling Dr. Crowe, I want to see some identification."

This was the kind of moment that made Gareth Messenger's law enforcement career enjoyable. He unbuttoned his suit jacket, making certain that Miss Beatrice Webster, the receptionist, saw the Smith and Wesson revolver he carried under his left armpit. He then retrieved and displayed his Baltimore City Police Department Detective badge and paper credentials to her. Clearly unimpressed, she then replied, "What about the other two gentlemen?"

Gareth turned to Murphy and Martin. "Gents, you heard the young lady."

Murphy displayed his FBI badge and credentials. Then Martin showed his bronze and blue shield with the emblazoned words, "Agent US Naval Intelligence."

"Very well, then," she said. "I will buzz Dr. Crowe."

Crowe sauntered into the reception area. Miss Webster said, "Dr. Crowe, these three have not filled out the Visitors Log, but given the nature of their credentials, I figured I'd better ask you whether they should sign in or not."

In a mirthful voice, Crowe replied, "Why, thank you, Miss Webster. Of course they should sign in. We are all on the same team, are we not, men?"

Gareth responded first. "Why, yes, we are, Dr. Crowe. Yes, we are!" Shaking Dr. Crowe's hand, Gareth announced, "Detective Gareth Messenger, BCPD." One after the other, Murphy and Victor shook hands and introduced themselves. They each signed in and followed Dr. Crowe to his office. To their surprise, Clarence Walker and Captain Charles McLaughlin had arrived before them and were seated at Crowe's conference table drinking cups of coffee. Neither of them had signed the Visitors Log. Crowe closed the door and asked the three newcomers to sit down at his conference table. "Would any of you like some coffee? I had a fresh pot prepared for you."

All three nodded yes and they got down to business. Gareth said, "Agent Walker, what a pleasant surprise! Has something come up that we should know about before we get started?"

"No, Detective Messenger. Please proceed," said a stolid Walker.

Gareth turned to Crowe and said, "How come there are no entries for Walker and McLaughlin in the Bendix visitor logbook? I thought that we were all on the same team."

Dr. Crowe replied, "We all are on the same team. It is just that some members of the team need to remain anonymous to preserve the fiction that this is an ordinary security review. Walker and McLaughlin will be leaving the building before you meet other Bendix employees and conduct the standard audit."

Captain McLaughlin glared at Gareth. "Is that clear enough for you, Detective Messenger?"

Gareth grinned. "Perfectly clear, Sir."

"Good," said Captain McLaughlin. "I would not want you to feel uncomfortable with a little operational ambiguity, Messenger!"

"Why, thank you, Captain. I appreciate your being so considerate."

Gareth reviewed their plan with Crowe and asked the Bendix executive whether he thought that they needed to add any areas to their security audit. Dr. Crowe answered, "No, you have 920 East Fort Avenue covered well enough. However, I suspect that the area which you will be most interested is the complex under construction out in Towson. I can review the plans for the buildings out there and take you to the site if you so desire."

Gareth replied, "Thank you. Once we finish our work here, we would appreciate your overview of the Towson buildings and a tour of the new site. Dr. Crowe, before we begin our review, we have a subject that we need to discuss with you and you alone."

Dr. Crowe, putting the tips of the fingers of his right and left hands together, looked down at the table and replied, "Go on, Detective Messenger."

"We would like to know whether or not Bendix is presently doing any research, development, or manufacturing work on radio-wave detection and tracking devices for either the Army or the Navy."

Crowe replied, "At the present time, we are not. However, it is a line of business that we would want to get into in the future."

Gareth followed up with another question. "Are you aware of any US companies or government entities conducting research, development, or manufacturing of such radio-wave detection and tracking devices?"

Crowe replied, "Yes. The US Naval Research Lab in Washington, DC; the US Army Signals Corps Laboratory in Fort Monmouth, New Jersey; Bell Labs and RCA."

Messenger: "But not Bendix, correct?"

Crowe: "Correct. Not at the present time. I will now take you to meet with the Bendix personnel who will assist you in conducting your security review for the next two to three days."

Gareth, Murphy, and Martin followed Crowe. McLaughlin and Walker remained in the office. When Dr. Crowe returned, Walker advised him of the deception plan involving the fraudulent report and Coleman. Walker then questioned Crowe about whether his cardiologist brother would assist them with the heart attack phase of the operation.

Crowe exclaimed, "Yes. A very elegant plan, I must say. My brother will enjoy being a part of such chicanery. He will keep his mouth shut, too. You should visit him today and tell him precisely what you want him to do. I will call him now and set up your appointment. What name should I use?"

Walker: "Mr. Smith. Please advise him that this meeting will have to be completely off the books—no visitor log entries, no secretarial diaries, etc. The meeting, for all intents and purposes, will never have happened."

Crowe: "No problem. When will this operation take place?"

Walker responded, "Given the current risk to Coleman's security, we would like to implement the plan this Wednesday, November 22nd."

Crowe replied, "Fine with me. The day before Thanksgiving. How appropriate! Let's call my brother."

As Richard Crowe predicted, his brother enthusiastically accepted the invitation to assist some of Richard's government friends. He reserved from 4 to 5 PM to meet privately and discreetly with Mr. Smith.

Crowe then asked Walker, "Should I have Coleman summoned to my office to be briefed by you?"

"Yes. We need to prepare him for this mission," replied Walker.

A few minutes later, Coleman entered Dr. Crowe's office and shut the door. Walker informed Coleman that the Japanese were pressuring Dr. Ames for sensitive information from Bendix and getting suspicious of Coleman's apparent lack of productivity gathering intel.

Walker told Coleman, "For your protection, the US Government is prepared to make a sensitive document available for you to transmit to the Japanese spy ring this coming Wednesday. To further protect your credibility with Dr. Ames and Katsuie, Dr. Crowe will have a medical emergency on Wednesday requiring him to be taken by ambulance to Johns Hopkins Hospital. You will take this opportunity to take a document marked Secret from Dr. Crowe's briefcase and mix it in amidst your Bendix employee math course homework papers. After work, take the document to Dr. Ames's home. Relate the events that gave you the opening to access the document with Ralph. Carefully photograph the document in Dr. Ames's home using the camera provided to you by the Japanese. Give the exposed film to Dr. Ames. He will probably use Junius to courier the film to his Japanese contact in DC. We are confident that this mission should eliminate whatever concerns the Japanese may have about you. Do you have any questions?"

Coleman replied, "No. I understand the mission and what I must do."

Walker closed the meeting by saying, "Coleman, pay close attention to Dr. Ames. Ames should hold you in high regard after the film of the document gets transferred to the Japanese and they have some time to assimilate the document's contents. However, if after you provide the film to Dr. Ames, he becomes critical of you or somewhat distant, signal us through Dr. Crowe. We will be watching, but you must be alert to this short-term threat. Rest assured, Coleman, we will protect you from Ames and the Japanese. OK?"

Coleman replied, "OK. I can read Ames quite well now. He is a sensitive man who craves acceptance. At times he loses control over his emotions. If anything appears to be out of the ordinary with Dr. Ames, I will let Dr. Crowe know. I really do think, however, that the plan will work and Dr. Ames and I will continue to get along just fine."

Captain McLaughlin reacted to Coleman's remarks. "Young man, do not become overconfident. Ames, as you know, handles firearms frequently and well. He is a committed supporter of the Empire of Japan and wants to overthrow the government of the United States by force. If he suspects you of being a mole, he will kill you. If his Japanese masters order him to kill you, he will kill you whether he likes you or not! This is the spy business, Coleman. I admire your bravery, but please, do not overestimate your abilities or underestimate the danger posed by the likes of Ames and Katsuie."

Coleman acknowledged Captain McLaughlin's comments. "Understood, Captain."

And that was that.

Phase One of the Bendix security review proceeded uneventfully. The team noted that the physical barriers to outside intrusion were robust. A lattice of metal bars protected each of the thick glass windows on both floors of the Bendix building. Bright lights surrounded the building, effectively eliminating any dark corners in which an intruder could hide. Bendix's numerous uniformed armed guards provided significant security by routinely patrolling the interior and exterior of the facility throughout the day and night. Access to documents relating to government programs were strictly controlled by Bendix employees. When government program documents were not being used by company engineers and technical personnel, they stored the sensitive materials in substantial safes located in each department. At the close of business, office desktops were cleared of paper and all desk drawers and filing cabinets were locked. Signs warning employees to be security conscious were conspicuous throughout the Bendix facility. All wastepaper was incinerated daily. Gareth, Murphy, and Martin found no significant exposures on day one of their audit.

The team's plan for day two involved interviews of the Director of Bendix Radio Corporation Engineering and Research and each of the project engineers reporting to him who were responsible for managing high-frequency radio transmitter, receiver, and antenna programs. Most of these individuals had advanced degrees in physics and electrical engineering from elite schools, such as the Massachusetts Institute of Technology and Johns Hopkins University, as well as experience working at government laboratories such as the Naval Research Laboratory in Anacostia (DC) and the US Army Signal Corps' lab in Fort Monmouth, New Jersey.

Reinforcing the Bendix technologists' security consciousness would be Goal No. 1 for the trio. Goal No. 2 was to learn as much as they could about radio-wave devices from these seasoned experts.

Martin took his leave of Gareth and William to have dinner with Gertrude one hour prior to the couple's 7 PM meeting with Rabbi Elkanan. When he arrived at Sun Radio, Martin observed that Shalom had his right arm around Gertrude's shoulder as she sat sobbing in her swivel chair. Martin viewed such public displays of sadness as a sign of weakness. What could possibly have happened to elicit such weakness from Gertrude—the toughest woman he had ever met?

Shalom Cohen answered Martin's unasked question. "Lieutenant Victor, your future wife's family reacted to the news of her engagement to you as predicted. They banished Gertrude from their abode in Patterson Park, and her father and brothers exhibited incredibly bad judgment by continuing their harassment of her at my place of business. They refused my order to cease, desist, and depart my premises, so I called the police. When the trespassers called me a kike and made threatening gestures toward me, I took off my suit jacket. The sight of my licensed handgun took the wind out of their sails and they left my premises, apologizing to the late-arriving Baltimore City constabulary for being 'out of line.' Gertrude conducted herself bravely during the altercation, but I think the delayed impact of these events now weighs heavily upon her."

Martin felt the one emotion members of the Victor family permitted themselves to feel: rage. "Shalom, thank you for defending Gertrude when I should have been the one to do so." Taking both of Gertrude's hands in his hands, Martin said, "Did any male in your family lay a finger on you, Gertrude?"

She ceased crying and said in a strong voice, "No. They know better than that!"

Martin then said, "Please describe how all of this happened."

Gertrude answered, "This morning before work, I told my mother that I was in love and that I had accepted your marriage proposal. I showed her the engagement ring that you gave me. When she asked, 'Who is the lucky guy?', I told her. When she asked about your family and where you lived, I told her. She slapped me across my face and ran to tell my father. Things went downhill from there." Gertrude then pointed to a large suitcase alongside her desk. "Everything else was pretty much as Mr. Cohen described it."

Martin squeezed Gertrude's hands. "Do not worry, Gertrude. All will be well."

Looking at Shalom Cohen, Martin asked, "May I make two local calls from the telephone in your office?"

Cohen nodded yes. Martin dialed WO-8844 and spoke to Grace Basswood in hushed tones, summarizing the facts and asking for permission to let Gertrude occupy his apartment while he set up residence with Milton. Grace said, "Of course. I will tell Henry."

Martin then dialed SA-0697 and spoke to Milton, conceding that his older brother was "right, as usual, about the troubled state of Polish-Jewish communal relations."

Milton smirked and laughed over the phone and said, "I will make an ice cream soda special for you tonight. You sound like you could use one. Martin, this really is all for the best. It is good to get such unpleasant things sorted out sooner rather than later. You and Gertrude are going to have a great life together."

Martin thought, *Milton must really like Gertrude. He doesn't believe in the institution or sanctity of marriage at all.* Martin was correct in his assessment. His brother had created a "Gertrude Exception" to his iron-clad rule against marriage. It was the only such exception on the subject that Milton would ever make.

Martin returned to the salesroom and said, "Gertrude, let's grab a sandwich and go visit Rabbi Elkanan. I think he will be helpful to both of us tonight."

Shalom Cohen agreed. "Gertrude, everything is going to be just fine. We are your family now!"

Gertrude thanked Cohen and apologized for the disruption. Shalom replied, "I needed a little excitement. No big deal. Gertrude, this is Baltimore!"

And that was that.

Gertrude and Martin crossed North Howard Street and entered Bickfords Restaurant. They agreed to share a club sandwich and a Coca-Cola. Gertrude spoke first.

"Martin, *Kochanie*, I am causing you trouble when you are busy doing important things for our country. Forgive me."

Martin shook his head. "You have done nothing for which I or anyone else needs to forgive you. Gertrude, you have been mistreated for falling in love with me. Do not aggravate yourself. I never want to see you weep again. Whatever comes, we will be strong together. Nothing can hurt us!"

Gertrude listened but knew better. Martin was being "optimistic Martin." She adored him for being relentlessly positive. Nonetheless, Gertrude Kowalska believed that the world would not tolerate her being happy for very long. She carried this dark secret deep within her and shared it with no one until the day she left this world.

They walked to the synagogue on Eutaw Place. Alone with Rabbi Elkanan, Gertrude discussed her family's casting her out over her relationship with Martin. The rabbi listened intently to Gertrude and uttered not a sound until she finished her story. He then spoke.

"Gertrude, I am surprised that you have not shed one tear during the telling of this profoundly troubling tale. How are you able to maintain such composure? Do you not care about the anger, hurt, and damage triggered by your desire to convert to Judaism and marry Martin?"

Gertrude replied, "Rabbi Elkanan, at first, I became emotional when my mother, father, and brothers reacted to my news with anger, hatred, and intimidation. I do not, however, feel remorse, because I do not believe that

I have done anything wrong or that I am doing anything wrong. I am fully prepared to follow Jewish laws and customs. My parents and brothers have chosen to disagree with my decision. They chose to be hateful, not me. My future is with Martin. We intend to have children. We intend to be a close family. As we have discussed, without faith, there can be no family. There must, therefore, be no difference between Martin and me regarding religion."

Rabbi Elkanan thought for a moment, then replied, "Gertrude, why don't we commence our studies with the Book of Ruth?"

Over the next two hours, Elkanan, Kowalska, and Martin read the text and discussed its meaning and its relevance to the three of them. At 9:30 PM, Rabbi Elkanan concluded the lesson.

"So you see Gertrude, Gillith—a Moabitess—chose to become Ruth, a Jewish woman of impressive faith and the grandmother of King David. I sense in you the strength of character and determination of a Ruth. I am honored to be your rabbi. Our next conversation should be about the fundamental purpose of the Jewish Sabbath and how we observe the Sabbath day each week. Would the two of you be available this Wednesday evening at 7 PM? As an incentive, I promise to serve tea!"

Gertrude said, "Yes. If you have the time, we have the time."

Elkanan replied, "For you, Gertrude and Martin, I most certainly have the time."

And that was that.

Gertrude and Martin took a cab to 14 South Broadway. Grace and Henry were waiting for them in their living room, listening to a recent recording of Arturo Toscanini conducting the NBC Symphony Orchestra in a powerful performance of Beethoven no. 5 in C Minor. Henry lifted the arm off the turntable and turned off the audio "machinery"—his term for any device he owned that drew electrical current.

Grace said to Gertrude, "Please have a seat next to me. Can I bring you a glass of warm milk, or whatever you would like?"

Gertrude replied, "Warm milk would be perfect. Let me accompany you to the kitchen."

After the two women departed, Henry asked,

"How bad was it?"

"It could have been worse, Henry," replied Martin. "Shalom Cohen, Rabbi Elkanan, and you and Grace saved the day!"

"We have no choice but to stand together and do what is right, Martin." replied Henry.

Martin could never quite understand how wiry Henry could produce such a deep-bass–sounding voice from that tiny chest cavity of his.

"Henry, thank you for all of your assistance. I must get over to Milton's place. I have a full day of work in front of me tomorrow and I have to be at the top of my game."

"Martin, you do whatever is necessary to beat those Jap bastards to death."

Martin thought, *Hypocratic Henry*. He then walked into the kitchen, kissed Gertrude on the cheek, and said, "Dear, I have to go to Auchentroly Terrace. Get a good night's sleep and I will see you after work tomorrow."

Gertrude would not settle for a mere peck. She embraced Martin like a female brown bear. Then she said, "Now you can leave, *Kochanie*!"

More than a little embarrassed, Martin looked at Grace and said, "I think we are in love."

Grace responded, "I should say so, Martin."

And that was that.

8:30 AM WEDNESDAY, NOVEMBER 22, 1939; BENDIX RADIO CORPORATION, 920 EAST FORT AVENUE, BALTIMORE

As they pulled into the Bendix parking lot, Dr. Crowe rehearsed the fake chest pain scenario with Coleman one last time. "Coleman, at 8:40 AM, I will be at my desk drinking a cup of coffee. We will be discussing the second order linear homogenous differential equation problem that you were assigned for homework last night. Initially, I will complain of indigestion. Then I will tell you I have a stinging pain in my chest and start experiencing shortness of breath and a pain in my jaw. I will tell you to call my brother, Philip, a cardiologist at Johns Hopkins Hospital. You will call him and recite each of my symptoms. He will tell you that he is sending an ambulance to pick me up and bring me to Johns Hopkins Hospital. You will dial the Bendix receptionist and tell her that I told you to call my cardiologist brother at Johns Hopkins and that an ambulance will be arriving shortly to take me to the hospital. Tell her that you are staying with me and that she should bring the ambulance attendants to my office. I will be driven off and you will take advantage of my absence to search my unlocked briefcase and find the Secret document. Put the document in your homework papers and go about your business. After work, take the document to Dr. Ames, answer his questions about how you obtained it and photograph each page using the equipment supplied to you by the Japanese. Give the exposed film to Ames and he will hand it off to Junius Johnson. I will call you on Thursday morning and ask you to bring my briefcase to my home as soon as possible. I will call the head of Bendix's Security Department and instruct him to let you into my office to retrieve my briefcase. I will also tell him that you will take my car, sitting in the Bendix parking lot, and drive it and the bag to my home in Roland Park. Drive the car to Dr. Ames's place, retrieve the document, put it into my briefcase, and then drive to my home. Mrs. Crowe will order a taxi for you to get you back to your apartment. Are we clear?"

Coleman replied, "Clear. Let's get this over with, Sir!"

The plan went off without a hitch. That evening, Dr. Ames examined the document closely. He had Coleman repeat the sequence of events that transpired at Bendix that morning three times, clearly comparing each recitation for inconsistencies and factual deviations. Satisfied that his agent had performed well under pressure and gotten a gold mine of intelligence out of Bendix, Dr. Ames said, "Coleman, you have done us all proud. Use your camera and two separate rolls of film to make two copies of this report. Make certain that there is adequate lighting when you photograph the document. No slip-ups. Do it now. You are going to have to return this original document to Dr. Crowe real soon, I bet."

Coleman told Ames, "Got it. This should take me an hour."

Ames said, "I will call Junius and tell him that he and I are going to drop the two rolls of film off at the Japanese embassy tonight!"

Coleman got to work. Dr. Ames called Junius. "Hello, I will pick you up at 7:30 PM."

Junius replied, "See you then, Dr. Ames."

Ames left his home and went to a nearby pay phone booth to alert the Japanese agent monitoring emergency calls at the embassy.

"Good evening, Sir. I need to speak with Miss Hara."

The agent replied, "She is in a meeting. Could you call back later?"

Ames: "Yes, it is not urgent. I will call her back in three hours—say, 9 PM?"

The agent responded, "I will advise Miss Hara to expect your call at 9 PM. Thank you."

The FBI agents monitoring Ames's home phone, as well as pay phones in a six-block radius of the doctor's street address—alerted Walker that all was working according to plan. To assure that the rolls of film arrived safely at their destination, several relays of FBI vehicles covered Ames and Junius's journey to the embassy. At 9 PM, Junius handed the film to a tall, well-dressed Japanese man who greeted him as soon as he stepped inside the embassy. They shook hands and Junius recoiled a bit when he realized the fellow had only three fingers.

Junius returned to Ames's car and they drove back to Baltimore. "Junius, we have accomplished something significant. I have had my doubts about Coleman. However, he appears to have come through for us splendidly. It will take a while for our friends in Tokyo to digest the document we just put into their hands. I can tell you, Junius, I have read it cover to cover—twice—and it contains the information our Japanese allies wanted us to get."

Junius replied, "Dr. Ames, we still have a lot more to accomplish. The people with whom I am closest—my parents, the faculty, and the administrators at Frederick Douglass High School—are just plain fools. They worship FDR and his wife. I struggle constantly to keep my thoughts to myself and echo their stupidity about the United States. They think this is a great country. I want to ask them, *What the hell is so great about America?* But I cannot blow my cover. So I keep my mouth shut. I feel just like a pot on a stove that is filled with boiling water. My lid is rattling, Dr. Ames! How do you maintain your composure? What can I do to maintain my composure?"

Ames smiled. "Junius, I just think about the day when what we have done brings this slave house called America down! You and I will be like Samson in the Bible. Keep focused on the future. Imagine FDR pulling you in a rickshaw around the streets of Washington. Think of Mrs. Roosevelt picking cotton for a Negro plantation owner one day. These dreams, and many more like them, will only come to fruition if people like us help the Japanese defeat the United States in a war."

Junius replied, "Amen, Dr. Ames. Amen."

After depositing Junius at his parents' home, Dr. Ames returned to North Carrolton Street and was pleased to see Coleman deeply engrossed in an advanced radio engineering textbook. "No rest for the wicked, eh Coleman?" said Ralph in a booming voice.

"No, Dr. Ames. No rest at all. I must confess that I enjoy the Bendix in-house math and engineering courses. How did your trip to DC go?"

Ralph replied, "Smooth as silk, Coleman. Junius handed the two rolls of film to a Japanese naval attaché and got unsettled shaking hands with a three-fingered man. He gabbed about the man's deformity the entire drive back to Baltimore. Like a lot of teachers, Junius can't see the humor in anything. Be that as it may, Coleman, I have got to tell you again how much I admire the take-charge attitude you displayed today at work. I know how most nonmedical professionals get upset when a co-worker or relative or friend suddenly experiences extreme pain and calls out for help. In an acute situation like that, it takes a different kind of man to hold and act on two inconsistent ideas like you did. Getting that white executive some medical attention and simultaneously stealing something sensitive from him was just plain inspired on your part. I suspect that you will be rewarded handsomely for your work. Katsuie might even find a little extra pocket change for me too."

Coleman responded, "Thank you Dr. Ames. I appreciate your patience and understanding while I positioned myself to accomplish something big. I hope that you, as well as I, get recognized for contributing to the cause in a major way."

Ames: "Yep. I predict another big steak dinner and Hendler's ice cream dessert in our future, Coleman. Did you hear anything about the condition of your boss while I was out?"

AJAX: "I have not received any news concerning Crowe."

Ames: "Well, do not fret over him. The doctors at Johns Hopkins Hospital are among the finest in the world. If they could not help him, then he could not be helped. Tomorrow is Thanksgiving. Odds are you will not hear anything about him for at least a day or two. Enjoy your Thanksgiving dinner with the Dixons and remember to give me a full report of their table talk."

Coleman, feigning a mixture of pride and submissiveness, replied, "Will do, Dr. Ames."

Then Coleman asked Ralph, "What will you be doing for Thanksgiving?"

Ralph: "I will be looking after patients at Provident Hospital. I don't celebrate Thanksgiving. That's for pilgrims, and Lord knows that I ain't one of them. I will celebrate a new kind of Thanksgiving when we win the war against the descendants of the pilgrims."

AJAX: "Dr. Ames, I admire your dedication to your profession and healing people in need."

And that was that.

The lights in Captain Masuji's embassy office burned brightly into the morning. On his first reading of the US Navy report Katsuie's agent had purloined from Bendix, Benkei could barely contain his elation. He analyzed the report over and over again, questioning its verisimilitude with each reading. Finally Masuji concluded that the report had to be authentic and worthy of being transmitted to Tokyo. He personally prepared the document and his analysis of it using an improved IJN code released in early June of 1939. As instructed by Admiral Toyotomi Mitsuhide in August, Masuji ordered a diplomatic courier to hand carry the super-enciphered document to Lieutenant Ito Yuji in Tokyo.

This will be of great interest to the IJN. I should get a medal for this achievement, thought Masuji. *Resources can now be prudently allocated by the IJN to develop more lethal shipboard weapon systems for our warriors, not wasted on costly crash programs to entertain electrical engineers.*

The Captain unlocked his safe, put the Secret file folder on the top shelf, and locked the safe's heavy steel door.

Miss Hara appeared at Masuji's door. "Your tea, Captain Masuji."

She had heard whispers from other clerical staff about Benkei's late night activities. Hara feared that he might be in a foul mood. To her relief, she saw Benkei smiling broadly as he said, "Please enter, Miss Hara. A beautiful morning, don't you agree?"

Miss Hara bowed low and, of course, agreed.

Masuji continued. "I doubt that there will be much work for you today. The Americans will be intoxicated, overfed, and absorbed in their spectator sports today and tomorrow. Leave work early, clean your apartment, do your laundry, enjoy yourself!"

Miss Hara honored Benkei's attempt at humor with a high-pitched feminine faux giggle. *Works every time!* she mused as she bowed and backed out of the office. Once outside the door she thought, *What is that beast up to?*

NOVEMBER 23, 1939; THANKSGIVING DAY

At 8 AM, Coleman received his call from Dr. Crowe. Ralph Ames, ready to drive to Provident Hospital, overheard Coleman say, "That is good news, Dr. Crowe. Why, of course I will. I will get on it right away. Take care of yourself. See you soon."

Dr. Ames asked Coleman, "What was that all about?"

Coleman replied, "It appears that Dr. Crowe suffered just a severe case of indigestion that presented itself like a heart attack. Dr. Crowe's brother, Philip, gave him a clean bill of health, discharged him from Hopkins Hospital, and drove him home early this morning. Crowe asked me to bring his briefcase to him at his home right away. I am going to have to put the report back where I found it and close his briefcase so he does not get suspicious."

Ames said, "Let me drive you to Bendix. Let's not keep the man waiting too long. He is probably nervous that he left an important document in an unsecured condition. Good! Your cover will remain intact. Don't mind me saying this, but your Dr. Crowe is a pussy. Imagine a grown man getting panicked over a tummy ache. Well, good for us."

The FBI agents monitoring the conversation were amused by Dr. Ames's crudeness. One of the agents said, "Dr. Crowe is not going to like being called a woman's organ of regeneration by the likes of Ralph Ames. Old Ralphie will not like the way he is treated in prison when he is convicted of committing espionage against the United States of America."

Coleman drove Dr. Crowe's Imperial to his home and handed him his briefcase. "Thank you, Coleman. Everything OK?"

"Yes, Dr. Crowe. Everything is OK, but we are up against some really bad people."

"Coleman, don't worry. They are out of their depth. You will see. Just be cautious in your words and your deeds. This will all be over soon."

"I hope so," said Coleman, suddenly feeling the effects of the pressure that he had been under for the past 24 hours.

Coleman called Dr. Dixon soon after he arrived home.

"Coleman, so good to hear your voice. Judith is cooking up a storm here. How about if I pick you up around 4 PM? Lucille will accompany me."

Coleman replied, "Now that IS good news. See you soon."

In DC, Horan, Walker, Zangara, Hercules, Clyde, and McLaughlin celebrated Masuji's taking the bait and bet that Lieutenant Yuji and Admiral Mitsuhide too would succumb to the siren song of the fictitious NRL report to the US Navy's CNO. The party ended abruptly when a flash telex arrived from Agents Dennis and Foster, reporting that their thorough search of Westphal's house provided evidence suggesting that one of Friedrich's friends at Glenn L. Martin, a young Baltimore Bund member named Jurgen Huber, intended to surreptitiously damage flight controls and electrical wires installed on twin-engine medium bombers being assembled for the French Air Force and the British Royal Air Force in a building in Middle River. Huber's plan was for the controls to fail in flight, causing the airplanes to crash, killing everyone onboard.

"Let's get Gareth, Murphy, and Martin to assist Dennis and Foster on this case," said Horan. "Who knew that Baltimore could be so exciting."

At 14 South Broadway, Grace and Henry Basswood, Gertrude Kowalska, Martin Victor, Milton Victor, and Rabbi Meir Elkanan gathered for Thanksgiving dinner. Milton commented favorably about the flavor of the turkey. "Grace, this bird is outstanding! My compliments!"

Grace replied, "Milton, you have Gertrude to thank for the delicious turkey. Wait until you taste the apple pie she baked! Best I have ever tasted!" Everyone raised their wine glasses to toast Gertrude. Blushing, Gertrude accepted their accolades.

"I am so glad to be sharing this wonderful day with you. You are all so very dear to me."

Grace then spoke. "And we feel the same about you, Gertrude."

Henry added, "Hear, Hear," and all repeated his toast.

Milton whispered to Martin, "You finally did something right, *Maishe!*"

Martin whispered back, "Milton, whatever happens to me, take care of Gertrude."

Taken aback, Milton replied, "Now there is no need for that kind of talk. Don't you worry about a thing, little brother."

That same evening, during a delightful dinner at the Dixon's residence, Lucille charmed Judith, Jonathan, and Coleman with humorous tales of her law professors deftly employing the Socratic method to pillory students publicly. Coleman could not see the value of such classroom hijinks. The truth be told, Coleman could not see the value of lawyers or the legal profession.

At the end of the day, he thought, *nothing tangible or beneficial comes out of a law school, a lawyer's office, or a courtroom. Nothing.*

Where he worked, people designed, built, and serviced useful advanced technology products that consumers, businesses, and the government needed. The engineers and physicists at Bendix applied their brilliant scientific minds to solving complex problems in innovative ways. Coleman kept his mouth shut and laughed along with the crowd. But deep down, he believed that the silly, game-playing esquires were not all that smart.

Coleman also thought, *These people have no idea that their country is under attack by subversive forces within their own community. Lucky for them that heroes like my uncle Hercules are out there on the front line, protecting them and the nation from its enemies.*

When dessert arrived—a delicious pumpkin pie baked by Judith Dixon—Jonathan Dixon said, "Coleman, why are you so quiet? Has this budding lawyer scared you into silence?"

"No, Sir," said Coleman, "I am mesmerized by Lucille's lucidity!"

Lucille knew when she was being mocked. "Coleman Braxton, you better watch out! I know you are toying with me."

"Now, Lucille," Coleman replied, "I would never do such a thing! I am just a simple, straightforward Baltimore engineer entranced by a skilled orator."

"There you go again, Mr. Braxton. Wait till I get my hands on you!"

Coleman replied, "Oh, Lucille, I would like nothing better!"

At this point, Judith jumped into the conversation. "Now let's simmer down, young folk. I am not sure you are headed in a proper direction!"

Then Jonathan commented. "Judith is right. Let's change the subject. Lucille, what do the people on your campus think about the current world situation?"

Lucille replied, "Most support President Franklin Delano Roosevelt and will fight to defend the country against the Nazis and the Japanese. Some, however, do not see the Japanese as enemies of Negroes. To me, if the Japanese are allied with the racist Nazis, then they are no different than the Nazis. So I support our President. What do you think, Coleman?"

Coleman answered, "Why, I agree with you, Lucille. Your logic is impeccable."

Judith, smiling, said, "Now isn't this an intelligent, civilized conversation, Dr. Dixon?"

Jonathan replied, "Mrs. Dixon, you took the words right out of my mouth!"

The four Thanksgiving celebrants howled with laughter. They agreed to celebrate Christmas Eve together, attend church, and enjoy Judith Dixon's home cooking. After dinner, Lucille accompanied Judith into the kitchen, ostensibly to assist with the cleaning and drying of dishes, glasses, and silverware.

After she commenced running water into the sink and started to scrub, Judith said, "Lucille, how are things going with you and Coleman?"

Taking the dish handed to her by Mrs. Dixon and toweling it dry, Lucille said, "I do not know. He appears consumed with his work and his studies, but I sense that he has other things on his mind. Coleman keeps his thoughts to himself and I do not press him for more information. I suspect that part of his problem stems from living under the same roof with Dr. Ames. Once I suggested that he move to a new apartment and he replied that he got along fine with Ralph Ames and that he did not have the time to engage in a search for a new place. Mrs. Dixon, I love Coleman and I am confident that he loves me. We just seem to be stuck. We are not moving forward in our relationship, and we are not moving backward either."

Mrs. Dixon thought carefully about what she had just heard. "Lucille, a good man like Coleman or my Jonathan tends not to share his problems with the woman he loves. They try to shield us from the danger and horror they see in the world by not talking about it. Where Coleman works, they see a war coming. The folks at Bendix are dedicated to their mission of providing America with the tools necessary to fight and win. He does not want you to worry about things over which you have no control. When Jonathan went off to Europe during the Great War, and even after he returned home, he refused to talk about any of it. He still doesn't talk about it. But here he and I are! Lucille, you stick with Coleman and things will move forward. That is what happened in my experience."

Lucille put down the plate she had dried and hugged Judith. "I do not intend to lose Coleman. Somehow I am going to get that engineer to propose to me!"

Judith exclaimed, "HA! That's the spirit, Lucille! You lasso that stallion, get him in your corral, and train him right!"

The two women roared at each other's earthiness.

Dr. Dixon and Coleman talked man-to-man in Jonathan's office. Puffing on his pipe, Dixon probed much the same territory as Judith did with Lucille. "What is going on with you and Lucille, Coleman?"

Coleman replied, "Between my being busy at work and her studying in DC, we do not communicate much. We sort of depend on our get-togethers with you and Mrs. Dixon to keep our relationship going."

Dr. Dixon pointed the stem of his pipe at Coleman. "Son, do you love Lucille?"

Coleman replied, "Of course I do, Dr. Dixon!"

Dixon then asked, "Can you see yourself married to Lucille?"

Coleman answered, "Yes. Certainly."

Probing further, Jonathan asked, "Coleman, do you want to have children with Lucille?"

Coleman replied, "More than anything, Dr. Dixon!"

Jonathan, in all earnestness, then said, "Well, why don't you move forward with her? You have a good job. She has a bright future. What is holding you back?"

Coleman replied, "Dr. Dixon, you know that I am involved in Hercules's business and that danger lurks everywhere about me. I cannot subject Lucille to any of that at this time. When everything is resolved, I intend to propose to her. But not now!"

Dr. Dixon took a puff, looked up at the ceiling, blew a smoke ring, and said, "Coleman, Lucille has two more years of law school. Do you think this 'business' you have with Hercules will continue beyond her graduation?"

"No. I think things will wrap up sometime in 1940," replied Coleman.

Dixon: "Then you propose to Lucille as soon as this Hercules matter concludes! I want to see you on your knee asking that fine young woman to spend her life with you! You buy her an engagement ring with some of that money you have been accumulating and you tell her the wedding will take place when she graduates from Howard University School of Law. Son, do not take counsel of your fears. The world may be a dangerous place, but you can handle it. Especially with Hercules Boulanger as your backup."

Coleman squared his shoulders and tightened his abdomen. "Dr. Dixon, may I call you 'Dad?'"

Jonathan replied, "Yes. I thought that you would never ask."

The two men shook hands just as they heard Judith and Lucille cackling from the kitchen. "We better check on those two," said Dr. Dixon.

Coleman and Jonathan walked into the kitchen. "What is all that racket about?" asked the doctor.

"None of your business, Jonathan," replied Judith.

"That's just what I thought you would say, woman!"

"Then why did you ask?" said Judith.

"A man might be wrong every now and then. I thought maybe you would 'fess up to whatever it is you two are plotting," replied Dr. Dixon.

"Not a chance, you old sawbones." came Judith's reply.

"Well, in that case, can Coleman and I get a cup of coffee?"

"Sure. Pour it yourselves." said Judith tartly.

"You ladies want some coffee too?" asked Coleman.

"Why, yes," said Lucille. "You can serve us in the dining room."

Dr. Dixon put his arm on Coleman's shoulder and said, "You see, Coleman? These modern women mean to dominate our lives."

Lucille and Judith both replied, "You are damned right."

The laughter could be heard down the block.

And that was that.

18

With the Masuji radio-wave device threat contained for the moment by the fraudulent document transfer, the FBI/ONI/BCPD team focused its attention on the Westphal-Huber espionage conspiracy targeting the 215 Glenn L. Martin Maryland 167 A-3 medium bombers being built in Building C in Middle River for the French Air Force. Delivery of these desperately needed aircraft to French Air Force depots in North Africa was scheduled for December 15, 1939.

Westphal and Huber exercised caution by covertly conducting their conferences concerning committing acts of espionage against the Maryland 167's solely within the confines of Westphal's home—a place they thought would be secure from surveillance. Their conversations, of course, were recorded by the listening devices planted by FBI Agents Dennis and Fowler. The transcripts of their talks disclosed that Bund member Jurgen Huber, the son of naturalized American citizens who had emigrated from Germany, argued with Bund member Westphal about preventing Glenn L. Martin bombers from being delivered to the French Air Force.

"I have relatives living in Germany, Friedrich. So do you. How could we live with ourselves knowing that we contributed to our kin being murdered by French airmen dropping bombs from airplanes built by our employer?" bellowed Huber in a transcript dated November 26, 1939. Westphal did not raise his voice in response to Huber's argument that they had to act at once to disable the aircraft before they were shipped to the French Air Force.

"Jurgen, I appreciate your concern and I feel your anguish. However, what you propose will not change anything. Damaging a few Maryland medium bombers will not prevent most of them from being repaired and hundreds more of them from being transferred to France. If your conscience plagues you, request a transfer to the group working on the PBM, a plane that will never be used to bomb or torpedo anything other than an enemy combatant's warships at sea. You will be caught if you attempt to sabotage the aircraft in Building C, and you will be imprisoned for a long period of time. Now what good will that do, my friend?"

Huber exploded in response to Westphal's logical arguments. "Friedrich, you are a disgrace to the Fatherland and the German people. You might as well be a filthy Jewish banker backing Franklin Roosevelt as he stabs Nazi Germany in the back. To defend the Reich and Aryan Germans, I intend to do as much damage to those Maryland medium bombers as possible, with or without you. You cannot hide your cowardice, Friedrich. You are afraid to protect your race. For shame!"

Restraining himself, Westphal replied, "Jurgen, calm yourself. Insulting me is not a rational way to weigh the facts facing us. Raising your voice will not persuade or intimidate me. I will not fight with you, Jurgen. I am asking you to consider carefully the path that you propose to follow."

On the 27th of November, Jurgen called Friedrich at home from a pay phone booth in Middle River, Maryland and announced, "Friedrich, I have to do what I have to do. The 167's are to be transferred during the first three days of December." He then hung up the telephone before Westphal could utter a sound.

Huber, a foreman in Building C, had unrestricted access to the plant floor 24 hours a day, seven days a week. He could pick and choose his time to damage flight-critical components in difficult-to-detect areas within the Maryland 167's. Given his intimate knowledge of the aircraft, Jurgen Huber could work quickly and unobtrusively using a handful of tools from his Glenn L. Martin tool kit. The bugged telephone conversation provided conclusive proof that Huber, an ardent Nazi sympathizer, had decided that the 167's about to be shipped to North Africa had to be sabotaged sometime between December 1 and December 3.

To make the prosecutors' case easier to prove at trial and to maximize Jurgen Huber's prison sentence, the team concluded that Huber ought to be allowed to damage one plane before they swooped in to arrest him. Hercules believed that Westphal could be persuaded to testify against his friend and might provide useful intelligence to the team regarding the Nazi government's efforts to encourage espionage in the United States.

In a meeting at the Baltimore FBI office, Hercules explained his thinking to Walker, Dennis, Fowler, Gareth, Murphy, and Martin.

"Huber has discussed with Westphal his plan to sabotage aircraft built by Glenn L. Martin. Friedrich, however, refuses to alert either security at Glenn L. Martin or law enforcement officials about Jurgen's intentions. Westphal could be charged as Huber's co-conspirator, as he has knowledge before the fact of the planned sabotage. However, Friedrich's lawyer will argue that his client never agreed with Huber to do anything and therefore Westphal cannot be guilty of conspiracy. All of this is nice lawyer stuff that the Department of Justice lawyers may overcome at trial, but clearly, Westphal is not in the same league as Jurgen Huber when it comes to the crime of espionage. Give Martin and me a chance to turn him to our advantage. If we cannot convince Westphal to work with us and testify against Huber, then let's put him up against the same wall as Huber and I will command the firing squad."

Walker replied, "I see your logic, but wouldn't the probability of success be increased if we sent Gareth and Murphy instead of you and Victor?"

Hercules, channeling Socrates, said, "You miss my point, Clarence. If Westphal is a hard-core Nazi, he will take one look at me and Martin and go down fighting like his pal, Jurgen. If Friedrich talks politely to the likes of me and Martin and cooperates with us, the man is definitely not a hard-core goose-stepper and can be converted to our cause."

Walker, turning to Victor, asked, "What do you think, Martin? In your estimation, will Hercules's plan work?"

Martin answered, "When has Hercules's judgment or instinct been wrong? I defer to him."

Walker then asked Murphy the same question. Murphy seconded Walker's notion that if the objective was to co-opt Westphal, the odds of success would be greater using Gareth and himself. "Why risk having Friedrich go 'Nazi nuts' when he sees a Negro and a Jew on his doorstep?"

Gareth disagreed. "Clarence and Murph, in my experience, you cannot reliably turn a true believer. Nazis, Communists, State Shintoists, and Fascists are not like street hoods or Mafia foot-soldiers and capos. They will not turn on a Hitler, a Stalin, a Hirohito, or a Mussolini. They will find a way to subvert our plans. So I would smoke out Westphal using Hercules and Martin. See if he genuinely is as rational and non-ideological as his transcripts indicate. If he is, we own him. If deep down Westphal is a Nazi fanatic, we lose nothing."

Walker nodded his head toward Hercules. "OK, Hercules. We will do it your way. But do not promise Westphal that we will not prosecute him. He has to earn his way out of this situation into which he got himself!"

Hercules nodded his head in agreement.

Gareth then added, "Clarence, you have a commitment to Captain Giles Renaud of the Baltimore City Police Department to alert him in advance of any planned takedown that poses a risk of gunplay. Trust me, Clarence, you do not want Renaud to first learn about an FBI espionage arrest at Glenn L. Martin from a front-page headline in *The Baltimore Sun*. He will never forgive you, and my career will be forever compromised."

Walker told Gareth, "You go visit your boss and brief him now. Invite him to join us in making the arrest. Tell Renaud that the FBI press release will specifically mention that this was a joint BCPD and FBI covert operation. Thank him from me for facilitating your secondment to the FBI-ONI team."

Gareth replied, "Clarence, this is the kind of consideration that will pay big dividends down the road. Baltimore relationships are built on a voluntary flow of reliable, back-channel communications concerning future events that benefit the recipient of the information. I will get right on it."

Clarence Walker called Edwin Coar on the executive's private line. In his most buoyant voice he said, "Hi, Ed. How are you doing on this fine day?"

Coar replied, "I was fine until this call. What is about to go very wrong in my life?"

Walker continued pitching Coar, using the FBI version of an automobile salesman's bonhomie. "Ed, we are about to remove some rats from your factory at no cost. You should be pleased."

"Oh, I am excited. Will you be shooting the rodents in my plant or will you just trap them humanely and carry them out to a waiting paddy wagon without injuring some innocent Glenn L. Martin employee bystanders or damaging Glenn L. Martin property?" Coar asked.

"Ed, there will be no gunplay in your workplace. There will be one arrest made, probably after most of your workers have gone home," replied Walker in a more FBI-agent-professional tone of voice.

Coar: "When will this blessed event transpire?"

Walker: "Not precisely clear just yet, but sometime between December 1 and December 3 in Building C."

Somewhat incensed, Coar exclaimed, "Christ Almighty, Walker! Do you know I have a big order of medium bombers going out to our French friends at that time?"

Walker: "Oh, do I ever, Ed. Two hundred and fifteen magnificent Maryland 167 A-3's, right?"

In a calmer tone, Coar replied, "You have been doing your homework, Clarence. I am impressed."

Walker: "Ed, I am a committed public servant and your buddy."

Coar: "Is this where you tell me some Nazi has to damage one of my bombers so you can win at trial and put the kraut away for a long time?"

Walker now knew that Coar would not object to the FBI's tactical plan. In his happy voice, Clarence said, "Precisely, Ed. I can see that you too have done your homework."

Coar laughed and agreed to Walker's request to position FBI "heavies" ahead of time in Building C to arrest Jurgen Huber after he sabotaged one—and only one—Maryland 167 bomber. "Real pleasure doing business with you, Clarence."

Walker replied, "Look at it like this—no Nazi, Jap, Commie, or Fascist will go near Glenn L. Martin when they see what we do to Huber in federal court. We are going to make an example of his sorry Reich rectum to deter other creeps cogitating committing espionage in Mr. Martin's domain."

Coar replied, "I will pass along the good news to Mr. Martin."

Walker: "Thanks. Give him Mr. Hoover's sincerest regards."

Coar: "I will do that. When would you like to go to the Cosmos Club again, Clarence?"

Walker, dreaming about consuming another gratis glass of expensive scotch with Coar, said, "How about in mid-December?"

Coar: "I will be in town on December 16th. Does that work for you?"

Walker: "As long as I am not in a Baltimore hospital recovering from gunshot wounds, it works for me. Seven PM at my office, and we can walk over together."

Coar: "Great. Stay safe. See you soon."

At 7 PM on Friday, December 1, Jurgen Huber found himself facing Dennis, Fowler, Gareth, and Murphy with their guns drawn, yelling at him to drop his tools and lie facedown on the shop floor next to the plane he had just sabotaged. Jurgen moved a little too slowly for Gareth, who used the butt of his revolver to "tap" the saboteur's carotid, knocking the Nazi to the ground. Captain Giles Renaud stood in the background, admiring Gareth's adroit use of overwhelming Baltimore Logic on the saboteur. After the handcuffs were tightly locked around Jurgen's wrists and the dazed Nazi hauled off, Renaud put his arm around Gareth and said, "I am going to the Commissioner's office to make my report. You want to accompany me?"

Gareth replied, "Of course. However, whatever works best for you, Boss, is OK with me. If you want do a solo briefing, my feelings will not be injured."

Renaud replied, "Gareth, I want the Commissioner to see that you and I are a team. We share the glory when things go right. When things go wrong, we share responsibility for the failure and do not point fingers at some scapegoat."

Gareth shook hands with Renaud and said, "Let's go impress the Commissioner."

Following the arrest of Huber, Boulanger and Victor received the green light to visit Westphal at home and chat him up. Hercules rapped on the front door and announced, "Open up, this is the FBI."

A surprised Friedrich Westphal took one look at Hercules and blurted out, "You are not FBI. You are colored."

Hercules flashed his badge and countered with, "*Herr* Westphal, this is your lucky day! My friend here, Lieutenant 'Cohen' from the US Navy, and I want to talk to you about a Mr. Jurgen Huber. Ever hear of him?"

Westphal replied, "Yes, I know Jurgen Huber."

Pleased that Friedrich was cooperating already, Boulanger continued. "Mr. Huber has been arrested for damaging a Maryland 167 medium bomber in Building C that was about to be shipped overseas to the French Air Force.

You know anything about his plan to commit this dastardly act of espionage? As you can see, my German-American Bund friend, you are potentially facing a lot of time in federal prison if you were involved in any way with Jurgen's misdeeds. Now, we would like to help you out. However, we need your cooperation in order to spare you the torment presently being inflicted on Mr. Huber. Jurgen has been booked on charges of espionage and assaulting an officer. He will, no doubt, be charged with additional crimes as a large team of experienced Department of Justice prosecutors is now reviewing, in minute detail, everything he has ever said or done during the past seven years. What do you think, Mr. Westphal? You want to invite us into your home and help us and yourself out? Or should we arrest you right here in front of all your neighbors and take you downtown for processing and an unpleasant weekend in jail?"

Westphal replied, "Gentlemen, why don't you come in so we can discuss this complex matter properly?"

Hercules smiled and said, "Wise choice, Mr. Westphal. We do not make offers like this twice."

To prepare for this encounter, Hercules and Martin had read the transcripts of every bugged conversation between Westphal and Huber, as well as the surreptitious entry reports submitted (but not officially filed) by Dennis and Fowler. The two federal agents were also well aware of Westphal's Carleton Hotel Bar dispute with Elizabeth Robertson. Armed with this background information, they intended to ferret out with whom Westphal and Huber were working. They would also ascertain the veracity of Friedrich Westphal.

Once inside his row house, Westphal turned left into his living room and asked if he could sit on the sofa. Although they knew the location of Westphal's weapons, Hercules asked Friedrich for permission to search the couch before Friedrich sat down. Westphal agreed and Martin thoroughly examined the piece of furniture. Satisfied that there were no guns or blades secreted in the sofa, Martin gave a thumbs-up signal to Hercules.

"Please be seated, Mr. Westphal," Hercules said in his gravelly voice. After Westphal sat down, "Lieutenant Cohen" completely closed the curtains to the window on the wall behind the sofa. Hercules and Martin sat on chairs facing Friedrich, their suit jackets open and their revolvers in their holsters plainly visible.

"Mr. Westphal, how long have you known Jurgen Huber?"

Clearing his throat, Westphal replied, "I met Jurgen the day the *Hindenburg* flew two circles over Baltimore: Saturday, August 8, 1936. Max Schmeling, my favorite heavyweight boxer, was aboard the *Hindenburg*."

Boulanger smiled and said, "My, you have a very precise memory."

Westphal smiled back at Hercules. "I have an excellent memory, Mister…"

"Call me Hercules."

"OK, Mr. Hercules. That night I visited the Deutsches Haus for a Bund meeting and I had a beer or two with Mr. Huber. We discovered that we had much in common. For example, we both attended Kreuzkirche Lutheran Church, graduated from Polytechnic High School, worked at Glenn L. Martin, loved airplanes, and, of course, enjoyed German beer!"

Hercules, still smiling, said, "I see. So would you say that you became close friends?"

Westphal: "Correct."

Hercules then asked, "Friedrich… May I call you Friedrich?"

Westphal: "Certainly."

"Friedrich, were you aware of Mr. Huber's intention to damage Glenn L. Martin aircraft?"

Westphal replied, "I was very aware of his ethical concerns about building bombers for the French Air Force."

Hercules: "Ethical concerns? Could you explain Jurgen's ethical concerns to me?"

Westphal: "He has family in Germany—Berlin, to be exact—and he feared that the Maryland bombers he was building for the French Air Force would be used injure or kill his family members."

Hercules: "And did you share Mr. Huber's 'ethical' concerns?'"

Westphal: "No. I work in the PBM Mariner seaplane program, not the Maryland medium bomber program. My aircraft do not bomb cities or civilians. The PBM is a purely defensive weapon system to defend America's coastline, harbors, and shipping against attacks by foreign navies. I saw no moral issue arising from my particular line of work."

Hercules was not about to let Westphal evade the essential issue, so he followed up with the question, "Did you agree with Jurgen as far as his work was concerned?"

Intellectually agile, Westphal responded, "Over time, I came to understand my friend's painful dilemma. I never agreed, however, with his solution to that dilemma. For a considerable amount of time, America appeared to be staying neutral regarding the conflict in Europe. Our Congress restricted arms shipments to all European belligerents. But as time passed, it appeared to most German-Americans I know that FDR favored Britain and France against Germany. Some American political and business leaders, representatives of numerous American groups, as well as officials from the German embassy and our relatives in Germany, complained openly about this lack of balance in US foreign policy. Even people from the US State Department expressed their concern about America's movement from neutrality to confrontation with Germany. Specifically, a female State Department official named Elizabeth Robertson accompanied a speaker from the German embassy named Joachim Lansdorff to a Bund meeting in Baltimore that Jurgen and I attended, and she strongly criticized FDR's offer to Great Britain of 'all aid short of war.'"

Boulanger asked, "Do you recall when this Elizabeth Robertson spoke at this Baltimore Bund meeting?"

Westphal replied, "I do not recall the precise date of the meeting, but it was soon after the Wehrmacht entered Poland in September of this year."

Resuming his main line of questioning, Hercules asked, "I hear you, Friedrich, but did you come to agree with Jurgen that direct action had to be taken to prevent Maryland medium bombers from being shipped to the French Air Force?"

Westphal: "Mr. Hercules, I personally could not go on to the shop floor and damage airplanes produced by Glenn L. Martin. Unfortunately, I could not convince my friend—who was motivated out of sense of moral outrage—to stay his hand. Mr. Hercules, I know that I should have done more to stop Jurgen."

Hercules: "Friedrich, you need to tell me about the full extent of your involvement in Mr. Huber's actions."

Westphal: "I met with Jurgen on several occasions here at my home, where he discussed his intentions with me. At no time did I agree to assist him in damaging a Glenn L. Martin product. When I was approached by German embassy people to provide information about the PBM, I refused to cooperate. When the State Department woman attempted to recruit me to help Germany and commit acts against the PBM program, I refused. Even though America and Glenn L. Martin intend to sell PBMs to the RAF, I refused to take any action contrary to the commercial interests of my employer. Although I feel strongly about Germany, I resisted embassy pressure to help them. They are not my friends. Jurgen, unfortunately, is my friend. And while I would not assist him, I could not betray him."

Hercules: "Did Jurgen meet separately with German embassy officials about his intentions?"

Westphal: "Yes."

Hercules: "Were you with him when he met with them?"

Westphal: "No. He told me that he had one such meeting, after it occurred. You will have to ask him for the details. He did not tell me the name or names of the person or people with whom he met. I do not know when the meeting took place. I do not know what was discussed."

Hercules: "Did he meet with the woman from the State Department?"

Westphal: "If he did, he did not tell me about it. Again, you will have to ask him."

At this point, Hercules said, "Friedrich, thank you for being so frank about this emotionally complex situation. To protect you from reprisals, we would like to take you into protective custody. You are not under arrest and you can refuse to come with us. However, I must tell you that you are now a 'loose end' in what appears to be a German government conspiracy against the United States. They do not like loose ends and, in my experience, they will do grievous harm to you to prevent you from talking to us and providing evidence against them."

Visibly shaking, Westphal replied, "May I bring a suitcase with me? I need some clothing, toiletries, and the like."

Hercules smiled and said, "Friedrich, we will take care of all your personal needs. The US Government is very generous to its friends."

Westphal, his hands trembling and his eyes glistening, said, "Let's go."

Hercules asked to use Friedrich's telephone to make one call. Friedrich agreed and Hercules received instructions from Karl Dennis about the location of an FBI safe house in Garrison, Maryland.

The three men got into Hercules's car and drove to Garrison, Maryland. Lieutenant Cohen, aka Martin Victor, who remained silent throughout the entire interview process, awed by Hercules's persuasive powers and cunning deceitfulness. Hercules had no authority to make any commitments to a potential co-conspirator in an espionage case, but he had cleverly sandbagged the US government with his offer of witness protection. Martin thought, *Tactically brilliant. Gutsy. Productive. I have a lot to learn from Hercules Boulanger!*

Martin called Henry from the safe house. "Henry, would you mind taking Gertrude to Rabbi Elkanan's synagogue on Saturday? I am involved in something significant and will be unavailable for the next few days."

Henry replied, "Martin, Grace and I would be delighted to assist you and Gertrude. Will I read about your activities in *The Baltimore Sun,* or hear about it on the radio?"

Martin replied, "Thank you. As you know, Gertrude must attend services regularly as part of her conversion process. As for your question about my activities, I cannot confirm or deny anything."

Henry: "I understand. Martin, protect yourself. Remember, if someone comes to hurt you, kill them first!"

Martin thought, *Hippocratic-Oath-Henry strikes again*!

8 AM SATURDAY, DECEMBER 2, 1939; GARRISON, MARYLAND, FBI SAFE HOUSE

Clarence Walker initiated the inquisition by showing Westphal the front page of *The Baltimore Sun*. The headline above the fold read, **Huber Faces Charges As Saboteur For Damaging Martin Planes**.

Friedrich read the article and sobbed. "I tried to reason with him not to damage any aircraft. I begged him not to do it. I warned him that he would get caught and spend a long time in prison. Now he is front-page news. What is going to happen to Jurgen?"

Walker replied, "First, the Government of the United States is going to impoverish Mr. Huber with legal expenses. Next, Jurgen will be fined at least $20,000, plus he will have to reimburse the cost of repairing the airplane he damaged. Mr. Huber will be tried and sentenced to a minimum of twenty years imprisonment in a federal prison filled with vicious men of all races and ethnicities who hate Nazis. Jurgen's life is essentially over. Now, if you want to avoid his fate, you must answer my questions accurately and completely. Hold nothing back. Mr. Hercules told me about your conversation with him and "Lieutenant Cohen" yesterday. He says that you want to help us get to the bottom of this case. Frankly, Friedrich, you have no choice but to assist us. Nazi agents have already been dispatched to silence you. Last night, the FBI detected two sinister-looking men park their automobile in front of your home. Their car had DC diplomatic license plates. Both men left the car and one of the gentlemen knocked on your front door. When there was no response, the other thug picked your lock in less than twenty seconds and the two of them searched inside your home you for 30 minutes. They then moved their vehicle to the corner of Kenwood Avenue and Baltimore Street and waited two hours for you to return. When you did not return, they drove back to the German embassy in DC, presumably to report to their boss.

"Friedrich, to protect Mr. Huber and the network of Nazi agents active in the United States, these men and others like them will hunt you down and kill you. Only the US government can stop them and save you at this point. The more you tell us about these Nazi agents and their US supporters, the easier it will be for us to eliminate them and protect you. Do you understand?"

Westphal replied, "I understand completely. I will tell you everything that I know."

Walker: "Good. Let's begin. Here are photos of the two men who visited your home last night. Do you recognize either of them?"

Westphal: "The man with the dueling scars on the left side of his face is the bodyguard of Major Joachim Lansdorff, an official at the German embassy. I do not know his name. As I told Mr. Hercules last night, Major Lansdorff and a Miss Elizabeth Robertson—an officer in the US State Department—attended a Bund meeting in Baltimore in September, just after the Wehrmacht entered Poland. The bodyguard accompanied Lansdorff at that meeting. Miss Robertson and Lansdorff circulated through the crowd and complained loudly about FDR's efforts to circumvent the US Neutrality Acts and provide Great Britain with 'all aid short of war.' Jurgen Huber was attracted to Miss Robertson and attempted to engage her in a more social conversation. She would have none of it. However, when Jurgen mentioned that he worked at Glenn L. Martin, she signaled Lansdorff and he joined the conversation. Robertson and Lansdorff attempted to get information from Jurgen and me about our work. I walked away. Jurgen stayed and spoke with them. However, he never told me anything about his private conversation with Robertson and Lansdorff that night."

Walker: "Yesterday, you told Agent Hercules that you did not know with whom Jurgen communicated about committing acts of espionage. Are you amending your previous statement?"

Westphal: "Yes, but only to the extent that I neglected to mention that Jurgen spoke to Lansdorff and Robertson privately at the Bund meeting in Baltimore. I did not know then, and I do not know now, what the three of them discussed at the Bund meeting after I walked away from them. Look, last night I was nervous, upset, and not thinking clearly at the time. As I said to you before, I intend to cooperate fully with you and will not withhold any information from you."

Walker: "OK, Friedrich. I cannot stress strongly enough that any communication that you have with us must be accurate. No games! No evasion!"

Westphal: "I understand. No games. No evasion."

Walker then showed a photograph of Captain Masuji to Westphal. "Ever seen this fellow?"

Westphal: "No, I have not. I would certainly remember a face like that one."

Walker put a photo of Ulrike Koch before Westphal. "How about her?"

Westphal replied, "I have seen that one with Joachim Lansdorff."

Walker asked, "Please elaborate. Where did you see her? When did you see her? And what happened when you saw her?"

Westphal: "This is an important story that I did not get to tell your men yesterday. I got a call at work from Elizabeth Robertson on Tuesday, November 7th, inviting me to have dinner with her in DC on Tuesday, November 14th. She asked me to pick her up at her apartment at 6 PM and gave me her address. I figured that Miss Robertson must be interested in me in a social kind of way, so I agreed. On November 14th, I left work early and drove from Baltimore to DC, thinking I was going out on a date with an attractive and sophisticated woman. However, when I got to her apartment, Lansdorff and that woman in the photo—I recall her name now: Ulrike Koch—were already there waiting for me. I knew instantly that I had been set up. Before I could say a word, Robertson said that Major Lansdorff wanted to speak with me privately before she and I would go to the Carleton Hotel for dinner. Koch and Robertson then left the apartment. Lansdorff tried every trick in the book to get me to agree to give him information about the PBM Mariner Program and anything else I know about programs at Glenn L. Martin. First he told me that it was my duty as a German to help the Fatherland. I said, 'Nothing doing!' Then, he offered me money—$500 a month—to become his agent at Martin. I told him, 'Absolutely not!' Then he offered me Miss Koch. I said, 'Are you nuts?' Finally, he asked if I enjoyed the company of men instead of women and offered an all-expense paid trip to New York to meet attractive German men! Sickened by the thought of what he was suggesting, I told him that I wanted nothing to do with him, Koch, and Robertson and that I was going back to Baltimore. He apologized profusely for being so forward and said that I would not hear from him or see him ever again. He left. Robertson returned to the apartment alone and apologized for Lansdorff's behavior. She told me that she should at least take me out to dinner. Like an idiot, I agreed. We went to the Carleton Hotel Bar. I ordered a hamburger and a Coke. She got drunk and loud, criticizing the American government's military aid to France and Great Britain and FDR's bias against Germany. I begged her to quiet down. She refused. I got up to leave. She paid the bill and I drove her home. Then I drove back to Baltimore. And that was that. I have not communicated with Lansdorff, Robertson, or Koch since."

Walker: "Mr. Westphal, why did you not report any of this to Martin's security department, or the FBI?"

Westphal: "I should have. I knew that these people were sick in the head. However, when Lansdorff told me that I would not hear from him again, I figured that he meant what he said. I hoped that this was the end of the matter.

I thought that I had not done anything wrong, and that now the whole thing would go away."

Walker: "But Friedrich, you still had your friend Jurgen to deal with! Did it not occur to you that Mr. Huber might be in league with Lansdorff? Didn't it seem to you that Jurgen was, as you put it, *sick in the head,* just like Lansdorff and his cronies? Friedrich, you are an educated engineer. Couldn't you see that Jurgen meant to endanger the lives of Glenn L. Martin test pilots and other employees by tampering with the Maryland 167 bombers that were about to be shipped to France? Did you not recognize that your company's reputation and business prospects would be damaged by the crash of one or more Maryland bombers? Why did you not alert the Security Department at Glenn L. Martin, or call the FBI to try to prevent Jurgen's espionage against your employer and against your nation?"

Westphal put his head in his hands and burst into tears. "I am a weak man. I am a fearful man. I am a cowardly man. I could not betray my friend Jurgen even though I could see that he intended to do wrong. I could not bring myself to blow the whistle on Lansdorff and Robertson because I feared their reprisals and because I feared possibly losing my job for associating with such bad people. I am an American citizen and yet, I went along with crowds of German-Americans who support Hitler—a man who hates everything the US stands for." Hitting his head with both of his hands, Westphal shouted, "I am just plain worthless, worthless, worthless!"

In a mild, pastoral voice, Walker said, "Friedrich, I can see that you are trying to redeem yourself. Please calm down. I have one last question for this morning. Think carefully: Did Jurgen ever indicate to you in any way that he may have met with Lansdorff, Robertson, Koch, or anyone else from the German embassy on his own without you?"

Westphal thought for a while and said, "No. Jurgen never told me that he was in contact with Lansdorff or Robertson after that one chance encounter that he and I had with them in Baltimore. He always seemed to be acting on his own to protect his family members in Germany. He never indicated to me that he was receiving money, gifts, or favors of any kind in exchange for conducting espionage activities at Glenn L. Martin."

Walker: "OK. We will talk later today, say around lunchtime. Let me know then if you recall additional information that we should know about concerning Glenn L. Martin, Jurgen, Lansdorff, Robertson, Koch, or other individuals who may be engaged in espionage."

Westphal: "I will reflect carefully on all of this terrible business."

And that was that.

Walker, Hercules, and Martin convened outside the safe house. "What is your assessment of Westphal's credibility, Hercules? Do you believe his story?" Walker asked.

"I think Friedrich is leveling with us now. He has diagnosed himself correctly. Westphal is a yellow-belly through and through. But he is our yellow-belly! The Nazi wolves have his scent and they are on his trail. We should stake Westphal out like a lamb and let the wolves come for him here in Garrison, Maryland. Then we can kill or capture a few hard-case Nazis. Assuming Friedrich survives, we can use him as a prosecution witness in Jurgen's trial...provided Huber survives long enough to go to trial."

Walker turned to Martin. "OK. Lieutenant Victor, what do you have to offer?"

"Agent Walker, Westphal's statements square with the facts we have collected during this investigation. Additionally, we now know that Lansdorff and Robertson are working together to commit acts of espionage. What we cannot confirm through Westphal directly is whether they were involved in Jurgen's plan to commit sabotage against the Maryland 167 bombers destined for the French Air Force. I think we need to have a run at Jurgen to pin down this part of the story. Perhaps we can combine this effort with Hercules's 'Westphal Wolves Gambit' to achieve a prompt, more efficient outcome."

Walker looked at Martin as if he were from another galaxy. "Would you mind explaining more precisely the details of the plan you are proposing?"

Martin replied, "Sure, Clarence. If we dangle Westphal in front of Huber as an FBI witness prepared to testify against him, perhaps Jurgen will feel betrayed and blurt out his version of events. We may get some new leads and some new facts from him to run down. I sure would like to know, for example, whether Masuji was involved in Jurgen's little frolic in Building C. Even if Huber clams up, you can just bet he will tell his German-embassy-financed mouthpiece that Westphal is a rat in need of a visit by some Nazi pest control operators. This will certainly amp up the Nazis and, as Hercules has suggested, give us an opportunity to bag some hard-core Hitler youth, one or two of whom might give us some useful intel."

Hercules enjoyed this interchange. "Walker, this Baltimore boy catches on quick, doesn't he?"

Walker, shaking his head, replied, "What hath Quantico wrought! I will run this by our team members Gareth, Murphy, Dennis, and Fowler and see if they agree and have any other ingredients that they would like to add to this witches' brew you two have cooked up."

Hercules and Martin reentered the safe house to babysit Westphal, and Walker headed to the Court Square Building in downtown Baltimore.

At 10 AM, Walker arrived at the FBI office. Two well-dressed, high-priced lawyers—one from a Baltimore law firm and one from a DC law firm—were demanding to see their client, Mr. Jurgen Huber, immediately. Huber's arraignment before a federal magistrate was scheduled for 2 PM that Saturday afternoon. The US attorney handling the case reviewed the bona fides of the defense counsel and Huber confirmed that he wished to consult with counsel. A room was set aside for this attorney-client privileged conversation to take place at 10:30 AM. Unbeknownst to the US attorney, the FBI had installed a listening device and a recording device in the conference room.

In manacles, Huber was brought to the conference room by two beefy US marshals. They denied the request by the lawyers to have the steel jewelry around Huber's wrists and ankles removed. The DC lawyer, Albert Benoit

Helm, protested. "This is outrageous. I will raise this cruel and highly unusual treatment of my client with the magistrate."

The marshals did not reply.

Helm introduced himself as a partner in the law firm of Helm and Fannon. The Baltimore lawyer introduced himself as Rainer Brennan, a partner in the law firm of Brennan and Gunther. Helm asked, "Jurgen, how have you been treated by the federal authorities?"

Jurgen replied, "Aside from one of the arresting officers knocking me to the ground for no reason and the atrocious swill they call food here, I have been treated OK."

Helm inquired, "Did anyone ask you any questions or pressure you to answer any questions?"

Jurgen answered, "No. No one has said much of anything to me."

Helm responded, "Odd that they did not at least try to get you to make some incriminating statements, or try to trick you into giving them some information with a worthless promise that 'things' will go a lot easier for you if you cooperate with them. Did you volunteer any statements or information to the FBI?"

Huber replied, "No. I spoke not a word!"

Helm: "Good. Have you ever been arrested before?"

Huber: "No, Sir. Never."

Helm: "Have you ever gotten into any kind of trouble with a school, an employer, a woman?"

Huber: "No, Sir. I have a perfectly clean record and reputation."

Helm: "All right. The magistrate is going to inform you of crimes for which you are being charged—espionage, sabotage, attempted murder, assaulting an officer, etc. He is going to ask you how you plead, 'Not Guilty' or 'Guilty.'"

Huber asked, "Well, they caught me carrying tools that were used to damage a Maryland 167 medium bomber. Can I plead Not Guilty under these circumstances?"

Helm: "Sure you can. Have you ever seen a doctor, Jurgen?"

Huber: "Yes. I had my tonsils removed. I fell off a ladder trimming a tree and got a concussion. That is pretty much it."

Helm: "Did you get hospitalized for the concussion?"

Huber: "Yes, I did. I was kept in a dark room for days at Johns Hopkins Hospital. It took weeks for me before I could go back to high school. I actually had to repeat my senior year at Polytechnic."

Helm: "Have you had any problems associated with the concussion since? Have you had difficulty with your attention span, for example? Have you had to go back to your doctor at Johns Hopkins for further evaluation?"

Huber: "Yes. I see the same doctor who first treated the concussion. I do get headaches. Migraines, the doctor calls them. Sometimes they are so bad that I cannot go to work."

Helm: "Can you describe what 'bad' means in this context?"

Huber: "It is like, I cannot stand any kind of light or sound. Sometimes I get dizzy and a little confused about what day it is or who the mayor of Baltimore is. You know."

Helm, "Do you remember the name of the doctor?"

Huber: "Yes. He is a good German. His name is Dr. Horst Dittman. But what has all of this got to do with today's court proceeding?"

Helm: "Jurgen, it sounds to me as though you might have grounds to plead Not Guilty on account of your diminished capacity from that fall you had. Of course, we will need some time to examine all of the details, but for now, I think you can reasonably plead Not Guilty. We will ask for some time to talk to your physician and other people who know you well. What is your relationship like with your parents?"

Huber: "Close. I live with them. Did they call you? Are they paying for your services for me?"

Helm: "No, your parents did not call us. Your parents are not paying for our services."

Huber: "Well, who is paying for all of this?"

Helm: "Your friends at the German-American Bund."

Huber: "Really?"

Helm: "Really! Now, Jurgen, did you talk to anyone about any plans you may have had regarding the Maryland 167 medium bombers you work on?"

Huber: "Well, just my close friend Friedrich Westphal. He works at Glenn L. Martin too, in the PBM Mariner Program. He tried to talk me out of doing anything to the 167's."

Helm: "Did you talk to anyone else?"

For the first time since the conversation began, Huber looked uncomfortable. He composed himself and then replied, "No. Just Friedrich."

Huber lied to his lawyers about discussions regarding his espionage plans in order to keep his promise to Major Lansdorff never to tell anyone about the two secret meetings he had had with Joachim and his chauffeur/bodyguard subsequent to the Bund meeting in Baltimore. During these encounters, Jurgen received a commitment from the German government to exfiltrate him from the US to Berlin after he damaged the Maryland bombers, find him an engineering position in Heinkel Flugszeugwerke—a German firm located north of Berlin that produced bombers—and open up a secret gold account for him in the Deutsche Reichsbank equal to $20,000.

Helm: "Good. You are certain about this?"

Huber: "Yes. Just Friedrich."

Helm looked at Brennan and said, "Rainer, what do you think?"

Brennan replied, "I think that we need to tell the magistrate that Mr. Huber needs to get a thorough neurological and psychological evaluation.

Based on what we have heard so far, Mr. Huber has grounds to plead Not Guilty and to ask for bail, as he will be living within his parents' home and he has no record of any previous criminal conduct. Mr. Huber, do you have a passport?"

Huber: "No. Why would I need one of those?"

Brennan: "You have never traveled outside the US?"

Huber: "No, I have not."

Brennan: "Where have you traveled in the US?"

Huber: "I go to Ocean City, Maryland, every summer with my parents. I went to the University of Maryland in College Park to pursue my engineering studies."

Brennan: "Ever been to DC?"

Huber: "Can't say that I have. I am a Maryland kind of guy."

Brennan: "Albert, I think Mr. Huber should be bailed out of here today."

Helm: "I agree, Rainer. Today."

Walker and Dennis had heard enough of this "privileged conversation" to decide to conduct a little psychological warfare against Jurgen, his two lawyers, and their Nazi backers. The two FBI men requested an opportunity to speak with the defendant and his counsel before the arraignment. Helm and Brennan agreed to the meeting on the condition that they and their client would only listen to what the FBI had to say, period. If, after the lawyers discussed the FBI's proffer privately with their client, a further conversation was deemed necessary, they would get back to Walker and Dennis. The two FBI men agreed to the conditions.

Before the meeting with Huber and his counsel, Dennis asked Walker, "Don't you think you ought to talk to the US attorney prosecuting this case about any of this?"

Walker told Dennis, "No. Maybe we will discuss it with him later. Then again, maybe we will not. Does this trouble you, Agent Dennis?"

Dennis replied crisply, "No, Sir, not at all!"

Walker nodded and said, "Good."

Walker and Dennis listened to the "private" conversation Helm and Brennan then had with Jurgen, informing him of their discussion with the two FBI agents.

Helm: "Jurgen, the FBI agents want to talk to us before the arraignment. We have agreed to listen to what they have to say to us. They will transmit. We will receive. Do not say a word to them, no matter what! Mr. Brennan and I informed the two agents that if we wanted to follow up with them after we had time to consider their statements in private, then we would let them know. So, let's go down the hall and listen to Mr. Walker and Mr. Dennis. Remember, Jurgen, these people are not—repeat, not!—your friends. They are not—repeat, not!—trying to help you. These guys make a living locking people up. They get promoted for locking people up. They enjoy locking people up. They are your enemies. Nothing you say to these people will help you. Do you understand?"

Jurgen: "Completely, Sir. My lips are sealed."

Walker and Dennis greeted Jurgen and his lawyers as they entered the conference room.

Walker commenced. "Thank you, Mr. Huber, for agreeing to meet with us. We have some information we would like to convey to you and your counsel prior to appearing before the magistrate this afternoon. First and foremost, we want to hear your side of the story regarding yesterday's events at the Glenn L. Martin Complex Building C. Second, we have compared the tool marks on damaged metal surfaces and wiring on the Maryland 167 medium bomber with the tools in the kit you were carrying at the time of your arrest and they match. Third, we have photos and videos of you entering and leaving the Maryland 167 aircraft where we arrested you. Fourth, we have statements from a Mr. Friedrich Westphal, a friend of yours who also works at the Glenn L. Martin in Middle River, that you communicated your intent to tamper with as many Maryland 167 aircraft as possible to prevent their being used by the French Air Force against German civilians. Mr. Westphal further told us that you attempted to persuade him to join you in sabotaging Maryland 167 aircraft. He informed us that he refused to join you in damaging any Glenn L. Martin products and that he attempted repeatedly to dissuade you from engaging in such illegal conduct. Mr. Westphal further told us that you accused him of being like a 'cowardly Jew banker' for not aiding him in his effort to protect German nationals from Martin 167 medium bombers that would be flown by the French Air Force. Finally, Mr. Westphal says that he saw you conversing with representatives of the German government in Baltimore and that they may be involved in some way in your endeavors. In our judgment, Mr. Westphal appears to be a credible witness, but our minds remain somewhat open and we would appreciate hearing your perspective regarding your friend's statements to us."

Mr. Helm could see that Jurgen's face had become cherry red. The lawyer put his hand on Jurgen's and politely told Walker, "We thank you for sharing this information with us. Per our agreement, we would like to return to our private conference room with our client to discuss your request to interview him."

Walker again expressed his appreciation for their meeting with the FBI on such short notice. The defendant and his counsel then left the room.

Once inside the bugged attorney-client privileged room, Jurgen screamed, "That coward! That traitor! That Judas son-of-a-bitch!"

Helm at once placed his hand on Jurgen's shoulder and in a calm, professional voice said, "Jurgen, I told you that these are vicious people. They deliberately antagonized you so that you would display anger in front of the magistrate. They want to argue that you are a dangerous person who should be denied bail. Do not let them win, Jurgen. Remember, it is perfectly legal for these so-called 'law enforcement officers' to lie to you. For all we know, Mr. Westphal did not speak with them at all, or told them a totally different story. Rest assured, Jurgen, we will soon find out whether Mr. Westphal intends to testify against you, and precisely what he intends to say in the event he does appear as a prosecution witness. Our goal for today is to walk you out of here on bail. You must remain a calm, rational manufacturing engineer, a responsible foreman at Glenn L. Martin. You are a young man who lives with his parents, has no criminal record, and has never set foot outside the state of Maryland. Jurgen, do you go to church?"

"Yes, I attend Kreuzkirche every Sunday."

Helm asked, "Would the reverend leader there vouch for you, if asked?"

Jurgen: "Certainly."

Helm's intervention significantly settled his client's mental state. The suave and sophisticated lawyer gently placed his hand on Jurgen's shoulder and said, "Good. Now, Jurgen, the FBI has made a big mistake giving us this information in advance. They may have other dirty tricks up their sleeves, but now you know the nature of these scoundrels with whom we are dealing. Keep calm! We will get you out of here on bail and we will work with you day and night to prevail at trial. Any questions?"

Totally in control now, Jurgen asked, "What about my folks? My parents must be overwrought over this situation."

Helm replied, "Jurgen, Mr. Brennan and I have already spoken with your parents and told them not to overreact to the reports they hear on the radio or read in the newspapers. You must compartmentalize your thoughts and emotions, Jurgen. Focus on winning your case. Do not concern yourself with what other people—even your own parents—might think or feel about the allegations against you. You are presumed innocent. Never forget this! Rely on Mr. Brennan and me only. We are one hundred percent on your side, and we know how to handle complex legal situations like this one. OK?"

A reassured Jurgen replied, "Thank you, Mr. Helm and Mr. Brennan. I understand. I just never thought that my friend would turn on me."

Helm smiled at Huber like a father consoling a disappointed son and said, "Jurgen, trust no one other than the people in this room with you. Talk to no one about this matter other than Mr. Brennan and myself. There will be other hard lessons for you to learn as this case moves forward. Your job is to control your emotions and level with us completely and exclusively as we prepare your defense. We will handle the rest."

Jurgen smiled back at Helm. "I understand. I will be restrained and relaxed in the courtroom and quiet everywhere else."

Helm: "You got it, Jurgen!"

In another room, Walker looked at Dennis and said, "That Helm is a good criminal lawyer. The SS, the Gestapo, the Wehrmacht, the *Kriegsmarine*, the *Luftwaffe*, and every Doberman and Rottweiler kenneled in America will soon be out in force hunting for Friedrich Westphal. You want to bet on Huber getting released on bail?"

Dennis replied, "Nope. The magistrate will almost certainly cut Jurgen loose. However, I think that Huber's days outside of prison walls are numbered."

Walker replied, "Land of the Free and the Home of the Brave, Karl!"

The arraignment went as Helm predicted. The magistrate released Huber on $50,000 bail based on his clean record, not being a flight risk, and respectful demeanor in the courtroom. Bond was posted and Jurgen walked out of the building with his lawyers. The three men drove away in Helm's Cadillac limousine. First they went to the Huber residence, where his tearful parents hugged him and told him how much they loved him. The Kreuzkirche reverend leader arrived shortly thereafter and counseled Jurgen and his parents to be strong, pray, and follow the lawyers' instructions to the letter. Helm asked Huber's parents if they would mind Mr. Brennan and himself taking Jurgen to another location to work on their son's legal defense. They, of course, gave their assent. The defendant and his counsel then motored to Brennan's office in the Munsey Building on Calvert Street for a thorough debrief in an office not yet bugged by the authorities.

Brennan's seventeenth-floor office in the southeast corner of the eighteen-floor building impressed Huber. From the office windows, he could see the bustling Baltimore harbor. Inside the office, Jurgen marveled at the sharpened pencils and legal pads perfectly placed in front of each of the eight leather chairs that were positioned around his lawyer's rich mahogany conference table. But what impressed Huber most were Brennan's credentials and achievements prominently displayed throughout the office. Behind Brennan's desk, Huber observed an imposing array of diplomas, including a master's degree in chemical engineering from the Massachusetts Institute of Technology, a Juris Doctor summa cum laude from Harvard Law School, and other certificates containing phrases like *Order of the Coif; Editor, Harvard Law Review;* and *Member of the US Supreme Court Bar.* Additionally, there were rows of autographed photographs of Brennan standing next to important people like Supreme Court Justices Oliver Wendell Holmes Jr. and Charles Evans Hughes, as well as numerous framed newspaper accounts of trials and appeals the lawyer had won.

How did I get so lucky? Jurgen thought. He also thought, *And Helm seems even more impressive than Brennan!*

Brennan asked Jurgen, "Would you like me to make a cup of coffee for you? How do you take your coffee, Mr. Huber?"

"Thank you, Mr. Brennan. I would appreciate a cup of black coffee, if it is not too much trouble for you. Are we the only people in this office?"

"Yes. Just you, Mr. Helm, and I are the only people in this law firm today, so we can work with no distractions. In any event, it is no trouble at all for me to brew you a cup of coffee, Mr. Huber. You have had an exhilarating 24 hours or so and probably could use some caffeine at this point," replied a courteous Brennan. "Mr. Helm, would you like a cup of coffee too?"

"No, thank you, Mr. Brennan. Perhaps later," muttered an impatient Mr. Helm, who added, "Let's get cracking. Mr. Huber, this alleged friend of yours—Mr. Westphal. How would you describe him?"

Jurgen thought for a few moments and reviewed his personal history with Westphal with his two lawyers. Huber then summed up the facts as follows: "In my opinion, Friedrich is insecure, has a low opinion of himself, and craves acceptance and approval. Worst of all, he has no convictions for which he will stand up and fight. Friedrich is the kind of German who will attend Lutheran services only if they are led in the German language, hang swastikas pennants all over Gwynn Oak Park on German Day, drink only German beer, sing the "Horst Wessel" song with gusto, attend German paramilitary camps, memorize quotations from *Mein Kampf*, pledge his loyalty to Adolf Hitler with tears in his eyes, and then agree to testify against his German Aryan friend who wants to protect innocent German women and children from being bombed by the French. I know that he met with members of the German embassy staff and a US State Department officer sympathetic to the German cause in DC not too long ago to discuss Glenn L. Martin programs. He did this on his own. I did not accompany him. However, he ran and hid from them, fearful of being arrested and charged with espionage. Basically, I think what the FBI agents told us about Friedrich's statements to them is probably accurate. He will testify against me. Of this I have no doubt. To please his newfound FBI friends and to avoid prison, he will say just about anything they tell him to say."

Neither Helm nor Brennan listened intently to Jurgen's soliloquy. Neither lawyer asked him any questions, nor did they take any notes regarding his remarks about Westphal.

Picking up a pencil, Helm then spoke. "Jurgen, let's move on to your medical condition. Please provide us with the name of your neurologist and, if you have seen a psychiatrist, his name too."

Sheepishly, Jurgen admitted that he had seen a psychiatrist at Johns Hopkins Hospital and had been diagnosed with depression. In mid-1939, he consented to his psychiatrist and neurologist treating his depression with a new, experimental therapy created in the mid-1930s by two doctors from Italy. Called "shock therapy," or more formally "electroconvulsive therapy," Jurgen's depression disappeared after four treatments. Both Helm and Brennan took detailed notes as Huber described in minute detail his medical condition and care.

"I guess you must think that I am nuts after hearing all of this," Jurgen said to Brennan and Helm.

Helm gently replied to Huber. "No, Jurgen. Not at all. Do not be embarrassed or ashamed. Everyone—even lawyers—encounters bumps along the road of life. Your condition and your treatment may well help us parry the FBI and Justice Department thrust aimed at you. What you consider a 'deuce' could be our 'ace' in this regard. We need to gain access to your medical records and interview your doctors. Would you mind making the rounds of your physicians' offices with Mr. Brennan and me on Monday morning to achieve these objectives? I believe that your medical records and testimony from your doctors will help us mount a very powerful defense."

"Sure, Mr. Helm. What time should I come here on Monday morning?" said Jurgen.

"To avoid exposing you to members of the press and their meddlesome questioning, Mr. Brennan will pick you up at 8:30 AM at your parents' home. Now remember, Jurgen, you are to talk to no one, not even your folks, about anything to do with this case," said Helm firmly, but politely.

Brennan then spoke. "Jurgen, you get a good night's sleep and relax at home on Sunday. We will be busy around the clock from Monday forward."

"Mr. Brennan, would it be OK for me to go to Kreuzkirche Lutheran Church with my parents on Sunday?" asked Jurgen.

Brennan replied, "Yes. But return home immediately after services."

Jurgen felt confident now that these lawyers would keep him out of prison. Brennan drove him to his home. They talked about engineering and physics the entire time. Jurgen deeply enjoyed the stimulating conversation. *I am one lucky guy*, thought Huber.

Helm returned to DC. He paid close attention to automobiles that might be tailing him. For two hours, he took unexpected turns, backtracked, went up one-way streets the wrong way, varied his speed, and kept moving until he found himself alone on a stretch of road in Chevy Chase, Maryland. Satisfied that he had shaken any surveillance, he stopped at a pay phone booth, dialed a number, let the phone ring six times, and hung up. He then drove to a lonely cemetery in rural Virginia where he waited for Joachim Lansdorff. The Nazi military attaché arrived in less than an hour in a Mercedes Benz driven by his menacing bodyguard. "No one followed me, *Herr* Helm, but let us keep this conversation brief."

Helm replied, "You have a nontrivial problem. Westphal is in FBI protective custody. He most certainly is cooperating with the Feds and will testify for the prosecution against Huber. The good news for you is that Huber is a mental case. He suffers from depression and has been treated for some time by doctors at Johns Hopkins. On Monday morning, Brennan, Huber, and I will visit the relevant doctors' offices, examine Jurgen's medical records, and possibly speak with his physicians. When we return to Brennan's office, I will work diligently alongside Mr. Brennan to prepare a first-rate legal defense for Mr. Huber. Brennan, of course, has no clue that this is all a sham intended to fix Huber's location for you and your hit team. Brennan's office is one floor down from the top of the 223-foot-tall, eighteen-floor Munsey Building in downtown Baltimore. Huber will be in the office assisting us beginning on Monday and throughout the week. Whatever happens to Huber next is up to you."

Lansdorff replied, "Thank you. Very helpful, as always. Forty thousand dollars in 1935 Swiss gold twenty-franc coins produced by the Bern Mint will soon be deposited into your secret numbered Swiss bank account by an untraceable source. Your customary fees for legal services, of course, will be paid to you and your firm separately and openly for tax purposes. Enjoy the charming city of Baltimore. *Auf Wiedersehen, Herr* Helm."

And that was that.

When Lansdorff returned to the German embassy, he found Dr. Heinz Engel from the New York consulate smoking a cigar in his office.

"Dr. Engel, how good to see you. Would you mind savoring your cigar somewhere other than in my office?" Lansdorff snarled.

"*Entschuldigung!*" replied Engel. "I forgot how sensitive you Wehrmacht officers can be about smoke, Joachim!"

Lansdorff replied, "You will see how insensitive we can be soon enough, Professor *für Ingenieurwissenschaften* Engel!"

"*Gut,* Major Lansdorff. What can my men and I do for you?"

Lansdorff explained to Engel the situation in Baltimore and that Jurgen Huber and Friedrich Westphal had become expendable pawns in the espionage game. Lansdorff provided Huber's precise coordinates in Baltimore to Engel, in addition to informing him of Jurgen's mental infirmity. "However, Heinz, Mr. Westphal appears to be hidden in an FBI safe house. We do not know the location of this safe house and we do not know how heavily Westphal is being guarded. What do you think you can do about tying up these loose ends?"

Engel replied impassively, "Mr. Huber will fall like an acorn onto the street below the Munsey Building. The pressure resulting from the criminal prosecution will appear to have been too much for his fragile, depressed mind to handle. We will pick the optimal time to implement the final solution for the Huber problem, but no later than Thursday he will have jumped to his death. Obviously, Westphal is a more complex problem. We have strict orders from Berlin not to kill FBI agents on US soil under any circumstances. Therefore, a frontal assault on a safe house, assuming we can find it, is not an option. Instead, we have a skilled sniper who can perform wonders with his Mauser K98 rifle and 4x scope. So, for the moment, we will pursue a 'one-shot, one-kill' solution for the Westphal problem. We will have to be patient. The odds are that Huber will become part of the Baltimore urban landscape before we deal definitively with Westphal. The FBI will, in all probability, expose their protectee, Friedrich Westphal, in order to catch and identify us. If the FBI follows this path, my specialist will put a 7.92mm round in Westphal's brain from a range of 1,000 meters and vanish before Hoover's men can arrest him. Is this acceptable to you, Lansdorff?"

"*Ja!* Your concepts are acceptable. We ought not to be seen in DC together. I will meet you at your home in Brooklyn, New York, after you and your team complete your missions in Baltimore," replied Joachim.

Engel, looking disappointed, said, "We cannot even have a little party tonight?"

"*Nein*, Engel. Best that you depart DC and commence your hunt for Westphal."

"Pity. See you in Brooklyn, Joachim."

Despite Lansdorff's entreaty that Engel leave DC, Heinz's plan was to remain in DC. To shield the identity of his prize mole within the FBI Field Office in New York City, Dr. Engel did not disclose to Lansdorff that he had already obtained Westphal's safe house address. Since 1934, when Abwehr Officer Engel arrived in the US under the diplomatic cover as First Secretary to the German Consulate in New York City, he constructed and controlled an exquisitely crafted agent network of pro-Nazi American citizens living and working in northern New Jersey and New York City. Meticulous about security matters, Engel kept virtually no written records, rarely spoke more than a coded sentence or two on the telephone, and rarely met with his agents.

Engel's rules for the few face-to-face meetings he attended were simple: (1) never meet with more than one agent; (2) always meet late at night in one of the many dimly lit German-owned bars in New York's predominantly German Yorkville neighborhood; (3) receive information, do not transmit information; (4) never meet for more than ten minutes; and (5) never leave through the door you entered. Nondescript in appearance and mannerisms, Dr. Engel's nickname within Nazi intelligence circles was *Geist* [Ghost]. Lansdorff had no idea that Engel had loosed his assassins on Huber and Westphal hours before he lit his cigar in the Wehrmacht Major's office. Engel had no intention of Lansdorff (or anyone else, for that matter) knowing more than he absolutely needed to know about *Der Geist's* sources and methods.

At the FBI safe house in Garrison, Maryland, Walker set the schedule for providing protection for Friedrich Westphal. On Sunday, December 4,

Dennis and Fowler would serve as the last line of defense inside the house. Murphy would scout the surrounding neighborhood in his radio-equipped car and call in the cavalry from the downtown Baltimore FBI office in the event the Germans attacked in force. A similar configuration would be employed on Monday, December 5, with Hercules and Martin inside the safe house and Gareth scouting. Zangara would remain in DC, monitoring Koch and Hara for any intel regarding German or Japanese espionage activities concerning Glenn L. Martin and Bendix Radio. Clearly, the team needed more manpower to cover the emerging threats. Walker and Horan committed themselves to acquiring two additional agents—one from the FBI and one from ONI. In the meantime, however, the team had to make do with the resources they had, which meant that neither Joachim Lansdorff nor Elizabeth Robertson had agents tailing them.

Gareth and Martin privately decided to have an unofficial conversation with Sergeant Alexander Ioffe at his office in the Maryland State Police HQ in nearby Pikesville, Maryland. Gareth told Martin, "We cannot defend this position against a sudden surprise attack by a German hit squad with the small number of 'swinging dicks' we have at the present time. Adding Alex will improve our odds. He is the equivalent of two men. I hope that he will be in the neighborhood on Monday. Martin, give him a call. I will have an off-line talk with Hercules about Ioffe. We should bring Hercules with us to meet Alex. I do not want any friendly fire incidents in the event things go sideways at the safe house."

Martin liked Gareth's idea and the two of them drove to the nearest pay phone with Hercules after the meeting ended. Victor dialed Ioffe's private number and after one ring, he heard, "*IOFFE!* Whoever you are, what do you want on a Saturday? This better be important!"

Martin replied, "Sorry to bother you on *Shabbos*, Alex. But an important law enforcement matter is developing up the street from you. Do you have a little time to talk face-to-face with Gareth Messenger, another FBI agent, and me?"

Alex answered, "For you, *Reb Martin*, sure. How far away from the State Police HQ in Pikesville are you?"

Victor: "Ten minutes, assuming no traffic."

Ioffe replied, "Well, come on down. I'll brew some Eight O'Clock and we can have an *Oneg Shabbos!*"

Martin then cautioned Ioffe, "Alex, the FBI agent who will be with us is a Negro named Hercules Boulanger. Will we encounter any, uh, 'difficulties' with your fellow troopers when we come in through the front door?"

Ioffe: "Good thing you alerted me to this unusual personnel issue. I will be out front waiting for you and escort you in. Do not worry, I will smooth things with the locals. I have a way with people, don't you know?"

Martin: "You are a regular Hillel, Sergeant Ioffe. Thanks."

Ioffe, resplendent in his freshly pressed, bemedaled, and braided sergeant's uniform, approached Boulanger and shook his hand.

"Pleasure to meet you, Agent Boulanger. Welcome to the Maryland State Police Headquarters! Let's go inside, grab some Eight O'Clock, and get to work."

The four men strode into a conference room adjacent to Ioffe's office. Alex closed the door and poured their coffee. "OK, gents. What can Sergeant Ioffe do for you?"

Martin laid out the tactical problem for Ioffe. "We have a cooperating witness in protective custody in a safe house on Montrose Avenue in Garrison, Maryland, off Reisterstown Road. The house is about thirteen hundred square feet, three bedrooms, two stories. There are a few other homes in the area, but the residents appear to keep to themselves. The German government does not want our witness to testify against their espionage agent, a young fellow who used to work in Middle River whom you may recently have read about in *The Baltimore Sun*. The Nazis do not know where we are hiding our protectee yet. However, the rumor on the street is that the Teutons can be very aggressive when threatened."

Ioffe, grinning from ear-to-ear, interrupted Martin. "You mean I might get to plug some Nazi invaders who resist arrest after we apprehend them in the act of attempting to commit murder in the State of Maryland? This is just great, Martin. I love it!"

Hercules slapped his right knee and added, "Nice to know that there is someone in the Maryland State Police who is anti-Nazi!"

Ioffe mildly corrected Hercules. "There are a few of us, Agent Boulanger. I am, however, by far the most anti-Nazi trooper in this HQ!"

While Martin appreciated Hercules's and Ioffe's brio, he wanted to concentrate on logistics and tactics. He outlined the schedule of the meager forces dedicated to protecting Friedrich Westphal.

"Alex, do you think you can make yourself available for some scouting duty this coming week? Also, you might want to beef up the arsenal in your automobile in the event a squad of heavily armed German assassins refuse to be taken prisoner."

Ioffe nodded and said, "I will give you guys the State Police radio frequency. If you need me, just call for 'Sergeant Ioffe, Code Blue.' I will keep an eye on Reisterstown Road. You guys focus on Montrose and the interior streets. Give me your radio frequency and I will call you on 'Victor, Code Blue' should I have something important to report. Anything else that comes up, call me on the phone number you used this morning."

Martin thanked Alex for his assistance, although no thanks was necessary. Ioffe, as much as Hercules, Gareth, and Martin, wanted to win a close-quarter gun battle with Nazis in Garrison, Maryland—or anywhere else, for that matter.

And that was that.

19

10 AM SUNDAY, DECEMBER 3, 1939; RABBI MEIR ELKANAN'S OFFICE, EUTAW PLACE, BALTIMORE, MARYLAND

Meir Elkanan admired Eliezer Ben Yehuda, a lexicographer and the reviver of the Hebrew language who had died of tuberculosis in British-controlled Palestine in 1922. Elkanan believed wholeheartedly that the creation of an independent, Hebrew-speaking nation in the land promised by God to his people in the Old Testament would lead to a glorious rebirth of Jewish culture and dignity. The rabbi conveyed these beliefs to Gertrude and Martin. Gertrude grew to adopt Elkanan's views. Martin, on the other hand, found Meir's affinity for Hebrew and Jewish culture unappealing. He loved classical Greek history, language, myths, philosophy, and culture. Nonetheless, from Gertrude's first Hebrew language lesson with Elkanan on December 3, 1939, until shortly before her passing at age seventy-nine on December 11, 1990, she studied the Hebrew language for at least 30 minutes each day. Gertrude became the rabbi's favorite language student and they remained close until his death in May 21, 1948, six days after the establishment of the modern State of Israel.

After their first language lesson with the rabbi, Milton picked up Gertrude and Martin in his gleaming DeSoto and took them to dinner at Haussner's.

"You look mighty happy, Milton," observed Gertrude.

"That is because I am happy! Gertrude, on Friday I won an impossible jury verdict for my client, a company that insures landlords. A sympathetic World War I Army veteran who purportedly had lost a leg in combat alleged that my client's policyholder, a landlord, had negligently maintained the apartment recently rented by the handicapped man. The plaintiff demanded $90,000 in damages for serious cranial injuries that he alleged he sustained from a fall proximately caused by a loose toilet seat in the apartment's only bathroom. Now, how could an insurance company possibly prevail in this particular case when a typical Baltimore jury is composed of twelve kind-hearted 'New Dealers' who hate their own landlords? Mind you, even the insurance company estimated its probability of winning at below twenty percent and authorized me to settle the case for $45,000! Well, Gertrude, justice prevailed! I won! The plaintiff got nothing, not one penny! During the trial I relentlessly cross-examined and thoroughly discredited the lying 'war hero.' The plaintiff admitted to the jury that he had (1) never served in the US Army, (2) lost his leg in an Amusement park accident in 1925—long after World War I had ended, and (3) had been under the Influence of narcotics at the time he fell in his apartment and fractured his skull. The jury convened for a mere 30 minutes and unanimously found no negligence by the landlord. A grateful insurance company rewarded me handsomely for my efforts and now I am celebrating the victory with you and Martin!"

Martin coughed "Uh, Milton, who contacted the US Army and got you the evidence that the plaintiff had lied when he said he had served his nation in uniform during World War I?"

Milton smiled and said, "Why, you did, Martin. Thank you."

Continuing, Martin inquired, "And who got you the evidence that the plaintiff received a substantial settlement from an insurance company in 1926 for the limb he lost at an amusement park?"

Milton again smiled and said, "Why you did, Martin. Thank you."

Martin now asked, "Who tracked down the emergency room doctor at Johns Hopkins Hospital who produced the medical records that the plaintiff had injected heroin into his bloodstream shortly before his fall?"

Smiling even more broadly, Milton said, "Why, you did, little brother! And I thank you for your efforts."

Milton hit the dashboard of his car with his oversized right hand. "Martin, it is a pity that you chose to serve in the military instead of pursuing a legal career."

Gertrude could not help but laugh at this Milton-Martin comedy routine. "You two are the best!" she said. "You ought to be in the movies!"

Dining at Haussner's added to everyone's happiness. Milton asked Martin, "So what is going on in your cloak-and-dagger life?"

Martin looked around the room and said, "You know I cannot tell you anything. However, if you read the newspaper, you might have some idea."

Milton lowered his voice and said, "I suspected as much. I am proud of you, Martin. You ought to put these Nazi bastards under the courthouse, not in it!"

Martin replied, "Let's move to another subject. You know Gertrude started learning Hebrew today with Rabbi Elkanan."

Milton whistled. "Gertrude, Grace and Henry Basswood will be absolutely thrilled. How are you getting along with the good rabbi?"

Gertrude replied, "Quite well, Milton. I have never met a person whose faith is founded on such a powerful combination of brains and hope. I enjoy studying with him and Martin, although your brother—for obvious reasons—seems preoccupied."

Milton responded, "Get used to Martin's lack of religiosity. The fact is that no one in the Victor family has ever been much concerned with Judaism. Hopefully you will be the first, Gertrude."

Putting her hand on Martin's hand, Gertrude said, "I will try, Milton, and maybe Martin will surprise us too."

The trio each had a cup of coffee. Milton lit a victory cigar and drove the couple to 14 South Broadway. As Martin and Gertrude got out of the DeSoto, Gertrude said, "Thank you, Milton. No sister-in-law could ever have a finer brother-in-law than you."

Once again, Gertrude managed to move Milton emotionally with her sentiments in a way to which he was utterly unaccustomed. "You take care of yourself, Gertrude. If you and Martin need anything, you just call me."

Martin told Milton that he would spend a little time with Gertrude and the Basswoods before returning to Auchentroly Terrace.

"Milt, I will see you this evening. On Monday I have a predawn mission that will run through Tuesday morning. A colleague will pick me up early in front of your place. You would be impressed with the professionalism of the men on my team."

Milton pointed his right forefinger at his brother and said, "Martin, you stay alert. Depend on yourself. No matter how strong you think your team may be, in the final analysis, you are the last line of your defense!"

And that was that.

6 AM MONDAY, DECEMBER 5, 1939; THE FBI SAFE HOUSE, MONTROSE AVENUE, GARRISON, MARYLAND

The shift change went smoothly. Dennis, Fowler, and Murphy informed Hercules, Gareth, and Martin that Westphal had behaved himself and that there had been no suspicious movements in or around the neighborhood. After the Sunday crew departed, "Lieutenant Cohen" engaged Westphal in conversation while Gareth walked around the exterior of the safe house. Hercules drove along Montrose Avenue, traveled less than 100 yards, and then turned right on Turnlee Road. He saw nothing but small, nondescript one-story homes built in 1911. Driving on, he made a right onto Harden Avenue and then stopped to make a right turn onto Reisterstown Road. At the intersection of Harden Avenue and Reisterstown Road, Hercules waved at

Ioffe parked in his Maryland State Trooper sedan. Alex waved back. Hercules then drove back to Montrose, where he turned right, and shortly thereafter turned left into the driveway of the safe house.

Gareth walked over to Boulanger's car. "What's going on in Garrison, Maryland?"

Hercules replied, "Quiet. Rural. Easy to notice things that do not belong. I saw Sergeant Ioffe parked south of here on Reisterstown Road. I am going to expand my patrol route down to Greenspring Valley Road where it intersects Reisterstown Road. See you in a few minutes."

This time, Hercules continued straight on Turnlee Road and parked briefly where Turnlee intersected with Greenspring Valley Road. He studied the same dull landscape, put the car in gear, and turned right on to Greenspring Valley Road. He stopped at the intersection of Reisterstown Road and Greenspring Valley, where he saw two severe-looking men in suits and ties parked in a black 1939 Chevrolet Master Deluxe coupe with Virginia license plate number 357-139. The men appeared to be studying a map. Hercules turned right on to Reisterstown Road and made a right on to Harden Avenue, a left on Turnlee Road, and then back to the safe house on Montrose. Hercules got out of his car and walked toward the front porch, where Martin sat on a wicker chair built for two people.

Sitting next to Martin, Hercules calmly said, "Martin, call the FBI office downtown and have them check who owns a Chevrolet coupe with Virginia license plate number 357-139. We may have some German scouts nearby. It has been years since I killed me some Germans, but I know 'em when I see 'em. And I saw two of 'em in a black Chevy not far from here."

"Roger that, Hercules," said Martin.

"Martin, while you are at it, tell Gareth I need to speak to him."

Gareth came out of the house and sat down next to Boulanger. "What's going on, Hercules?"

"Gareth, I think somebody leaked the address of this safe house to the Germans. Right now we have the numerical edge, four of us to two of them, but they will figure that out soon enough and call in more troops. Germans are experts at infiltration tactics. I learned long ago to thin them out before they can mass for an attack. Take my vehicle and go out to Reisterstown Road, head south, and see if a black Chevy Master Deluxe coupe with Virginia plate 357-139 has moved from the southeast corner of Greenspring Valley Road and Reisterstown. Get a look at the mugs on those two men. If they ain't Nazi torpedoes, I am Josephine Baker."

Gareth chuckled. "You got enough gasoline in the car for this reconnaissance mission, Josephine? I mean Hercules!"

Hercules did not laugh. He replied, "If you see those two krauts, you turn around and head back north on Reisterstown Road and see if you can rustle up Ioffe, who is parked in his State Police cruiser where Harden Avenue intersects Reisterstown. Get him and get back here pronto."

The two men in the Chevy coupe remained at their post. Gareth figured that they were waiting for reinforcements and possibly nightfall before they attacked. He found Alex right where Hercules said he would be.

"Alex, Hercules wants to invite you to a surprise party on Montrose Road. Looks like a Black Forest cake with at least two candles on it will be served sometime soon."

Ioffe, grim-faced, replied, "Let me go get a friend of mine, Officer Thompson, to help us greet our guests." He opened the trunk of his vehicle and came back with a Thompson .45-caliber submachine gun and two 50-round drum magazines. Alex looked at Gareth and said, "Think this will be enough?"

Gareth replied, "I certainly hope so."

They drove back to the Montrose safe house. Hercules approached Ioffe's car, saw the Thompson, and said, "Glad you could make it, Alex. That is one nice trench sweeper sitting on your passenger seat."

Alex replied, "Nothing but the best for Nazis."

Martin now came out of the house. "Hercules, the car is registered to Wolfgang Pieper, an international trade lawyer who works in DC. What is our next move?"

"So, if that is Pieper out there, he has no diplomatic immunity. I say we go out and roust them," replied Hercules. "Alex will park his car in front of their Chevy and approach them in his uniform. Gareth, you take my car and pull up on them from behind. Take Martin with you. I will guard Westphal. Good hunting!"

Ioffe used the front bumper of his car to block the front of the Chevy coupe. Simultaneously, Gareth put his front bumper an inch short of the rear bumper of the Chevrolet coupe. Swaggering up to the driver's side door of the coupe like John Wayne in the movie *Stagecoach*, Alex barked out, "I want to see your license and registration!"

Meanwhile, Gareth positioned himself close to the rear right fender of the Chevy while Martin stood behind the rear left side of Pieper's car. Gareth and Martin each had their right hand on the grips of their S&W .357 Magnums.

The driver of the coupe protested in German-accented English. "Vot iss zee problem, Officer?"

Ioffe repeated his instruction. "Your license and registration, now!"

The driver replied, "May I get out uff my car?"

Ioffe: "No, you may not get out of your car. I will arrest you if you do not hand me your license and registration immediately."

The driver fumbled, getting his documentation. When he finally produced his papers, it was none other than Wolfgang Pieper. Alex snarled, "*Herr* Pieper, what brings you to Garrison, Maryland?"

Pieper erupted. "I am a lawyer, Officer. I know my rights. You haff no right to harass me like ziss. I haff done nothing wrong. I do not haff to answer your impertinent questions."

Ioffe shook his head. "*Herr* Pieper, we received a report that a vehicle with Virginia plates had entered Maryland and that its occupants were illegally transporting firearms across state lines. Are you carrying any firearms in this car of yours, *Herr* Pieper?"

Livid, Pieper blurted out, "And vot iff I do?"

Ioffe pulled his weapon from his holster and shouted, "Both of you get out of the car. Keep your hands high where I can see them. *NOW!*"

Gareth stepped forward quickly with his revolver in his right hand and opened the passenger door. The passenger got out and Gareth ordered, "Lean forward! Keep your feet apart! Place your hands on the front fender of the car! Keep your arms all the way out!"

Gareth closed the door to the coupe and proceeded to pat the passenger down. He found a Walther P-38 semi-automatic pistol in the man's shoulder holster. "Put your head on the car roof and your hands behind your back!" Gareth shouted as he manhandled the passenger into a position where he could handcuff him.

"Look what I found!" Gareth announced as he held the weapon up in the air for Ioffe and Martin to see.

Martin moved around to provide backup for Alex, who needed no backup. Alex yelled at Pieper, "Arms behind your back, head on the roof. Spread your legs. Do not open your mouth! Martin, open the trunk!"

The trunk was unlocked. Inside, Martin found a bolt-action rifle with a scope on it. He held the Mauser K98 in the air and said, "Now, is this any way for Germans from Virginia to visit the State of Maryland?"

Alex searched Pieper and found a Luger in Wolfgang's shoulder holster. Alex also found a dagger with a swastika on its handle in a scabbard hanging from the international lawyer's suspenders. "*Herr* Pieper, you and your *freund* are under arrest. Welcome to the State of Maryland!"

Ioffe used the radio to get backup from Pikesville. He escorted Pieper and Josef Fuchs, a "vacationing" German mechanic employed at a small automobile component manufacturing firm in Munich, to Maryland State Police Headquarters for booking at 10 AM. Gareth and Martin drove back to the safe house and reported the incident to Hercules.

"Damn shame those two Nazis did not resist arrest. You just wait. We are going to have to go all the way back over to Europe sometime soon to kill them when we could have finished 'em off here. Anyway, sorry I missed all the fun. I guess we ought to tell the story to Westphal and see if he knows either Pieper or Fuchs."

Friedrich did not handle the news well. "It's a miracle they did not get me!" he said, shaking like a leaf.

"It is no miracle at all, Friedrich," replied Hercules. "We nabbed them before they got anywhere near you. Now sort yourself out, young man!"

Westphal, nervously wringing his hands, complained, "What if they send more men and try to get me again?"

Hercules replied, "Then we will intercept and pick off their follow-on force, Friedrich. Stop being a little baby about this! We got you covered. You should be relieved that your security detail has matters well in hand. You should be glad you did not remain in your house! If you had, the Baltimore police would be fishing pieces of you out of the harbor right about now!"

This made sense to Westphal and he calmed himself.

Later that day, at around 6:30 PM, Jurgen Huber "jumped" to his death from the roof of the Munsey Building, disrupting early diners' dinners at Bickfords Restaurant located nearby at 3 North Calvert Street. Coincidentally, Milton Victor was walking to Bickfords to meet his old high school chum, Leon Neuberger, for dinner at 6:45 PM. Leon, a laconic and phlegmatic Food and Drug Administration chemist, witnessed Huber's body strike the street. Amidst the sirens, police lights flashing, and women crying, Milton arrived and asked Leon, "What is going on around here?"

Neuberger replied, "I saw a person hit North Calvert Street at high velocity. Then I heard a police officer say that a man had fallen off the roof of the Munsey Building and died."

Milton: "Well, thanks for the fact-filled report, Leon. Very informative. Let's go somewhere else to eat. It is too chaotic around here. Any ideas where we should dine?"

Neuberger replied, "Miller Brothers."

Milton nodded his head and said, "Leon, excellent choice."

And off the two old friends went to talk little and eat much.

And that was that!

Albert Benoit Helm, Esq., and Rainer Brennan, Esq., expressed shock, surprise, and grief to the gruff Baltimore City Police Department Detective who informed them that their client, Mr. Jurgen Huber, "took a header from the Munsey Building into North Calvert Street." Helm let Brennan take the lead in responding to the Detective's numerous routine questions concerning the events leading up to the tragic event. Throughout the two-hour inquisition, Helm consistently nodded agreement with Brennan's statements. Brennan then escorted the Detective around the law firm and introduced him to each of the lawyers and secretaries. The Detective asked each of them about Huber. They knew nothing about the man. No one recalled seeing him leave the office.

At 10 PM, as the Detective prepared to exit the law office, he spoke to Brennan and Helm. "Just to review the facts, you both spent the day with your client, Mr. Huber."

Brennan: "Correct."

Detective: "Mr. Huber was charged on Saturday with violating federal laws against espionage, sabotage, and resisting arrest."

Brennan: "That is right."

Detective: "Mr. Huber had a history of mental depression."

Brennan: "Yes, Detective."

Detective: "You accompanied Mr. Huber to visit his doctors, including his neurologist and his psychiatrist, at Johns Hopkins today."

Brennan: "Yes, Detective."

Detective: "And in the course of your visit, you reviewed Huber's medical history with his doctors and interviewed his physicians about his current mental state."

Brennan: "Yes, Sir."

Detective: "The records and the doctors confirmed that Mr. Huber suffered from depression and that he was under their care."

Brennan: "Yes, Detective."

Detective: "According to his doctors, Mr. Huber was aggressively treated for clinical depression in the past, and he seemed OK to them and to you today."

Brennan: "You probably should question Mr. Huber's physicians directly for their personal views. However, from my perspective, Jurgen Huber appeared fine and never once indicated that he had any intent to injure himself. In fact, Jurgen verbalized his gratitude for the thorough legal work that Attorney Helm and I were performing on his behalf and expressed optimism that the defense we were preparing would exculpate him."

Helm nodded his head in agreement with each of Brennan's statements.

Detective: "Mr. Huber never mentioned to either of you that he intended to go up to the roof of the Munsey Building."

Brennan: "Correct. He got up from the table where the three of us were working and told us that he needed to go to the bathroom. We thought nothing of it. We got concerned after approximately 10 minutes when he did not return to the conference room. We searched each of the men's bathrooms on the seventeenth floor and every office and closet belonging to the law firm and could not find him. We asked each person present in the office if they had seen Mr. Huber. No one saw him leave the office."

Detective: "Mr. Huber lives…uh, lived with his parents and they expressed no concern to you about his mental state."

Brennan: "Correct. Will you be informing the parents of this tragedy?"

Detective: "Another officer has already notified the family and will get the parents to identify what is left of Mr. Huber. I will, however, be the law enforcement officer in daily contact with them as the investigation proceeds."

Brennan: "If there is anything we can do to be of further assistance to you, just ask!"

Detective: "Gentlemen, you and the people in your firm I interviewed could not have been more cooperative, informative, and forthright. Rest assured that my report will reflect this! If I or any other officers need additional information, we will contact you."

Brennan: "Thank you, Detective. Nothing like this has ever occurred at Brennan and Gunther. It is all so very distressing."

Albert Benoit Helm, however, felt relieved. Dr. Heinz Engel and his minions had dealt with their "loose end" promptly and efficiently without involving Helm in any of the dirty work. Jurgen had been lured to the roof by a note passed to him at Kreuzkirche Lutheran Church services on Sunday morning. Joachim Lansdorff's driver had been standing at the front entrance of the church when Jurgen and his parents arrived. Jurgen recognized Joachim's bodyguard from their past covert encounters and nodded his head when the scar-faced man smiled at him. At the end of the Sunday service, as members of the faithful stood in line to shake hands with the clergy, the driver inserted a single sheet of folded paper in Huber's jacket pocket. Jurgen read the note instructing him to go to the roof of the Munsey Building late Monday afternoon, where he would receive further instructions from Joachim. The end of the note read, "Burn this after reading." Jurgen, of course, followed orders. No one in law enforcement ever saw the Nazi note.

Earlier in the day in Pikesville, relations between the Maryland State Police and the two disarmed German citizens they wanted to question were not at all amicable. Placed in separate interview rooms at Maryland

State Police Headquarters in Pikesville, Wolfgang Pieper and Josef Fuchs adamantly refused to answer any questions put to them by teams of interrogators. Both men demanded access to a telephone in order to call a lawyer. When separately permitted to make a call to their respective counsel, both men dialed the same number in Washington, DC, and by 2 PM, a pair of elite criminal lawyers—one from Baltimore and one from DC—arrived in Pikesville to provide legal counsel to their two clients. The lawyers requested that the police cease and desist from any efforts to interrogate their clients.

The German embassy soon registered a formal complaint to the US State Department, objecting to the unlawful arrests of Pieper and Fuchs, the illegal search of Mr. Pieper's automobile, the illegal seizure of property in the trunk of Mr. Pieper's automobile, and the vicious, anti-German behavior of a "Gangster Jew" Maryland State Trooper Sergeant named Alexander Ioffe. The embassy demanded that "the Jew, Ioffe" be severely punished for his verbal and physical mistreatment of Messrs. Pieper and Fuchs. A call by Baltimore's *Kamaradschaftbund*, and a host of other German-American civil, economic, and religious groups, went out for the entire community to march on Pikesville the next day to protest police state tactics targeting Germans.

The local and state political representatives of predominantly German districts too were inundating the State Police, the governor of Maryland, and even the mayor of Baltimore with pointed questions about official hostility directed against German-Americans. In short, the entire State of Maryland was in an uproar.

Alerted to Pieper's and Fuchs's predicament by a phone call to his hotel room from his agents' DC counsel, Dr. Heinz Engel began organizing an escape for his two agents. He assumed that the German embassy and his German contacts would likely be under close surveillance, so he hailed a cab and went directly to the front entrance of the Japanese embassy. There he asked to see his Japanese Army Intelligence counterpart in the US, Colonel Asano Nagamasa.

Colonel Nagamasa, a polished, pathologically vicious man proud of his participation in the Nanking Massacre in December of 1937, welcomed Dr. Engel into his unadorned basement office. "What a pleasant surprise. You must be pressed for time. What can I do for you, *Herr Doktor*?"

Engel replied, "I need to exfiltrate two of my agents from the United States within the next 36 hours. Presently they are in the custody of the Maryland State Police and, no doubt, the FBI. Their precise location is the Maryland State Police Barracks in Pikesville, Maryland. They should be arraigned and released on bail within 24 hours. Can you assist me?"

Nagamasa thought for a moment and replied, "Give me a moment." He walked up two flights of stairs to Benkei's office and, without saying a word, gestured for Captain Masuji to follow him. Benkei and Nagamasa returned to the windowless basement office and closed the room's heavy door. Nagamasa announced, "We can talk openly here. Captain Masuji, I want to introduce you to Dr. Heinz Engel, a senior officer in the Abwehr who needs our assistance in exfiltrating two of his German agents from the United States within the next 36 hours. His men are being held by American authorities in a jail northwest of the city of Baltimore. These agents should be released on bail shortly. Are you able to help us humble the American authorities by making these men disappear once they are no longer in police custody?"

Masuji knew that if he performed this service, both the Imperial Japanese Army and the Abwehr would be profoundly indebted to him and the Imperial Navy. "Yes, of course, Colonel Nagamasa. I would be delighted to help you and our Third Reich comrades-in-arms. These two men of yours are under heavy surveillance, correct?"

Engel: "Very heavy! The FBI wants to insult the Reich by publicly treating these men very badly."

Masuji: "Good. This will make their successful flight from the US even more embarrassing and humiliating. Dr. Engel, do these men have lawyers who can be trusted?"

Engel: "The average American is a coward. The average American lawyer is even more cowardly than the average American. None of them can be trusted. The most I can promise you is that the American lawyers will drive the two agents to a law office in Baltimore once they are released on bail."

Masuji replied, "*Doktor* Engel, I will need the precise location of this law office. Someone from the German embassy will have to inform your agents that my men, two experienced professionals, will transfer them to a Japanese merchant ship, the *Kinka Maru*, due to depart a pier near the American Sugar Refinery in Baltimore harbor in 36 hours. I trust that your agents will enjoy the delights of Yokohama, the ship's destination."

Engel responded, "Excellent. But do you need to verify the availability of this *Kinka Maru* vessel for our purposes, Captain Masuji?"

Masuji: "Dr. Engel, I am a Captain in the Imperial Japanese Navy. Just get your man from the German embassy to the law office in Baltimore and have him inform your two agents of the extraction plan without their American lawyers present. The Empire of Japan will make your men disappear."

Engel shook hands with Masuji. "I will call Colonel Nagamasa from a pay phone and give him the Baltimore lawyer's name, the name of his law firm, and the firm's street address, building name, and floor number. Thank you, Captain Masuji."

Benkei: "My pleasure."

Nagamasa then spoke to Engel. "If you do not object, I will have my adjutant serve as your chauffeur tonight. I suspect that you will need to use several phone booths in Virginia, Maryland and possibly DC in order to communicate securely with your exfiltration team. I think it best for you to lie on the floor of my adjutant's vehicle until he tells you that he is not being tailed by the FBI."

Engel: "Fine with me. The Reich will be forever in your and Captain Masuji's debt!"

Masuji thought, *The Reich and you most certainly will be indebted to me.*

And that was that.

The 4 PM arraignment of Pieper and Fuchs did not go smoothly. The magistrate expressed serious concerns about the potential danger these men posed to the community and the considerable risk that they might flee to Nazi Germany, a country unlikely to honor any US requests for their extradition.

The Baltimore counsel for Pieper and Fuchs argued vigorously that neither man had ever been arrested in any jurisdiction prior to this incident in Garrison, Maryland. The lawyer told the magistrate, "Your Honor, I had the rare privilege of serving as a clerk to Supreme Court Chief Justice William Howard Taft, who—as you well know—was the twenty-seventh President of the United States prior to his becoming Chief Justice. I learned much about the Constitution—particularly about the Bill of Rights and the Fourth and Fourteenth Amendments—from him and the other esteemed Justices on the Supreme Court. I have argued and won over a dozen cases before US Courts of Appeals, as well as the US Supreme Court, defending individuals against abusive police tactics that infringed on their constitutional rights against unreasonable search and seizure and false arrest. Your Honor, in my professional experience, I have never encountered unconstitutional conduct by law officers as egregious as in this case. I have advised my clients that under US law, my judgment is that they have an excellent chance of prevailing on the merits. Nonetheless, in order to address the concerns of this Court, my clients will surrender their passports to you today to demonstrate that they are committed to appearing in court to defend their rights—the rights the US Constitution extends to all individuals within the jurisdiction of the United States of America. As further evidence of their intention to remain in Maryland and contest these charges in court, Mr. Pieper is prepared to leave his new 1939 automobile in the possession of this Court (or whomever the Court desires to maintain custody over said vehicle) this very day. Furthermore, Your Honor, my clients will agree to reside at the Emerson Hotel on North Calvert Street in the city of Baltimore from now until the time they are vindicated at trial. They will leave the Emerson solely for the purpose of assisting in the preparation of their defense with me and co-counsel in my law firm's offices located nearby on North Calvert Street in The Equitable Building."

The magistrate responded, "You have not mentioned bail, Sir. Suppose I set the bail for each of them at $100,000."

"Your Honor, I believe that bail in that amount is excessive."

The magistrate replied, "Take it or leave it, Counselor!"

"We will take it," answered the lawyer.

After the arraignment, Pieper and Fuchs were hustled out of the courtroom by their lawyers and driven to The Equitable Building. It was 6 PM when they arrived at the law office on the sixth floor. Dr. Engel called the DC counsel for Pieper and Fuchs from a pay phone in Alexandria, Virginia, and received a detailed report of the events in court, as well as the extraordinary commitments the lawyer made to get the two Germans out on bail. Engel expressed his appreciation for the legal team's fast footwork with the magistrate.

Engel then said, "This Emerson Hotel, does it have a quiet place where I might have an associate of mine meet my men for a private chat?"

The lawyer said, "Well, the Chesapeake Room in the basement of the hotel is not particularly well lit and the food is quite good. There is also a basement exit to a side street if you wish to maintain your privacy."

Engel replied, "Thank you."

Doktor Engel promptly advised Nagamasa of the location of the law firm and the Emerson Hotel next door. Nagamasa advised Engel to call a pay phone number in Georgetown in two hours for further details about the extraction plan. Nagamasa then met with Masuji and provided him with the information that he had previously requested from Engel. The two Japanese embassy spies proceeded to construct an exfiltration plan that would be executed by Dr. Ralph Ames and Junius Johnson.

Masuji received Engel's call at the phone booth in Georgetown and communicated the proposed plan to *"Der Geist."* The German spymaster enthusiastically approved the plan. Dr. Engel then briefed Klaus Schmitz, a trusted Abwehr agent operating under deep cover as a member of the German embassy legal staff. Engel ordered Schmitz to go to the law firm office in The Equitable Building in Baltimore first thing Tuesday morning and alert Pieper and Fuchs to the plan for them to depart America surreptitiously Tuesday night.

To make certain that the plan would be executed properly, Captain Masuji decided to take the risk of meeting with Dr. Ames face-to-face to go over the details. At 7 PM, he asked Miss Hara to alert his driver that he needed to leave the embassy in five minutes. She followed his command and, as always, asked no questions. If Benkei wanted her to know something, he would tell her. Prying into the Captain's meetings, memoranda, or movements would raise his suspicion, and possibly his ire. Hara kept her mouth shut.

Masuji instructed his driver to drive evasively for 15 minutes to assure that they were not being followed. Confident that there were no tails, Benkei ordered the driver to take him to 1514 Division Street in Baltimore. At Rhode Island Avenue and 5th Street NW, Captain Masuji directed the chauffeur to stop at a pay phone booth. The Captain made one brief phone call to Dr. Ames's hospital office. The switchboard operator connected the call. When Ralph Ames picked up the phone, Masuji spoke slowly and clearly. "Dr. Ames, please go to a pay phone and call this number." Masuji gave the phone booth number and area code to Ames. Ralph left the hospital and dialed Masuji from a nearby pay phone.

"I am a friend of Kimura Katsuie. I need to meet with you tonight, Dr. Ames. Please wait outside the main entrance of Provident Hospital at 8:30 PM. I will be in the left rear seat of a chauffeur-driven, black four-door Lincoln Zephyr with diplomatic license plates. Please enter the right rear seat. Understood?"

Ames replied, "Understood."

Anticipating action, Ralph called Junius at home from a pay phone within the hospital and said, "Junius, this is Ralph. Tell your folks that you are a little dizzy at 10:30 PM tonight and that you are going to call me for assistance. Call me on my Provident Hospital phone line and complain about experiencing vertigo. I will come by and brief you on the mission. Understood?"

"Understood," replied Junius.

Ames got into Masuji's vehicle as soon as it stopped near the hospital on Division Street. Looking straight into Benkei's cold eyes, Ralph said, "What can I do for you?"

Masuji replied without disclosing his name. "Dr. Ames, the Empire needs you and your assistant, Mr. Junius Johnson, to perform a vital service tomorrow evening. Two German men, a Mr. Pieper and a Mr. Fuchs, need to be taken to a ship, the *Kinka Maru*, docked at a pier near the American Sugar Refinery in Baltimore harbor. Do you know this place, Dr. Ames?"

Ames replied, "Yes. It's off Key Highway. I have been in that area many times."

"The two Germans expect a young Negro male—Mr. Johnson—to greet them at 9:15 PM in the basement hallway of the Emerson Hotel, just outside the Chesapeake Room restaurant. Do you know this place, Dr. Ames?"

"Yes. I know exactly where it is. White democrat politicians meet there frequently to plot their political deals with each other. Mr. Johnson should not have a problem at 9:15 on a Tuesday night standing in a basement hallway pretending to be a chauffeur for white men," replied Ralph.

"Good, Dr. Ames. Get Pieper and Fuchs out to the American Sugar Refiner dock promptly, but strictly obey all traffic regulations. These men need no further encounters with the police! The Captain of the *Kinka Maru*, Captain Yonai, will be expecting two German passengers. Leave the pier as soon as the Captain shakes hands with the two men."

"Got it. What should we do if we encounter any difficulties?" asked Ames.

Masuji replied, "Use your judgment, Doctor. But these two men must not be taken prisoner again by the American authorities."

"I understand," replied Ralph.

As instructed, Junius called Dr. Ames at Provident Hospital at 10:30 PM. Isaiah and Frances were pleasantly surprised when Dr. Ralph Ames stopped by their home late at night to examine their son.

Ralph briefed Junius about the details of the operation and said, "Junius, this is a big deal. The Japanese would not entrust a mission this important to anyone in whom they did not have total confidence. No one, not even Coleman, can know of our involvement in this operation. This will be front-page news—a huge public defeat for the US government—but you and I will be the only Americans to ever know who pulled this thing off. Understood?"

"Yes, Dr. Ames. Totally."

"OK. Junius, I am going to tell your parents that you appear all right, but that I will see you in my office tomorrow evening just to be certain. The story for tomorrow will be that you checked out fine and I prepared a late dinner for you afterward at my home."

At 9 AM on Tuesday, the Abwehr Agent Schmitz, posing as an in-house embassy legal counsel, arrived at the lawyer's sixth-floor office in The Equitable Building. He asked to speak privately with the two German nationals about their treatment by the US legal system.

In a small conference room, the "embassy counsel," in hushed tones, told the two German agents, "Dr. Engel sends you his regards. This evening at eight PM, you will dine alone together at the Chesapeake Room restaurant in the Emerson Hotel's basement. Wear the suits and ties you are wearing now. Bring no luggage of any kind. Do not consume any alcoholic beverages. You need to be ready for action. At 9:15 PM, you will leave the Chesapeake Room. A young Negro man will greet you in the basement hallway. Say nothing to him. Follow him to a vehicle driven by another older Negro male. Go with them. You will be taken to a Japanese freighter that will take you far away from the United States. Talk to no one about this conversation that I am having with you, especially your lawyers. *Verstehen Sie?*"

Fuchs and Pieper both repeated, "*Ja. Wir verstehen!*"

The extraction went off without a hitch. By 10 PM on Tuesday, Pieper and Fuchs were onboard the *Kinka Maru*, hidden in a secret compartment near the ship's kitchen in order to confuse the senses of any police dogs that might be sent by US authorities to search the vessel. No such search ever took place. The defendants' lawyers dutifully reported to the Maryland State Police that Pieper and Fuchs failed to arrive at their offices by 11 AM on Wednesday. A search of their hotel rooms indicated that all of their belongings had been left behind. The FBI, US marshals, State Department investigators and Maryland State Police participating in the hunt for the two German bail jumpers received no cooperation whatsoever from the German government. The Third Reich's official position was that the two men were private citizens and that the embassy had no idea where Pieper and Fuchs were.

No US law enforcement or intelligence officer even hypothesized that the Japanese facilitated the escape of the two German agents. The FBI pursued every imaginable German, German-American, Italian, and Italian-American lead and found nothing. Newspapers, magazines, and even members of the House of Representatives and Senate had a field day fulminating about the incompetence of the FBI and law enforcement for losing two dangerous Germans the day after they were arrested by the Maryland State Police.

It was not until the morning of May 11, 1940, that the FBI became aware of the details of Dr. Engel's twin master strokes in the city of Baltimore—the assassination of Huber by one of *Der Geist's* German hit men and Pieper and Fuchs's escape via a Japanese merchant vessel, courtesy of Japanese embassy officials with diplomatic immunity. Ulrike Koch learned the true facts from an inebriated Klaus Schmitz while he posed nude in her apartment on the night of May 10, 1940. She informed Al Zangara at 4 AM on May 11, after Schmitz finally staggered out of her premises. By then, the grim news of Nazi Germany's Blitzkrieg victories over the combined forces of The Netherlands,

Belgium, France, and Great Britain had erased from the American public's memory the bail jumping by two German nationals awaiting trial in Baltimore and the apparent building jumping suicide by a clinically depressed German-American, also in Baltimore. The bitter memories within the FBI of its embarrassing counterintelligence failures in Baltimore remain until this very day, however.

Clarence Walker received a dressing-down from the FBI Assistant Director not long after Zangara got the report from his CI, Ulrike Koch. "Clarence, you figure out precisely how this counterintelligence failure happened. You put procedures in place so that nothing like this ever happens again. The Germans, the Japanese, and their Fifth Column American agents who flouted US laws and authority must be made to understand that their despicable deeds will not be forgotten, that there will be a Day of Reckoning. Your career is on the line here. Do you understand?"

"Yes, Sir! Leave it to me. I will take care of it. All of it!" replied Walker.

9 AM MONDAY, MAY 13, 1940; 10TH AND CONSTITUTION AVENUES: BLOOD, TOIL, TEARS, AND SWEAT

Before Clarence Walker reviewed with the team the information gleaned from Zangara's CI and commenced the process by which he would address each of the the Assistant Director's mandates, he welcomed the return of Lieutenant JG Martin Victor from his brief honeymoon trip to New York City with his wife, now over four months pregnant.

"Gentlemen, our best marksman has returned to duty and it is my understanding that his aim was as true in the Lord Baltimore Hotel in Baltimore as it was in the FBI range at Quantico, Virginia!"

Gareth shouted, "Martin, we knew you had it in you! Now Gertrude knows too!"

Hercules added, "All those marriage classes you and your wife took with that Rabbi Elkanan must have worked!"

Walker reasserted control over the unruly crowd. "Enough! Lieutenant Victor, every member of this team enjoyed attending your wedding and meeting your family and friends. Most of all—and I know that I speak for every man in this room, as well as Captain McLaughlin—we are in awe of Gertrude. Martin, you sure know how to pick a wife!"

Everyone in the room shouted, "Here! Here!" Martin got up from his chair and bowed slightly. He then spoke.

"Ten months ago, I could not imagine my life amounting to very much. Today I am amazed at my great, good fortune. Thank you. From the bottom of my heart, thank you!"

With that, he sat down. In Martin's mind, however, swirled the lyrics from Cole Porter's, "Do I Love You?" Gertrude and he heard Ethel Merman and Ronald Graham sing the song when they attended the musical, *Du Barry Was a Woman*, at the 46th Street Theatre in New York. The newlyweds decided that this would be their song. Martin's heart ached when he sang to himself that he would never leave his beloved Gertrude.

He knew that he had to focus on counterintelligence matters now. Martin submerged his emotions. He was good at that.

Walker returned to the important matters at hand. He presented the details collected from the debrief of Zangara's Confidential Informant concerning the aftermath of the arrest of Jurgen Huber at Glenn L. Martin's Building C. "The Assistant Director believes the opposition outmaneuvered us. We have been directed to analyze the causes of our poor performance and revise our procedures to eliminate the possibility of our suffering another such humiliation in the future. Walker decided that after his entire team accomplished these tasks, he would privately assign just Boulanger and Zangara the mission of educating the Nazi and Japanese espionage elites that they would not be permitted to violate US laws and sovereignty with impunity.

The rest of the day and evening were devoted to constructing a detailed timeline of events and identifying what decisive moves by the opposition were missed by the FBI/BCPD/ONI team members.

By 10 PM, a clear picture emerged of what the Nazis and Japanese had done right, what the US team had done wrong, and the new tactics necessary for the team to preclude any similar enemy successes in the future. With the entire team present, Hercules summarized their findings with Walker at 9 AM on Tuesday, May 14.

"In war, and we are at war, you win by persistently taking the initiative. You lose when you let up on your adversary and allow him to breathe, to think, to plan, to move freely, to collaborate with others, and to execute missions. We lost the initiative when we failed to smother Huber, Pieper, and Fuchs with surveillance after their release on bail. We should have allocated at least two people to watch over Huber on Saturday. Instead, we overprotected Westphal and did not commit even a single agent to cover Jurgen Huber. We repeated this error on Monday after we bagged Pieper and Fuchs, the Nazi hitmen sent to snuff out Westphal. Once we had those German assassins in custody, Westphal had served his immediate purpose for us. Instead of turning Friedrich over to the US Marshal Service for protection as a witness in an espionage conspiracy case, we high-value counterintelligence 'knights' wasted our time by continuing to protect a pawn whose relative value had declined significantly. By not surveilling Huber, we made it easy for a Nazi hitman to give Jurgen a flying lesson off the roof of the Munsey Building. It has been months and we still do not know the identity of Huber's assassin! By not surveilling Pieper and Fuchs, we missed an opportunity to publicly take down a Jap-Nazi spy alliance operating inside Baltimore and Washington. Had we arrested Dr. Ames, Junius Johnson, and the Captain of the *Kinka Maru* in the act of assisting Pieper and Fuchs to flee from prosecution, we might have been able to trap Masuji and Engel taking a subsequent run at freeing or killing all five of their agents before trial. We might even have learned the identity of the mole inside the FBI who leaked the safe house address to that son-of-a-bitch Dr. Engel.

"To sum up, Clarence, we failed to reprioritize our targets after initial contact. Had we done so, our surveillance skills and tactics applied to the correct targets would have resulted in a win and not a loss. From now on, the team will build into its operations a continuous assessment and reassessment of its surveillance targets and use this prioritization process to manage its allocation of resources.

Walker replied, "I appreciate that the team did not whine that it needed more agents and more resources in order to avoid this humiliation in Baltimore. I concur with your analysis and conclusions. I look forward to your presenting to me a written set of operational procedures for implementing these improvements to our management of espionage cases by the close of business today. Murphy, you will lead the team in this effort. I must temporarily reassign Hercules and Al to an urgent new matter. They will likely need the rest of the day to handle it. Carry on."

"Al and Hercules, please come with me to my office."

Walker instructed his secretary to hold all calls and closed the door to his inner sanctum. "We have been asked to educate our foreign and Fifth Column adversaries about the consequences of conducting their operations in the US like gangsters rather than gentlemen spies. Our goal is to deter the governments of Germany and Japan from engaging in such bad behavior in the future. I want you two to analyze this problem in all its dimensions and solve it definitively without any blow-back to the Bureau. I do not need to know any of the details. You are on your own. Understood?"

Hercules and Al replied simultaneously: "Understood." They left Walker and sealed themselves off from humanity in the conference room adjacent to Zangara's office. After placing individual 8 x 10-inch photographs of Dr. Engel, Major Lansdorff, Captain Masuji, Dr. Ames, Junius Johnson, Elizabeth Robertson and Attorney Helm in a straight line across the center of the conference room table, Al announced: "Let's rank these individuals by the extent to which they are culpable for the assassination of Jurgen Huber." Carefully weighing the facts from the recently constructed chronology, Al and Hercules concluded that Dr. Engel bore primary responsibility for engineering the Huber hit.

The two FBI agents then followed the same procedure to assess the blameworthiness of each of the seven subjects for the exfiltration of Pieper and Fuchs. Again, they concluded that Engel ranked number one. "This German engineer has impressive organizational skills." Said Hercules. "He effectively manipulated all of the lawyers, the court, German Embassy officials and even Imperial Japanese Army and Imperial Japanese Navy Intelligence operators to do his bidding. The man has talent."

Finally, Boulanger and Zangara considered the seriousness of the threat that each of the subjects posed to US national security for the foreseeable future. They took little time deciding that Dr. Engel could and would inflict the greatest harm to the US as he commanded a small army of anonymous killers capable of deploying rapidly and executing costly attacks against high value targets within America.

At 5 PM, Alphonse Zangara told Clarence Walker that Hercules and he had a productive day and that they were leaving the office to have dinner. Walker wished them well and said, "See you in the morning."

And that was that.

Hercules and Zangara dined together at "Maison Boulanger" that night. Each ate a "Cheeseburger a la Hercules," one-half pound of ground porterhouse steak, grilled medium rare with cheddar cheese and bacon, served on a deluxe seeded roll. They listened to the radio and heard a recording of Winston Churchill delivering his first speech as Prime Minister to the British Parliament. Boulanger smiled when Churchill told his besieged citizenry that he had "nothing to offer but blood, toil, tears and sweat" in waging war against the bestial Nazis. However, when Churchill announced that "victory" was the sole aim of his government: "Victory at all costs. Victory in spite of all terrors. Victory, however long and hard the road may be, for without victory there is no survival," Hercules hammered his fist into his kitchen table. "That man knows how to motivate people! Damn!"

Zangara agreed. Then he said, "Herc, let's take a walk."

Hercules knew what would be coming next.

Alone together on U Street on a clear, 70-degree night, Al, said, "Hercules, here is my plan. Analyze it and tell me if you see any problem. We know from Miss Koch that Dr. Engel frequents Stewart's Cafeteria at 116 7th Avenue in New York City to find athletic males with whom he can later engage in intimate acts at his luxurious home in Brooklyn. I know a man of prodigious strength with considerable underworld experience who long ago took a solemn vow of silence and noncooperation with law enforcement. This unchivalrous paladin owes me a favor... actually, many favors. When Engel encounters this powerfully built man at Stewart's, he will desire him, and invite him to his home. Assume that things just do not go well for Heinz Engel while entertaining this "cavaliere Oscuro" in his Brooklyn boudoir. Assume further that the nature of the crime scene leads the local constabulary to conclude that a crime of passion occurred, the kind of passion the Nazi consulate in New York would not want publicized. In other words, assume that there will not be a diplomatic row between the German government and the US government over this regrettable event and the NYPD will find other, more important crimes to solve with their limited manpower and resources."

Hercules replied, "As long as I am not the powerfully built man to whom you are referring, it sounds like a righteous plan to me."

Zangara responded, "Hercules, you are an excellent friend and a great American!"

Hercules laughed and said, "I try to be, Al. I truly try to be."

JUNE 4, 1940

Addressing Parliament, Winston Churchill roused his nation with a clarion, savage war cry:

"...to defend our island whatever the cost may be. We shall fight on the beaches, we shall fight on the landing grounds, we shall fight in the fields and in the streets, we shall fight in the hills; we shall never surrender."

Late that night in New York at Stewart's Cafeteria, Dr. Heinz Engel met a mature *übermensch* who, in his youth, might have been a strongman in a circus. After a brief conversation, Engel invited the tall, dark man —wearing size seventeen brogues— to his home. On the afternoon of June 5, the New York Consul General, Dr. Manfred Froelich, dispatched Dr. Engel's secretary to Brooklyn when Heinz failed to attend a mandatory embassy staff meeting and did not answer numerous phone calls made to his home. The secretary entered Engel's abode using the keys Heinz had deposited with the Consul General. She found Dr. Engel's lifeless nude body on the floor of his bedroom. Horrified and sickened by the sight of her deceased boss, the secretary called Consul General Froelich, breaking down completely when she attempted to describe the scene in the charnel house. Froelich contacted the German embassy in DC and alerted the ambassador to the preliminary facts as reported to him by the distraught secretary. The embassy contacted the US State Department, which promptly informed the US Attorney General and the Director of the FBI. J. Edgar Hoover. Director Hoover called the head of the FBI New York office with the news, ordering the SAC to "get to the bottom of this mess." The New York Agent in Charge then called the NYPD Commissioner, the New York Medical Examiner, and the New York District Attorney, advising them of the fraught diplomatic situation brewing in Brooklyn and that "Mr. Hoover" would be arriving to assess the situation on June 6.

By early evening, forty law enforcement personnel were scouring the home of the late Dr. Heinz Engel, as well as the surrounding neighborhood, for evidence and clues. By late evening, the Reich Foreign Ministry in Berlin issued an order to the German embassy and the German consulate, forbidding any interviews of German personnel by American federal, state, or local authorities regarding Dr. Heinz Engel.

The total lack of cooperation by the German government triggered a "freedom of the press" response by the New York Police Department. Copies of Dr. Engel's framed photos of nude males engaged in a variety of erotic poses like those depicted on Fifth and Sixth Century BC Attic Kylixes somehow found their way into the hands of the editors in chief of prominent New

York newspapers. The identity of the American cleaning woman retained by the late Dr. Engel became available to members of the Fourth Estate, and Mrs. O'Shaughnessy provided numerous, detailed interviews confirming the Bohemian character of her late employer. The apogee of the Third Reich's public relations nightmare came when *The New York Times* published an article hinting that Dr. Engel's true profession involved espionage and quoting a Deputy Medical Examiner who said, "It should come as no surprise that a man like Engel came to a violent end."

Despite the extraordinary allocation of investigatory resources, the demise of Dr. Heinz Engel decayed into a cold case, unsolved to this day. Coincidentally, Alphonse Zangara reconciled with his father in June of 1940 and the two celebrated Thanksgiving and Christmas together each year until Mario's passing of natural causes at his home in Bridgeport on May 5, 1961, while watching astronaut Alan Shepard successfully pilot the Freedom 7 spacecraft on its suborbital mission.

Ulrike Koch continued to supply intelligence to Zangara until Hitler declared war on the United States on December 11, 1941. A man almost seven feet tall, wearing a blue fedora, was observed by a guard at the German embassy walking arm-in-arm with *Fraülein* Koch to a car driven by a Negro male, also wearing a blue fedora. The Nazis never saw her again. A Miss Ellen Carson moved to Lewiston, Montana, in the spring of 1942. She opened a photography store, which became famous for displays of her vivid photos of rugged cowboys, ranch life, mountain ranges, and people trout fishing in the Judith River. Though somewhat reclusive, Miss Carson celebrated the anniversary of V-E Day, May 8, 1945, every year by hosting a party at her ranch. Four reserved, imposing male friends of hers would routinely attend "Ellen's Gala," rooming at her place for a few days before returning to their homes in Maryland and the District of Columbia. Carson committed suicide with a 9mm Luger in the fall of 1967 after amyotrophic lateral sclerosis robbed her of her ability to ride her prized stallion, named "Al."

Captain Masuji never believed that the motive behind Engel's murder involved sex. Benkei reasoned that the death of Dr. Engel was an act of retribution by someone in the US government. "If Engel caused me to lose face the way he humiliated the FBI in Baltimore, I would have killed him too!" he told Colonel Nagamasa shortly after Engel's death. Nagamasa concurred with Captain Masuji. The Colonel had personally decapitated Chinese citizens for merely looking at him in a disrespectful manner.

Pondering the situation, the Colonel said to Masuji, "What troubles me most is not knowing how the Americans learned about Dr. Engel's involvement in the Baltimore operation. Engel never surfaced in Baltimore. He handled the Glenn L. Martin matter remotely, with an admirable economy of communication. How could the Americans have detected him? Could we or the Germans have a mole?"

Masuji replied, "My thinking is that there is a mole operating out of the German embassy. We have surveilled everyone intensively in my office, even secretaries, and concluded that all of them are clean. Perhaps I will ask Major Lansdorff to look deeply into his organization, if he has not done so already."

The Japanese Colonel answered, "You do that, Captain Masuji."

Major Lansdorff discussed the mole issue with Masuji over a round of golf. "I see your point, Captain. Berlin wants this Engel business buried and would not approve of me speaking with you about it. However, I will review who knew the details of the operation, ask a few questions, and determine whether we have a security breach or not. Do you have anyone in mind who you suspect, Captain Masuji?"

"Elizabeth Robertson," replied Benkei.

"I will investigate. But let us not discuss this subject ever again," snarled Lansdorff.

"I understand fully, Major," said Masuji.

The Major returned to the embassy after his encounter with Captain Masuji. Klaus Schmitz saluted Lansdorff, clicking his heels together loudly.

Joachim returned the salute, said, "*Heil* Hitler," and asked Schmitz to come into his office and close the door.

"Klaus, one of the most repellent people I ever encountered, Dr. Heinz Engel, died a well-deserved death. Today, the next most odious individual I have ever known, Captain Saigo Masuji, ordered me to hunt down a mole in our employ whom he suspects is responsible for Engel's murder. Can you believe the insolence of that ape? Masuji's prime suspect is Elizabeth Robertson."

Schmitz shook his head in disgust. "Major Lansdorff, I could not agree with you more. Only a devious Asiatic could question Miss Robertson's loyalty to the Third Reich. If a mole exists, the creature dwells in the embassy of Japan. Do not trouble yourself, Sir. Never again will Engel smoke cigars in your office, dropping ashes on the floor. Never again will Engel attempt to seduce men in the embassy. As for our Japanese 'allies,' I have arranged payment in full for the exfiltration from Baltimore of our two Aryans orchestrated by Masuji and the other rabid simian, Nagamasa. You will not have to concern yourself with these allies unless we absolutely need access to another one of their ships."

Joachim thanked Klaus for his work and asked, "What reward did you arrange for them?"

Schmitz replied, "I have organized a tour of selected technical enterprises in Germany for a few of Japan's top military and scientific personnel. They will see only what our leaders in Berlin want them to see, nothing more. As the Americans would say, we are giving them the sleeves off our vest!"

Lansdorff chortled and patted Klaus on his shoulder. "Good man!"

And that was that.

20

8 AM TUESDAY, JUNE 18, 1940; CAPTAIN MASUJI'S OFFICE, THE JAPANESE EMBASSY

Saigo Masuji did not enjoy reading the front page of *The Washington Post* that morning. The headline read, **Measure for 84 New Warships Is Presented to House, Senate**. The American government announced that another $1.2 billion would be added to the federal budget to build a "two-ocean" Navy. This 23 percent increase in the size of the US fleet would make the American Navy the largest in the world. But what concerned the Imperial Japanese Navy Captain most appeared in the continuation of the article tucked away on page two, column three:

> The President named a nine-man National Defense Research Committee [NDRC] composed of Dr. J.B. Conant, president of Harvard University; Dr. Richard C. Tolman, of the California Institute of Technology; Dr. Karl Compton, president of the Massachusetts Institute of Technology; Conway P. Coe, United States Patent Commissioner; Dr. F.B. Jewett, president of the National Academy of Sciences; the Secretary of War [Henry Stimson], and the Secretary of

the Navy [Frank Knox]. Dr. Vannevar Bush, president of the Carnegie Institution, previously was appointed chairman of the group.

Captain Masuji recognized that FDR had created an organization composed of a who's who of American scientific, technical, industrial, military, and political talent capable of mobilizing and focusing the vast resources of the United States of America to fight a war of annihilation against Japan. Benkei knew, but would never admit to anyone, that his nation could not possibly prevail in a war with a United States fully committed to victory. Captain Masuji, the son of an ancient samurai family, distinguished graduate of the Etajima Naval Academy, decorated Imperial Japanese Navy hero at the Battle of Tsushima, and, most importantly, a Japanese man limitlessly indebted and devoted to the sacred Emperor of Japan, preferred death to submission, surrender, or defeat! He would go down fighting, doing as much damage as he possibly could to thwart this NDRC.

Thus, Benkei directed Hiroaki Shima to establish, with all deliberate speed, a comprehensive research, analysis, and reporting system regarding the NRDC with the aid of the embassy's science and technology attaché and Miss Hara. "Shima, I want to see everything published each day about the NDRC, Vannevar Bush, and each of the NDRC board members."

"*Hai!*" replied Shima. He turned and scurried to his office to organize a system capable of meeting Benkei's requirements.

Masuji asked Miss Hara to come into his office. She bowed low before him. "Miss Hara, I have asked Mr. Shima to track very closely a new US threat to Japan. You will assist him and the science and technology attaché in this endeavor with all of your skills and with total devotion to your duty to the Emperor and Japan. If Shima has not called you in two hours, call him and ask to be briefed on your role in this matter."

Miss Hara bowed again and backed slowly out of Benkei's office. After one hour, she called Shima. "Mr. Shima, Captain Masuji says that you have an important assignment for me."

Shima: "Yes, I do. Please come to my office."

Miss Hara joined Shima and the S&T attaché, Professor Acai, in a discussion concerning the NDRC research project that lasted for a full hour and a half. She had much to report to Al.

On Saturday, June 22, Kinuyo walked from her apartment to the National Zoo. Hercules, Clyde, and Zangara detected no surveillance. Al picked up Miss Hara near the zoo on Connecticut Avenue. As they drove to an FBI safe house in Culpeper, Virginia, a concerned and excited Kinuyo described the current status of Captain Masuji's operation targeting the NDRC and its chairman.

"Benkei is consumed by the danger this organization poses to Japan. The Captain views this Professor Bush as a uniquely intelligent and capable man. I fear that Saigo intends to harm the professor before he can harness the full might of American science and technology to crush the Empire of Japan. I overheard Masuji speaking with Kimura Katsuie about putting surveillance on Bush. They know that he and his wife live at the Wardman Park and are using Katsuie's agents from Baltimore to study the extent to which Bush is being protected. Benkei desperately wants to know which weapons programs Bush and the NDRC plan to pursue. Even though Benkei detests Elizabeth Robertson, he is considering using her connections within the State Department to learn more about Dr. Bush and his committee. Al, in just four days, Masuji has set much in motion."

Al attempted to calm Kinuyo. "The faster Benkei moves, the more mistakes he will make. We will stop him before he hurts anyone, Kinuyo. If you want to leave the embassy today and become an American citizen, just tell me. As far as I am concerned, you have done all that anyone could have expected you to do. If this double life you have been leading has become too difficult for you to manage, I completely understand."

Zangara then pulled the car off the road and turned off the ignition. He took a surprised Kinuyo by the hand and said, What I am trying to say is, if you will have me, I would be honored to be your husband."

Neither Kinuyo, nor even Alphonse Zangara, were prepared for this outburst of candor and emotion. A tearful Miss Hara gently replied, "Yes, Al. I would be most honored to be your wife. However, I must stay at the embassy until you and the FBI close down Masuji's operation. If I leave before you act, he will understand instantly that I betrayed him. He will remove his sword from his scabbard and cause as much bloodshed as he can in order to die while washing away the stain of his unbearable dishonor."

Al replied, "Sweetheart, this episode must end soon. The NDRC is too important for us to permit a person as dangerous as Masuji a prolonged opportunity to plan ways to damage it and its personnel. You must not arouse any suspicion by behaving differently than you always have at work. Are you confident that you can remain composed for another month or two?"

Kinuyo answered, "Of course, Al. I am Japanese, you know."

Al laughed. "You are going to make an outstanding mother as well as a wife, Miss Hara!"

Kinuyo bowed her head and smiled at such pleasant thoughts.

And that was that.

1 PM SUNDAY, JUNE 24, 1940; 10TH AND CONSTITUTION AVENUES

Clarence Walker, Alphonse Zangara, and Hercules Boulanger met to discuss Miss Hara's startling revelations concerning Masuji and the NDRC. Walker asked Al, "Are you confident in the accuracy of your CI's report?"

"Yes. Miss Hara is member of Captain Masuji's team working this NDRC matter. She has a front row seat at all of the meetings."

Walker then asked, "Do you believe that Masuji intends to harm the chairman of the NDRC?"

Zangara replied without hesitation. "Yes. If Captain Masuji determines that he can materially impede America's preparations to fight a war with Japan by removing a particularly gifted individual, he will do so."

Walker: "I have heard from my source at Glenn L. Martin that this Dr. Vannevar Bush is essential to our war effort. Clearly, the President of the United States agrees. Under these circumstances, I must inform the Assistant Director of the threat. He will, no doubt, ask me what our plan is to contain Masuji. You two are my brain trust. What do you recommend?"

Zangara glanced over at Hercules and said, "What do you think?"

Nonchalantly, Hercules proffered a list of recommendations and rationales. "First, we need to secure the chairman. Put a few fine-looking fellows in fedoras like Fowler and Dennis around him. Whoever is watching Bush needs to know that if they attempt any rough stuff, they will die in a hail of .357 Magnum bullets. Martin and I will serve as an invisible outer security ring identifying who Masuji's watchers are. Gareth's job—one at which he excels—will be to make an example of one of the watchers Martin and I pick up. If hospitalizing one of these potential aggressors fails to deter the others, then let Gareth make an even more serious example of the next watcher we identify. Additionally, Clyde could put a few rounds into Masuji's personal vehicle late at night…when the car is parked and no one is in it, of course. Sooner or later, even a somewhat deranged samurai like Masuji will understand that the US government means to aggressively protect the NDRC chairman. Second, we need to prevent the Japanese (or the Germans, for that matter) from knowing where the chairman is going and with whom he is meeting. He may be associating with people—say, British people—concerning topics that we want to keep confidential. Murphy would be a perfect diplomat to coordinate with the keeper of the chairman's calendar so we can decide when these extra precautions need to be taken. Third, Elizabeth Robertson needs to be dealt with now. Get the State Department to assign her to a job rejecting visas for diseased peasants at a consulate in Turkey or some other awful out-of-the-way place where she can't provide support to her Nazi and Japanese friends and cause us any trouble."

Walker, mildly amused, responded, "Is that all you have, Boulanger?"

"That is all I have…for now," Hercules replied.

Walker saw Zangara smirking. "Alphonse, do have anything to add to Boulanger's list?"

"No, Sir. Hercules's plan addresses the threat as we understand it today."

Walker told Zangara and Hercules that he would get back to them after he spoke to the Assistant Director. "However, I think that this issue will go to the Director. Where it goes after that, I do not know. Without causing a disturbance, keep an eye on the NRDC chairman until I get back to you."

Al and Hercules took a walk past the White House and then toward the Lincoln Memorial. "Hercules, thank you for keeping Miss Hara's security out of the discussion. I did not want to receive an order from Walker directing me to leave Kinuyo in place at the Japanese embassy no matter how great the risk may be to her safety. I would never obey such an order, but I would prefer not having to be insubordinate. If Masuji becomes demonic as we grind down his operation, you and I are going to have to extract Kinuyo before the Captain cuts her into little pieces."

Hercules replied, "Al, I will personally shoot Masuji in his scrotum if he so much as lays a finger on your fiancée. This is America, my friend!"

Al chuckled. "Always aim for the center of mass, Hercules. Remember Koch's photo of Masuji!"

"Do I ever!" replied Boulanger.

And that was that.

By the first week of July of 1940, research and development of radio-wave devices (called RADAR by the US Navy for "**RA**dio **D**etection **A**nd **R**anging") had become a top-secret priority for the NDRC. A Section D, headed by Chairman Karl Compton and Vice-Chairman Alfred L. Loomis, a wealthy polymath (lawyer and PhD physicist), had been secretly established within the NDRC to manage all radar R&D projects. The FBI Director and the Attorney General approved a slightly edited version of Hercules's list of security recommendations. Walker had omitted any mention of Gareth and Clyde in the official document; however, he told Al and Hercules that Gareth's and

Clyde's roles were in the plan as far as he was concerned. The NDRC scientists and staff understood and accepted the importance of maintaining strict security in the office, in public, and at home. As Hercules predicted, Murphy's management of relations with the NDRC minimized friction between the fedoras and the top hats.

The first hint that Masuji had that his NDRC operation might be compromised occurred when Elizabeth Robertson received a "promotion" to serve as the Assistant Chief of the Visa Unit at the US embassy in Ankara *before* she could provide the Japanese naval attaché with any inside information about Vannevar Bush and the NDRC. The second sign that Masuji might not accomplish his objectives occurred on Monday, July 29, 1940, when Junius got too close to the Wardman Park Hotel where Bush, Loomis, Compton, and Jewett were having a private dinner meeting to discuss microwave technology as it applied to radar. Martin recognized Junius Johnson, and with one finger, vectored Gareth to the target.

Gareth intercepted Junius and said sternly, "Do you live or work here?"

Johnson said, "What right do you have to ask me such a question?"

Gareth smirked and said, "Show me some identification, now!"

Johnson again attempted to bluff Gareth. "I have done nothing wrong. Why do I have to show you anything?"

Gareth had had enough. "This is your final warning. Turn around now and walk away!"

Junius walked forward instead and Gareth hit him in the solar plexus, knocking the wind out of him. Hercules flashed his Metro PD Detective's badge to an investigating patrol officer and said, "You need to arrest that fellow struggling for air over there." He pointed at Junius. "I think he tried to strike a security guard." He pointed at Gareth.

The officer put handcuffs on Junius and asked Gareth if he was all right. "I am fine, Officer. This young man apparently did not understand that he cannot intrude on a private dinner at the Wardman Park."

The officer said, "So he was trespassing?"

Gareth: "You could say that, Officer. But the real problem here is that some government people are trying to have a private working dinner. This guy is not on the guest list. He refused my polite request to go somewhere else and then he moved forward and bumped me."

"Oh," said the officer. "He assaulted you!"

"You could say that, Officer," replied Gareth. "I just want this punk out of here."

By now, Junius had caught his breath and he began to protest. The officer was having none of it. "You agree to move along and I will take the cuffs off. You continue to be disruptive and I will leave the cuffs on and run you in. You really do not want to get booked and spend the night in the DC lockup. What is your decision?"

Junius agreed to leave to avoid getting an arrest record. He reported to Dr. Ames about the high level of executive protection at the Wardman Park. Ralph Ames called Masuji and was heard by FBI wiretappers saying, "The Feds are not fooling around. They got physical with Junius over the slightest provocation. One cracker cop appeared to know a little anatomy. Punched Junius right in the solar plexus and temporarily incapacitated him."

The Captain called Katsuie and asked for reinforcements from New York. Katsuie refused. "What is your plan, Captain? What do you intend to accomplish? You need to find a better, more subtle way."

Masuji hung up on him. "What is going on here?" he asked himself. After contemplating his options, Benkei called Dr. Ames back.

"Dr. Ames, please speak to Mr. Coleman Braxton and have him investigate if any relationship exists between his firm and the NDRC. Give him the names of the following people: Dr. Vannevar Bush, Dr. James Conant, Dr. Richard Tolman, Dr. Karl Compton, Conway Coe, and Dr. Frank Jewett. Have him determine whether Bendix Radio has consulting contracts or informal contacts with any of these men. Perhaps Coleman's superior, Dr. Crowe, has access to the NDRC, or professional relationships with some of the men I named. Get back to me after you discuss this matter with Mr. Braxton."

When Coleman arrived home from work, Ralph reviewed the situation with him, including the incident involving Junius. He had Coleman write down the initials "NDRC" and the names. Then he said, "Coleman, Captain Masuji sounds concerned. Please make this a priority so that I can get back to the Captain by Wednesday, July 31st."

"Will do, Dr. Ames," Coleman replied. "How is Junius doing? The cops did not injure him seriously, right?"

Ames, scowling, said, "Coleman, anytime a white man mistreats you, it leaves a scar. Junius is OK physically, but psychologically, I am sure that he got hurt."

Coleman asked, "Would it help if I called him?"

Dr. Ames replied, "No. I will tell him that you are concerned. If he needs a little help, he will call you. We cannot coddle people in our line of work, Coleman."

Coleman answered, "I understand."

The FBI wiretap teams relayed the substance of the July 29 conversations to Clarence Walker immediately.

TUESDAY, JULY 30, 1940; BALTIMORE

Coleman shook hands with Dr. Crowe and got behind the wheel of the Imperial. As they drove toward Bendix Radio, Coleman announced, "Sir, the Japanese are seriously interested in the National Defense Research Committee, NDRC. They want me to snoop around and see if Bendix Radio or you have any connections to the NDRC, Dr. Vannevar Bush, and a few other individuals whose names Dr. Ames dictated to me. Ralph wants an answer from me tomorrow. I think we ought to contact Clarence Walker about this."

Dr. Crowe replied, "I know Dr. Bush and most of the members of the board of the NDRC. We must contact Walker first thing this morning about this. Got any other good news for me, Coleman?"

Smiling, Coleman replied, "Other than the Orioles won a double-header yesterday over the Buffalo Bisons, no, Sir."

Crowe: "Now that is more like it, Coleman."

When they arrived at Bendix, Dr. Crowe's secretary announced that a Mr. Walker had called and requested a return call from him at his earliest convenience. "Please get Mr. Walker for me. Thanks."

Once the door was closed, Crowe said to Coleman, "This is not good."

Walker asked Crowe, "Do you know why I am calling?"

Crowe: "Yes, Coleman mentioned that Dr. Ames and the Japanese want to know about anything that Bendix has going on with the NDRC and everything I know about Dr. Bush and each of the NDRC board members."

Walker: "Correct. Now I know you are wondering how I could be so well informed about a conversation Coleman had with Ames. Do not concern yourself about such technical law enforcement matters. The less you know about such things, the better. Is Coleman with you?"

Crowe: "Yes."

Walker: "Could you have him pick up the other phone in your office, please."

Crowe: "Sure."

The three-way conversation did not last long. Crowe would not discuss anything about the NDRC or Dr. Bush to anyone not cleared to know. Walker told Crowe to sit tight, that he and another agent with top-secret clearance would arrive at Bendix in about an hour.

When they walked through the front door and into the foyer of the Bendix Radio building on Fort Avenue, Walker and Zangara were not asked by the receptionist to sign the Visitors Log. Dr. Crowe escorted them to his office. Coleman was already seated at the conference table. Zangara asked Coleman to repeat word for word what Ames had told him the night before.

After Coleman repeated what Zangara and Walker already knew, Walker asked Crowe, "Does Bendix have any contracts with the NDRC at the present time?"

Crowe: "No. However, we are having discussions with Dr. Jewett and Dr. Joliffe about electrical communications devices, radios, and mechanical and electrical equipment for aircraft."

Walker: "Anything specific?"

Crowe: "Mainly a study involving interference between aero-engines and radios."

Walker: "Anything classified as secret or top secret?"

Crowe: "No, not yet."

Walker: "Who is your contact at NDRC?"

Crowe: "Dr. Jewett."

Walker: "Talk to anyone else about this project, like, uh, Vannevar Bush?"

Crowe: "No. Just Jewett at this point. For what it is worth, Dr. Vannevar Bush was dean of engineering at MIT and my PhD thesis advisor."

Walker: "Have you heard rumors about any NDRC projects?"

Crowe: "No. The NDRC management and staff are very secretive and security-conscious people."

Walker: "Do you have any official documents from NDRC?"

Crowe: "Just a letter inquiring about our interest in bidding on some research in the field of airborne radios."

Walker: "That's it?"

Crowe: "That is all."

Walker: "OK. Let's work up a story with these facts for Coleman to pass on to Ames."

In 30 minutes, a factually accurate, entirely credible, and totally useless tale had been created for the purpose of further frustrating Masuji. To create the mirage of thoroughness and circumspection, Coleman would not present the story to Dr. Ames until July 31.

Walker ended the meeting by saying, "Coleman, Dr. Ames may pressure you to take a trip to DC to do some reconnaissance with him or for him. Do not refuse his order. Just do it."

Coleman: "OK, Sir. But I do not want to get beat up like Junius Johnson did!"

Walker: "I cannot guarantee that. You must give the appearance of being on Ames's team. If Ralph directs you to go over the line a little bit, a policeman or security officer might get physical with you. As long as you make no threatening gestures with a weapon, like a knife, a club, or a gun, no lawman will use his firearm against you. Do not carry anything that could be misconstrued as a deadly weapon. Do not resist an officer who decides to arrest you. Follow these rules and you will not be severely or permanently injured. I can guarantee that you will not have an arrest record after the dust settles."

Coleman: "Well, that makes me feel just fine. Thanks for the guidance and assurance!"

And that was that.

Driving back to DC, Zangara said to Walker, "Why did you lay it on so thick with Coleman Braxton?"

Walker replied, "I am thinking about an endgame with Masuji that might briefly put Coleman in danger. I needed to see whether he would wilt or not if placed in a combat situation."

Zangara whistled. "Tell me more, Boss."

Walker: "Suppose that Captain Masuji is led by Coleman to believe that he—the Captain—has an opportunity to get close to the NDRC chairman in a secluded location in DC? What if Masuji thinks that Coleman will be driving Crowe to a private meeting with Dr. Bush? Now assume that instead of the

NDRC chairman participating in this meeting, an FBI agent who looks like Dr. Bush, backed up by Hercules, Clyde, Gareth, Murphy, Martin, Dennis, Fowler, and you show up. What do you think will happen next, Alphonse?"

Zangara whistled again, only louder. "Clarence, you know that Masuji is a talented fanatic. In my estimation, the probability of Benkei killing or severely injuring one of us before we finish him off has to be at least fifty percent."

Walker replied, "That is why I will be observing the takedown from a safe distance, Al."

Zangara: "You sound like a DC bureaucrat, Boss. Are you going to run this Rising Sun firing squad plan by Hercules?"

Walker grinned. "I already did. He loved it."

Zangara laughed out loud. "You are so much more sinister than you look, Clarence."

Walker: "That is the key to my meager success in this business. Al, I do not mind you discussing this plan with Hercules, but do not tell the rest of the team members about it. Except for Hercules, Gareth and Clyde, this will likely be their first authentic knife-and-gun fight. I need to assess their performance under worst-case conditions. The cowardly, weak, or slow ones will be washed out."

Zangara: "Or Masuji will save you the effort of 'laundering' your personnel by killing or maiming them."

Walker said, "Good point, Al. Fidelity, Bravery, and Integrity."

Zangara: "Listening to you, I feel like a priest taking confession from Bohemond of Taranto after the Siege of Antioch."

Walker: "Thank you for the compliment. In all candor, however, I kind of see you as Bohemond, not me."

Zangara decided to deflect and replied, "How about those Orioles taking a double-header from the Buffalo Bisons the other night?"

Walker smirked.

And that was that.

MID-AUGUST 1940; WASHINGTON, DC

In mid-August, Prime Minister Winston Churchill assembled a group of Great Britain's leading scientists and technical military experts under the leadership of mathematician and physical chemist Sir Henry Tizard to prepare to transfer top-secret military technologies to the United States. A primary objective of the Tizard Mission was to hand deliver to the American defense establishment every British breakthrough in radar technology. The Walker-and-McLaughlin Baltimore Team now had to assure the security of NDRC Section D's evolving "Radar Alliance" with the British and protect it from Captain Masuji.

Before Tizard's arrival at the Shoreham Hotel in DC on August 22, 1940, Captain McLaughlin met privately with Martin and gave him the following guidance.

"Whatever is necessary for you to do to protect this NDRC program and the Tizard people, DO IT! Whatever risk you must take to accomplish this mission, TAKE IT! Martin, you have seen that counterintelligence matches are fought with no holds barred. Fight to win, Martin. It is us or them! Do you understand?"

"Yes, Sir. Understood. Baltimore Logic. Baltimore Rules."

McLaughlin then said, "OK. Congratulations again on your recent wedding. When is your baby due?"

Martin replied, "Second week of September, Sir, plus or minus a week, according to the doctor at Johns Hopkins."

The Captain replied, "Good for you and your wife, Martin. I hope you have a healthy boy. See to it that he goes to Annapolis and not some second-rate Maryland college or university's NROTC program."

Martin, smiling, said, "Aye aye, Sir!"

"Dismissed, Victor."

14 SOUTH BROADWAY, BALTIMORE, MARYLAND

While Captain McLaughlin met with Martin on Constitution Avenue in DC, Gertrude sat somewhat uncomfortably in Henry and Grace's kitchen, having breakfast. Grace, gazed approvingly at Gertrude's increasing girth, said, "Gertrude, you look beautiful! Henry, don't you agree?"

Henry looked up from the awful news about Hitler's rapid conquest of Europe on the front page of *The Baltimore Sun*, glanced at Gertrude, and replied, "Exceedingly healthy young woman, no doubt about it!"

Gertrude could feel her first-class passenger kicking and punching her. "Grace and Henry, this restless fellow wants to come out and meet everybody! Martin somehow must have transmitted his Quantico training to him. Grace, put your hand on my abdomen. Is that a foot or a hand?"

Grace felt something solid pushing outward and said, "I don't know, but we will have our hands full when this ruffian emerges."

Henry commented, "In my opinion, we will not have a chance against him. He is going to be big, strong, smart, fearless and totally independent-minded."

Gertrude slowly got up from the table and announced that Shalom Cohen wanted her to stop working, now that she was a month away from delivery. "I still feel fit enough to work, but he insists."

Grace agreed with Mr. Cohen. "Gertrude, you can help me out with Henry's books and other paperwork. We will keep you occupied until we all go up together to Hopkins Hospital in a few weeks."

Henry lowered his classes on his nose. "There's probably a lot of errors for you to correct in those books of account, Gertrude."

Irritated, Grace glanced at Henry and thought, *One day I am going to brain that husband of mine!* However, she said to Gertrude, "And you and I can continue to study with Rabbi Elkanan right up until the day the physician presents us with your mystery guest!"

Gertrude thanked them both for being such good friends and so very helpful. "OK, I will stop working at the radio store on Friday."

And that was that.

THE TIZARD MISSION

On Wednesday, August 22, 1940, Sir Henry Tizard arrived alone in DC. The remaining six members of his mission would not join him until September 11. Sir Henry checked in to the Shoreham Hotel, two imposing nine-story brick buildings united by a connecting walkway. Adjacent to Rock Creek Park, the Shoreham contained 132 apartments mixed with 250 hotel rooms.

Within walking distance of the Shoreham was the Wardman Tower, home to NDRC Section D Vice-Chairman Alfred Loomis, as well as the residence of many powerful US government officials such as Robert Jackson (Attorney General), Frank Knox (Secretary of the Navy), and Cordell Hull (Secretary of State). Secretary of War Henry Stimson, a cousin of Alfred Loomis, lived near the Shoreham Hotel in the Woodley Mansion. The White House, a place Tizard would soon visit, was a short drive from the Shoreham. Optimally situated, members of Tizard's team would forge links with their American counterparts that would ultimately revolutionize warfare. The innovation and industrialization of VHF, UHF, and microwave radars would allow for a broad range of applications, including air defense, surface naval vessel gunfire control, anti-submarine warfare, navigation, strategic air offensive bombing, and even proximity fuses tucked into artillery munitions.

Captain McLaughlin learned of Tizard and his mission through his superior, the Director of the ONI, who dined with Sir Henry on his first evening in Washington, DC. The next day, Thursday, August 22, the ONI Director and Secretary of the Navy Frank Knox met to discuss the details for executing the technology exchange. Providing adequate security for the growing number of secret meetings being arranged for Sir Henry Tizard challenged the manpower limits of McLaughlin and Walker's team. For example, on Monday, August 26, Tizard met privately with President Roosevelt to discuss radar development. Later that same day, Sir Henry met secretly with Secretary of War Henry Stimson, who strongly suggested that he meet with Vannevar Bush, Karl Compton, and Alfred Loomis to pursue radar issues. On the evening of Wednesday, August 28, Sir Henry dined with Dr. Bush at the Cosmos Club. The two scientists got along quite well and Bush advised Tizard to begin building close ties with the US military. From this Cosmos exchange came a meeting the next day with the leadership of the Naval Research Lab, where Tizard learned of American technical advances in radar about which he had been wholly unaware.

On August 30, Walker went to McLaughlin's office for an off-the-record chat about the number and scope of Sir Henry's radar technology meetings. They concluded that once the rest of Tizard's team arrived in DC in mid-September, the probability of Masuji learning about the growing alliance would approach the number one. To eliminate this risk to a top-secret program approved by President Roosevelt himself, Walker broached an aggressive plan to entrap and eliminate Masuji with Captain McLaughlin.

"Now you are talking my language, Agent Walker!" said a sinister-looking McLaughlin. "Once Masuji is out of DC, it will take the Japanese months to find a suitable replacement. It will take years before Masuji's successor can learn the job and threaten our lead in radar-based weapons systems. By then we will be at war with Japan, fighting and winning our way across the Pacific using an advanced technology that the IJN does not have! Clarence, how soon can we have this party?"

Walker replied, "I like September 11th. Tizard's crew will just be moving into the Shoreham on that day. We can lure Benkei into a secluded area within Rock Creek Park, where he can attempt to harm a senior US government official. Hopefully Masuji will surrender when he sees that he is enveloped by our overwhelming numbers and firepower. Then, we can get him declared *persona non grata* and wave bye-bye to Benkei. Of course, if he resists, we will ship his ashes back to Tokyo in an urn on the bow of a slow-moving garbage scow."

McLaughlin: "I am beginning to think that you do not like Captain Masuji."

Walker: "And you would be correct in having such thoughts, Captain McLaughlin."

The two men shook hands. Walker returned to his office. "Get me Zangara and Hercules…please," he called to his secretary.

"Gentlemen, welcome," intoned an ebullient Walker in a faux British accent when Hercules and Al walked into his office. "Please close the door. Captain McLaughlin and I have decided to have a team party early in the evening on September 11th in Rock Creek Park. Our special guests will be IJN Captain Saigo Masuji, an FBI agent who looks a lot like the chairman of the NDRC, Dr. Richard Crowe, and his chauffeur—Coleman Braxton . You two should reconnoiter Rock Creek Park and find a secluded location with adequate light at 6 PM to get proper gunsight alignment. Also, the location should offer little opportunity for bullets to wound innocent bystanders, should someone discharge their weapon and miss Masuji, or if some lead passes through Benkei's body and keeps going. Any questions?"

Hercules replied, "Nope." Zangara and Boulanger left Walker's office. To the amusement of Clarence's secretary, Hercules imitated Paul Robeson singing "Old Man River" as the two men walked to the elevator.

Walker said to himself, "You cannot beat those two. Nothing like them in the entire FBI!"

Al and Hercules found a wooded path that met all of Walker's tactical requirements. "Just the right place for Masuji to make the biggest error of his life," Hercules growled. "Benkei is going to think that he and Coleman can corner Dr. Bush and Dr. Crowe in this isolated area without any bodyguards to protect them. The samurai's murderous instincts and sense of absolute duty to his Emperor compel him to make an assassination attempt. All Walker has to do is create a plausible scenario that will convince Masuji that the NDRC chairman wants to do a favor for one of his former PhD advisees by handing Crowe a secret radar contract offer to give to Bendix."

On Saturday, August 31, Walker surveyed the ambush site with Hercules and Zangara. "OK," said Walker. "Get the team to this spot and rehearse your tactics. The only person who I can accept getting injured in this operation is Saigo Masuji. I will handle getting a Dr. Bush doppelganger for you and drawing Benkei into this location at 6 PM on September 11th. If you get this thing done right, everybody on our team will get promoted and into new assignments. Screw it up and you can spend the rest of your careers hunting bank robbers in International Falls, Minnesota, in the winter."

Hercules cleared his throat and said, "Clarence, I think we should lower the risk of casualties by disabling the firing pin mechanism on Masuji's semi-automatic pistol sometime before the 11th of September. The Captain will probably engage in some target practice shortly before the day he intends to plug a US public official, so we will have to wait before we turn his gun into a paperweight."

Walker replied, "Hercules, your suggestion is sound. I will see to it that Masuji's 8mm popgun will not pop on September 11th. But do not tell anyone on the team about this trick we intend to play. The men need to be razor sharp. Preparing for a full tilt knife-and-gun fight with a killer like Saigo will concentrate their minds, hone their reflexes, and increase the likelihood of a quick and decisive neutralization in Rock Creek Park. Are we in agreement?"

Hercules and Zangara responded, "Agreed."

SUNDAY, SEPTEMBER 1, 1940; 14 SOUTH BROADWAY

Martin, Gertrude, Milton, Grace, and Henry enjoyed breakfast together at the dining table in the Basswood's cramped living room. Henry played his favorite 78-rpm phonograph recording of Debussy's *La Mer* to relax Gertrude. Martin's mysterious overnight missions in Washington, DC, concerned her. His efforts to quell her anxiety failed. Gertrude knew that Martin was on the front lines fighting an undeclared war with dangerous adversaries. She understood the importance of what he was doing, and that he and his fellow agents were well-trained and motivated. She accepted that the world had gone mad and surrender was not an option, particularly for Jews. Nonetheless, reason and reality could not allay her fear of losing her man. Gertrude desperately wanted their baby to arrive now. She wanted Martin to see and hold their child before some awful event ended her *kochanie's* life and forever closed his magnificently lively eyes.

Grace had come to love Gertrude as the child that God had deprived her from having. Teaching "her daughter" how to prepare for the Jewish holidays, going with "her daughter" to Rabbi Elkanan's religion classes, and sharing so many intimate conversations with "her Gertrude" brought out a sensitive side in Grace's personality that Henry had not known existed.

Henry restrained himself from making cynical comments about his wife's sudden softness. He observed and appreciated "the Gertrude effect" in silence.

Like Gertrude, Milton knew that this "goodness" was too good to last. He steeled himself for the inevitable catastrophe that would take his beloved brother from him. He committed himself to protecting what would remain. In the meantime, he pretended to be happy. What else could he do?

The Basswood phone rang. Henry picked up the handset. "Dr. Basswood speaking!" he said coldly. He listened and handed the phone to Martin.

Martin listened for one minute and said, "Roger that. See you tomorrow at 6 AM, Gareth." He then placed the handset in the cradle. All eyes were on him—he had to say something.

"Training exercise. Starts tomorrow, ends September 11th, and then I have leave for the rest of the month of September."

Milton said, "My tax dollars going up in smoke! You government employees work half a month and get paid as if you worked all of it! This country is going socialist, no doubt about it."

Gertrude smiled. "Martin, you will be here when our baby is born. This is such a relief!"

10 AM, SEPTEMBER 2, 1940; BALTIMORE, 920 FORT AVENUE

Clarence Walker, Alphonse Zangara, and Coleman Braxton sat silently around the conference room in Richard Crowe's office waiting for the good doctor to wheel in a fresh pot of coffee and coffee mugs. *No use in making small talk with these two*, thought Coleman.

No use upsetting the kid before his boss is there to hold his hand, thought Walker and Zangara.

Christ, I hope those two don't rattle Coleman when I am not in the office, thought Crowe.

Counterespionage equilibrium had been achieved in Dr. Crowe's office without making a sound.

After the coffee arrived, Zangara launched into his pitch. "Dr. Crowe and Mr. Braxton, the time has come to conclude the career of IJN Captain Saigo Masuji, Japan's master spy tasked to steal US radar secrets. We need your assistance and cooperation to achieve this objective. We have devised a plan to expose Masuji's nefarious activities, have him declared *persona non grata* by the US government, and have him recalled to Tokyo. Any questions before I go into the detail of how this operation will proceed?"

Both Crowe and Coleman shook their heads no.

Zangara continued. "We need Masuji to hear from Coleman that the chairman of the National Defense Research Committee will be meeting secretly in DC with his former PhD advisee, Dr. Richard Crowe. Masuji must be led to believe that at the meeting, the NDRC chairman will provide Dr. Crowe with the draft of a lucrative contract for the development of a new shipboard device capable of detecting other surface vessels at a range of 20 miles through the transmission and reception of radio waves. Furthermore, Masuji should be told that the chairman wants to help his former electrical engineering acolyte at MIT get promoted by top management at Bendix by signaling how much Dr. Crowe is trusted by the NDRC."

Dr. Crowe asked, "Where and when will this meeting take place?"

Al replied, "In Rock Creek Park at six PM on Wednesday, September 11th. You will meet the NDRC chairman in the parking lot and walk to an isolated area for a brief conversation about the project before he hands you the document."

Crowe asked, "Why not do this in an office in DC?"

Zangara replied, "Masuji should think that the chairman is operating a little outside of regular government contract protocols because he wants to bring a new, nongovernment-owned and -controlled firm into this radio-wave device business. Masuji should be told that the government employees inside the various Army and Navy research laboratories are opposed to admitting private industry into their secret technology preserve at this time. The chairman wants to avoid the bureaucratic delays that will occur if the in-house labs learn that 'an outsider' is invading their turf. So the chairman is using unconventional methods and meeting places to keep the in-house labs in the dark."

Crowe nodded his head. "I see. This makes sense to me. It should make sense to Masuji too. What happens next?"

Zangara replied: "We have reliable information that Masuji wants to harm the NDRC chairman. We anticipate that news of this private meeting involving unarmed civilians in a remote place will draw him out. He will assume that Coleman will assist him in his plan to harm Dr. Bush and yourself. Disguised as a tourist or businessman, Masuji will probably position himself in Rock Creek Park before you arrive and follow you into the secluded area. Nine camouflaged, highly trained, heavily armed agents will arrest Masuji for possessing weapons and threatening a US government official the moment he enters the clearing where you will be meeting. The Japanese ambassador will be notified by the US State Department of the arrest, as well as the serious criminal charges that will be filed against Masuji. To prevent yet another embarrassing incident involving a deranged Japanese official from becoming public, the ambassador and the Government of Japan will commit to having their unbalanced naval attaché whisked back to Tokyo forthwith, never to return to the US again. Since the Japanese government will not want to lose face over this action by their rogue agent, your identities will be kept confidential and out of the news."

Crowe turned to Coleman. "Any questions or comments, Coleman?"

Coleman: "I have just one question. Will my uncle Hercules be one of the agents waiting to take down Masuji?"

Zangara replied, "Absolutely, Coleman. Hercules has reviewed this plan and approved of it. He and his men will be rehearsing this arrest at a site within the FBI training grounds at Quantico, Virginia, for the next ten days. They will be as sharp and quick as humanly possible when September 11th comes around."

Coleman then said, "Fine with me. But what about Dr. Ames and Junius? What happens to them?"

Zangara answered, "Coleman, nothing will happen to them. The arrest and rapid deportation of Masuji will cause them to seriously reconsider their dalliance with the Japanese, and instead concentrate on pursuing legitimate lives and careers. Your uncle and I will, of course, be visiting Dr. Ames and Mr. Johnson and explain to them that rarely do people assisting foreign espionage agents get a second chance. They will be warned to leave you alone and that any return to their anti-US, pro-Japanese ways will result in their immediate arrest and prosecution. Dr. Ames will have to agree to surrender his firearms and ammunition to us and make no further weapons purchases. He will have to resign from the Patriot Outdoor Sportsman's Club. Ames and Junius will be under surveillance for a while to assure that they do not stray from the path of righteousness."

Coleman: "OK. I hope they respond appropriately to your being so lenient."

Zangara: "I hope so too, Coleman. So, gentlemen, will you assist us?"

Crowe and Coleman nodded yes.

And that was that…almost.

After Coleman returned to his office, Walker explained to Crowe that Dr. Bush did not know anything about either Captain Masuji or the counter-intelligence operation plan to take down Benkei. Walker further informed Crowe, "A doppelganger will be used in the NDRC chairman's place. The Bush look-alike will be an armed FBI agent with extensive shoot-out experience involving submachine-gun–toting Midwestern bank robbers during the mid-1930s."

Crowe was relieved to hear this. "No need to trouble Dr. Bush or put him at any risk. The man is a national treasure! Agent Walker, is there anything else you neglected to tell me about during the initial meeting with Coleman?"

Walker replied, "No, Dr. Crowe. Just drop to the ground and lie flat when you hear a very loud voice shout, 'Freeze!'"

6 PM TUESDAY, SEPTEMBER 3, 1940; DR. AMES'S HOME, NORTH CARROLTON AVENUE, BALTIMORE

Coleman entered Dr. Ames's home and saw Ralph standing in the kitchen contemplating the dinner menu for the evening. "Coleman, you want to have a bacon, egg, cheese, and tomato omelet with me?"

Smiling, Coleman replied, "Thank you, Ralph! Can we have some Eight O'Clock, too?"

Ames smiled back at Coleman. "Of course. Coming right up!"

Once seated, Coleman said, "Ralph, something related to radio-wave devices came up at work today. I think it's important."

Dr. Ames looked up from his omelet and said, "Well, go on, Coleman. I am all ears."

Coleman: "Dr. Crowe has been asked to meet privately in DC with Dr. Vannevar Bush, that big-shot you said Captain Masuji was interested in. Remember back in July I told you that Bush had been Crowe's PhD thesis advisor at MIT, but that Bendix had no major contracts with Dr. Bush's organization and that Crowe had not spoken with Bush in a long time? Well, now, Dr. Bush wants to talk to Crowe and Dr. Crowe wants me to drive him to the meeting."

Dr. Ames took a tiny pad of paper from his shirt pocket and put it on the table. He then took cap off of his fountain pen and began to write. "Coleman, do you know when and where this meeting in DC will occur?"

Coleman: "Yes. September 11th at 6 PM in Rock Creek Park."

Ralph asked, "Why meet in a park in DC at dinnertime?"

Coleman: "I do not know for certain. Dr. Crowe mumbled something about the NDRC chairman not wanting government lab folks to know that he was bringing private industry in to do research and development of these new devices. Apparently, Bush is concerned that the government lab people will obstruct the entry of any competitors into their field."

Ames: "I can just imagine! These white people do not like competition. They have been shutting us out of the professions, businesses, and government since colonial times. Coleman, this is important. I am going to alert Katsuie and have him contact the embassy attaché right now. Enjoy the rest of your dinner. I will be back soon."

Dr. Ames drove to a nearby pay phone and called the Katsuie contact number in New York City. He left the pay phone number with the Japanese operator. In a few minutes, he heard Kimura Katsuie's voice say, "Hello, Ralph."

Ames said that he had just learned something important from Coleman and proceeded to read aloud the notes he took during dinner.

"I will pass this news to the Captain," replied Katsuie. "Either he or I will get back to you. Stay where you are."

In ten minutes, the pay phone rang. Ralph picked up the handset and heard Masuji's voice. "Good evening, Dr. Ames. Would you mind repeating the information to me that you provided to Mr. Katsuie a few minutes ago?"

Ames did as he was told. Masuji thanked him profusely. "Dr. Ames, may I come to your home the morning of Saturday, September 7th, at seven AM? I would like to speak directly with Mr. Braxton and you about this matter."

Ralph replied, "Yes. My pleasure. Would you like to have breakfast with us?"

Masuji answered, "Coffee will be fine."

And that was that.

Ames returned home and related the conversation with Masuji to Coleman. "Coleman, this is really important. I am proud of you!"

6 AM, SEPTEMBER 4, 1940; QUANTICO, VIRGINIA

The entire Sicinnus Team plus the doppelganger, Agent Brock J. Price, assembled to rehearse the arrest of Captain Masuji. Price fit in well with everyone. An Eagle Scout in his youth, Price possessed the same angular features, height, build, hairstyle, and three-piece suit as Dr. Bush. Even his New England accent sounded like the NDRC chairman's. Hercules played the role of Benkei and Walker stood in for Coleman. Initially, Hercules's quick draw with a handgun and skill with a knife confounded the takedown team. By the end of the day, repeated practice yielded a smooth, efficient disarming and arrest of "Masuji" with no casualties. The team practiced all day on September 4 and 5, with the same positive results achieved. Walker decided to provide a rehearsal break on September 6 and 7. Firearms practice and hand-to-hand combat drills were used to keep the men sharp. Rehearsals resumed on the ninth and tenth.

"I want this perfect," Walker admonished the team.

Everyone was ready. At 3 PM on September 11, each man was hidden in his assigned position in a semi-circle around the clearing where the meeting was to take place.

Captain Masuji's breakfast meeting with Dr. Ames and Coleman on Saturday, September 7, lasted less than one hour. Benkei began by saying, "Gentlemen, this mission will be our last. Mr. Braxton, you and I will leave for Japan aboard a freighter departing Baltimore harbor the morning of September 12th. Dr. Ames, it will take months before my replacement will arrive in Washington. When he does, he will contact you through Mr. Katsuie. Advise Mr. Junius Johnson on September 16th that you and he have been temporarily deactivated as agents for a few months. He may speculate that Mr. Braxton and I were involved in what will be a front-page news story, and that this event triggered this hiatus in service. Do not confirm or deny any theory he may posit. He has no need to know any details about this operation. Tell him to be disciplined and pursue his teaching career until the Empire reactivates him. Do you have any questions?"

Both Ames and Coleman merely shook their heads. "Good," said Masuji. "Now, let us discuss a few operational details. Mr. Braxton, you will need a firearm on September 11th. Dr. Ames, do you have a weapon for Mr. Braxton that cannot be traced to you?"

"Yes, Captain Masuji. I have an easy-to-conceal, lightweight 2-inch barrel five-shot .32-caliber Smith & Wesson Safety Hammerless pistol with no serial numbers or markings of any kind."

"Good, Dr. Ames. Please provide this revolver and fifteen rounds of ammunition to Mr. Braxton after I leave today. Coleman, I will dispatch Dr. Bush first and then tend to Dr. Crowe. I will move quickly, but if Dr. Crowe attempts to interfere with me or run away, shoot him. Do you think that you can perform this task?"

Coleman replied, "Yes, Sir. I can and I will."

Benkei smiled. "Dr. Ames, Mr. Braxton is, as you Americans say, 'a good hire.'"

Ralph agreed. "Indeed, Captain Masuji. Indeed."

Masuji shook Ames's hand and then Coleman's. "Mr. Braxton, you will like Tokyo. There are many opportunities for engineers with your education and experience. You will enjoy Japanese women, too. When Japan and Germany conquer America, you will return to the United States as a hero and a political leader."

Coleman replied, "I look forward to such a future. See you on the 11th."

After Captain Masuji departed, Dr. Ames told Coleman that he needed a few more minutes of his time. "Coleman, doesn't the prospect of participating in the killing of Dr. Crowe and leaving everything and everybody— especially that young lady friend of yours—behind in Baltimore bother you?"

Coleman looked Ralph square in the eye and said, "Of course it bothers me. It bothers me greatly. Nonetheless, when I volunteered to serve Japan in order to overthrow the United States government and fundamentally change American society, I knew that I might have to give up my life for the cause one day. Well, that day has arrived and I will support Captain Masuji in accomplishing his mission. If we succeed, living in Tokyo for a few years will not be the worst thing that could happen to me. If we fail, I shall have honorably sacrificed myself for a greater good. Hopefully I will see you back in Baltimore after the war is won."

Dr. Ames shook Coleman's hand and replied, "You and Captain Masuji will prevail. I admire your courage, Coleman. I will miss you when you are in Tokyo and will look forward to seeing you return to Baltimore as a conqueror."

Also looking forward to the future were the FBI agents monitoring the surveillance devices in Ames's home. They smiled with the satisfaction of spectators anticipating a one-sided bullfight in Seville, Spain.

And that was that.

SEPTEMBER 11, 1940

During much of the drive between Baltimore and Washington, Dr. Crowe and Coleman remained silent, lost in their respective thoughts and concerns about what awaited them in Rock Creek Park. Twenty minutes before they arrived at their destination, Dr. Crowe spoke.

"You know, Coleman, this is a courageous thing that you are doing. Remember, when you hear a loud voice scream 'FREEZE,' drop to the ground immediately. I suspect that the Japanese naval officer will never surrender, despite his immunity as a diplomat. He would rather die than give up or admit failure. That is how they are raised. That is how they are trained. So bullets will be flying at his torso and his head, not at his feet. Stay low and hug the ground. Do you understand?"

Coleman, holding the Imperial's steering wheel tightly, said, "I understand. Don't worry about me. Follow your own advice and we will both drive back to Baltimore as heroes in a war few people have any idea is going on. I will tell you this, Dr. Crowe. I am going to ask that woman law student to marry me this weekend. We have a date this Saturday—the 14th, my lucky number."

Crowe replied, "You mean Lucille Dixon? Good for you, Coleman. You will invite Mrs. Crowe and me to the wedding, won't you?"

Coleman, relieved, answered, "You are family, Dr. Crowe. You and your wife have to attend."

As they pulled into the parking lot at Rock Creek Park, they saw Agent Price. "He certainly looks just like Dr. Bush!" said Dr. Crowe. "Truly, just like him!"

Coleman opened the door for Dr. Crowe. They walked over to Agent Price. Price shook hands with Dr. Crowe. "How are you, Van?" said Crowe loudly.

"Just fine. Great to see you. Let's take a little walk."

Price and Crowe walked ahead of Coleman. Coleman felt the snub-nosed revolver in his pocket and wondered, *Why don't I just shoot Masuji myself before he can hurt Dr. Crowe or me?*

That thought lingered as Captain Masuji, dressed in khakis and wearing leather boots, suddenly leapt out from behind a tree and blocked the path a good five yards from the clearing where the "Bush-Crowe" meeting was supposed to take place. Benkei had an odd-looking semi-automatic pistol in his hand. He pointed the weapon at Price's head at point-blank range and pulled the trigger. Nothing happened. Masuji quickly cleared the semi-automatic pistol's chamber of what he thought was a dud cartridge, loaded a new round, and pulled the trigger. Again, nothing happened.

Alphonse Zangara thundered, "FREEZE, MASUJI! YOU ARE UNDER ARREST! DROP YOUR WEAPON OR WE WILL SHOOT!"

Crowe dove for the ground. Price remained standing as Benkei produced a *kunai* and, with blinding speed, buried it into Price's abdomen, neck, and thorax before the FBI agent could reach his revolver. Mortally wounded, Price fell in a fetal position.

His blade slick with Price's blood, Masuji then turned toward the prone Dr. Crowe. Instinctively, AJAX did a push-up, rising to confront the oncoming Japanese executioner. Coleman drew Dr. Ames's revolver from his pants pocket just as small arms fire crackled from several points along the path. One round hit the young engineer in the left temple, taking virtually the entire top of his head off. He died instantly.

A .357 Magnum round fired from Martin Victor's revolver entered Masuji's right knee, destroying the joint and its surrounding muscles, ligaments, and cartilage. Despite the catastrophic damage to his right leg, Benkei attempted to charge forward and dispatch Crowe with his *kunai*. This movement completed the amputation of the limb. The samurai collapsed, soaking the soil with his blood.

One of the three previously situated ambulances carried Coleman's body to Freedmen's Hospital on Bryant Street, NW, between 4th and 6th Streets. A member of the medical team from one of the remaining ambulances placed a tourniquet around Benkei's thigh and the vehicle sped him to the George Washington University Medical School and Hospital. The third ambulance slowly transported the lifeless body of Agent Price to the morgue at George Washington University Medical School and Hospital. Agent Walker drove a distraught Dr. Crowe to Sibley Memorial Hospital on North Capitol Street for an evaluation by one of Clarence's few friends, Dr. Russell Kincaid.

"What the hell happened out there?" Crowe yelled at Walker.

"We did not anticipate Masuji using the tree as his launch point. We could not move to new positions before Masuji initiated his attack on you, Price and Coleman. Furthermore, Masuji adjusted very quickly to his firearm malfunctioning and he probably set a world record for puncturing Price's vital organs with that nasty dagger of his. Finally, Coleman did not follow his instructions and stood up just as the shooting started, instead of lying on the ground."

Agitated, Crowe responded, "Agent Walker, you have lost two good men due to inadequate planning and preparation. Coleman tried to save me from that madman Masuji and got killed by friendly fire. Something is very wrong, very deficient at Quantico. You had plenty of time to choreograph this operation. Jesus Christ, Clarence, the FBI can't properly take down one middle-aged Japanese naval officer in the capital of the United States! This was a monumental screwup, a Keystone Kops farce. My God! My God! Noble young Coleman is dead. We utterly failed him. Masuji should have been shot as soon as he pointed his gun at Agent Price, not after he perforated the poor man with a knife. Price's blood is on our hands, Agent Walker."

Crowe wept bitterly and said no more until he was examined by Dr. Kincaid, a psychiatrist who had studied and treated American shell shock patients during and after World War I.

Following his hour-long conversation with Kincaid, Dr. Crowe regained his balance. He apologized profusely to Agent Walker for his undisciplined outburst. "I guess I am not as tough as I thought, Agent Walker. I know that you are hurting too. And I know that you and your team will thoroughly review today's events, identify specific areas for operational improvement, and prepare training exercises to avoid similar problems in the future. An Annapolis grad should never lose his composure, as I most certainly did, and start pointing a finger at 'the man who was in the ring,' as President Theodore

Roosevelt used to say. Please accept my apology. Coleman and Price died as heroes serving their grateful nation. We must take solace in this."

Agent Walker replied, "No need to apologize, Dr. Crowe. A close-quarters knife-and-gun fight in which men die violently challenges the nerves of even the most resilient and best trained warriors. You were correct to point out my command failures. I must live with the loss of men for whom I was responsible. I assure you that every error will be identified and rectified. All any of us in this counterintelligence business can do after a day like today is to look deep within our souls, ask God for his forgiveness, and pray for Him to give us the strength and courage to carry on."

With that, both men shook hands, and Clarence arranged for two FBI agents to take Dr. Crowe home.

Hercules accompanied AJAX's body in the ambulance. He spoke to his dead nephew. "Coleman, Coleman, my brave young lion, you died honorably. I am proud of you. I wish you had followed your orders to stay down, but you could not lie still while your comrade was in peril. You will be buried in a plot next to mine at Saint Augustine's cemetery. Father Sykes will officiate at your funeral. I will miss you, but we will be together with Genevieve in heaven in God's good time."

And that was that.

Agent Price's wife and three children were informed of his death by a personal visit by the Assistant Director of the FBI responsible for counterintelligence operations. "Your husband died heroically serving our great nation," he said to the distraught widow. "Your father was a great man," he said to the weeping children. "His gallant sacrifice and your profound loss were not in vain." Agent Price became classified as an FBI Service Martyr.

Due to Agent Walker's adroit planning, the news media did not connect either Dr. Crowe or Coleman Braxton to the bloodbath in Rock Creek Park. "The official story" held up that two US government agents were, without any provocation, attacked by a berserk knife-wielding Japanese naval attache' whom they had under surveillance as part of an ongoing espionage investigation. For security reasons, the identity of the sole surviving agent who shot and wounded Imperial Japanese Navy Captain Saigo Masuji was withheld. A joint investigation of the incident by both the US Department of Justice and local District of Columbia law enforcement promptly concluded that the discharge of one round of ammunition by the anonymous agent in response to the brutal assault on his partners had been entirely justified.

Privately, Captain McLaughlin and Clarence Walker awarded Martin Victor with a hastily contrived "Sansei Medal" in a small conference room within the Navy Department Building. While pinning the award on Martin's US Navy uniform, Captain McLaughlin announced to the team and Catharine, "Martin, a sansei is a diminutive mythological Japanese one-legged, frog-eating demon. Though your shooting should have been a bit higher on September 11th, 1940, the gallantry you exhibited in your first knife-and-gun fight fully merits this unique award. Regrettably, future generations will not and cannot know of your heroic conduct in Rock Creek Park. Nonetheless, everyone here today wants you to know how honored we are to serve alongside you in this undeclared war in defense of our nation."

"Speech!" called out the irrepressible Hercules Boulanger.

Martin Victor looked into the faces of his comrades. "While deeply grateful, I cannot help but feel sorrow over the loss of Coleman Braxton and Agent Price. The next time, I vow that I will shoot sooner and higher. I look forward to protecting our British visitors and the US technologists who will be working together to give us an edge over the Nazis and the Japs when we finally do get into this war."

"Hear, hear," called out Hercules. Everyone applauded.

No diplomatic row ensued from the incident at Rock Creek Park. ONI stations in Cavite, Pearl Harbor, and DC intercepted and decoded Japanese diplomatic radio traffic clearly indicating that the government of the Empire of Japan had no advance knowledge whatsoever of Captain Saigo Masuji's rogue assassination mission. The Japanese ambassador officially, but privately, disavowed the actions of the naval attaché and personally apologized to the

US Secretary of State for the "unfortunate acts committed by a deranged citizen of Japan." Furthermore, the Japanese government paid an indemnity of $350,000 for the damage caused by Captain Masuji. The Director of the FBI saw to it that the family of Agent Price received a significant portion of the proceeds from the indemnity.

As soon as his medical condition permitted, Benkei returned home on board a Japanese merchant vessel commanded by Captain Sanada Nobunaga, a former Etajima classmate of Saigo's. Captain Masuji retired from the Imperial Japanese Navy prior to December 7, 1941. He committed *seppuku* not long after hearing Emperor Hirohito's August 15, 1945, speech announcing Japan's surrender to the Allies. Captain Nobunaga served as Benkei's *kaishakunin*, expertly severing all but a thin band of flesh which held Saigo's head to his body.

Miss Hara failed to show up for work at the Japanese embassy on September 12, 1940. She married Special Agent Alphonse Zangara at Saint Augustine's on Christmas Day, 1940. Hercules Boulanger served as best man. Father Sykes officiated. Mario Zangara stood in between Special Agents Walker and Horan during the wedding service and sat between them at dinner that night at Frank Abbo's "Roma" restaurant on Connecticut Avenue. Walker and Horan escorted Mario Zangara to the train station the next day to assure that he returned to Bridgeport, Connecticut, and did not linger in DC. Mario Zangara Junior, the first of Kinuyo and Alphonse's five sons, was born on August 19, 1941. Mario Zangara Senior got to know Walker and Horan quite well as they escorted him to (and from) each of his grandsons' baptisms, communions, and school graduations during the next twenty years. Walker and Horan attended Mario Senior's funeral in Bridgeport in 1961. Reflecting on his father's FBI "Honor Guard," Alphonse remarked, "This is the most ironic and poignant moment of my life, and I have had a life rich with irony and poignancy."

On September 14, FBI forensic analysis determined that the bullet that killed Coleman Braxton came from FBI Agent William Murphy's service revolver. Overcome with remorse, Murph requested a meeting with Clarence Walker and Hercules Boulanger.

"In light of my poor performance on September 11th, I think it best for me to resign from the FBI. Hercules, I know that no apology or acceptance of responsibility on my part will bring your courageous nephew back to life. I know that nothing I say or do will ease your grief. Nonetheless, Hercules, I wish with all my heart that I could undo the past, and I pray that in time, God will provide you with his comfort."

Hercules replied, "Agent Murphy, I have killed many men in my time, including fellow American soldiers in friendly fire incidents. I too feel remorse beyond measure for the damage that I have done. However, in war we do not get to resign because of inadvertent, unintentional errors we make in the heat of battle. You would be doing a great disservice to Coleman, to me, to the team, to the FBI, and to yourself and your family if you walk away from your duty to protect America. We need you. We need your smarts and your body in this fight. Murph, I forgive you." Hercules then hugged a tearful William Murphy.

Walker added, "Murph, I agree totally with Hercules on this matter. We need to improve. We will scrutinize the events in Rock Creek Park and correct all our deficiencies. Now, let's move forward. I want no more negative thinking from you or from anyone else on this team."

Agent Murphy nodded his head in agreement and served honorably and well until his retirement from the FBI in 1968.

On Monday, September 16, 1940, at 5 AM, Alphonse Zangara and Hercules Boulanger rang the doorbell to Dr. Ralph Ames's home. The physician, smartly attired, clean-shaven, and fragrant with cologne, greeted them. "I have been expecting you, gentlemen. Please come in," said a very poised Dr. Ames.

"Thank you, Ralph," replied Hercules in his early morning gravel-voice. Zangara remained silent, ominous, and ready to put a bullet in Ames's heart if the Japanese agent made a false move. Ralph understood completely the grave situation in which he found himself. He did not want to die. He did not want to go to prison. He did not want to be humiliated. He wanted to make a deal.

So did the FBI.

Seated at Ames's dining room table, Hercules made the pitch.

"Ralph, you have the blood of my nephew, Coleman Braxton, on your filthy hands. You have the blood of an FBI agent named Price, a good husband and loving father of three children, on your filthy hands. You have corrupted the soul of Junius Johnson and compromised his future by facilitating his participation in seditious acts against the United States of America. What have you got to say for yourself, Ralph?"

Clearing his throat, Dr. Ames glared at Hercules and said, "I do not know your name, Sir. But all the sins and all the crimes you have alleged against me are true. I contest none of it. While you no doubt know why I have done what I have done, I have no legal defense or justification for my conduct. All I can offer you is my complete cooperation in your investigation of the Masuji-Katsuie spy network. In addition to records that I have maintained concerning Japanese espionage efforts in the US, I am prepared to assist you in identifying and entrapping each foreign and domestic agent working on behalf of the Empire of Japan against the Government of the United States. Finally, I will forfeit to the US government every dollar I have been paid by the government of Japan over the years of my involvement with them: approximately $75,000."

Hercules scowled and replied, "And what do you want in exchange for betraying your Japanese buddies and paying such a paltry fine?"

Ames answered, "I want to be able to continue practicing medicine and treating members of my community in the city of Baltimore. I want immunity from prosecution."

Hercules leaned forward and said, "We do not immunize people who conspire to overthrow the government and who also participate in a conspiracy to assassinate US government officials. However, we do have a deal for you to consider. You will have five minutes to accept it or reject it. If you reject our generous offer, the rest of your life will be behind bars in the worst prison we can find in the Deep South. Here is our nonnegotiable proposal: You do whatever we ask you to do whenever we ask you to do it. You give us everything you have got on the Japs. You give us every dollar in your bank and checking accounts. We walk out of here with every firearm and round of ammunition you possess, and you resign from the Patriot Outdoor Sportsman's Club. You agree to plead guilty to a charge of tax evasion and serve six months in a federal country club up north where it might be cold, but you will be treated kindly. When you are released from prison, you will serve as a physician for two years in a Negro Army division being formed, now that President Roosevelt has so wisely reinstituted the draft. The duration of your military service may be extended should the US get involved in a war with Germany, Japan, or Italy. However, once you have rehabilitated yourself through government service, we will support your reentry into your medical practice here in Baltimore. OK, Ralph, you decide your fate in the next five minutes."

Dr. Ames looked out his front window at the park across the street. He accepted Hercules's offer.

"Wise man, Ralph. Now call Junius Johnson and invite him over for a little chat before he goes to school."

Ames called and Junius came running. When Junius realized that he had been ambushed, he started to cry. Dr. Ames, stern-faced, said nothing. Agent Zangara, impassive, indifferent, and as uncaring as a matador, said nothing.

Hercules contemptuously barked, "Enough bawling, Mr. Johnson. Enough! I have in my hand a Selective Service notice for you. Congratulations, you passed your physical and mental exams. You are ordered to report to Fort Huachuca in Arizona for military training in two weeks. Show this notice to your principal and your parents. Keep your nose clean in the US Army and you will not be prosecuted for the despicable crimes you have committed against the United States of America. Talk about this deal, or any of the activities in support of the Empire of Japan you performed to anyone, and you will spend the rest of your life in prison. Do you understand?"

J3 nodded his head.

"Now get out of my sight, Junius!" growled Hercules.

J3 took off and did what he was told. He ultimately became a Lieutenant in the 2nd Battalion, 366th Regiment of the 92nd Infantry Division. Junius was killed in action on Christmas Day, 1944 near the Town of Barga in Italy. He received a bronze star for leading the defense of his platoon's position, which stopped the advance of a significantly larger German infantry unit. Lieutenant Junius Johnson was buried with full military honors at Arlington Cemetery. Until their own deaths, Junius's parents visited his grave each year on his birthday and on Christmas Day. The couple held hands, wept, and told their decorated, martyred son how proud they were of him, how much they missed him, and how they looked forward to hugging him in heaven.

Dr. Ralph Ames served six months in the newly built, minimum-security Danbury Correctional Institution in Connecticut. By all accounts, he was a model inmate who ably assisted the physicians who manned the prison infirmary. Upon his release, Dr. Ames became a US Army Medical Corps officer serving Negro troops stationed in Arizona. Though they were aware of each other's presence at Fort Huachuca, he and Junius never communicated with each other. Ultimately, Dr. Ames served in the 93rd Infantry Division, providing medical care to men injured in combat in Bougainville Island, Morotai (Dutch New Guinea), and Zamboanga (Philippine Islands). Attaining the rank of major, Dr. Ralph Ames returned to his medical practice in Baltimore after being demobilized in 1946. By the time of his passing in February of 1972, Dr. Ames's tax problems had long been forgotten and he was remembered as a fine, caring physician and a pillar of Baltimore's African American community.

On Tuesday evening, September 17, 1940, Hercules Boulanger visited the office of Dr. Jonathan Dixon. The psychiatrist's red-rimmed eyes and poor posture moved an immoveable Boulanger. Hercules hugged his friend and whispered, "Jonathan, you, Judith, and Lucille do not deserve the pain and loss that I have caused you. I cannot tell you any facts beyond the official police report that Coleman Braxton was murdered by an unknown assailant in Rock Creek Park. All I can tell you, and just you, is that my nephew died a hero defending our country. I wish I could have been killed instead of him, but God has his plan for each one of us. It was Coleman's time, not mine."

Dr. Dixon whispered in response, "Hercules, my dearest friend, I am a broken man not because of anything that you did or did not do. My patients' suffering, my failures, my inability to produce children, the loss of dear Coleman, and the institutionalization at Crownsville Hospital of poor Lucille have brought me low. I will try to get over this. Give me a little time. Let's get together on Veteran's Day in November. By then, I will be back to my old self."

The two men parted. Jonathan Dixon died of heart failure in early October, 1940. Hercules attended the funeral. Judith refused to speak with him, blaming Boulanger for the death of her husband and Coleman Braxton.

NOON THURSDAY, SEPTEMBER 19, 1940; JOHNS HOPKINS HOSPITAL, BALTIMORE

Dr. Nicholson J. Eastman, Obstetrician-in-Chief at Johns Hopkins Hospital since 1935, managed the delivery of 9-pound Adam Victor. "Mrs. Victor," the world-renowned physician said to his patient, "you and your husband have brought a fine young lad into the world. Congratulations!" Gertrude kissed the doctor's hand as she gazed upon the magnificent child she cradled in her left arm. Grace, Henry, Martin, and Milton were permitted to enter the recovery room for a few minutes. "Ten fingers. Ten toes. Two eyes. Two ears. Two arms. Two legs. A good start, Gertrude," said serious Grace Basswood.

Henry, the urologist, could not resist adding his own observation. "And a large penis, Grace. Do not forget that! It's also part of a good start for our man Adam!"

Milton punched Martin in the arm and said, "You had better thank the Lord above that this handsome child looks like Gertrude, not you!" For once,

Martin said nothing. He just looked on in wonder and allowed his tears of joy to flow.

Thursday evening, Henry, Milton, and Martin sat together in the tiny fenced-in garden adjacent to 14 South Broadway. Milton produced three Cuban Montecristo cigars. Blowing a stream of smoke from the lit cigar, Henry looked at Milton and said, "Thank you. This thing will keep me alert for hours!" Turning his head slightly and fixing his eyes on Martin, Dr. Basswood said, "Damn shame about that Japanese naval attaché losing his leg in a shoot-out in Rock Creek Park a week or so ago, Lieutenant Victor. I wonder, does the government reward its employees for crippling a lying, murdering Jap bastard?"

Savoring his Cuban cigar, Martin replied, with a smile, "I wouldn't know anything about that, Doc!"

Henry replied, "I figured that a nice Jewish undercover agent like you who totes a .357 Magnum would never get involved in a violent encounter like that in a public park right around dinnertime. But you know, both Grace and Gertrude thought for certain that their sweet Martin must have done the outdoor surgery *sans anesthesia* on Captain Masuji. I tried to reason with the two of them, but once they got that strange idea like in their noggins, I just could not disabuse them of it!"

Milton chimed in. "Well, maybe if you spoke English better, you could have made more progress with them, Dr. Basswood."

Dr. Henry Basswood took great pride in his command of the English language. An avid reader who taught English to new immigrants and who had carefully maintained a detailed daily diary of his life since entering medical school, Henry took umbrage at Milton's verbal *banderilla*.

"An ambulance-chasing lawyer such as yourself may communicate effectively with twelve ignorant, uneducated, and inebriated Baltimore jurors, but face it, Milton—you lack the literary skill to impress people possessing average to slightly above average intellect."

Milton loved to needle Henry and Grace. He knew that he had hit a vital nerve now judging by Basswood's angry response.

"Yep, all those syphilitic sailors and prostitutes you treat must really appreciate your knowledge of Shakespeare!" Even Henry had to chuckle at Milton's riposte.

"So, Martin, as I was saying before I was so rudely interrupted, will you be getting any time off from your job of increasing prosthetic device sales in our nation's capital?"

Ignoring the doctor's effort to pry loose information from him, Martin replied, "Henry, my boss ordered me to attend a meeting for him in a location north of New York City on September 28th. So I have liberty in Baltimore until I shove off for early in the morning on the 28th."

Henry turned serious. "Martin, you must pay close attention to Gertrude and Adam. They need you as much as your country needs you. Maybe they need you a little more."

Martin nodded his head. "Dr. Basswood, I always live up to my responsibilities. I will not let anybody down."

Milton did not appreciate Henry browbeating his little brother and interjected, "Christ Almighty, can you end this guilt session, Dr. Basswood? Henry, you know damned well that Grace will watch over Gertrude and Adam like a hawk. If there is anyone on this planet better than Mrs. Basswood at caring for a new mother and her child, I would be surprised. Martin, you do what you are ordered to do by the US Navy, and the rest of the time you can devote yourself to your family. Dr. Basswood, never tell a soldier or a sailor to question or disobey an order. And Henry, stay the hell out of Grace's way while she tends to Gertrude and Adam. If you or Grace need me, by the way, you have my number. Just call me!"

Stunned by Milton's assertiveness, Martin and Henry shrugged their respective shoulders and puffed on their Montecristos.

"You want some scotch?" Dr. Basswood inquired.

Milton replied, "It is about time you extended us a little hospitality, Dr. Basswood!"

And that was that.

21

SEPTEMBER 28, 1940; CAMDEN STATION, BALTIMORE

At 7:38 AM, Gareth and Martin boarded the B&O Washington Express train to New York City. They sat alone together the entire trip. Wearing dark blue suits and fedoras, these two hard men, who had been hardened even more by their recent experience in Rock Creek Park, projected a baleful aura that passengers boarding the train instinctively avoided.

"Martin," Gareth said jocularly, "we are clean-shaven, healthy men bathed in Old Spice aftershave lotion, and no one comes near us. Why do you think this is so?"

Martin, with a serious look on his face, replied gravely, "Gareth, you look Jewish and they are all anti-Semites. That is why they want nothing to do with us."

Gareth responded, "Martin, I am not circumcised. Do you think that if I just unzipped my trousers and allowed 'Jumbo' to get some air, we might become more popular, at least with the ladies?"

"Gareth, that would frighten our fellow train riders even more," said Martin.

"You are correct, Lieutenant Victor. Let's discuss the plan for our babysitting the British and American scientists at Alfred Lee Loomis's Mansion and laboratory at Tuxedo Park."

"OK, Detective Messenger. What's on your mind?"

"Martin, I do not know much about electricity, radios, or radio waves. This is your field of expertise. So when the genius physicists meeting at this multi-millionaire Loomis guy's Tuxedo Park palace start discussing stuff like Ohm's Law, oscillators, and antennae, you take notes and teach me about whatever I need to know when we get some free time. OK?"

Though astonished by Gareth's underestimation of his capacity to grasp technical matters, Martin decided not to debate the issue with his partner. He simply agreed to honor Detective Lieutenant Messenger's request. "Fine, Gareth. No problem. However, I am depending on you to read these Nobel Prize contenders' faces, body language, and statements for signs that they might be Axis moles or careless with confidential information. According to Captain McLaughlin, the Brits—Dr. John Cockcroft and Dr. Edward Bowen— possess a device that will fundamentally alter the nature of warfare. Our primary mission is to protect these gifted men and the priceless 'toys' they have with them. Furthermore, Alfred Loomis is a first cousin of Secretary of War Stimson. We have got to protect him at all costs. Our secondary mission is to impress upon these gentlemen that the work they are doing is top secret and must be treated as such. I do not see this as a serious problem. These scientists understand the implications of losing control over a war-winning technology that they invented."

Gareth leaned back in his seat and remarked, "Martin, did you ever think when you were at Baltimore City College High School that you would ever get to do anything that actually mattered? I know that I didn't."

Martin shook his head. "Gareth, we may be in way over our heads, but we understand something the big-shots from Boston, DC, and London will never get. You know what that is?"

Gareth laughed. "Yep. There are some problems in life that can best be solved by the judicious application of force."

Martin replied, "Correct. And our Baltimore Logic is what will going protect these vulnerable wise men and the USA from characters like Engels and Masuji."

A New York-based FBI agent met Gareth and Martin at the Liberty Street Station at 11:30 AM and drove them 50 miles along the Hudson River to Alfred Loomis's Mansion in Tuxedo Park. The FBI agent informed them of a newsflash that his office received that morning. Nazi Germany, Fascist Italy, and Imperial Japan had signed a "defensive" agreement in Berlin, committing each of the three nations to provide military, political, and economic assistance to any one of the three signatory states should it be attacked by the United States.

"Looks like the pot is boiling now," said the New York agent.

"The Nazis and the Japs have been working together against us for quite a while," said Gareth. "We will be at war with them within the next two years. I do not intend to learn German, Japanese, or Italian, so we had better do all we can to win it," he concluded.

Martin thought, *You just have to admire Gareth's clarity of thinking.* The New York FBI agent said not another word for the duration of the trip.

When they arrived at Loomis's estate, a housekeeper greeted Martin and Gareth. "Lieutenant JG Victor and Detective Lieutenant Messenger," said Martin to the servant who checked their names against a printed list on a clipboard he carried. The housekeeper showed them to their separate bedrooms and then escorted the two agents downstairs to join the scientists on a guided tour of the premises conducted by Dr. Loomis. After the orientation session, Gareth and Martin were asked to join the physicists and engineers for a sumptuous dinner at 7 PM.

"This is the life!" remarked Gareth to Martin.

"Yes, it most certainly is," replied Martin, "but I wish we had tuxedos like the other guys. I feel so out of place."

Gareth responded, "It would take more than a monkey suit and a top hat to make either of us fit in with this highbrow crowd."

The evening ended with a theoretical discussion led by Dr. Cockcroft of the decisive military advantage that possessing a monopoly on "powerful, pulsed centimetric-length microwave radio detection and ranging systems" would confer on a nation's armed forces. Before they went to bed, Gareth asked Martin to decode Cockcroft's message. Ever the public high school teacher, Martin began his tutorial by simplifying and personalizing the subject matter.

"Gareth, imagine that it is late at night and you are the pilot of an interceptor airplane ordered to locate, engage, and shoot down enemy bombers before they can attack a US city. How would you find your targets and shoot them down in the dark?"

Gareth replied, "I have no idea."

Martin continued. "Well, our dinner companions do have an idea how to accomplish such an airborne interception mission. Apparently, transmitted radio signals striking a ship or a plane can reflect back to a receiver. Dr. Cockcroft believes that a system capable of transmitting and receiving radio signals with wavelengths that are ten centimeters or less could be used by pilots flying interceptor aircraft in the dark of night to locate and attack enemy bombers. Cockcroft's conceptual system consists of five components sufficiently compact and light in weight that they can all be mounted on a small interceptor aircraft. The first component of their hypothetical system would be a very powerful 15-kilowatt transmitter capable of generating microwave pulses ten centimeters (or less) in length. The second system component would be a small directional antenna that can transmit these centimetric-length microwave pulses into the sky. Through a third component called a 'duplexer,' the same antenna can also receive signals, which are echoes of the transmitted ten-centimeter (or less) microwaves reflected off the fuselage of an attacking bomber. The fourth component of the system—the receiver—will process the signals or transmitted waves reflected off the enemy bomber and forward them to the fifth system component, a cathode ray tube display inside the cockpit of the interceptor aircraft. This display will allow an interceptor pilot to visualize the range and direction of the attacking bomber hiding in the dark, or in the rain or in fog, or in clouds or in smoke. With this information, the enemy bomber can now be located, attacked, and shot down regardless of weather or light conditions.

"Gareth, this is a big deal. This kind of system could also be adapted for use on our warships to locate enemy vessels at great distances in the dark. As a shipboard system, it could be engineered to aim the main batteries of our battleships, cruisers, and destroyers to deliver 16-inch, 8-inch, 6-inch, or 5-inch projectiles with devastating accuracy at ranges far beyond those possible with today's optical sights and rangefinders. Just think of the advantage such a system would give our Navy in a gun battle with Japanese or Nazi ships that are relying solely on optical sights! The theoretical system the scientists discussed tonight might also be engineered to function as a warship's anti-aircraft spotting system and control the firing of smaller caliber anti-aircraft guns with greater accuracy than anything currently in the US fleet. And I see no reason why scouting aircraft could not use this kind of centimetric microwave system to locate and attack distant submarines that are charging their batteries on the surface of the ocean. I suspect that this system could be developed to detect a submerged submarine's periscopes peeking through the surface of the water, trying to target merchant ships and warships."

Gareth, as always, got right to the point. "Martin, what's the catch? Why don't we have pulsed one-centimeter or ten-centimeter microwave ranging and detection systems in our aircraft right now?"

Martin replied, "Gareth, we do not have vacuum tubes capable of producing 15 kilowatts of pulsed power output at short wavelengths, like ten or three centimeters. We can probably generate enough power with today's vacuum tubes to produce ten-meter-length high-frequency radio waves, or maybe one-meter-length very-high-frequency radio waves, but you would need large land-based antennae, or antennae that would take up considerable real estate on a warship, for this kind of HF or VHF ranging and detection system to work. Interceptor aircraft are a fraction of the size of a naval vessel and can only accommodate smaller, shorter antennae that will not interfere with their aerodynamics."

Laughing, Gareth said, "I bet old Peg Leg Captain Masuji would love to be here with us right now in Tuxedo Park!"

Martin replied, "I wish I had hit him just about a foot higher and about six inches to his left."

Gareth winced and said, "OUCH!"

SUNDAY, SEPTEMBER 29, 1940; "THE SECOND BIGGEST SHOCK OF MY LIFE," TUXEDO PARK

British Prime Minister Churchill's two military technology emissaries—John Cockcroft and Edward Bowen—were superb showmen who knew how to awe an audience of American plutocrats responsible for preparing their hesitant nation to fight and win a global war. The Brits had waited one day after arriving at Tuxedo Park to present an odd-looking electrical device called a "resonant cavity magnetron" to their US colleagues. Invented by John Randall and Harry Boot, two British professors working at the University of Birmingham, this compact high-power vacuum tube could do precisely what Martin had just told Gareth could not be done—produce 15-kilowatt pulsed microwaves ten centimeters in length. With this breakthrough technology, a crash program employing America's and Great Britain's finest physicists and engineers could make compact, lightweight centimetric airborne and naval radar systems available in time to bring Nazi Germany and Imperial Japan to their knees. Unlike England, the United States possessed the financial resources and secure research and production facilities, far removed from day and night raids by German bombers, which could get the complex R&D and manufacturing job done quickly.

Martin whispered to Gareth, "Next to the birth of my son Adam, this is the second biggest shock of my life!"

Gareth shook his head at the wonder of it all. He whispered back to Martin, "I never would have appreciated any of this had you not provided me with your tutorial last night. Thanks, pal."

On October 2, 1940, Dr. Loomis traveled to Woodley, Secretary of War Stimson's home in Washington, DC, where he briefed his cousin on the technological breakthrough disclosed by the British and its strategic implications. In November of 1940, Vannevar Bush's NDRC opened the US Radiation Laboratory at MIT to secretly develop centimetric radar systems for three major applications: airborne interception, long-range navigation for bombing, and "gun-laying" (i.e. the directing of accurate anti-aircraft and artillery fire). Professor Lee DuBridge, the thirty-nine-year-old chairman of the University of Rochester Physics Department, and Isidor I. Rabi, a world-renowned physics professor at Columbia University, were recruited to serve as Director and Associate Director of what become known as MIT's "Rad Lab." By the end of World War II, the Rad Lab employed 3,500 people and had developed over 100 radar systems. Dr. Loomis, a Harvard Law School–educated Wall Street lawyer, financier, and PhD physicist, played a major role in bringing Bell Labs, Radio Corporation of America, Westinghouse Corporation, General Electric, Sperry, Philco, and Bendix Corporation into this burgeoning, top-secret radar enterprise. The significance of the joint effort by the United States and the United Kingdom to develop radar can hardly be exaggerated.

The security requirements and associated manpower necessary to protect this mammoth technological and industrial undertaking—as well as other top-secret efforts like the Manhattan Project—far exceeded the capabilities and the capacity of the small FBI and ONI group originally established to blunt the efforts of Captain Masuji and his collection of amateur spies operating in the Baltimore and Washington area. The Sicinnus Team was soon disbanded and most of its members reassigned to new and larger groups within the federal government responsible for conducting counterintelligence operations and protecting America's industrial security.

By December of 1940, Gareth Messenger had returned to working full time at the Baltimore City Police Department. By virtue of his intellect and physical stamina, as well as his deep understanding of human psychology (both normal and abnormal), he rose to become Chief Inspector of the BCPD, reporting directly to the Baltimore City Police Commissioner. Karl Dennis and Donald Foster resumed their previous roles in the FBI office in Baltimore. Clarence Walker, Gilbert Horan, William Murphy, Louis Clyde, Alphonse Zangara, and Hercules Boulanger became legendary figures in the FBI's growing counterintelligence empire. They continued their successful hunting of Axis spies throughout World War II and transitioned to pursuing Soviet bloc spies from 1945 until each of them retired from government service.

22

9 AM TUESDAY, NOVEMBER 12, 1940; THE NAVY DEPARTMENT

Captain McLaughlin summoned Martin into his office. "Close the door, Lieutenant. We have some important matters to discuss."

As always, Martin followed orders. He closed the door and stood at attention, eyes forward, without uttering a word.

"Victor, you need a new job, a new mission. I have one question for you. Answer just "Yes, Sir" or "No, Sir" to my question. If your answer to my question is "No, Sir," leave my office and you will receive new orders from your new commander whenever he gets around to issuing them. Here is my question: Do you want to continue working for me?"

Martin replied, "Yes, Sir!"

"Excellent," replied McLaughlin. "At ease, Victor.

"Martin, I know you like operating US Navy radios and that recently you have become infatuated with radar. But do you like US Navy aircraft?"

Without thinking much about what Captain McLaughlin had asked him, Lieutenant Victor replied, "Yes, Sir. Very much, Sir."

"Excellent," replied McLaughlin. "Why don't you take a seat in front of my desk?"

Martin sat down. McLaughlin then asked, "Would you like to hunt Nazi submarines threatening the East Coast of the United States?"

"Yes, Sir. Very much, Sir."

"Perfect," replied McLaughlin. "Let me tell you about your bright future in the US Navy, son."

Martin had never heard Captain McLaughlin address him as "son" before. He thought, *Things are looking up.*

"Lieutenant Victor, in 1927, at the tender age of thirty-eight, I earned my naval aviator wings at the Naval Air Station in Pensacola, Florida. In my graduating class at Pensacola, there was a forty-nine-year-old Captain named Ernest J. King, an outstanding naval officer of uncommon intelligence with the craftiness and temper of Neptune himself. The rumor in this building is that Vice Admiral King, now Commander of the Atlantic Squadron, will soon be promoted to full Admiral and CINCLANT, Commander-in-Chief Atlantic Fleet. Martin, this is no mere rumor. It will soon be a reality. Admiral King has asked me to oversee the new Glenn L. Martin PBM Mariner seaplane air wings and squadrons that will conduct anti-submarine patrols in the Atlantic Ocean, and ultimately hunt down and sink Nazi U-boats threatening merchant ships and US Navy warships. I want you, a man I know to be one hundred percent reliable and loyal to me, to assist in effectively and efficiently deploying these airborne assets to conduct so-called 'neutrality patrols' out to 300 miles from the US coastline. To expedite your entry into naval aviation, I have organized an anti-submarine warfare curriculum for you, concentrating on seaplanes (particularly the Martin PBM Mariner), sensors (particularly a British airborne radar called the ASV Mark II that works on seaplanes), air-dropped munitions such as depth charges, bombs and torpedoes, and weapons like the .50-caliber machine gun). Any questions?"

A very excited Martin Victor answered, "When do I start?"

McLaughlin laughed. "Good question. Today, Lieutenant, today. Not too far from here is Anacostia Naval Air Station, where US Navy, Naval Research Lab, and Royal Air Force personnel are testing an ASV Mark II radar on a PBY Catalina—an older, less-capable seaplane than the Martin Mariner PBM. You and I are going to drive over there today and learn a little about the ASV Mark II radar. My understanding is that Norfolk Naval Air Station will be installing this device on Martin PBM Mariners in June of 1941. In any event, we will take a ride on the PBY today and see how the radar improves our ability to locate enemy submarines and surface vessels. Ever take off and land on water, Victor?"

Martin replied, "No, Sir. But it sounds like great fun."

McLaughlin said, "Oh, it is fun all right. Now, here is a US government life insurance policy with your name on it. Martin, if you die serving our great nation, your family will get $10,000, a carefully folded US flag, and the right to visit your grave in Arlington Cemetery any time they like."

Martin appreciated McLaughlin's sense of humor. It inspired in him a devil-may-care courage he carefully hid from the people who cared about him the most. He replied, "Thank you, Sir. It is reassuring to know that my commanding officer is so concerned about the well-being of my family."

Without missing a beat, Captain McLaughlin replied, "Lieutenant Victor, someone has to look out for them!"

"Good point, Sir."

And that was that.

Captain McLaughlin and Lieutenant Victor were chauffeured to Naval Air Station–Anacostia. A British Royal Air Force officer, a US Navy pilot, and a US Naval Research Lab civilian with a PhD in electrical engineering welcomed them into a secure area for their top-secret briefing on the British seven-kilowatt, non-microwave 1.7-meter wavelength radar before boarding a nearby Consolidated PBY seaplane to flight test the device.

Commander Lucas Breault, USN, presented the overview of the ASV Mark II. "Gentlemen, this radar can detect a battleship at a range of 36 miles. Our tests further establish that it can detect a destroyer roughly 18 miles away and a submarine charging its battery on the surface of the water 9 miles away. The radar's minimum range is one mile, so a final attack run to bomb, torpedo, depth charge or machine gun a Nazi or a Jap ship will have to be accomplished using your eyesight, not the ASV Mark II."

Using large photographs of the PBY Catalina as demonstratives, Commander Breault pointed out the location of the ASV Mark II transmitter, receiver, and Yagi antennae. He showed McLaughlin and Victor a physical model of the ASV's "L-Scope" used by the radar operator to visualize the direction and range of the target.

At the end of the briefing, Breault announced, "Based on our testing and reports from the Royal Air Force, we believe that equipping the Consolidated PBY Catalinas and the larger Martin PBM Mariners with ASV Mark II's will materially improve the ability of our Atlantic Ocean Neutrality Patrols to locate surfaced Nazi U-boats. Should the President permit the Navy to attack Nazi submarines, our radar-equipped seaplanes will, in many cases, be able to bomb, torpedo, or depth charge the U-boats before (or shortly after) they can dive beneath the waves to avoid destruction. Thus, the ASV Mark II equipped PBM's and PBY's pose a mortal threat to *Kriegsmarine* vessels presently targeting British and American ships off the East Coast of the US."

Restless for action, Captain McLaughlin said, "Thank you, Commander. Now, let's take a spin in your PBY and see whether or not this British radar can pick up any contacts in the Chesapeake Bay."

Commander Breault saluted and said, "With pleasure, Sir!"

Martin had never flown in an airplane of any kind before. To him, the high-wing, twin-engine PBY Catalina appeared ungainly, maybe even a little bit ugly. The thin support struts connecting the 104-foot-long wing to the port and starboard sides of the 64-foot-long fuselage looked like an engineering afterthought to Martin. The two glass canopies on the port and starboard sides of the PBY near its tail section reminded him of a bullfrog's eyes. And the decibel level of the noise inside the seaplane's cabin produced by the two Pratt & Whitney R-1830 engines exceeded anything he had ever experienced.

However, as the Catalina rose from the water to an altitude of 10,000 feet, Martin became totally exhilarated. Cruising at 115 miles per hour, the seaplane had a range of 1,400 miles when carrying 2,000 pounds of bombs. Breault took the plane down to 2,000 feet and ordered the radio man/radar operator to fire up the ASV Mark II. Sitting next to the sailor, Martin observed a blip on the L-Scope and admired the method used to vector the Catalina toward the unsuspecting US Navy light cruiser 15 miles away. After an hour and a half of flying and locating five ships in the Chesapeake Bay, including a small destroyer escort, both McLaughlin and Victor were sold on the utility of the ASV Mark II.

The water landing, though bumpy, thrilled Martin. He thought, *If Gertrude were here, she would just love this! Milton would hate it! This is so much better than the rides at Gwynn Oak or Carlin Park.*

Commander Breault thanked Captain McLaughlin and Lieutenant Victor for visiting the Anacostia Naval Air Station. McLaughlin shook hands with Breault and said, "Outstanding demonstration, Commander. Now I understand why the Navy wants to purchase thousands of radars like these from companies like Philco."

McLaughlin and Victor then headed back to the Navy Department, where the Captain completed his description of the courses he had arranged for Martin to take over a late lunch of bacon, lettuce, and tomato sandwiches and Coca-Colas.

"First, the good people at Glenn L. Martin are going to give you a three-week program on the capabilities and performance of the PBM Mariner. You will see the planes being built in Building B in Middle River. The engineers will provide you with an overview of the training program they provided this past October and November to two PBM squadrons that are presently based in Norfolk, Virginia. Focus on anti-submarine mission–related information.

I have been told that a PBM carrying 2,000 pounds of bombs can fly 2,100 miles on one tank of aviation fuel—that's 700 miles farther than the PBY. We need detailed PBM performance data in order to plan our campaign against the Nazi U-boats in the Atlantic, Martin. Use your lawyer and counterintelligence-agent skills to get me everything I need from the manufacturer. There is a Glenn L. Martin executive in Middle River named Dr. Ed Coar who worked closely with Clarence Walker on our German spy case in Baltimore not too long ago. Dr. Coar is smart, in the know, and patriotic. Develop him as a key contact. Any questions?"

Martin replied, "No, Sir. I have got it."

"Good," said McLaughlin. "I am in a hurry and do not have time for insecure slowpokes. You ever been to Florida, Martin?"

"No, Sir."

"Well, you are going to enjoy Banana River Naval Air Station. The trainers there will show you how the US Navy operates and maintains PBM seaplanes. You will get to drop some depth charges, bombs, and torpedoes. If you are nice to them, they might let you light up some targets with the PBM's nose- and waist-mounted .50-caliber machine guns. I would be interested seeing whether your marksmanship skills with a handgun scale up to a .50 cal., son!"

Ah, that word son *again!* thought Martin. The noun, as used by Captain McLaughlin, motivated Martin by making him feel loved for his latent lethality. "Sir, I look forward to finding out. I would enjoy ventilating the torso and head of U-boat Captain standing on his sub's conning tower with a .50 before sinking his ship and killing his crew with bombs, torpedoes, and depth charges!"

"Lieutenant, not until the President gives us orders to shoot Nazi submarines on sight, or some German bastard foolishly shoots at you first. I know you are itching to mix it up with the Nazis, but you have to follow the rules of engagement."

"Yes, Sir," replied Martin. In his heart, he yearned to get a medal for sending a U-boat and its entire crew to the bottom of the Atlantic.

"Lieutenant Victor, after twelve weeks at Banana River, you will be assigned to Norfolk Naval Air Station to get some actual experience flying patrols with members of the VP-55 and VP-56 patrol squadrons. Following your training at Norfolk, you will get one week to see your family. Then you will work with me out of my new office here in DC. By then, hopefully before then, I should be a Rear Admiral."

"Congratulations, Captain McLaughlin. You deserve it!"

"I agree, Martin. If you perform up to your potential and make me look good to my superiors, perhaps you will be the first Lieutenant Commander in the US Navy to have ever graduated from Saint John's College. Go home, Martin. Regards to your wife. Gertrude, right?"

"Yes, Sir, Gertrude."

"And Adam, your son. Right?"

"Yes, Sir, Adam. Future Annapolis Class of 1961, Sir."

"Good man, Victor. Now get out of here."

Not long after Martin left, Catharine entered McLaughlin's office. "You like that Lieutenant, don't you, Charles?"

Captain McLaughlin looked at her tenderly and with a tinge of sadness in his voice said, "Catharine, the probability of that Lieutenant surviving the coming war is so low that I cannot afford to like him too much. Victor reminds me of Hector in *The Iliad*. He is skilled, courageous, family-oriented, and patriotic—truly an admirable man. However, he is no match for the fanatical demigods that Admiral Karl Donitz has trained to command his U-boats. So while I genuinely appreciate Lieutenant JG Martin Victor, I try not to get too attached to him. Darling, what little emotion I have got, I give it all to you."

Smiling ruefully, Catharine replied, "You are such a sweetheart, Rear Admiral."

"Captain, for now, Catharine. The only rear I want is yours—this evening."

"Is that an order, Captain?" Catharine replied coquettishly.

"No, ma'am. You have to volunteer," Charles said with a salacious leer.

"Sign me up," said Catharine as she executed a crisp about-face and walked out of the office, swinging her hips.

"Just cannot get enough of that woman," said McLaughlin, shaking his head.

7 PM TUESDAY, NOVEMBER 12; BALTIMORE, 14 SOUTH BROADWAY

Martin Victor hurried home from the train station, hoping to see Adam in Gertrude's arms. As soon as he opened the door, he could hear Gertrude speaking to Adam in her warm way. Mother and child were seated on the couch in the Basswood's living room. Adam's bright blue eyes were riveted to his mother's face. Grace sat to Gertrude's right. Henry was nowhere in sight.

Grace saw Martin standing tall in his uniform and let loose with her standard line. "Look what the cat dragged in, Adam!"

Martin growled, "Where's my Adam?" Instantly, Adam turned his head to his right, saw his father in uniform, and started bouncing up and down excitedly on his mother's lap. Martin put both of his arms straight out, with the fingers of each hand curled as if grasping for a victim. He proceeded to walk forward, rocking robotically and making monster noises like Boris Karloff playing *Frankenstein* in the movies. Adam went wild when his father picked him up and held him at arm's length. Martin gently put his right hand behind Adam's neck and his left hand carefully around the infant's lower back, bent over, and rocked Adam between his legs as if the little boy were on a swing or in a cradle. The look and the sounds emanating from the little boy could best be characterized as "ecstatic," but truly defied description.

Gertrude summed up the event by saying, "Adam, your papa really loves you!"

Martin stopped rocking Adam and hugged his son, squeezing his eyes shut so that he could absorb the physical presence of the boy within his nervous system for all eternity.

Grace observed, "Finally, Martin is behaving in a dignified fashion. You do not want to turn this child into a wild animal."

Gertrude put her arm around Grace and consoled her. "Grace, boys will be boys!"

Grace replied, "That, Gertrude, is the problem!"

Adam yawned, turned toward Gertrude, and put his arms out.

"Somebody wants to sleep," said Gertrude, and she whisked him up to his crib upstairs.

Henry returned from a medical meeting at that point, saw Martin, and asked, "So what do you think about the British sinking the Italian fleet at Taranto?"

Martin shrugged his shoulders and said, "From what I read in *The Baltimore Sun* and *The Washington Post*, it sounds like the Royal Navy caught the Italians napping and torpedoed their fleet while they were in port."

Henry asked, "Could that happen to us? Could our fleet in Pearl Harbor get crushed like that?"

Martin replied, "I doubt it, Henry. My understanding is that Pearl Harbor is too shallow for torpedoes dropped from aircraft to cause any damage to our warships. The 'fish,' as sailors call torpedoes, will get stuck in the mud in the bottom of the harbor after being dropped and therefore be unable to 'swim' into the sides or bottoms of our warships. Also, we have around-the-clock patrols operating far out at sea and in the air in order to provide adequate warning against any approaching Japanese sneak attack. However, Henry, you never can be certain in war."

Just then Gertrude returned, hugging and kissing Martin passionately. "Now, that's enough of that," said Grace. "Calm down. You just had a baby, Gertrude!

"Grace, can I help it if I am attracted to a man in a uniform?" said Gertrude.

"Yes. You can restrain yourself!" replied Grace.

Henry joined in. "Martin, we seem to have a difference of opinion between our womenfolk. Let's move on to a new topic."

Martin took this opportunity to inform Gertrude, as well as Grace and Henry, of his new assignment. "My old unit successfully completed its final mission and got disbanded. This exposed me to being reassigned to a new posting, possibly in the Pacific. Well, my former commander is being promoted to a new position and he requested that I work for him in DC for the foreseeable future. I accepted his offer, so I will not be going to Pearl Harbor or Guam, or Wake Island or the Philippines."

Thus, somewhat less than fully informed about the nature of her husband's new job, Gertrude breathed a sigh of relief. Grace asked, "Can you tell us more precisely what you will be doing, Martin?"

Martin thought carefully before answering this question. Then he replied, "I will assist in managing President Roosevelt's Neutrality Patrols. I cannot say more. I will be working in Baltimore for the next three weeks at Glenn L. Martin, learning technical aspects of the equipment utilized to conduct the patrols, so let's make the most of it!"

Gertrude squeezed Martin's hand and said, "Martin, you do what the US Navy orders you to do. You protect us, and we will carry on and wait patiently for you to return."

Martin looked at Gertrude and thought, *I think I better not discuss the $10,000 life insurance policy with her at this time.*

Gertrude gazed upon her Martin and thought, *We truly need to make the most of each moment together.* She fought the cloud of impending loss impinging on her soul by holding her Lieutenant tight that night, and every night thereafter.

7:30 AM WEDNESDAY, NOVEMBER 13, 1940; GLENN L. MARTIN, BUILDING B, MIDDLE RIVER, MARYLAND

Ed Coar greeted Martin Victor warmly. "Delighted to meet you, Lieutenant. Clarence Walker, a man I consider to be a model FBI agent, spoke very highly of you. I want you to know that based upon his recommendation, you will receive the full cooperation of Glen L. Martin in your quest to learn everything there is about the Martin PBM Mariner seaplane!"

"Thank you, Dr. Coar," Martin said as he shook Coar's hand.

"Call me Ed," replied Coar.

"Call me Martin," replied Victor.

Martin put his cards on the table. "Ed, my commander—soon-to-be-Rear Admiral Charles McLaughlin—wants to move out smartly running the Atlantic Neutrality Patrols. He has ordered me to gather as much information from you as I can about the Martin PBM Mariner's anti-submarine capabilities."

Coar replied, "Martin, on November 1st, the Navy ordered 379 new model PBM-3 Mariners, ninety-four of which will be tailored to perform anti-submarine patrols. These ASW aircraft will be called the PBM-3S. Deliveries should commence in mid-1942. For now, let's concentrate on the new PBM-3S aircraft, which will have significant enhancements over the initial twenty PBM-1's already purchased by the Navy. The PBM-3S, fully loaded with either four 650-pound bombs or four 325-pound depth charges, can fly 2,725 miles—200 miles farther than the PBM-1 and over 1,000 miles farther than a PBY Catalina carrying half the bomb load of a PBM. A technical advance called 'Shannon Vortex Airfoils' will improve the stability of the Mariner PBM-3. Furthermore, the addition of self-sealing fuel cells in the PBM-3 series will prevent fuel from leaking and igniting if the aircraft is hit by enemy fire. The PBM-3S will also have twin .50-caliber flex guns in the bow of the plane and a single .50-caliber gun in the tail, so you can say hello and then goodbye to Nazi U-boats before and after you drop bombs or depth charges on them. Finally, for security reasons, the British ASV Mark II airborne radar, scheduled to be installed soon on PBM-1's at the Norfolk Virginia Air Station, will also be incorporated into the PBM-3S in Norfolk. The ASV radar will alert the PBM pilot and crew to the presence of a submarine on the surface of the ocean from a maximum range of about nine miles and provide a significant opportunity to surprise and sink the target. Now, let's walk through the manufacturing line and, at the end, examine the inside of the fuselage of a finished PBM-1 from bow to stern."

The architect designed the well-lit, 135,000-square-foot Building B in Middle River to allow the simultaneous manufacture of several of the large PBM Mariner aircraft. A Mariner was 80 feet long, 27 feet high, and had a wingspan of 118 feet. The disciplined army of workers busily assembling these massive flying machines greatly impressed Martin.

"Ed, this makes you proud to live in Baltimore," Martin said earnestly.

Ed Coar and Martin climbed aboard a recently completed PBM-1. For the next hour and a half, Dr. Coar provided a thorough engineering analysis of the seaplane and its capabilities to Martin. Coar pointed out the uniquely designed ordnance bays located in the PBM Mariner's engine nacelles. He also explained in considerable detail the Mariner's communications systems and showed Martin where the ASV Mark II radar equipment and radar operator station would be located in the future.

"Martin, you want to see Baltimore and the Chesapeake Bay from the air in a PBM 1?" asked Dr. Coar.

"I would be delighted!" replied Martin. While waiting for the pilot and copilot to arrive, Martin reflected on how the seaplane, with its gullwing and dihedral horizontal stabilizer, appeared like a giant pelican eager to pounce on its U-boat prey. *How appropriate*, he thought.

Two Glenn L. Martin test pilots introduced themselves to Martin and went through each preflight step in the flight manual with him before takeoff. He sat in the radio operator's station behind the copilot. Dr. Coar sat in the navigator's station behind the pilot. Once again, Martin experienced the exhilaration of ascending from the water into the beautiful blue November morning sky. The flight plan followed Lieutenant Martin Victor's personal journey through life. Flying over East Baltimore, he could see "The Castle on the Hill," Baltimore City College High School. Heading southeast, the PBM flew over Saint John's College and the Naval Academy. Martin's mind briefly conjured up the first US Navy uniform he wore as a Naval Reserve Officer Training Corps cadet. He thought about drilling with World War I–era rifles on Saint John's athletic fields. Winging west over Washington, DC, he could see the Department of Justice Building, the White House, the Navy Department, and Rock Creek Park. The seaplane turned southwest, flying over Quantico, and then flew southeast along the Potomac River and Chesapeake Bay. Soon, Martin saw Norfolk Naval Air Station, where one dozen PBM-1's were lined up neatly near a large concrete ramp leading to the water. The pilot then headed north, flying over Fort McHenry, where Martin could see the Bendix Radio building and South Broadway.

Inside this war plane, Martin admitted to himself that forces far beyond his control might take him away from Gertrude and Adam forever. He thought, *I am but a pawn. I cannot retreat. I can only move forward one space at a time. My value comes from my willingness to be sacrificed to achieve the strategic objectives of my command authority.*

While this existential reflection hurt, Martin felt fortunate to have come this far in life, and comforted himself with the knowledge that Grace, Henry, and Milton would look after his two loved ones if God wanted it that way. "So be it," he murmured. As the pilot brought the PBM in for a smooth landing on Middle River near Glenn L. Martin, Lieutenant Victor pushed the negative thoughts of his being mortal aside. He wanted to sink several U-boats before his ticket got punched. To accomplish this goal, he needed to master this "killer pelican" and work with Rear Admiral McLaughlin to send squadrons of PBM's out into the Atlantic Ocean to hunt down German subs and sink them. This was Martin Victor's mission now. He determined to focus solely on accomplishing his mission.

Ed Coar said, "Lieutenant, what do think about the Mariner?"

Victor replied, "Sure beats the PBY!"

Coar responded, "Now that is what I wanted to hear. I will pass statement on to Mr. Glenn L. Martin himself!"

Martin grinned. "You do that. If I had any money, I would buy stock in your company!"

Coar laughed. "I am going to report that comment too, Lieutenant Victor."

Martin replied, "You do that!"

For the next three weeks, Martin Victor arrived at Building B at 7:30 AM and rarely departed before 7 PM. He absorbed every lesson about the PBM Mariner aircraft proffered by Dr. Coar. Martin read every PBM manual and studied Glenn L. Martin's product development plans for the Mariner series and how technological improvements in propulsion, flight controls, materials, electrical systems, and weaponry would be inserted in subsequent models of the seaplane that he and Rear Admiral McLaughlin would be taking to war against the *Kriegsmarine*. On Monday, December 2, 1940, Lieutenant Victor submitted to the admiral his 30-page, single-spaced report regarding his activities at Glenn L. Martin and his thoughts about optimally employing PBM aircraft in anti-submarine warfare.

After listening to Martin present the key points of his paper, McLaughlin snarled, "Victor, not too long ago, you shot a leg off an IJN officer for me. Now I want you to sink a Nazi submarine, drown its Captain and his entire crew. Would you do that for me, son?"

Martin, steely-eyed, said, "Sir, I will do it for the both of us! And I intend to destroy more than one Nazi U-boat!"

"Good man, Victor. Good man. Commencing December 9th, there is a class for PBM-1 flight observers that I want you to take at Banana River NAS in Florida. It will take about three months for you to complete the program. You have a little less than a week to spend with your family before you report for duty. Extend my apologies to your wife and son."

"Sir, they will understand!"

"Good man, Martin. Good man."

And that was that.

DECEMBER 3 THROUGH DECEMBER 6, 1940; BALTIMORE

On December 3, Gertrude celebrated her twenty-ninth birthday with Adam, Martin, Grace, Henry, and Milton. Wearing colorful conical hats, everyone—including the boisterous three-month old Adam—joyously sang "Happy Birthday" as Martin presented Gertrude with her favorite dessert, a Silber's Bakery peach cake. Henry took a photograph of the family with his new Anniversary Speed Graphic camera. The sudden bright light from the camera's flash attachment made Adam roar with laughter. The magnificent moment memorialized in the photograph remained on Gertrude's dresser top until her passing at age seventy-nine on December 11, 1990, the first night of Hanukkah—the Jewish festival she and Adam loved most.

On December 4, Martin and Milton took a radiant Gertrude to Haussner's for dinner while Grandpa Henry and Grandma Grace watched over their pride and joy, Adam. The three talked and poked fun at each other for two hours.

At 8 PM, Gertrude announced, "Guys, I have to return to 14 South Broadway. My breasts are telling me that it is time to feed my little bruiser, Adam." Martin and Milton restrained themselves from making an East Baltimore comment in response to Gertrude's rather forward statement about her mammary glands.

However, after she disappeared upstairs to nourish her son, Martin said to his brother, "Adam will be spoiled for life by those sublime breasts. I doubt that he will ever find anything like them on another woman!"

Milton, aghast, said to Martin, "The Navy has corrupted you. A little decorum, Martin!"

Martin looked around to make sure that neither Henry or Grace were in earshot and said, "Milton, I will be getting some pretty intensive training in Florida and Virginia between December 9th and March 9th. Please look in on Gertrude and Adam while I am away." Handing his older brother an envelope, he said, "If anything happens to me, here is a $10,000 government life insurance policy. Gertrude is the beneficiary. I know that you will take care of Adam and Gertrude. You have no idea how much you mean to me, Milton."

Milton, his eyes glistening, placed his right hand on Martin's shoulder and applied his vise-like grip. "*Maishe,* my brother, nothing is going to happen. God protects reckless romantics like you. But in case I am wrong about you and God, everything I have belongs to Gertrude and Adam while I live, and after I myself am gone. They will want for nothing. Now let's stop talking about such somber things before someone overhears us. No need to upset anyone other than ourselves."

On December 6, 1940, Lieutenant Victor boarded a southbound train to Florida. On March 7, 1941, Martin became the oldest man in his program to earn the US Navy Naval Aviation Observer Badge. His positive attitude, practically eidetic memory, radio skills, excellent physical conditioning, and superb marksmanship with a .50-caliber machine gun made him popular with his classmates and instructors. From December until March, Martin had risen before every other student in the morning to study, and he kept studying long after every other student had gone to sleep. To please his commanding officer, Martin totally committed himself to graduating at the top of his class. He graduated second, however, behind a recent graduate from the California Institute of Technology.

Rear Admiral McLaughlin attended the graduation ceremony at Banana River. Shaking Martin's hand and admiring the shiny new flight wings on the Baltimorean's uniform, McLaughlin said, "Son, you have yet again exceeded my expectations. Congratulations. Keep up the excellent work when you get to Virginia."

When Martin Victor arrived in at Norfolk Naval Air Station, the members of the VP-55 and VP-56 squadrons soon came to appreciate his thorough knowledge of the PBM Mariner and his aggressively creative insights concerning anti-submarine warfare. Rumors about Martin's ONI exploits in Rock Creek Park further reinforced his stature with the intrepid naval aviators and aircrews. Every pilot and crew wanted Lieutenant Victor to fly with them on Neutrality Patrols because they knew Victor wanted to sink Nazi subs, not just observe them. They missed him when he went to Baltimore for one week's leave and then disappeared into Rear Admiral McLaughlin's lair in the Navy Department Building on Constitution Avenue.

In a private telephone conversation on May 21—the day President Roosevelt proclaimed to the nation that an Unlimited National Emergency existed—the commanding officer of VP-55 said to McLaughlin, "Martin Victor is too good a naval officer to be shackled to a desk when a war at sea could erupt at any moment. A man with his abilities and warrior spirit belongs in the air!"

The Rear Admiral replied, "You think so?"

"I know so, Sir! I want him. My entire squadron wants him."

"We will see, Captain. I have logged your request."

23

EPILOGUE

On September 4, 1941, U-652, a Type VII C German submarine, fired a torpedo at the USS *Greer*, a US Navy destroyer patrolling in the North Atlantic. While the torpedo missed the *Greer*, President Franklin Roosevelt had had enough with Nazi Germany. On September 11, 1941, FDR authorized US warships to "shoot on sight" any German submarines or surface raiders found in waters deemed "necessary to the defense" of the United States. The gloves were now off officially.

Rear Admiral McLaughlin partially assented to the VP-55 Squadron Commander's May 21 request and ordered Lieutenant Victor to observe firsthand the unit's operations under the new presidential directive. Additionally, McLaughlin directed Victor to "recommend such alterations in tactics and procedures you deem necessary to assure the effectiveness and safety of patrol aircraft and their crews engaging hostile surface and subsurface vessels in combat."

Martin's orders were effective September 20, 1941. Rear Admiral McLaughlin wanted him to be able to celebrate Adam's first birthday in Baltimore on Friday, September 19. Now walking and talking, Adam provided hours of heart-pounding "entertainment" for Gertrude, Grace, Henry, and Milton. Grace nicknamed Adam "Houdini" in recognition of the child's extraordinary ability to escape the custody of any adult charged with supervising him. Adam enjoyed being the center of attention at his party, grabbing his slice of Silber's Bakery vanilla-frosting angel food layer cake with both hands and smearing it all over his face, neck, and clothing.

"Behaves just like his father," commented Milton.

"Yes," replied Gertrude. "Isn't he beautiful?"

Gertrude maintained her stalwart and stoic demeanor when Martin departed early the next morning before Adam awoke, but she cried the entire day after Martin took the cab to the train station. Henry asked Grace to console Gertrude.

"Won't do any good, Henry Basswood. She will have to cry this out of her system. God help us all if anything happens to that man of hers... That man of ours."

Henry, dressed for Sabbath synagogue services, replied, "I pray for him three times a day, Grace. What more can we mere mortals do?"

Grace had no answer.

Other than familiarizing himself with the ASV Mark II radar system recently installed in his aircraft, Martin's first patrol on Monday, September 23, proved uneventful. Every aircraft in the squadron had been secretly upgraded with the ASV in July by technicians at Norfolk NAS. While the radar and the radar operator on Martin's PBM performed well, no radar or visual contacts of Nazi U-boats or surface vessels occurred. This situation was about to change. The unit and its seaplane tenders received orders to move their base of operations from Norfolk to patrol for trouble in the high northern latitudes between Iceland and Greenland.

On October 13, the radar in Martin's seaplane detected a vessel on the surface of the water eight miles away in the Denmark Strait. The pilot decreased altitude to 2,000 feet as they closed to within one mile of the target on the ASV Mark II's display. Using the powerful binoculars provided to him courtesy of Rear Admiral McLaughlin, Martin saw the profile of a Type VII C Nazi U-boat moving at approximately 15 knots on the surface of the sea.

The radar detected several larger objects another ten miles from the submarine—British merchant vessels carrying cargo from Canada and the US to England. Clearly, the U-boat's intentions were not at all honorable. The pilot looked at Martin and, without a word being spoken, Lieutenant Victor gave him a thumbs-up. Through his binoculars, Martin saw men running on the U-boat's deck.

He told the pilot, "They have spotted us!"

The pilot informed the crew, "We are going to attack the Nazi sub. Bombardier, we will drop all four of our depth charges. Set the intervalometer at ten feet and drop the ordnance when the bombsight gives you a good solution on the target. Front turret gunner, hit them with everything you have got as we approach. Waist gunner, you pick up where the front gunner leaves off. I will swing around and we will rake the U-boat with more gunfire after the drop."

Just then, the U-boat's two double-barrel 13.2mm Breda anti-aircraft machine guns opened up on the low- and slow-flying PBM. Tracer rounds, cycling at 500 rounds per minute from each of the Bredas, raced toward the American plane.

Over the intercom, the pilot ordered, "Radio operator, alert all squadron aircraft of our coordinates and call for assistance. Advise them that we have been fired upon by a Type VII C Nazi submarine."

The PBM's twin .50-caliber guns fired into the submarine from stern to bow. The depth charges dropped in a straight line, ten feet apart, also from stern to bow. Two of the 325-pound devices buried themselves into the deck of the 220-foot-long U-boat.

Rounds from the submarine's guns came through the floor of the sea plane. One bullet entered Martin's left leg, ricocheted upward off his thigh bone, tore through his groin, and exited through his right clavicle. Lieutenant Martin Victor died without making a sound.

The U-boat Captain cleared the deck of sailors manning the anti-aircraft guns. He then descended into his sub and ordered a crash dive. When the

U-boat dove 50 feet, the two depth charges embedded in the submarine's deck exploded, killing all four of the ship's officers and its crew of fifty-six enlisted men.

After witnessing the underwater explosion, the PBM pilot circled the site for 20 minutes and concluded that there were no survivors from the ship. He ordered his radio operator, "Report time and coordinates regarding the sinking of the U-boat. Report all hands aboard the submarine KIA. Advise that we have one USN officer KIA onboard our aircraft. No other US casualties."

After a few seconds of reflection, the pilot announced over the intercom, "Lieutenant Victor would be proud of what we accomplished here today." Not a word was spoken for the remainder of the flight to their temporary base near Reykjavik, Iceland.

Rear Admiral McLaughlin ordered that Lieutenant Victor's body be properly prepared at a morgue in Reykjavik for shipment to Arlington Cemetery for burial. Charles McLaughlin always kept his promises.

The Nazi ambassador met with the US Secretary of State to discuss the incident. "Your Excellency," he said, "a German submarine with sixty men on board is missing somewhere in the Denmark Strait. Its Captain reported that his ship was under attack by a large, two-engine seaplane that he thought was a Martin Mariner PBM with US Navy markings. We have not received any further reports from the Captain and the Reich presumes that he, his ship, and all hands were lost at sea. My government concludes that the Captain, fighting for his life, misreported the nationality and type of the attacking plane. We further conclude that the attacking aircraft was a Royal Navy PBY Catalina since the United States and Germany are not, and should not, be at war with each other. May I report to Berlin that you have heard this message from me and that your government will not issue any official statements contradicting the conclusion the Reich has reached regarding the sinking of its U-boat?"

The American Secretary of State gazed indifferently at the Nazi diplomat and said, "We will not comment on this incident." After the Nazi left his office, the Secretary of State called the White House.

"As we suspected, the Nazis do not want to open up yet another front while fighting in the Soviet Union. They are attributing the loss of their U-boat in the Denmark Strait to a Royal Navy Catalina seaplane."

"Excellent. Please see to it, however, that the US naval officer killed sinking the Nazi U-boat is awarded a Navy Cross, and that the citation for the medal is classified for national security reasons. I want him posthumously promoted, too, and his family treated generously."

"Yes, Mr. President. I will inform Chief of Naval Operations Admiral Stark."

On October 30, 1941, Lieutenant Commander Martin Victor was laid to rest with full military honors at Arlington Cemetery. Rabbi Elkanan and a Jewish Navy chaplain presided over the religious service. Rear Admiral Charles McLaughlin spoke of Lieutenant Commander Victor as "the American equivalent of Lysander: A heroic warrior totally devoted to victory. He set the standard by which all US naval officers should be judged."

Later, Milton wrote a heartfelt letter to the Rear Admiral stating, "Nothing would have pleased my brother more than to be ranked with Lysander by his commanding officer, a US Navy Rear Admiral."

Attending the funeral were the entire Sicinnus Team, the crew of the PBM on which Martin flew into his Valley of Death, Edwin Coar, Richard Crowe, the dean of the University of Maryland School of Law, the dean of Saint John's College, the principal of Baltimore City College High School, and Shalom Cohen. Gertrude, though crushed by grief, clutched the folded flag from Martin's coffin with her left hand and held Adam with her right.

Milton drove Gertrude, Adam, and Grace and Henry Basswood home from Arlington. For the remainder of their lives, Grace and Henry cared for Gertrude as if she were their daughter and doted on Adam as if he were their grandson. Contributing common stock in Glenn L. Martin Corporation and Bendix Corporation, Edwin Coar and Richard Crowe jointly established a trust fund naming Adam Victor as sole beneficiary. Coar, Crowe, and Gertrude were appointed trustees of the fund. At age twenty-five, the trust would be liquidated and all proceeds would belong to Adam.

Gertrude's relationship with Milton matured into marriage. Rabbi Elkanan conducted their wedding ceremony on October 14, 1945, in his synagogue on Eutaw Place. In his toast to his bride, Milton said, "Adam needed a father. Gertrude and I needed to fill the holes in our hearts from Martin's passing. So now we have solved all of our problems, although I must confess that I got the best of this bargain. I say this because no man could ever measure up to my beloved brother. And no woman on earth can ever measure up to Gertrude. I promise you, dearest Gertrude, that I will devote myself each day to being the best second-best man in your life that I can possibly be."

In Gertrude's toast to her husband, she said, "Milton taught me to transcend tragedy. Together, we honor our great loss by rising above it."

Adam worshiped his mother and Milton, even during his difficult teenage years. Adam's mystical relationship with Martin, the biological father he never knew except through the tales told to him by his living parents, grandparents Grace and Henry, a Baltimore City Police Chief Inspector named Messenger, and a US Navy Vice Admiral named Charles McLaughlin. A photograph of a robust, smiling US Navy Lieutenant standing proudly in front of a Martin Mariner PBM at the Norfolk Virginia Naval Air Station hung in Adam's bedroom and shaped the lad's life.

On June 7, 1961, President John F. Kennedy addressed the graduating class of the US Naval Academy, which included one Ensign Adam Victor who graduated third in his class with a double major in physics and electrical engineering. Gertrude and Milton Victor, accompanied by Vice Admiral (Retired) Charles McLaughlin and his wife Catharine, smiled with pride as Martin Victor's final remaining promise to his commanding officer was kept. Clutching his late father's Navy Cross, FBI Possible Club membership card, and the makeshift Sansei Medal in his left hand close to his heart, Ensign Adam Victor looked up into the sky and said, "Dad, there are no happy endings, just happy beginnings. I hope I have made you happy and proud today. I promise that there will be other such happy beginnings for me to share with you…"

Then, tossing his graduation cover high into the air, Adam finished his sentence. "…until you and I meet and finally begin again together forever."

Not Quite The End.